THEMES

THEMES

BY

JAY DUBYA

www.bookstandpublishing.com

Published by
Bookstand Publishing
Morgan Hill, CA 95037
4690_2

ISBN 978-1-63498-800-1

Printed in the United States of America

Other Books by Jay Dubya

Adult Fiction

Snake Eyes and Boxcars, Part II
UFO: Utterly Fantastic Occurrences
PLOTS
The Psychic Dimension
The Psychic Dimension, Part II
Modern Mythology,
First Person Stories

Young Adult Fantasy Novels

Pot of Gold
Enchanta
Space Bugs, Earth Invasion
The Eighteen Story Gingerbread House

Contents

Articles and Stories

Essay Manuscripts

Description

Themes is a collection of fifty-two short manuscripts: nineteen of which are articles and stories along with thirty-three of which are essays that reflect the author's personality and philosophy. Articles range from biographical sketches to the author's humorous adventures and the manuscript section is dedicated to the writer's observations about matters running the modern social spectrum from the *Iraq War* to inherent problems associated with American democracy. Some of the articles in this work originally appeared in the *Hammonton* (New Jersey) *Gazette* and the *Hammonton News*.

Part I:
19 Articles and Manuscripts

"A Tale of Two Counties"

I have always lived on the cusp and have immensely enjoyed doing so. I don't exactly mean that I was born between two astrological zodiac signs. I mean I live on the edge, and this pattern of behavior makes others (especially educational bureaucrats who fear on-a-mission teachers) "edgy" because of my proclivity for adventure and because of my inclination for challenging arbitrary executive decisions.

In my short history on this planet I have always exploited the maverick and the iconoclast role to the hilt. I generally root for the underdog and hope that he or she wins big over the favorite. I instinctively despise bureaucracy and prefer to pursue simplicity in all my mundane endeavors. As a rule, I like unusual things and topics, and I certainly am not a blustery politician or an impractical businessman. I don't have to "kiss-up" to anybody and I'd definitely prefer kicking someone's butt rather than smooching it. As Popeye would often say and maintain, "I am what I am, and that's all that I am."

Being a true-blooded "cusper" does have its attendant rewards. My teacher pension is secure after completing thirty-four years of dedicated public-school service. This new-found independence I cherish affords me unique privileges. I can write controversial *Hammonton Gazette* opinion columns and get local residents all riled up, I can author R-rated adult novels with relative impunity, and I have the opportunity and the luxury of sharing my self-gratifying singularity with separate newspaper and book readerships. I don't have to worry about losing my job because I have no job to lose, and I relish every moment of it. That's why both acquaintances and enemies regard me as a dangerous person. I just don't care what others think when I obey my moral compass.

I not only figuratively live on the cusp. I actually literally reside on the cusp, too. My house physically exists in two New Jersey counties. I like it that way. It adds variety to my life. My geographic status is consistent with my personality characteristics and with my life. This is how the entire two-county phenomenon spontaneously developed.

My wife and I had gotten tired of living in five-room apartments. First, we lived in Hammonton Arms on Valley Avenue when that project was new back in the late '60s, and then we lived several years in Della Court Apartments on Park Avenue just off Egg Harbor Road. It was time to get serious as parents and have our house built, but my

3

wife Joanne and I wanted our children to attend Hammonton Public Schools in Atlantic County (New Jersey) because we both taught there. We were in sort of a quandary about how to solve our minor dilemma but thanks to a stroke of good luck, we did.

Chris Rehmann, the Hammonton town engineer, performed a comprehensive survey of my father-in-law's (Joe Battaglia) farm property and discovered that Joe owned a hundred feet of land in Atlantic County that he never knew about. Joanne and I appeared before a local planning board and acquired fifty-foot frontage of additional land in Winslow Township by having one of my father-in-law's Camden County land parcels subdivided. Then we had our creative subdivisions approved in both Atlantic and Camden Counties to form a standard-size building lot and the tax assessors agreed that the Town of Hammonton would tax the home and the additional fifty-foot stretch of land would subsequently be taxed by Winslow Township.

The green "Now Entering Town of Hammonton" highway' sign on the White Horse Pike is not the true Atlantic/Camden County-Line. An observer must perceptively look at my house situated across the street from the boundary-line highway designation. The middle of my porch is the real county division, so when I pensively pace around inside my side screen porch, I inadvertently keep moving from county to county as I become thoroughly geographically disoriented.

Whenever a traffic accident happens on *Route 30* (which is referred to by locals as "the Pike"), I automatically dial *911* not thinking that someone might have hit a pole in Winslow Township, Camden County. My *911* street' address is hooked-up with Hammonton in Atlantic County, and I must commend the Hammonton Police Department because the officers will professionally and promptly respond to the emergency in Winslow Township, direct the four-lane highway traffic and attend to the accident victims until the Winslow Township Police arrive to take over those responsibilities.

Late last summer I was about to trim a large yew bush on the Hammonton side of my U-shaped asphalt driveway. I thought I had observed a big white bag stuck inside the yew shrub so I reached inside to grab and remove the object. I soon frightfully discovered that the circular white bag was a honest-to-goodness hornets' nest. Several nasty warrior wasps flew out of their well-constructed domicile and persistently buzzed around my head. I scampered rather frantically one hundred feet to the safety of my home's laundry room, wildly slamming the entrance door to my garage behind me. I soon realized that I had received a painful arm sting from one of the angry neurotic insects. My mind was naturally contemplating revenge.

After conscientiously applying a generous application of rubbing alcohol to my left shoulder I decided to wage battle against the ornery and undesirable wasp colony. I hopped into my *Buick LeSabre*, made sure that the power windows were up and then slowly drove the vehicle out of my garage, turned it around and next methodically progressed forward toward the White Horse Pike. I gently rammed the yew bush with my car's left front fender, intentionally and gleefully disturbing the seemingly tranquil hornet' colony.

I delighted watching agitated wasps swarm in a disorganized frenzy around my *LeSabre's* windshield. I felt protected and insulated from imminent danger. Feeling entirely safe, I cheerfully laughed at the insects' futility and at their general confusion and incompetence. I deliberately crashed into the wasp-hive nine consecutive times while I amply savored the annoyance I had initiated and the frenetic insect activity that enveloped my automobile. I was administering to the buzzing and incensed nervous critters a well-deserved intrusion. In my illustrious perception of ongoing events I knew that superior human intellect was successfully transcending primitive bug instinct. I was indeed the supreme master of my environment.

Finally, I determined that I had executed on the agitated wasps sufficient retribution for my still throbbing shoulder sting. I skillfully backed-up my' reliable auto' to the front section of my driveway. When I confidently halted my reverse movement, I quickly perceived that a hostile guard' wasp had somehow managed to wriggle its way inside the car. My cocky nonchalance suddenly converted into unbridled panic. My general conceited suaveness soon changed into an exasperating "fight or flight" mode. I discreetly chose "flight" as the more intelligent and discreet alternative. I had underestimated my all-too-determined instinct-guided opponent.

My body instantly exited my metallic blue *Buick* in a hurry and then I swiftly sprinted westward to avoid the disturbed insect's mounting wrath. All the while the furious wasp buzzed around my head, madder than a hornet. 'That angry hornet has a bee in its bonnet!' I remember thinking as I scurried onward. 'I need sanctuary quick!'

I dashed toward my mother-in-law's White Horse Farm Market with every iota of energy my legs could muster and anxiously scurried down the dirt road a full six hundred feet until the nasty territorial hornet abandoned its pursuit. I logically stopped my escape enterprise, extremely exhausted and completely out-of-breath from the arduous episode. Then I realized something rather significant. 'I'm really very lucky,' I rationally thought, 'because that hostile berserk out-of-control hornet was so angry that he had chased me clear into another county.'

"Identity Crisis Brewing in Author's Mind"

Yesterday morning I was peering into the bathroom mirror and as usual, my accurate reflection was predictably staring back at me. That simple everyday 7 a.m. act gave me adequate time to *reflect.* "I'm much better off than you are," I chuckled to my always loyal mirror image, "because I'm three dimensional and you're just a flat 2-D surface impression of the real me," I emphatically said as my eyes noticed my lackluster likeness's mouth stating the exact same inane jargon back to my unshaven face. I didn't realize it at the time but that bathroom situation was actually the start of a very vexing identity crisis.

I carefully stepped downstairs (for I had once fallen and double-sprained my left ankle), sauntered through the kitchen and den and then entered my two-story colonial home's laundry room. "Where are you going?" my wife inquired. 'You seem like a determined stubborn swallow looking for Capistrano."

"Over to my mom's place for breakfast," I half-guiltily replied as my mind contemplated my objective. "I'll stop at *Dunkin Donuts* and get something palatable to bring along with me. Maybe I'll buy a half-dozen double chocolates."

"Don't stop at that doughnut place," my spouse commanded in almost a military tone of voice. "You're getting too fat and old looking. You're a prime candidate for either diabetes or a cardiac arrest. And watch out for the black ice!" Joanne authoritatively commented. "February driving in South Jersey can be very hazardous!"

"I'll see ya' later," I defiantly answered my interrogator as I entered the laundry room door leading to the garage. I forcefully pressed the garage wall button in disgust and the electronic door opened. I was glad to escape my wife's criticism. My trusty car would be my perfect getaway vehicle from what I un-affectionately considered 'matriarchal tyranny.' I suddenly identified with why Rip Van Winkle habitually went squirrel hunting up in the *Catskill Mountains.*

I carefully pulled out of my U-shaped asphalt driveway onto the White Horse Pike and soon my characteristic rebellious nature rose from my subconscious. "I can't wait to buy those half-dozen high-calorie doughnuts," I said to my 2-D image in the flat rearview mirror. 'Instead of double-chocolate I might even buy the Boston cream kind without the holes in the center so that I get more delicious doughnut to munch on,' I thought and laughed while thoroughly enjoying my general naughtiness. 'Or maybe I'll purchase three and three.'

I flicked on my car stereo and heard The British rock group The Who singing and playing the catchy tune "Who Are You? Who-who, who-who!" The familiar music reminded me of my 2-D bathroom mirror reflection so I hurriedly switched stations, even though The Who are of "My Generation" and quite personally I really like most of the songs of Roger Daltrey, Pete Townshend, John Entwistle and Keith Moon.

I then realized something rather significant as I stopped for the traffic signal at the *Route 30* and *Route 206* intersection. That particular musical activity I was listening to was the continuation of a once more subtle identity crisis, which had originated a month before when I had spilled some *Coor's Light* onto my new shirt at a restaurant and my wife proceeded to criticize my ineptness (in her classic soprano voice) in the car on the way home, "You smell like a brewery! Take that shirt off when we get home so I can throw it into the washing machine and get rid of that ugly stain. You really know how to increase my daily workload! And be careful of the *206* intersection!"

My Walter Mitty mind exited its unpleasant recollection and I gingerly switched the radio station from Philadelphia's Oldies' WOGL-FM playing the Beach Boys' "Wouldn't It Be Nice" back to Trenton's WNJO's spinning of the equally rhythmic "Who Are You?" Then my in-progress reality check hit me like a crumbling concrete wall. "You smell like a *brewery*!"

My family name originally was Wiesnieski. But then the three-syllable Polish name was Germanized around 1900 into Wiessner. That transition (according to omniscient family historians) was done because during the turn of the twentieth century Germans were generally regarded as highly skilled workers and thus commanded higher paying salaries in Baltimore, Maryland than the newly arrived Polish immigrants did.

On the last leg of the drive to the local franchised doughnut outlet I recalled that my father's oldest sister Aunt Marie Mayor once told me that a prominent business had existed on Gay Street in downtown Baltimore appropriately named the John F. Wiessner Brewery. I remembered Aunt Marie showing me in her club basement several empty brown-bottle souvenirs that were officially labeled "The John F. Wiessner Brewery." 'I WAS named after a brewery,' I recollected with enlightenment as I approached *Dunkin Donuts*, 'and the strange irony is that my wife had just incidentally said I smelled like one!'

At that moment I needed to rationalize my most recent comprehension in a hurry. Remarkably there were only two cars ahead of me in the doughnut establishment's quick service lane. My frail ego had to defend its latest fracture and convince my mind that the coincidence was some type of weird anomaly.

"Ha ha!" I chuckled to my image in the rearview mirror while recollecting my wife's Saturday morning prattling about how especially dangerous it was devouring high-fat-content snacks. 'When I type in John Wiessner on *Google* or on *Yahoo Internet* search engines, my name usually comes up listed *before and ahead of* the famous John F. Wiessner Brewery. At last I'm more notorious than the brewery I had been named after. I have a higher *Internet* ranking than that defunct out-of-business brewery does!' I proudly concluded. 'Aunt Marie Mayor would definitely be proud of my accomplishment!'

It doesn't matter if my last name is spelled Wiessner or Weissner (my real last name follows the utilitarian spelling rule I had memorized in third grade, I before E except after C). My last name is sometimes misspelled Weissner because one of my credit cards spells it that way and when I had originally purchased my first computer, I had used that particular credit card. So, because of an accidental clerical error at the credit card company, my three e-mail addresses are also misspelled *Weissner* and consequently my last name appears on the *Internet* with two different spellings.

Despite the remembrance of that annoying difficulty my often-maligned family name (either Wiessner or Weissner) still commands more respect and patronage on *Google* and on *Yahoo* than does the brick and mortar John Frederick Wiessner Brewery that (according to Aunt Marie) my father and I had been named after. My Saturday morning existence was finally enjoying a moment of triumph.

"Did you know that I'm finally out of the shadow of the John F. Wiessner Brewery in Baltimore?" I told the suddenly startled and bewildered doughnut employee at the carry-out-window. The encumbered in-a-rush woman gave me a very peculiar look as she robotically handed me my white bag and my change through the opened drive-up window. The befuddled lady didn't even give me the courtesy of a perfunctory "Thank you!"

As I slowly drove to my mother's Marlyn Avenue residence an additional thought hit me like a ton of bricks and mortar. My author pseudonym *Jay Dubya* when typed on *Google* or *Yahoo* commanded much more respect than John Wiessner, John Weissner and the John F. Wiessner Brewery does all added together, but the really perplexing dilemma my brain was struggling with was this. 'I now have more identity as a "pen name" than I do as a real person, or as a real person named after an eighteenth-century brewery.' I reckoned. That grim realization only added misery to my already depressing identity quandary. 'The appellation *Jay Dubya* does not appear on my birth certificate!' I concluded.

As I steered my metallic blue *Buick LeSabre* from Bellevue Avenue onto Marlyn other bothersome-but-relevant ideas haunted my vulnerable psyche. My former high school (Bishop Egan) on the Levittown (Pennsylvania) Parkway has recently been demolished and no longer exists at its former location. The high school has merged and is now Conwell-Egan High in Fairless Hills, Pa. I had graduated in 1960 from Edgewood Regional High School but that institution is now called Winslow Township High School. In 1965 John Wiessner had graduated from *Glassboro State Teachers College*, which now possesses the designation *Rowan University*. Ironically much of my past both in Pennsylvania and in New Jersey has been erased.

I sat in my warm car in my mother's driveway and seriously evaluated the total puzzle. 'Nothing is easy in this world!' I decided. 'Sometimes I believe I should be living on a more favorable planet that accommodates dreamers.' Then my imagination adroitly put all of the pieces together.

I had been named after my father who had been named after a brewery once located on Gay Street in downtown Baltimore, Maryland. 'That's an undeniable fact!' my mind assessed. 'My pen name is more famous than my real name, which has two distinct *Internet* spellings. One of my high schools no longer physically or functionally exists and my other high school and my former college both have acquired different names,' I reminded myself. 'A good deal of my memorable past has been almost systematically eradicated from history.' I flicked the ignition into the "Off" position and grabbed my small bag of doughnuts.

Now you fully know and can amply appreciate precisely what has been "*aleing*" me and I hereby humbly solicit your sympathy. An identity crisis had been *brewing* deep inside my mind, inside my heart and inside my restive soul. I recklessly exited my *Buick* automobile and slipped and fell on the black ice that covered my mother's driveway.

"Oh well," I mumbled to my somewhat defeated spirit as I rose from the hard, cold driveway to my feet and gingerly reached for my white *Dunkin Donuts'* bag, "I'm still going to enjoy my delectable chocolate-covered Boston cream doughnuts and a few double-chocolate treats to boot regardless of who I might happen to be! Maybe I should have listened to my wife about icy February obstacles! Gee, I can already smell the aroma of Mom's coffee brewing from inside her home!"

"Local Legend Transcends Technology"

Jack Donio is not only Hammonton's Fire Chief for fifteen years but also the good-hearted citizen is a local living legend and a favorite hero of area mythology. Move over Jersey Devil. If big Jack Donio happened to be an American Indian, he would more-than-likely carry the name Chief Big-Heart. His widespread reputation is not only because of his extraordinary volunteer service to his town. You'll soon know why.

All kinds of fascinating tales abound about "Big Jack." For some inexplicable reason I always want to believe these incredible stories, no matter how exaggerated their redundancy may sound. Having a literature background, this former English teacher enjoys myths and relishes their perpetuation.

One popular tale has Jack Donio on his former Winslow farm surrounded by fifty silent and obedient migrant workers. Without making any announcement in either Spanish or English Jack holds two huge sledgehammers perpendicular to the ground. Standing erect, the mammoth man casually twists his wrists upward and the dual sledgehammers instantly rise to waist level right before his very amazed and spellbound audience. Then Big Jack Donio casually drops the dual heavy objects to the ground and departs the barn area in a nonchalant gait as the impressed and astounded farm employees chatter amongst themselves.

A garrulous farmer (of some credibility) had once told me that he had witnessed Big Jack pull into Folsom's C&E Cannery with an enormous load of Jersey tomatoes stacked in "five-eights' bushel baskets." The tailgate load was so large that when Big Jack stepped down from the cab, the truck's front tires immediately rose two inches above the asphalt. I don't care if it sounds too sensational and exaggerated to believe. The story propagates and verifies the behemoth's remarkable legend, which quite incidentally I too am guilty of perpetuating.

I could mentally picture Big Jack arm wrestling King Kong Bundy for hours over whose head was balder, and the intense contest would naturally end in a draw because the smoky bar they were in had to finally close down for the night. That's the kind of bizarre stuff my fertile mind imagines whenever I meet and converse with Big Jack Donio.

One particular Saturday night in late July of 2001 my wife Joanne and I and friends Mac and Denise Fascetta drove eight miles from

Hammonton out to Sweetwater Casino for dinner. After enjoying a terrific meal and some interesting conversation while seated at a table overlooking the historic *Mullica River*, the four of us had to exit the South Jersey establishment through an adjoining dining room. My perceptive eyes immediately observed stocky brothers Jack and Joe Donio seated at a table having dinner with wives Eugenia and Roseann.

"Uncle John," Joe enthusiastically greeted me in his familiar affable tone of voice, "how the heck are ya' doin'?"

"Great Uncle Joe," I returned, implementing *our* typically predictable salutation. "It's great to see two local farmers out feasting and enjoying themselves during the height of the summer harvest season."

"Sir," Jack said as he nearly disintegrated my right head in a firm handshake, "it's always an honor and a privilege to see you," the likeable giant stated rising from his seat while all four of our wives chuckled.

I was extremely flattered because the local legend Fire Chief regarded former English teacher John Wiessner as an important member of *his* community. Overcome by curiosity and desiring to learn some gossip, I inquired about the validity of one of his many adventures.

"Jack," I deviously began, "is the fantastic story true that you used to take two heavy sledgehammers on your Winslow farm and..."

"Forget about that trivia," the awesome hero politely interrupted with noteworthy authority. "That's history if ya' know what I mean. Here's a new story."

Big Jack told me that on one recent occasion he had been summoned to a massive local fire. The Chief felt sick, weak and dizzy after arriving at the scene of conflagration. Upon exiting his vehicle and stepping towards the blazing warehouse, Big Jack nearly collapsed to the ground. The Hammonton Rescue Squad arrived and immediately transported the afflicted Fire Chief to Kessler Memorial Hospital. Everyone who had been present during the emergency suspected that Big Jack Donio had suffered a heart attack.

"Wow!" I loudly exclaimed inside the handsomely decorated Sweetwater dining room. "Obviously you've survived your ordeal. What happened next?"

Big Jack took a deep breath to effectively heighten my suspense and then he dramatically explained that the hospital doctors told him his heart had lost its rhythm. It was fluttering and beating irregularly

14

and had to be stabilized. 'The rhythm must have sounded like a really bad rap song,' I thought but dared not comment.

"The doctors in the Emergency Room said that three things could happen to me," Big Jack nonchalantly emphasized. "And I'll always remember them."

"What were they?" I curiously asked. "I'm always interested in learning new information."

"Nothing would happen, I could live, or I could die," Donio tersely replied quite matter-of-factly. "They then said they had to use a ...."

"A defibrillator?" I interrupted as I inserted a direct object into his declarative sentence. "The medical device you're referring to is called a defibrillator."

"Yeah, that's it," Big Jack concurred with my accurate nomenclature, "they wanted to give me a powerful electric shock to get my heart workin' right again."

Big Jack next informed me that the concerned doctors then professionally administered several hard electric jolts to his immense sternum. Donio's huge barrel-shaped-chest did not respond to the potent stimulation and his body did not react by heaving up from the hospital table like viewers always see on TV hospital shows. "I stayed in the hospital for a full week but my damned heart never regained its proper rhythm," Big Jack stated in a feigned melancholy tone of voice.

"Well, how did you ever get it beating back to normal?" I inquisitively wanted to know as I glanced down at the gigantic steak that looked like half a cow lying in the center of Big Jack's dish.

"I went back to work as a wintertime highway supervisor. I was at a construction scene," Big Jack proceeded to elaborate, "so bein' bored I grabbed a jackhammer from a guy and started riveting concrete non-stop for six hours. Then I went back to the doctors at the hospital for a scheduled checkup, and they were astonished and said that my heart problem had miraculously been cured."

As I drove from the rustic Sweetwater Casino Restaurant back to Hammonton I thought about Jack's new tale and about my fantasy of him arm-wrestling King Kong Bundy for hours in that splendid imaginary smoky barroom. I then thought about the lyrics to a Jim Croce song.

"He's badder than old King Kong, meaner than a junkyard dog." Then while driving south past several expansive blueberry plantations I chuckled at my mind's fantasy. The pro' wrestler King Kong Bundy's family owned a South Jersey junkyard and they probably have several vicious mongrel dogs diligently protecting the premises. 'Heaven rest Leroy Brown and Jim Croce's souls,' I mused, 'and long

15

live King Kong Bundy and Hammonton's Chief Big-Heart. Now I know why the riveting road-shattering device is called a Jack-hammer,' I concluded with a smile.

"Keep your eyes on this winding road," my wife imperatively ordered. "How come you're smiling and giggling?"

"I don't know!" I prevaricated. "Sometimes I just simply enjoy acting stupid!"

"Williamsburg Field Trips"

Throughout my thirty-four-year teaching career I had been on over a hundred field trips, mostly with seventh and eighth grade *students*. Some of the more exotic destinations have been Philadelphia, Baltimore's *Inner Harbor,* Atlantic City, New York, *Hershey Park, Kings Dominion, Six Flags Great Adventure* in New Jersey, Luray Caverns, Washington DC, and on the emotionally traumatic Williamsburg/Washington DC field trip.

The three-day and two-night annual eighth grade field trip to Washington/Williamsburg was definitely the most harrowing misadventure that could easily whittle away at a teacher's life expectancy. At certain times on the bus the *children* would be screaming so loudly that I thought the juveniles were testing the malleability of my ears' tympanic membranes.

Some of the more obnoxious *students* would kick each other across the bus aisle, slap and punch the *children* sitting behind them or in front of them and put chewing gum (which was forbidden and against school rules) into girls' long tresses. Some of the more boisterous and aggressive *children* behaved as if they were rookies vying for starting positions in a professional football team's camp. A traveling sideshow class of a hundred and fifty fourteen-year-old *student* squealing demons could dramatically transform an ordinarily tranquil motel into a frenzied scene.

I do recollect one particular excursion down to Williamsburg, Virginia very well. Four buses were commissioned to transport the pint-sized eighth grade Philistines. I was assigned to Bus #1 along with another teacher Rob Renbeck and the superintendent of schools. "Where are you going to sit?" I asked the school system's chief executive before I boarded the bus.

"In the front," the superintendent replied. "I always like to sit in the front."

"Okay," I said, "I guess I'll be sitting in the back somewhere with Mr. Renbeck. First I'll take attendance!"

I stepped onto the bus while the superintendent was gabbing with the other chaperones, the principal and the school nurse. After surveying the caliber of *students* aboard I rearranged the *children*'s seats while I took the roll to make sure everyone on my Bus #1 roster list was safely aboard. I made sure that all of the worse behaved *children* were sitting up front with the superintendent and that the better-behaved *students* in the rear were sitting near the other teacher and me.

After an hour of motoring southward (we were then on the *Delaware Memorial Bridge* just before *I-95*), the ornery tendencies of the more-naughty rascals surfaced in the anterior of the bus. The *children* hooted, chanted and carried on, testing the mettle of the school system's chief administrative official. And before a person could recite the Russian alphabet the *children* seated toward the front of the vehicle then began singing popular television jingles with dirty words being substituted for the original rhyming ones.

Several of the boys started shouting and sounding like they were a covey of inebriated hoot owls while they explored the boundaries of being free of parental control. Many of the less illustrious *students* had never been out of New Jersey before and didn't know how to act civilized in public (or in private). In fact they acted like little spoiled scamps, just the same way they had always been behaving in school.

While the back of the bus was rather calm the front (where the superintendent had been sitting with *his* rigged audience) produced the racket of an ancient Roman gladiatorial contest. The mystified school superintendent turned around several times to get my attention but I ignored his eye contact, pretending to be taking in the blurred scenes flitting by my side window.

"The *super*' looks distressed!" I laughed to Rob Renbeck, my teaching comrade.

"The whole front of the bus sounds like a juvenile gang fight in a teenage cabaret," Rob answered. "I hope the superintendent knows karate!"

"He must think we're fantastic disciplinarians," I chuckled. "Rob, let's step to the front of the bus and settle the little urchins down so that we don't have to perform emergency *CPR* on the superintendent."

The superintendent was an intellectual philosophical type and he actually impressed me by showing a remarkable bit of disciplining skill while at the Williamsburg motel. The *children* had just finished swimming that evening in the motel's pool. Next the energetic lads and lasses had dinner at the motel and at ten p.m. everyone was supposed to be in their rooms. At ten-thirty the superintendent was telling Rob Renbeck, Joe Sacci (the music teacher) and me how he had surprised several *students* that had tried sneaking out of a Washington motel room back in 1950.

"I was down by the pool at the Washington motel, just like we're standing here right now," the superintendent explained to Rob, Joe and me. "Then I spotted two girls sneaking out of their motel room on the second floor and I yelled, 'Hey you up there'!" the superintendent bellowed and then indulgently laughed as he turned and pointed up to the motel's balcony without really looking up at it.

Well, it was a very unbelievable case of déjà vu. When the superintendent yelled out "Hey *you* up there!" with his back to the motel's balcony and then turned, two girls tried sneaking out of their room and had thought the superintendent had caught them in the act of escaping while he was telling us his 1950 story. The startled young ladies re-entered their room thinking that they would be seriously reprimanded. The superintendent had caught and indirectly disciplined two girls in Williamsburg violating the rules without his knowledge while he was cheerfully describing in 1977 a similar incident in Washington that had occurred way back in 1950.

"What's so funny?" the Socratic-type superintendent asked when noticing that Rob Renbeck, Joe Sacci and I were holding our stomachs while laughing so hard.

"You tell the funniest stories!" I answered as Rob Renbeck nearly lost his balance and almost tumbled backward and coming very close to launching Joe and him into the motel's swimming pool.

On another trip down to Williamsburg from New Jersey, some nutcase sniper (on the passenger side of a passing left-hand-lane car) had an air rifle and took a shot at the driver's side window. The glass internally shattered while the bus was going sixty-five miles-per-hour down *I-95* between Wilmington, Delaware and Baltimore. All four chartered class trip buses heading south stopped and we had to wait for the Maryland State Police to arrive so that an official report could be filed.

That same beleaguered bus driver should have read *his* horoscope before re-embarking toward Washington. As the driver of Bus #1 made a wide right-hand turn heading onto Independence Avenue toward the *Capitol Building* a taxi cab driver tried passing the bus on the right. The bus and the auto' turned simultaneously and *it* violently smashed the taxicab into a parked car.

The already stressed-out bus driver got into two heated arguments at the same time with the Iranian taxicab driver and with an Iraqi that owned the stalled parked car that had had its hood open. It was a unique dispute because neither the Iranian nor the Iraqi yelled and screamed in English while the accursed bus driver was bellowing an assortment of cuss words at the two foreigners using very understandable and graphic American expletives. The vehement yelling and cursing really entertained the *children* that had recently been evacuated from the bus after the collision.

The thought of the annual Williamsburg pilgrimage always made me shudder with apprehension. In 1978 the hundred and fifty screaming neurotic demons were impatiently waiting for entrance into a *Smithsonian Institute* exhibit area. A female teacher- chaperone brought it to my attention that the *students* were blocking the other tourists' access to the exhibit's ticket booth so I chivalrously commanded in a loud authoritarian voice for the eighth-grade *students* to "slowly shift to the right."

As I casually shuffled to the front of the *students'* irregular line a young married couple began shouting a stream of criticisms directly toward me. The pair of "civilians" apparently had become unhappy campers mixed up in the legion of eighth grade maniacs moving to the right and had been severely jostled around in the turbulent *student* migration. The young man bellowed in my ear, "Look buddy, your kids almost crushed my wife and me. We didn't appreciate being mauled and knocked about by your discourteous teenagers!"

"Sir, I was only trying to show the other tourists some courtesy by making the ticket booth accessible to them!" I answered. "I guess my maneuver backfired!"

An intimidating crowd of bloodthirsty fourteen-year-old *children* crowded around the man, his wife and me and began yelling, "Give him a shot in the nose Mr. Wiessner!" and "Teach him a little karate Wheesey baby!"

I immediately felt like a frustrated toreador at a bullfight that was geared to the emotional interests of aspiring juvenile delinquents. The *students* actually wanted to see their English teacher get into a wild fistfight with a simple disgruntled tourist and his equally distressed wife.

"Sock it to him Mr. Wiessner!" a young pugnacious-type fight enthusiast boisterously hollered. "Hit him upside his head!"

"Listen Mister, do you see this mob of screaming young devils!" I told the fellow as I pointed to the psyched-up crowd of rabid youths. "How would *you* like to take my place and be in charge of these young hellions?"

"No thank you!" the man instantly answered. "My wife and I have already felt their wrath!"

"God bless you!" the wife exclaimed as she and her husband voluntarily moved away from the ticket window vicinity to the back of the line.

Events that suddenly emerge out of nowhere can make long-distance overnight field trips about as desirable as a chicken hawk colony flourishing on a poultry farm. As the chartered buses rumbled through the federal government district of Washington D.C. I was amazed at the observations the more alert *students* were making while glancing outside their bus windows. None of the magnificent white marble monuments and obelisks that they had recently viewed at an eighth-grade *educational* slide presentation assembly in their school auditorium interested them in the least.

As the bus driver announced over the microphone, "There's the *White House* on your right!" several *students* looking in the opposite direction of 1600 Pennsylvania Avenue then yelled to their classmates, "Hey, look at that weird guy selling balloons!" and "Check out that drunk begging for booze money!" But that was not the rule for several of the more serious *students* that had asked when pointing at the *White House*, "Is that the *Capitol* or is it the *Supreme Court Building?*"

The basic purpose of the Williamsburg/Washington trips was to cultivate an appreciation of American history and of our nation's colonial heritage. But to the more nefarious-minded *students* the highlights of the daily educational itineraries were staying up all night, pounding on walls, and having wild pillow fights. The children also reveled in playing strip poker with members of the same sex, sneaking out of rooms at four in the morning and making the teacher-chaperones earn every cent of the money they weren't getting paid extra for.

If the social (sociological) experiences just mentioned were the culminating aspects of the *students'* trip, then why did the teachers have to transport them three hundred miles away from home? We could have simply rented a motel five miles from the school and saved fourteen hours of needless transportation back and forth from Williamsburg. After all, the social experience should transcend the dull academic learning agenda, shouldn't it?

"It's a good thing we have the rule that girls sit with girls and boys sit with boys on the bus!" Rob Renbeck stated to Joe Sacci and me.

"Yes, and the girls are on the second floor of the motel and the boys all on the first floor!" Joe added.

"Guys, the school field trip rules might actually be promoting homosexuality by keeping genders together without even realizing it!" I concluded, much to Rob and Joe's amusement.

That night we stayed at a motel on the Alexandria side of the *Potomac.* Several enterprising *students* somehow jimmied open a soda machine's door and the culprits emptied out the entire *Coke* dispenser (which had recently been filled) and distributed their booty among appreciative and already hyperactive classmates. When the hotel manager discovered the theft he really protested to the trip's

21

coordinator and naturally the school had to compensate the motel for the juvenile larceny.

Rob Renbeck and I had pulled the midnight to three in the morning shift to check rooms and curtail male *students* from sneaking out of their quarters and visiting members of the opposite sex on another floor of the motel. I noticed across a side street that someone was breaking and entering into a car so I reported the crime-in-progress over my room phone to the motel's office. The night manager came running up the concrete steps to the balcony overlooking the alleged crime scene.

"Look at that guy over there trying to start that car!" I told the night manager. "Mr. Renbeck here and I just saw the fellow break into the auto' three minutes ago!"

"Oh," the night manager replied, "that's not happening on the motel's property so I'm not going to worry about it and get involved!"

"But it's the stealing of an automobile!" I objected. "It's a major crime!"

"Do *you* want to come back to Alexandria and testify in court six months from now just to see justice served?" the motel night manager asked me.

"No, I don't think so!" I replied in astonishment. "I live a hundred and fifty miles away!"

"Well then, if I was you I would just forget that I had seen anything at all!" the night manager finished with a wink. "Now if you'll excuse me I have some important paperwork to do!"

Rob Renbeck and I looked at each other and we both shrugged our shoulders. We stood there and watched the entire theft transpire and gave the anonymous criminal mock waves as he drove the stolen vehicle by the motel balcony.

While we were in Williamsburg on that same trip a group of *students* was watching a colonial craft demonstration. A female Williamsburg employee dressed in 1700s garb was showing some of the *students* how pottery was made back in the time of George Washington. "Don't stick your hand near that spinning machine!" Rob Renbeck cautioned the *children.*

The last thing' in the world a teacher can tell fourteen-year-olds is "Don't do that!" or "Don't try that!" An eighth-grade girl stuck her right index finger in the spinning pottery and got it caught in the rotating lathe. Blood was squirting all over the place. The rotating pottery wheel had to be stopped and Rob Renbeck had to accompany the crying injured *child* to the nearest infirmary and then call the parents and get permission for stitches to sew up the wound. Renbeck had to spend five hours of *his* time making sure that all school procedures had been properly followed involving the case of "an unnecessary *student* emergency."

"Maybe that girl will grow up and become a *spinster!*" I told Rob that night in our motel room.

"I don't think so!" he tersely returned with a forced smile.

That night at the Williamsburg motel I was rooming with music teacher Joe Sacci and with Rob. Joe heard some ecstatic *students* yelling into the air vents and they were telling other *children* in neighboring motel rooms that big parties were to be held in rooms 211 and 223. Joe stood on a chair, skillfully disguised his voice and then yelled into the air vent, "The biggest party is goin' to happen in room 217 at three in the morning!" Joe informed his anonymous air-vent audience. "We have two big bottles of whiskey!" Sacci persuasively added.

At precisely three a.m. there was a gentle rapping at our motel room's door. Joe triumphantly opened the door and he, Rob and I yelled at the six astounded and shocked violators standing outside, "Busted! You're all busted!" in what was certainly the finest case of *student* entrapment I had ever been associated with on any overnight field trip.

On the way back from Williamsburg the buses stopped at the distinguished and eminent *Kennedy Center* in Washington. After a brief tour of the cultural arts' facility the *students* were conducted to the *Kennedy Center's* cafeteria. Some hungry *children* had beaten Rob Renbeck and me to the cafeteria, had opened up the wall menu ledger and then had mischievously rearranged some of the word' letters of foods available to diners. Servings of "Pussy Burgers" and "Dick Dogs" were suddenly imaginatively listed inside the *Kennedy Center's* cafeteria ledger. A cafeteria manager came over, saw the recently created obscenities inside the ledger and screamed, "Who's in charge of these juvenile delinquents?"

Rob Renbeck and I looked frightfully at each other, spun around and deftly hid behind two tall and wide red pillars so that the columns completely obscured us from the distressed woman's sight. The thoroughly appalled cafeteria manager eventually got the *children* to line up and then assigned a cafeteria employee to change the ledger language back to the normal "Hamburgers" and "Hot Dogs."

The trip coordinators showed up and had to listen to the cafeteria manager complain to Mrs. Finnian, the school principal and the superintendent, "This is definitely the most embarrassing and humiliating thing that has ever happened in *my* cafeteria! It was absolutely mortifying and a horrible public disgrace!"

When the four buses finally headed back north toward Baltimore, bus number two passed bus number one and the children got all excited about the little race the drivers were conducting. Rob Renbeck and I were on bus number one and watched in astonishment as a *student* on bus number two opened the roof-hatch and stuck his head out giving the middle finger to the mesmerized *students* on bus number one.

The buses were heading toward the tollbooths for the *Harbor Tunnel* before traveling under the *Patapsco River*. The wise guy *student* on bus number two (giving the royal finger to the tunnel-vision *students* on bus number one) was almost decapitated as the bus number two's raised hatch just made it under the *Harbor Tunnel's* tollbooth's pavilion roof. Everyone held his and her breath until the bus's roof hatch was finally closed. The *student* received three days of Office Detention for nearly beheading himself and for using obscene gestures (not "obscene jesters" as indicated in the Teachers Handbook) to his fellow classmates viewing the crazy spectacle from bus number one.

The Williamsburg three-day-trip was eventually shortened in the 1980s to simply being the Washington DC two day and one motel night trip. That move was done for costly economic expense reasons. The high school seniors that used to go to Washington for their pre-graduation trip now flew from Philadelphia to *Disney World* in Orlando, Florida so the eighth grade graduating class inherited Washington as its prime destination.

The first day of a 1990s eighth grade class trip was rather exhaustive as the students and chaperones visited and toured the *White House*, the *Capitol*, the *Washington Monument*, *Ford's Theater* and then partook of a night cruise with dinner on an entertainment ship down the *Potomac River*.

The very wary chaperones deliberately kept the *students* touring historic sites and monuments to tire them out so that the *children* would sleep the whole night instead of bugging the heck out of us. After we had toured the *Lincoln* and *Jefferson Memorials,* the buses finally headed across the *Potomac* where that year the *children* were staying at an attractive Tyson's Corner motel.

Since the volatile *children* had been fairly well' behaved on that particular Washington excursion, the chaperones rewarded them with a pizza party in the motel's Madison Room. When the pizzas and soda had been totally consumed five chaperones escorted the first half of the *students* back to their rooms, which were strategically located in a remote section of the huge suburban motel. The four remaining chaperones (including myself) escorted the second batch of seventy-five *students* from the Madison (mass dining) Room to *their* assigned accommodations.

Mac Fascetta and I made sure all of our *students* had evacuated the Madison Room and we brought up the rear guard of the second set of still boisterous fourteen-year-old *children*.

Suddenly a stocky male in his early twenties (chaperoning a Catholic high school sophomore class that was also staying overnight at the Tyson's Corner motel) came sprinting up to Mac and me nearly screaming the larynx out of his throat.

"Are *you* in charge of those wild kids on the other side of the building?" he hollered, apparently not used to the behavior of normal *public school* eighth grade *students*.

"Yes we are!" I politely answered. "There are five of our chaperones already over there' getting the *students* settled in their rooms!"

"Well your kids are banging on the walls and setting a bad example for my kids!" the young muscular fellow shouted with a crimson face.

"Look," I rather calmly answered, "I'm assigned to this group of seventy-five *students*. Our school already has five very capable chaperones over there to deal with *that* problem!"

Evidently the muscular Catholic high school chaperone didn't savor my explanation so he surprisingly took a huge swing at my face. I ducked down just in the nick of time and his blow glanced off the top of my head and knocked off my red *Phillies* baseball cap. Then Mac Fascetta latched onto the fellow's right arm and I firmly gripped his left one and the enraged chaperone' finally realized that *we* weren't exactly wimps and that my friend and I could effectively restrain him and defend ourselves if necessary.

So even while enjoying a pleasant field trip a teacher's existence might be endangered by a chaperone from another school losing his temper from excessive stress and then ultimately going ballistic. When Mac and I got back to our "Home sweet home!" motel quarters we heard a major disturbance sounding like glass being shattered (originating from the adjoining room).

Four of our eighth-grade *students* had indeed been pounding on the walls and had antagonized a drunken tractor-trailer driver that had been occupying the neighboring room. The noise had aggravated the inebriated fellow to the point where the big-rig operator was *climbing the walls* from the *students' pounding on the walls*. The totally upset man had entered the startled kids' room, had broken an empty bottle of *Southern Comfort* and the crazed tractor-trailer driver was in the process of threatening to slice up the throats of the suddenly shocked *students* with the shattered weapon being held in his right hand.

Mac and I convinced the intoxicated man that we were the *students'* unfortunate chaperones and then we humbly and respectfully apologized for any inconvenience the little terrors (presently being terrorized) had caused him. After Mac and I had promised that the "obnoxious *children*" would not bother the troubled gent again the somewhat appeased driver slowly staggered out of the boys' motel room muttering under his breath how he indeed would inflict serious injury if the reprehensible rascals persisted in the continuation of their annoying high jinks. Remarkably (and much to *our* relief) the boys' sensed that the irritated fellow meant business, abandoned their disturbing antics and soon went to sleep shortly after midnight.

The following morning after enjoying a scrambled egg breakfast at the Madison Room, the buses were boarded to tour some sites in metropolitan downtown Washington. Mac and I had pulled the difficult midnight to three a.m. shift and were tired the entire morning. After touring the *Vietnam Memorial,* Mac Fascetta and I returned to our bus only to find four eighth graders standing on the roof and being screamed at by at least twenty *Vietnam War* veterans (several of them were in wheelchairs) that the *children* had recently verbally antagonized. Police in the area arrived on the scene and adroitly broke-up the brief altercation and the incident was then reported to the school principal for further disciplinary action.

At noon the eighth graders ate in a cafeteria in downtown Washington. Several *students* were making fun of an old man sitting alone dining in the cafeteria. After noticing the old man reaching into his vest beneath his sport jacket and toying with an object that Mac and I believed was a handgun, my fellow teacher and I approached the boys' table and had them move into an adjacent dining room before any unnecessary tragedy might have happened.

While we were waiting for the buses to arrive Mac and I casually strolled through a shopping mall browsing at window displays. Three of our *students* raced by before I could yell out "Stop!" Then suddenly five motorcycle gang members in black leather jackets dashed by in hot pursuit of the three scampering *children*. Apparently, the *students* had made some irreverent remarks to the gang members, who then hopped off their motorcycles and chased the young renegades through the shopping mall. Obviously. the offensive *children* must have been in better shape than the burly motorcycle enthusiasts because the pursuers eventually gave up the hunt and disgustedly walked back past Mac and me in the direction of their parked *Harley Davidsons.*

At the *Smithsonian's Aerospace Museum* Mac and I showed some bona fide *students* the *Spirit of St. Louis* that had been flown across the Atlantic from New York to Paris by Charles Lindbergh and then we viewed several space capsule models. We were really fatigued from a lack of sleep so Mac and I did what we traditionally had done on all previous trips. We entered the *Smithsonian Aerospace Museum's* planetarium to rest our bloodshot eyes and our weary bones.

"Wake me up if I fall asleep," I told Mac.

"And *you* wake me up if I fall asleep," my chaperone friend requested.

Three fairly reliable *students* from our school were seated directly behind Mac and me so I figured I would ask them for a small favor. "Guys! If Mr. Fascetta and I both fall asleep," I said, "please wake us up after the planetarium show!"

"Don't worry Mr. Wiessner!" the three dependable *students* assured me. "We know you both must be real tired!"

The lights went out and fifteen minutes later I heard Mac snoring so I gave him a jolt to the ribs to bring him back to consciousness. Then ten minutes after that Mac gave me an elbow poke to alert me that I too had been snoring.

Fifteen minutes later I felt a hand shaking my right shoulder. A planetarium usher was vibrating both Mac Fascetta and me, waking us up from deep slumbers. The three reliable *children* had abandoned us after the astronomy show so we had to suffer the mortification of being irresponsible chaperones falling asleep on the job and having to be awakened by a thoroughly amused planetarium program attendant.

"A Young James Bertino"

I knew James Bertino several decades before he had matured and blossomed into Hammonton town councilman James Bertino. Jim has a twin brother John and their parents Anthony and Margaret Bertino owned "Twin Boys' Farm Market" on the White Horse Pike across from the Oak Grove Cemetery. My parents were proprietors of Pete's Farm Market in Elm, New Jersey, which is now owned by Dennis Donio. Being in the same retail fruit and produce business made *our* families' rivals but also friends.

From the years 1967-'81 I had co-owned boardwalk businesses in Rehoboth Beach, Delaware (a beach tee-shirt and gift shop) and in Ocean City, Maryland (a boardwalk arcade). It was an April Friday evening in the mid-1970s and I desperately needed a healthy young body to help me install twenty re-conditioned poker-card drums into Dealer's Choice machines at my Ocean City, Maryland boardwalk arcade. My brother-in-law Ollie Paretti had done his usual excellent repair work on the electromagnetic devices that rotated inside the cabinets' windows. I figured I would get in touch with the prospective assistant I had in mind.

I gave young James Bertino a call and the teenager was quite anxious to accompany me on the 175-mile excursion down the Delmarva Peninsula to Ocean City. I picked Bertino up at his parents' home in my green Pontiac station wagon and we were soon heading south on *I-295* toward the *Delaware Memorial Bridge*. I was already rather fatigued from teaching my grueling six English classes at the Hammonton Middle School so while motoring toward Dover I stopped at a McDonald's in Smyrna, Delaware where *we* could devour some much-needed carbs and enjoy mutual sugar rushes. I quickly learned that my callow friend and I were not-too-enamored with studying in school and teaching in a public school respectively.

Soon James Bertino and I were on our way east on *Route 13* heading toward Rehoboth Beach where my boardwalk' tee-shirt store was located beneath the high-rise Star of the Sea Condominiums. We dropped off several boxes of decals and a new heat-transfer machine. It was then after midnight and our eyes were already bloodshot. Our next task would be to deliver the rehabilitated poker drums twenty-five miles down the coast to 410 South Boardwalk, Ocean City, Maryland.

I was getting a little giddy and groggy from sheer exhaustion so I told Bertino a story John Rizzotte (the driver education teacher at Hammonton High School) had once related to me in the faculty room.

"John, what should I do if I'm ever stopped on the highway by a policeman?" I innocently had asked the driving instructor while retelling the anecdote to my rather apathetic passenger.

"That's easy John," Rizzotte told me. "You have to simply take away *his* psychological advantage. Ya' gotta' aggressively steal the initiative from him."

"What's that supposed to mean?" I persisted to my faculty room colleague. "Sometimes I don't know if you're being facetious or being honest."

"Well," Rizzotte continued with his little informative seminar, "as soon as you come to a stop, jump out of your auto' and go directly to *his* car. Respectfully ask the officer why he had stopped you. Cops are usually so used to being in control and walking over to your car that most won't know what to do or how to react when you break that regular pattern. Most policemen will then let you go without a ticket because you've successfully taken away their psychological advantage."

While articulating the story to young James Bertino I continued driving my green Pontiac wagon out of Rehoboth Beach onto the devoid-of-traffic Coastal Highway. My station wagon was soon heading due south through Dewey Beach, Delaware, a summer college bar town like Somers Point up in Jersey. Dewey Beach has a strict 25 mile-per-hour speed limit. I was wrapping up telling Bertino the instructions that John Rizzotte had confidentially told me in the faculty room.

Suddenly a police car's red beacon light became visible behind me in my rear-view mirror. Next my ears perceived a shrill siren blasting. Naturally I had to enact what I had just told my rider Bertino in the car.

I halted my Pontiac wagon, leaped out of the vehicle and briskly hustled toward the police cruiser. One burly Dewey Beach cop had already jumped out of the driver's side. He had thought that I was about to attack him so the patrolman roughly grabbed me, threw me up against the rear of my station wagon and directed me to keep my hands on the roof while he expertly frisked me for possible weapons. As the no-nonsense cop was performing that act another policeman stopped with a K-9 German shepherd, which began growling, snarling and ferociously barking at me while displaying a wicked set of fangs. At that juncture I was completely intimidated and quite cooperative.

The first cop asked me what was under the tawdry old blue bed quilt in the station wagon's rear storage area. I showed him the poker machine drums with their new regulation-sized cards recently glued on. My interrogator immediately suspected that the mechanisms were illegal Delaware slot machines, which were also perfectly legal licensed amusement gaming devices on the boardwalk in Ocean City, Maryland.

I then discreetly dropped a few names of some big shots I knew in Ocean City. Bill Purnell was my landlord and Jim Mathias was a good friend who owned another popular amusement arcade where players acquired and accumulated coupons to trade for prizes. Both gentlemen were prominent Ocean City councilmen. After the Dewey Beach cops made several radio calls, those influential Maryland names were verified as legitimate references. I was allowed to re-enter my green station wagon. All the while I was cursing John Rizzotte's non-sage advice under my breath.

The first cop apologized for the rough treatment he had administered to an honest hard-working midnight-traveling teacher-businessman. "Mr. Wiessner," the cop said with a grim expression on his countenance, "for your benefit I'd like for you to do me one small favor."

"What's that?" I solemnly and respectfully asked trying my best to be polite and sincere.

"Please sign your name on the back of your driver's license. It's not valid until you do. And then I'll call ahead to the Bethany Beach and to the Fenwick Island police so that you'll not be inconvenienced again. I guarantee you safe passage until you hit Ocean City."

I fired up the engine and slowly pulled my vehicle onto the highway. James Bertino was laughing so hard because a tough brawny policeman had very efficiently manhandled his former English teacher. I thought young Jim's appendages were going to fall off from excessive laughter. Needless to say I was very embarrassed.

"See," I said to my traveling apprentice as I drowsily motored down the coast through Fenwick Island toward my ultimate destination, "Mr. Rizzotte was right. I didn't get a traffic ticket after all!"

Bertino cackled and gasped for air in reaction to my timely comment. I imagined he was going to explode all over my dashboard and inside windshield. Truthfully, I have never seen a person laugh so indulgently.

Councilman James Bertino is presently employed in Hammonton being a key supervisor at Garden State Color Film Corporation on Fairview Avenue. I know he vividly remembers the bizarre Dewey Beach police/motorist incident. The man has a photographic memory.

"Good Grammar and Spelling Skills"

Being a former dedicated English teacher has its advantages. I can use my grammar, spelling, punctuation and logic skills to instantly detect *Internet* scams advanced by devious unscrupulous scoundrels. Con artists on the net' are so intent and thorough in organizing their reprehensible plans that in their mania they overlook simple basic communication rules. Honest business people understand that impeccable English is always necessary to make a good first impression; scamsters haven't yet mastered middle school level language arts.

Here are a few examples to illustrate exactly what I mean by the need to possess better than average grammar and spelling tools. Several weeks ago I received an "Urgent *Confedential* Request" from one Andrew Chidi, whose name appeared as Anyanwu Agu on his e-mail address bar. I immediately became suspicious when someone with a great name such as Andrew Chidi would coincidentally masquerade with a more complex e-mail name Anyanwu Agu. Besides not knowing how to spell the word "confidential," the e-mail solicitor stated that he was the Director of the Foreign Remittance Department of Du Banque Lome-Togo of West Africa, where apparently the need for good communications' skills is not too important.

I know for a fact that anyone who knows how to spell "Remittance" should easily know the simpler syllable construction "confidential." I automatically reckoned that a definite problem existed when Andrew Chidi's heading had the false-but-creative spelling designation "*Audeting* and *Accoting* Unit." Any imbecile with a decrepit-looking dollar paperback English Dictionary could easily research the words "Auditing and Accounting." Furthermore, good old lazy Andrew found out about John Wiessner "as a *relaible* person" by reading about me in a "West African *Chamber of Commerce* Business Directory." Unfortunately (for Andrew's sake) I was not impressed with the phony flattery represented in the suspect e-mail.

Now if that were the *Harry Potter Chamber of Secrets'* Business Directory instead of the West African *Chamber of Commerce* Business Directory being cited, I would have placed more credence in Andrew Chidi's awkward and grammatically flawed letter of introduction. The Banque Lome-Togo sounded more like the Bank of Money to Go (from MY pocket).

Andrew's form letter had a fairly interesting "hook." He indicated that a bad-luck American businessman had died in a November 1997 plane crash in Chidi's section of Africa, leaving the sum of 14 million dollars in an African Bank Account at the Banque Lome-Togo. 'What a fantastic coincidence!' I thought. 'The plane crashed in the same African country where the American entrepreneur's huge bank account existed! The millionaire victim's bad fortune just had to be preceded with fantastic good luck.' The poor deceased American had no relatives or heirs since according to Andrew Chidi's research findings no one has claimed the fourteen million-dollar-bonanza that was just sitting there collecting cobwebs in the Banque Lome-Togo.

According to my new friend Andrew, all I had to do was send him an affidavit falsely asserting that I was the plane victim's nearest next of kin. Presto-chango! My new African banking pal would then transfer the fourteen million to my Hammonton, New Jersey bank account. In a half a year's time Andrew and his "partners" would show up in town and claim 70% of the windfall, leaving me with a handsome commission of 4.2 million bananas. Rule Number 1 of *Internet* scam analysis and investigation: if the e-mail is not personally addressed to you and is prefaced by "Dear Sir," then ignore and delete it. Also, no legitimate business openly solicits your patronage over the *Internet* unless you have an account with them.

Andrew signed his fairly weird letter *Best Regard*. Now really intelligent fraud masters fully fathom that the second word in a letter's closing is never capitalized and that the correct nomenclature should have been "Best regards." I mean for heaven's sake Andy, don't insult my limited intelligence! First my solicitor wanted me to commit an international misrepresentation crime by pretending to be this dead man's closest relative. Then Andrew Chidi desired for me to commit nefarious international conspiracy. I know that I am occasionally stupid but I am infuriated to feel that the African gentleman (here a polite reference) thinks that I AM ignorant enough to fall for a frivolous e-mail caper. Any dunce knows that any bank deposit into my account over ten thousand dollars would automatically be reported to and investigated by the *IRS*. 'Certainly a mere fourteen million would never escape the IRS's intense scrutiny,' I facetiously reasoned!

A week later I received via e-mail another "Urgent Business Invitation" from one Tanko Bamiayi, who remarkably maintained that he had obtained my e-mail address from a widely used legitimate Internet Business Directory. In his lackluster missive Tanko introduced himself as the eldest son and heir to African Retired General Ishaya Bamaiyi (notice the different last name spelling), who had been the Defence Army Chief in the late Sani Abacha's regime. Now I became wary of the spelling of the word "defence" but I gave

Tanko the benefit of the doubt because the British spell "defense" that way, so I needed more grammatical evidence to justify my skepticism. Also, I had four questions nagging my ever-alert conscience. Who in tar' nation was Sani Abacha, and how did he die? Who really cares how Sani Abacha expired? Did Tanko and his father conspire and assassinate Sani Abacha? Why does Tanko spell his last name differently than his seemingly famous military father?

Tanko explained in his extensive letter that 46 million dollars would be meritoriously transferred to my bank account from profits that had been skimmed from illicit African Arms and Ammunition acquisitions. I could get to keep 20% of the booty, a cool 9.2 million. 'Who needs Andi Chidi's meager 4.2 million when I could reap 9.2 million from Tanko and his all-powerful pop!' I jokingly thought. 'If I go for both deals, I could accumulate a remarkable 13.4 million and be able to afford the legal services of a high-powered attorney like Johnny Cochoran when prosecuted by the *IRS*, the *CIA* and the *FBI*. If lucky,' I cleverly surmised, 'I might even be able to afford having O.J. testify in my behalf.'

A red flag went up when Tanko wrote and expounded, "Believe me, there is no one else but you (the random recipient of the form letter) that my father and I can trust." Give me a blessed break will you Tanko? Out of six billion or so humans on the face of the earth, Tanko and his compassionate and generous dad could only trust me, a perfect stranger passively living in the pinelands of southern New Jersey. 'And if I became an instant criminal by joining *their* international conspiracy,' I hypothesized, 'I could be safely assured by the all-too-truthful maxim: 'There is no trust among and between thieves and criminals'.'

My grammar and spelling theory about how to identify malicious fraud was finally proven in the weird letter's last paragraph. "You have nothing *to loose*." On the contrary Mr. Bamiayi, I have a pair of Bermuda shorts that are *too loose*! And the zany letter also stated that the windfall money would be *"dully* paid." 'I think Tanko really meant to express the terminology *"duly* paid" but perhaps I ought to consult a good dictionary before being too presumptuous and cynical. 'Mr. Bamiayi, I resent your attempt to capitalize on greed,' I concluded after looking up the word "duly" and carefully evaluating its definition just to verify what I already knew.

Scam artists are a definite downside to people doing legitimate business on the *Internet*. I believe that Andrew Chidi and Tanko wanted to each offer me a whale while trying to steal a trout from my personal bank account. "Holy mackerel!" I exclaimed without ever having seen a fish inside a church. "Those scam artists want my bank checking account number to tap into my records in order to electronically withdraw my hard-earned money. How villainous can wicked people get? They were on separate *phishing* expeditions."

I reported the scams to the FBI in Newark. I haven't heard from the Bureau. They're probably too busy now with terrorists and with anthrax threats to deal with international white-collar criminals. But one thing is certain: these low-life thugs operate outside the USA and consequently outside the jurisdiction of the *IRS* and *the FBI*. And they use electronic bank transfers from the bank accounts of greedy victims that have been hoodwinked by these somewhat imaginative get-rich-quick schemes.

Just yesterday I received an urgent e-mail from one Ibrahim Gwandu of Nigeria stating that......

"Misadventures in Furnitureland"

Every morning weather permitting I walk the asphalt roads in the Oak Grove Cemetery located about a quarter of a mile from my Hammonton, New Jersey home. The graveyard jaunt's distance is a little more than a mile if the serious trekker traverses the entire blacktop surface. The daily ritual is good therapy for both body and spirit and also for stabilizing the delicate harmony that exists between the two entities. My physical form experiences much needed exercise, and the invigorating activity energizes my remaining aging brain cells. 'A stroll a day keeps the psychiatrist away,' I often muse.

After my ritualistic morning hike, I habitually visit my mother's home on Maryln Avenue for a cup of coffee and usually consume my favorite treat, *TastyKake Butterscotch Krimpets*. Naturally my flimsy reasoning is that I must quickly replace those vital calories I had just burned-off while power walking around the cemetery. One such visitation to Mom's place happened last May.

"Hi Mom," I respectfully greeted after I knocked on and opened the back-kitchen door. "How's that new chair that was delivered yesterday afternoon? I'm anxious to try it out and give you my opinion about its comfort."

"I'm very unhappy with it," she answered in a disappointed tone of voice, "because I had ordered a recliner and the company sent me a recliner/rocker."

I stepped into the den and keenly scrutinized the object of discussion. "But Mom, the leather and color are identical to that which you had selected in the showroom. I was there, and I remember."

"Yes, but they switched chairs on me, and I don't want a rocker. I just want a recliner. But somehow things got scrambled and a rocker/recliner was delivered."

"You should've bought it from Mazza's Bassett Furniture Direct on the Black Horse Pike," I suggested in hindsight. "I know Frank and Gary and they wouldn't have pulled the old proverbial switcheroo on you. Sometimes it pays to spend a little more and get exactly what you want."

"Do you want your krimpets and coffee or not!" Mom threatened in the form of a parental reprimand.

"Okay, I'm sorry," I apologized, for I did not desire to forfeit my favorite morning snack over something as silly as an argument over a stupid recliner that rocks. "Forgive me for being so inconsiderate and unsympathetic."

Mom had purchased the chair using her *VisaCard,* and with the help of *Visa,* was able to get her money back without too much hassle. Who says that credit/debit cards are bad to have? A disgruntled customer has a month-long time frame to cancel-out a large-ticket purchase.

In July of that year my wife and I were shopping around for a hideaway bed for my computer room, which used to be my oldest son Joe's upstairs bedroom. We thought we had gotten a pretty good deal on a factory closeout, which included a queen-size sofa bed, a matching love seat, three tables and a color-coordinated rug. It all looked too good to be true. And when matters look too good to be true, as the saying goes.....oh well, *you* know what the hackneyed cliché states.

"Wow!" I told Joanne. "We really got a great deal on this ensemble. We only wanted a sofa bed and we have the whole room decorated for a few hundred dollars more. Who says we aren't accomplished bargain hunters?"

"Make sure all your horses are in the corral before you close the gate," my generally pessimistic wife curtly replied in her typical guarded tone. "Sometimes cynicism is more intelligent and desirable than enthusiasm."

Five weeks later the furniture delivery truck rumbled into my driveway. Two husky fellows appeared at my front door with an authorization slip. I invited the visitors inside, escorted them upstairs, sauntered down the hall and showed the men the large former bedroom that had been ingeniously converted into my personal writing quarters. "In here!" I proudly proclaimed. "Carry the new furniture in here!"

"Sir," one of the men qualified after clearing his throat, "the big queen-size sofa bed will not fit into this room. Even if we successfully make it up the stairs and turn the corner it's too long and it can only go through the doorway vertically. I can guarantee you that problem without even havin' to measure the area."

"Can't we just take the door off?" I asked, diplomatically trying to be constructive. "Surely you're often confronted with this type of scenario during the course of your job."

"No Sir, that idea of removin' the door won't make any difference," the second man interrupted. "The sofa is ninety-two inches long and your doorway is only.....only seventy-eight inches high," the fellow informed as he meticulously measured the aforementioned portal with his tape.

I was suddenly deeply depressed by the new negative-sounding information. "Is there any solution to this perplexing problem?" I defensively asked.

"Well now," the first delivery person responded with a forced smile, "the company has a technician that will come out and disassemble the sofa bed, take the parts upstairs and then put it all back together for you."

I became a little perturbed to add to my frustration and dissatisfaction. "Look at this bill from your furniture store," I insisted, exhibiting a degree of petulance. "The salesman's writing of ninety-two inches looks like seventy-two inches!" I futilely argued. "How much will it cost me to have a technician come out to my house and perform his service?"

"Around two hundred dollars," the very formal second furniture handler related rather authoritatively. "He maintains a busy schedule so I estimate that he'll come out here to Hammonton in a week or so. In the meantime Sir you can keep the bigger sofa bed stored in your garage."

I felt a trifle stupid and foolish having made such a dumb error in reading the store salesman's hieroglyphic-like handwriting so I reluctantly assented to the burly chap's recommendation. "Okay, but first carry the love seat upstairs. I'll call the store and arrange to have a technician come out to dismantle the sofa in the garage and then reassemble the piece upstairs."

My wife calmly contacted the furniture store and was given the phone number of the company's regional office. A voice at the other end told Joanne that our home was geographically situated outside the technician's service radius.

I frantically dashed up the steps and addressed the preoccupied deliverymen, who had just deposited the love seat (but not the queen-size sofa bed) in the computer room. "Stop!" I imperatively hollered. "We can't accept the furniture because according to your bosses at headquarters no technician is going to come out here to Hammonton."

"Well, ya' gotta' pay us cash-on-delivery for the furniture!" the second perturbed fellow grumpily demanded.

"That's what you think!" I angrily shouted back, a little out-of-character. "You two guys will have to come and sit on my queen-size sofa bed in the garage every day in January freezing your butts off and see how you'd like it!"

To make a long story short the furniture was returned to the company's main warehouse, and I had to suffer a hundred seventy-five-dollar penalty for refusing delivery. The next morning I visited my mother's place for coffee and my standard delectable butterscotch krimpets. "How do you like your new furniture?" she inquired.

'Quit busting on me!' I thought.

Looking for some family empathy I sadly related the nightmare misadventure in furnitureland that I had recently endured. "You should've bought the items at Mazza's Bassett Furniture on the Black Horse Pike," my mother suggested and reprimanded. "At least they would know whether or not the queen-sized sofa bed would fit in an upstairs bedroom."

I honored my mother's wisdom without too much accompanying embarrassment or loss of pride. And I must confess that Joanne and I are completely happy and satisfied with the new improved appearance and décor of the computer room. Thank you, Frank and Gary Mazza. You can come over to my place any time for tea and *krimpets*. I'm also thrilled to report that no February guests will have to sleep in my garage on the queen-size sofa bed.

"Mr. Charles B. Sipley"

Every so often an impact person (other than a parent) enters your life. You don't know when or where that person might appear to give guidance until he or she shows up. But that very special individual possesses dynamic qualities that have a genuine lasting impact. The Godsend person will inspire the beneficiary and his or her influence will dramatically affect the remainder of the lucky recipient's mortal tenure on this planet.

In the summer of 1960 I was privileged to come into contact with a retired high school mathematics teacher, Mr. Charles B. Sipley, who had a profound positive lasting impression upon my attitude towards the world. Mr. Sipley taught me the most valuable lesson of my young life. Forget self-esteem! He taught me how to overcome failure and self-imposed emotional adversity and concurrently the incredible man injected a healthy dose of resilience and confidence into my character.

In early 1960 my family had moved back to New Jersey from Levittown, Pennsylvania. My folks had an opportunity to purchase a home and a farm market and finally own a viable business. I had to transfer from *Bishop Egan High* (now Conwell-Egan) in Bucks County, Pennsylvania into *Edgewood Regional High School'* (now Winslow Township High School) in Tansboro, New Jersey.

Coming from a Catholic school tradition, I had excellent background in English and also in social studies. I was very adept at grammar, spelling, vocabulary, punctuation, literature and writing. Language arts, history and geography came exceptionally easy to me and I excelled in those subjects.

Conversely, after I had transferred into *Edgewood High* I soon discovered that I was extremely weak (compared to other *students* in the college prep' curriculum) in both science and advanced mathematics. Each day at *Edgewood* seemed very paradoxical to me. I would breeze through English, history and world cultures' classes and then dismally suffer through trigonometry and physics.

My mind and heart were in turbulent quandaries and my spirit shifted several times daily from the positive end of the achievement spectrum to the negative terminal. In late May of 1960 I found out from my guidance counselor that I had failed trigonometry. I was not allowed to graduate on stage with my class, and that punishment greatly disturbed me. I felt I had never had adequate preparation in my parochial school background in algebra and that I could not fairly compete with the other public-school *students* on a level math' playing field in trigonometry.

In 1960 at *Edgewood High*, if a *student* failed one major subject, that person had to attend summer school for remedial instruction. I was extremely demoralized and confused. I honestly believed that I was destined to be an incompetent failure for the remainder of my life and that my future had been adroitly sabotaged by Mr. Andrews, my strict and inflexible *Edgewood* trig' teacher. My English and social studies teachers were always touting me as one of the top *students* in the high school, and my science and trig' teachers evaluated my lackluster performance as being inferior and situated far below mediocre.

Since I was not permitted to graduate with my class-mates I had a serious choice to make to finally obtain my high school diploma. I could either attend summer school at *Haddonfield High* (twenty miles away from my home) or I could seek-out the services of a qualified tutor. I had heard about Mr. Charles B. Sipley from a friend so I gave the retired Hammonton High School teacher a call, explained my dire situation, and I was thrilled to learn that the man would accept me as his *student*.

When I first met Mr. Sipley face to face at his home I was deeply impressed with his demeanor. The retired teacher was not a huge man but he possessed a strong constitution that seemed to transcend physical prowess. My soon-to-be mentor had a powerful inner strength shrouded in a hard, outer mantle of Old-World values that somehow directly and immediately communicated with my inner-core-being. Mr. Sipley could motivate, inspire and influence me. Charles B. Sipley was confident that I could succeed and he would not accept "No I can't do this!" as an excuse. He soon masterfully transmitted *that* elusive confidence factor along with that special hard-to-define inspirational certainty to me.

At first, I was reluctant to open-up my soul to my mentor, trying to conceal and shield my shame and disgrace at failing high school from *his* scrutiny. After the first several tutorial sessions, under his calm strong guidance, I began to finally decipher the enigmas and codes that had previously made trigonometry a total mystery to my hungry cerebrum.

With Mr. Sipley's encouragement and expertise I soon became proficient in the fundamentals of sine, cosine, tangent, cotangent, secant and cosecant. I gradually understood the definite relationships between complicated mathematical formulas and the six trigonometric functions. Learning became easy and soon it became fun. Trig' was no longer an enigma.

In four short weeks I knew trigonometry as well as the average *student* of that subject and after the eight-week tutorial was over I had a terrific command of the advanced mathematics, thanks to my sympathetic, patient-but-tough mentor. Mr. Sipley *expected* me to succeed and master trig' and I had no alternative other than to fulfill *his* lofty expectation. His daily demands allowed me no wiggle room from his strict regimentation.

In early September I made a visit back to *Edgewood Regional High School* with a "Letter of Recommendation" signed by Mr. Charles B. Sipley. The neatly handwritten missive stated I had mastered the fundamentals and the mechanics of trigonometry and that I should "receive a minimum *adjusted* grade of B for the course." I proudly took the note to the main office and a secretary showed it to Mr. Pinkerton the *Edgewood* principal, who then shuttled me up to Mr. Andrews' familiar M-Wing classroom.

I handed the stern pedagogue Mr. Sipley's complimentary letter, and after reading its benign content Mr. Andrews became quite skeptical and said that the note could have been a clever counterfeit and that I still had to pass *his* awesome final exam' "to officially graduate." The mean-spirited fellow chuckled as *he* directed me to park my body in the last desk near the side windows, the same desk I had occupied as a failing student up to mid-June of 1960. Then Mr. Andrews handed me his toughest final examination as the twenty trigonometry *students* in the new senior advanced class chuckled and snickered at the Promethean task I was undertaking.

It took me a mere twenty minutes to solve all of the formerly complicated mathematical riddles, and after spending an additional five minutes checking over the more difficult test items I marched-up to the teacher's desk and handed the pedagogue my exam' papers. Mr. Andrews appeared momentarily shocked by my arrogance and by the new cocky confidence that I was demonstrating.

The extremely astonished trig' teacher intensively scrutinized my test paper, closely eyeballing every single answer with his mouth agape. Instinctively I knew that I had gotten every problem correct, but the obstinate disbelieving advanced math' instructor did not put any grade on my exam' paper. Instead he scribbled his name on Mr. Sipley's letter and addressed his comment to Mr. Pinkerton, "Give this former *student* a final grade of C on his report card."

Andrews handed me his notation that had been jotted on Mr. Sipley's courteous letter, which I carefully read with an element of resentment. I looked the instructor straight in the eyes, and somehow, his former formidable dominance no longer intimidated me. I felt that I had grown into a man at *that* precise moment. I felt like viciously punching the obstinate martinet in the face but I restrained myself from committing violence and thought, 'I'm gonna' attend *Glassboro State College* and become a teacher. Then I'll be able to help kids learn instead of trying to destroy their egos like some teacher I know!'

I accepted the *altered* letter', promptly brought it downstairs to the main office and soon a polite secretary inserted a "C" for "Trigonometry" on my report card and then expertly typed that grade onto my *Edgewood High* transcript.

I shook hands with Mr. Pinkerton, who like Mr. Andrews seemed diminished in stature and in potency now that I had also officially escaped *his* jurisdiction. I departed the high school with *that* chapter of my adolescence finally being closed behind me. I imagined a happy future devoid of annoying obstacles like Mr. Andrews and Mr. Pinkerton.

In retrospect, failure was a good experience for me. It provided me with determination to prove to Mr. Andrews that I could overcome the rigors associated with *his* most challenging subject. I believe that today's educators (including myself) are wrong when they pass undeserving *students* along and keep them rising on the academic escalator while simultaneously attempting to insulate lazy or weak-skilled kids from the reality of failure. Thanks to Mr. Charles B. Sipley, I had gained the math' ability I needed to effectively show Mr. Andrews that I was tougher than *his* toughest trigonometry test items.

Mr. Sipley was definitely an impact person who had entered my life at a most opportune time and had kindly rescued me from despair. It was because of my mentor's extraordinary example that I had vowed to become a public-school teacher and help others as he had so wonderfully assisted me. Mr. Charles B. Sipley extended to me hope once I was able to have faith in my ability. He had mercifully salvaged my spirit at a time when I seriously doubted my own potential and my own self-worth.

I decided to wait a full year before matriculating into *Glassboro State Teachers College*. During the twelve-month interim, my father got me a job as a welder's apprentice at *his* winter place of employment, Martin and Quade Stainless Steel Fabricating Company in Norristown, Pennsylvania. I quickly realized I needed a good education to learn a profession because I had no desire to breathe-in factory welding fumes for the rest of my working life. And besides, I did not savor the long hour and fifteen-minute commute from Elm, New Jersey to Norristown every workday.

My first assigned job at Martin and Quade was to operate a large seam-welding machine. Bulky sheets twenty-foot-long were mounted and then clamped upon *my* machine. The fabricating machine next folded each sheet into a circular tube ten inches in diameter. After polishing off the first batch of fifty stainless steel pipes, the plant inspector came to my workstation to examine the craftsmanship. He found many defects in the quality of the seams I had welded and my first instinct was that I had not followed directions and that I would be dismissed from real-life employment. Instead of rebuking my ineptness, the foreman patiently told me that I had to seam-weld the tubes a second time, which I carefully did. My second production easily passed the scrutiny of quality control.

In the past, American *free enterprise* has always emphasized individual accountability, responsibility and productivity. It is beyond my comprehension why modern public schools do not demand similar performance characteristics from *students*. Instead, twenty-first century American education uses the terms accountability, responsibility and productivity to describe the role of the teacher and not the function of the *student*.

Today's teachers are asked to experiment with innovative instructional methods and to *adjust* the curriculum to the needs of each *student*. Always the teacher and the system must accommodate the *student* when the situation should be the opposite and reflect the way the real world operates. And if the *students* fail to learn, it is now the teacher's fault for being ineffective. If a *student* fails to achieve a standard, the teacher is at fault and accountable and should be the one feeling guilt and shame. What a travesty modern education has evolved into since my invaluable learning experience (from failure) at *Edgewood High*!

When I was operating that seam-welding machine at Martin and Quade the shop stewards didn't care how that activity was satisfying *my* emotional and psychological needs. All industry in the American economic system would suddenly collapse if the board of directors of all major corporations all at once decided that production should be geared to "meeting the emotional and psychological needs" of each worker and be adjusted to the needs of *each* employee.

In today's American public schools, the needs of each *student* vary considerably and each *student's* specific needs cannot be accurately identified. To insist that the curriculum must be transformed to accommodate each individual *student* is both a sham and a charade, especially since the competitive American free enterprise society (that educators are preparing the *students* to enter) functions in a completely different and more demanding dimension than the "protective atmosphere" public schools do. The current "meet each *student's* needs" philosophy of our U.S. public schools is counterproductive (and anathema) to the needs of *our* competitive American quality-control economic system.

Instead of effectively preparing kids for the rigors of the real-world job market, public schools are attempting to mold and create a false reality making *the system* conform with the whimsical utopian fantasies geared to what liberal quixotic college professors think the future American society should be. By teaching young people that happiness is paramount in human endeavor and should easily be experienced and achieved in any classroom activity, and by advocating that quality production, healthy competition and failure are secondary values of human enterprise', our schools are committing a grave injustice to this country's future.

The present educational philosophy is slowly eroding away the vital main cogs that hold together the industrial wheel of our great American free enterprise economy. Giving kids A's and B's for doing mediocre work and C's and D's for doing inferior work is analogous to Martin and Quade paying *me* for welding and producing non-usable stainless-steel tubes.

Mr. Andrews had performed a valuable favor by failing me and Mr. Charles B. Sipley did me a much bigger favor by becoming my mentor. The Martin and Quade shop foreman helped my development by telling me that my job performance had been unsatisfactory and then giving me a second chance to succeed. Those three men helped me emotionally grow and mature by being truthful about my inadequate performance, and by making genuine demands and not providing false praise, the three individuals had contributed to me becoming a stronger and wiser person.

Compare Mr. Andrews', Mr. Sipley's and the shop foreman's methods with those that are currently being practiced by teachers in American public-school classrooms and you will understand why American education is failing our civilization. Schools are dishonestly passing students that are under-performing. Thanks, Mr. Sipley for showing me the light. Yes, forget self-esteem! Overcoming failure is a valuable learning experience that builds confidence. In the final analysis I truly believe that any success I'll ever achieve in life I'll owe to Mr. Charles B. Sipley.

"The Pain in Sprain Is Mainly on the Plane"

I know for a fact that the pain in sprain is mainly on the plane, even without ever even personally knowing actors Audrey Hepburn or Rex Harrison. I don't believe that Professor Henry Higgins and the uneducated Eliza Doolittle ever had severe ankle sprains to match several of mine. One such minor calamity occurred just before Christmas in 1974.

This writer observed that one of my three sons had accidentally tossed a small *Frisbee* onto my home's side porch roof and the object had been left resting halfway between the pinnacle of the A-frame and the back-rain gutter. Motivated with determination I dauntlessly ambled to the garage, removed my trusty aluminum ladder and then intrepidly ascended up onto the side porch's roof. 'I hope I don't get a bad case of shingles,' I haughtily laughed to myself. 'If this house didn't have shingles, I'd be more *roofless* than I really am,' I mused. Reaching the errant *Frisbee,* I adroitly flung the red plastic saucer back down to the ground, quite proud of my achievement and competency.

When I returned to where I had placed the aluminum ladder near my home's backyard, I soon realized that the wind had blown the object over onto the ground. 'Hard to climb that thing from way up here,' I brilliantly thought. 'My oldest son never locks his window. I'll get into the house by climbing through it,' I concluded.

Much to my aggravation Joe's bedroom window above the side porch roof was (perhaps for the first time) locked. Then I assessed the true nature of my mounting dilemma. The external temperature was fifteen degrees, a gusty wind was blowing and the wind-chill factor was about minus five. My mind reviewed my embarrassing predicament. I was stuck on the porch's roof, no-one else was home, the aluminum ladder was laying horizontal on the hard lawn, I was wearing an autumn-lightweight jacket, had no gloves on my almost numb hands, and felt rather foolish standing alone up there with the atmosphere cold enough to freeze an obese Eskimo's bellybutton.

I soon spotted my wife driving by on the White Horse Pike (also known as *Route 30*) heading west toward her mother's place. I desperately and frantically waved my arms as if I was a stranded *Robinson Crusoe* trying to get Friday's attention. Joanne whizzed by while focused on changing lanes and was completely unaware of my wild gesticulations. I motioned at other motorists traveling "the Pike" but they either ignored my plight or thought that I was over-zealously trying to be friendly. Several passing drivers', thinking that I was being friendly, honked their horns in recognition of my zany hand signaling. The frigid air was becoming un*bear*able, even for a thick-furred grizzly.

'Now I know how Gilligan must've felt every time he and the Skipper had been *almost* rescued from that isolated Pacific island,' I lamented. 'I gotta' get off this roof before I either turn into an icicle or an igloo.'

I glanced at the security light telephone pole situated five feet from the roof's back rain gutter and actually considered leaping onto it. 'If only I had worn gloves,' I woefully regretted. 'I don't need fifty splinters in each of my cold hands if my open palms make physical contact with the pole and then accidentally are compelled by gravity to slide down the vertical wooden object.' Being under great mental duress, I panicked, and without yelling "Geronimo" or some other inane nondescript parachutist jargon, I leaped ten feet from the roof down onto the Tundra-like frozen turf. I had severely injured my left ankle, and after examining x-rays that afternoon a local doctor diagnosed my impulsive self-inflicted new-found condition as a "double-sprain."

"What made you do such a stupid thing like climbing up on the roof when nobody else was home?" my Sicilian wife later criticized my unilateral decision.

"Sometimes I just really enjoy being stupid," I argumentatively snapped back. "Rene Descartes said he could prove he existed by saying, 'I think; therefore I am.' To me, intense physical pain is the true proof of existence," I stubbornly answered my spouse. "I have to live with the pain and you don't, so stop harassing me with your non-constructive remarks."

Two days later Joanne and I were scheduled for a Caribbean cruise on the *Cunard Adventurer*. My left ankle had puffed up to the size of a plump cantaloupe and I remember the excruciating pain my ankle endured as I dragged several pieces of luggage through New York's *Port Authority Bus Terminal*, and then later through *Kennedy International Airport*. But the biggest agony was sitting on the jet plane for the four-hour flight from the *Big Apple* to tropical San Juan. I put my set of earphones on, switched to the plane's Oldies audio-channel and then had to suffer through Chubby Checker's lively rendition of "The Twist" and ironically next the '50s classic tune, "The Bunny Hop."

Several decades after "the porch roof fiasco" I was showing an eighth grade class the movie *Bye, Bye Birdie* as a basis for a writing lesson where the students had to analyze the film's characters, settings and plots. In one humorous movie scene, the Russian ballet was formally dancing on stage as a segment of the *Ed Sullivan Show*, and the conductor had been given a special formula called "Speed-up." The maestro drank the powerful potion and then wildly swung his baton, which instantly made the stage dancers *speed up* to the now rapid-paced music.

I had always enjoyed spicing up video lessons to entertain my students so in the dark, I dashed to the back of the classroom and started dancing and wildly hopping around in front of the elevated television and *VCR*, acting like a demented nutcase to briefly amuse the class. A female *student* had neglected to place a thick textbook under her desk and when my left foot landed on the uneven surface, I immediately re-double-sprained my left ankle. The pain was excruciating.

This victimized English teacher hopped about the back of the classroom holding my raised left foot and the students all roared, obviously thinking that I was idiotically enacting some pre-planned theatrical exaggeration. I finally reached the Central Avenue side thigh-high bookshelf where I immediately parked my body. In quest of relief I winced with pain as the class laughed hysterically, still believing that I was dramatically acting-out false agony.

After the forty-five-minute class period finally ended I had one of my more-trustworthy Hammonton Middle School students go to the intercom and buzz the nurse's office. Mrs. Marie DeLaurentis eventually appeared inside the classroom three minutes later and had to cut off my newly purchased shoe with hand shears to examine my inflated left foot. Bill Amedio, the middle school custodian, was assigned by the Principal to drive me to the school physician's office. Dr. Nurkiewicz evaluated my foot and recommended that I be put on disability. So, I was the first Hammonton teacher to ever get injured on the job and collect disability.

Several weeks later over the *Thanksgiving* holidays *My Fair Lady* and I went on vacation to the Bahamas with several other teacher couples. On the ordinary flight from Philly' down to Nassau, I again became quite aware that "the pain in sprain is mainly on the plane."

"Growing-up in Hammonton"

I was born (not hatched as some acquaintances might believe) in 1942 at the Swenson Home on Horton Street on the north side of the railroad tracks in Hammonton, New Jersey. The town had no hospital back then so many other Hammontonians that were not delivered by midwives were also naturally born (or born naturally) at the Swenson Home on the "proper side of the tracks."

On December 7, 1941 Pearl Harbor had been attacked. *World War II* was in progress in the European and in the Pacific Theaters (where the war was playing). My father had volunteered his service after the Pearl Harbor sneak attack and was away training at U.S. military camps and later after 1943 had been stationed in France and in Germany during my early childhood. When Dad returned from the terrible conflict, he opened a small gas station/repair' shop next to the family's modest white bungalow, which was situated beside my mother's parents' Hammonton business, Square Deal Farm Market on *Route 30*, the White Horse Pike.

Grand-pop Tony had pioneered the farm market trade on that busy highway, which at the time was the major summer tourist link between Philadelphia and Atlantic City. Gramps would often drive me around South Jersey in his black stake-body truck to various fruit and vegetable farmers, where he would purchase corn, peaches, apples, blueberries, cucumbers, peppers, zucchini squash, tomatoes and other locally grown produce. Several times he even brought me to Dock Street in Philadelphia, which at the time was the area's major fresh food distribution center.

Antonio Giacobbe was a Sicilian immigrant who had come over to America via Ellis Island and settled with former Old-World Messina, Sicily relatives near Ninth Street in Philadelphia. Gramps started out in the American free enterprise system by vending fruit and vegetables from a pushcart around the Italian Market on Ninth Street. In a few years he earned enough money to invest in a five-acre tract on the White Horse Pike in Hammonton.

Italian immigrants were not too well received by the firmly entrenched and established English Hammonton WASPs. A year after my grandparents erected Square Deal Market during the mid-1930s' Depression, an influential farm family of British descent was determined to knock them out of business by building a similar farm market right next to Square Deal. When a customer would stop his or her automobile between the two properties, Grandma Annie would rush over and nail the fresh fruit shopper before the competition had a chance to react to the prospective customer's arrival.

Eventually Antonio Giacobbe prevailed and proudly bought the other market from his chief rival. My Sicilian grandparents on my mother's side had overcome 1930s WASP discrimination through hard work and personal determination. Perseverance was a good lesson I had learned at an early age. It has as much to do with human economic' survival as persistence has to do with human success.

Grandma Annie Giacobbe also had a difficult childhood. She had come from a very poor Sicilian family that lived beyond the end of Pine Road in an area known as Sandy Crossways. She had to wear her father's discarded tattered shoes with holes in the soles to school and was often mocked by the other children fortunate enough to have wealthier parents and better shoes. Young Annie vowed to elevate herself above poverty. She always remembered the emotional scars she had suffered in her impoverished childhood. After marrying Grandpa Tony, my grandmother gained self-esteem by running Square Deal Farm Market with steadfast precision and a terrific Old-World work ethic.

Kindergarten was not mandatory back in 1948. I remember entering first grade at St. Joseph School on Third Street in downtown Hammonton. I managed to master the fundamentals of reading and writing in four years of schooling, and when Grandpa Tony took me to buy produce I soon realized at a young age that I knew how to read and write and that he didn't. Grandpa would ask me on our excursions around South Jersey to read the various billboards and signs that dotted *Route 206, Route 54, Route 322* and *Route 30* and I would gladly oblige. All Gramps had mastered was how to scribble two letters, his initials "A.G.," which he used to certify his approval on sales receipts that verified his wholesale purchases.

No matter where Grandpa would drive me, he would always reiterate his reason for moving to New Jersey. The fat, bald-headed man knew very little English and repeated at least ten times to and ten times from our given destination, "Giovanni, there's too much true-bulla in Pencil-bania!" he would repeat in between smoking his huge *El Producto* cigar, before coughing like a tuberculosis victim. Then Grandpa Tony would again ask me the identification of words that puzzled him on various highway billboards. But Gramps knew his mathematics without the need of a pencil, eraser or adding machine. He could calculate and subtract figures in his head and would tell amazed commission house men the exact total of his purchases to the penny that took *them* minutes to figure out.

When I was six years old in 1948 Mom and Aunt Frances took me one Saturday night to The Rivoli Theater on Bellevue Avenue in downtown Hammonton to see the Otto Preminger film *Forever Amber*, starring Cornell Wilde and Linda Darnell. The movie had a very spectacular fire scene and at six years of age, I thought that the whole theater was engulfed in the inferno that was being shown up on the big screen. I panicked and started screaming my lungs out until Mom removed me from my seat, walked me to the foyer and soothed my alarm by buying some much-needed popcorn and soda.

The *Philadelphia Phillies* had won the National League Pennant in 1950 and I recall how psyched-up I was watching them on a small screen black and white TV play in the *World Series* against the *New York Yankees*. Joe DiMaggio hit the winning home run in game two and then the *Yankees* cruised to a four-game sweep in spite of inspirational play by *Phillies'* center-fielder Richie Ashburn, my boyhood hero.

During the summer months Gramps would take me north on *206* to Indian Mills where he would daily buy two thousand ears of freshly "pulled" Jersey corn. Then he would bury me up to my chest with corn' ears as I sat in a back *corn*er of his black Chevy stake-body truck. I got a thrill waving to surprised motorists and their passengers passing us going south toward Hammonton on *206*.

Grandpa Tony often took me in his large black truck to the Hammonton Auction Block where he would buy fruit and vegetables to resell at his farm market. Post *WWII* Hammonton was an agricultural town of around ten thousand inhabitants with a large Italian immigrant population and most of the farmers wore caps, flannel shirts, gray wool vested sweaters, baggy pants and had mustaches. Some older Sicilian farmers even still brought their crops to the auction "block" in horse drawn wagons. The local growers would line up their trucks and wagons in four lanes that passed through the "auction block." Lots were drawn to see which line would go through "the block" first, second, third and fourth. Commission produce brokers and independent buyers like Grandpa would bid on items after being shown "sample packages" of the fruit and vegetables up for sale.

Downtown Hammonton hadn't changed much since the late 1940s. Dad was away in Europe going up against Hitler's minions so Mom would take me onto Bellevue Avenue every Friday night to do shopping. During the daytime Monday to Saturday she would faithfully wait for the daily mail to see if a letter from France or from Germany was forthcoming. Many American kids grew-up in the mid-

'40s without fathers (that were in the military) around to give them guidance and discipline. So like many other young boys during that decade, I was more exposed to female nurturing than to male naturing.

The small town's early claims to fame were having Presidential candidate Teddy Roosevelt's campaign train arrive for a whistle stop speech and having noted anthropologist Margaret Mead living on Fairview Avenue during her younger days where she studied the cultural adaptations of Italian immigrants. Another important event in the town's history was when acclaimed virtuoso John Philip Sousa and his famous touring band gave a sit-down concert for local citizens at the Hammonton Lake Pavilion.

I remember that late '40s and early '50s Bellevue Avenue was crowded with enthusiastic shoppers. There were soda fountains all over the main street. Every drug store, five and ten and luncheonette had one. I recall Vega's Drugs on the corner of Third and Bellevue, Godfrey's Drug Store at Bellevue and Egg Harbor Road, Kern's Drugs at 2nd and Bellevue, J.J. Newberry's and Joanne's Restaurant on the main drag all having splendid soda fountains.

Grandpa Tony spoiled me rotten by taking a young J.W. to see the four a.m. freight train rumble past the intersection of Fairview Avenue and Egg Harbor Road next to Vet's Bakery. My biological clock would wake me up at 3:30 in the morning and then I would bawl and throw a tantrum until Grandpa put me in his black stake-body truck and transported me to the *Pennsylvania Railroad* tracks to see the steam locomotive, the tankers and boxcars and finally the caboose.

When Dad returned from overseas, he opened his small gas station/repair shop next to the little white bungalow, which was adjacent to Square Deal Farm Market. One day after supper Dad sent me on an errand. I had to fetch a bill of sale from his office desk inside the garage. I left the building closing the garage door very hard, and the descending object smashed down on my left foot, crushing my big toe. I was afraid to tell Pop of the catastrophe but since the pain was so excruciating, I finally had to divulge my self-inflicted injury.

Dad, who had seen all kinds of dead mutilated corpses in Nazi Germany, was horrified. He rushed me to Dr. Frazier Elliott's Office on Packard Street, two blocks from the center of Hammonton. Dr. Elliott was a remarkable man who inspected my ugly wound without batting an eyelash. Then he administered a needle and proceeded to cut the entire toenail off my big toe as if he were casually peeling a potato. Even at age ten I had to admire the fine dedicated small town doctor who settled me down, allayed my fears and kept his cool under very dire circumstances.

Saturday afternoons the Rivoli Theater at Bellevue and Third (across the street from Vega's Drugs) had matinee movies. I still vividly recollect seeing *King Kong, Mighty Joe Young, The Beast from 20,000 Fathoms, The Creature from the Black Lagoon,* and *The Day the Earth Stood Still* at the downtown movie house with St. Joseph School friends. The theater boasted an ornate ceiling with crystal chandeliers that made it a showplace for the proud small town in the '40s and early '50s.

Most '50s businesses were little mom and pop operations like Rescignio's candy store across Third Street from St. Joseph School and like Miller's Family Department Store on Bellevue Avenue. Then, highway custard stands began replacing main street soda fountains and malls started sprouting up knocking places like Miller's Department Store and Rescignio's Candy out of business. Finally, in the early '60s the popularity of a new medium, television led to the demise of the glorious Rivoli Theater.

In the early fifties Grandpa Tony would take me over to the Sons of Italy Garibaldi Lodge on North Third Street and park me on a barstool to drink all of the *Cokes* and eat all of the pretzels and potato chips I wanted. Gramps would then play an Italian fingers game with some old cronies, and if Grandpa had had a dispute with Grandma Annie, he was determined to win the fingers game. Then Gramps would become the Capa or Boss and appoint a Lieutenant. Everyone else who had lost in the fingers' game would have to watch Grandpa drink eleven beers on the table (paid for by the losers) and then appoint his lucky Lieutenant to drink the twelfth.

Many Saturday nights Grandpa' Tony arrived back home drunk and then tripped and stumbled in the dark over living room furniture on his way upstairs to bed. Later in life his bad case of diabetes had been compounded, which eventually led to wheelchair confinement. His excessive drinking and need to be the "beer Capa" and the nasty-looking bruises on his legs didn't help his physical condition any.

Downtown Hammonton in the early '50s was very similar to the way Bellevue Avenue appeared in the '40s. On Friday and Saturday Nights the Hammonton High School kids hung out on their side of town in front of Vega's Drugs and Augie's Sub Shop and Hamburger Paradise and across the street the St. Joseph High teens usually congregated in front of the Rivoli Theater. Bellevue Avenue acted as sort of a demilitarized zone separating the two rival factions. The Ramrodders greaser gang hung out in front of the Central Café on Egg Harbor Road three blocks away.

Certain business establishments were neutral territory where all three teen groups would share space. Those businesses were the Gem Burger Bar on Central Avenue, a block west of Hammonton High School, and DiDonato's Bowling Alleys and Royale Crown Custard Stand on the White Horse Pike on the Atlantic City side of Hammonton.

When I turned nine I became a friend of David Parkwell, whose family had a Farm and Garden Center across the White Horse Pike from Square Deal Market. David was two years older than I was, and I admired his mischievous nature.

"Slow John" DiAngelo was an elderly grower that owned ground behind Grand-pop Tony's five acres of peach and apple orchards. Several times I pretended that I had been naughtily-picking cucumbers in "Slow John's" field when the gimpy farmer was riding down a sandy road on his old *John Deere* tractor. This would infuriate the partially lame old grower. He would halt his tractor, leap off and then awkwardly chase me across twenty or so rows of cucumbers until I safely gained shelter in a nearby' woods.

While "Slow John" was pursuing his elusive nemesis, (who had also been wearing a Halloween Dracula mask), Dave Parkwell would quickly exit a clump of trees from the opposite side of the field, the woods located along the dirt road. Then my friend would hop onto the *John Deere* and drive it along farm roads through pepper and tomato fields until he parked the piece of machinery a mile or so away.

Dave and I would then reunite at my parents' snack bar located inside of Square Deal Market, and we would celebrate our dual mischief with "Electrocuted Hot Dogs" and bottles of *Ma's Old Fashion Root Beer*. Then I would furtively show Dave the neat Dracula mask I intended to wear next Halloween.

Dave convinced me to join the Hammonton Little League, which had the distinction of winning the 1949 Little League World Championship. He was the star of our team, DiDonato's Bowling. I played an occasional second base or left field.

In one particular night game a big kid named Rollie Cantrobone hit a towering fly ball to left field. I backed-up to the green wooden fence, held my glove up toward the blinding lights, and then defensively searched the night sky for the obscure baseball. A small miracle happened. The baseball plopped down into my glove as I shielded my face to protect it from the descending white object. The fans on both sides of the field erupted in a boisterous cheer in recognition of my fantastic accidental accomplishment.

I had a great time making and having friends at St. Joseph School on North Third Street. During recess we played marbles on the hardtop playground, and yo-yos were prized possessions, too. I invented the baseball card game known as "three-way matchies." Two close friends and I would simultaneously flip to the ground baseball cards with the images of major league players on the front and their' performance statistics on the other side. The owner of the odd-sided flip would win "the jackpot." If two cards showed their backsides, then the player that owned the face-up card would be declared the winner. My buddies and I spent hours of leisure school recess time perfecting and demonstrating our marble, yo-yo and "matchies" skills.

I remember when I was ten that all the Catholic school kids from grades three to twelve had to attend an assembly at the Rivoli Theater. We all walked by grade level classes from the Catholic school two blocks east to the movie house on the corner of Bellevue Avenue and Third Street. All that week the St. Joseph School Fillipini nuns and Pallottine priests had been talking about heavenly visitations from the Blessed Virgin Mary, angels and saints while hyping the new religious movie *Our Lady of Fatima*. The cinema presentation was an awesome experience to a ten-year-old kid. The film must have had a profound impact on my vulnerable subconscious. It probably also sparked my fertile imagination.

Sometimes I would sleep the night in the spare bedroom upstairs in my grandparents' red brick home, which was situated behind Square Deal Farm Market. A statue of St. Anne (the Virgin Mary's mother) dressed in a macabre black robe rested atop the brown mahogany bureau next to the bed. The statue's stern face was always peering down at me and I always had to go to sleep turning my body and my head in the opposite direction. St. Anne's hands held black rosary beads, suggesting that she was praying for the soul of the bed's occupant lying beneath her presence.

Every 16th of July the town of Hammonton celebrates the Feast of Our Lady of Mount Carmel with a large traveling carnival and an Old-World religious street procession. Statues of Jesus, Mary, Joseph and saints from St. Joseph Church are mounted on carts with drapes covering their frames and wheels and escorted by the faithful through the major streets of the community and then back to the Third Street church. Clusters of donations in the form of five, ten, twenty, fifty and hundred-dollar bills were hung from and adorned the statues. In the years after *WWII* fifty thousand visitors would attend the 16th of July Mount Carmel Festival. The pilgrims were mostly Italian immigrants or first-generation offspring.

Grandma Annie Giacobbe gave me a five-dollar bill to have pinned onto the statue of Our Lady of Mount Carmel. My grandparents did not trust banks because many had collapsed during the Depression, so they stashed cash in the mattress of an old bed stored in the brick house's attic. I discovered the cache (of cash) and stole five dollars from the attic mattress. I had received five dollars spending money from my parents and I also had in my pocket the *Abe Lincoln* my grandmother had given me' to have pinned on the Our Lady of Mount Carmel procession statue in addition to five dollars I had been saving for the carnival.

I met some friends at the carnival grounds, and the four of us bought popcorn, soda, pizza and cotton candy. Then we addictively played different games of chance and tried out various amusement rides. Before I knew it I had exhausted all the money in my possession including the five dollars I was supposed to have pinned on the Blessed Mother's statue.

"Did you pin the money on Our Lady's statue?" my grandmother asked.

"Yes," I lied, "and the man said 'Thank you'."

"Good boy," Grandma complimented. "Marie, I think your son is goin' to grow up and become a priest. He's such a *bona, belle* boy!"

That night I slept in the spare bedroom of the red brick house. As my guilty mind approached the drowsy state that usually comes before actual sleeping, I turned my head and thought I saw St. Anne's statue kneeling beside the bed, praying for my wandering straying soul. "You must return the ten dollars you have stolen," she commanded, "or else your soul will burn in hell!"

The next morning, I didn't know what to do. I entered the small white bungalow and saw my father's wallet on the kitchen table. While dad was in the bathroom shaving, I opened his wallet that contained only ten-dollar bills and removed one. That night mom told me I had to sleep in the red brick house because she and dad were going out to dinner.

I was tossing and turning in bed from the guilt of my third misdeed involving Dad's wallet. I had planned to go over to David Parkwell's parents' Farm and Garden business the following morning and have my pal change the ten-dollar bill into two fives, which I would then surreptitiously plant into the stuffed attic mattress since it contained mostly five-dollar bills.

As I feared, I opened my eyes around midnight and St. Anne was again kneeling beside the bed. "You've been a sinful boy again," the statue said to me while sobbing and weeping. "I don't want to see you

58

burn in hell for all eternity!" I turned my face and when I looked back, the statue was no longer on the floor beside my bed. It was again stationed up on the mahogany bureau.

My vernal heart and conscience were both in the same miserable quandary. How would I get twenty dollars to repay my debts to the Blessed Mother and to Dad? I prayed to St. Anne for a solution to my heartfelt dilemma. I was in for the surprise of my young life!

The next morning Steve Van Buren, an all-pro football player for the *Philadelphia Eagles* stopped at Square Deal Market to acquire some tomatoes, corn, blueberries and peaches on his way to the Jersey shore. I immediately recognized the famous sports' celebrity from *Eagle'* television football games and from sports' news clips I had seen at the Rivoli Theater.

I almost swallowed my tongue when Steve Van Buren and his wife approached the little candy/soda/hot dog concession where I had been standing behind the counter. They ordered *Pepsi-Colas* and hot dogs, which I began to prepare on the "Hot Dog Electrocutor." Then the football star and I struck up a casual conversation.

"Do you know who I am?" he casually asked while his wife chuckled in the background.

"I think you're Steve Van Buren, my very favorite football player!" I exclaimed.

"You're absolutely right," the tough athlete remarked. "Would it be all right if I signed and gave you an autographed picture? I have some in my car."

"Can I have one for my friend David Parkwell too?" I begged.

"Why sure, no problem," Van Buren returned. "I'll be right back with two of 'em."

I graciously and thankfully received the two unexpected gifts. I was thrilled to death to obtain them from the *Eagle* great.

After Steve Van Buren gathered his produce and then drove off with his pretty wife another farm market patron made his way to the concession stand.

"Wasn't that Steve Van Buren?" the man asked.

"Sure was," I answered.

"He's the best fullback in professional football," the man elaborated. "I'll give ya' twenty bucks for one of those signed pictures. What do ya' say?"

"Okay," I said, "but this is a big sacrifice," recalling a synonym I had learned for the word *bunt* in baseball.

"I'll cherish this picture for the rest of my life," the fellow commented. "I'll even have it framed."

That afternoon my father again was shaving. I sneaked into the bungalow's bigger bedroom, found his wallet on the bureau and replaced "the ten-dollar loan" I had borrowed. Then the next time I was in church I put five dollars in the collection basket. And finally, I replaced the five dollars I had pilfered from the attic mattress.

'Thank you, St. Anne!' I respectfully acknowledged as I rolled my appreciative blue eyes toward the ceiling. 'Now I'm off the hook!' And that's how David Parkwell never got his autographed Steve Van Buren photo' (which *he* never knew about).

My parents had purchased their first television in early 1953. I was forced to sit down for a "lesson in history" and watch the boring Queen Elizabeth Coronation in network black and white. Even at ten years of age I hated royal pomp and ritual. The ceremony went on for hours and hours. I thought to myself that the mere act of placing a crown on somebody's head (even a *Head* of State) should require no longer than fifteen-seconds. So even at age ten, I had already been exhibiting symptoms of cynicism towards the artificiality of "stupid" adult traditions.

In March of '54 I received some bad news. Dad explained that the family would be moving away from Hammonton, New Jersey to a newly constructed community, Levittown, Pennsylvania. "Levittown is closer to Norristown than Hammonton is," Dad explained. "Uncle Frank got me a good job as a stainless-steel fabricator at his company, Martin and Quade. It's an opportunity for advancement."

Before 1954 my life was rather nondescript. At age ten I was satisfied and content doing simple basic chores around Square Deal Farm Market. I felt threatened having to abandon the security of playing Little League for DiDonato's Bowling and of leaving the familiar halls and rooms of St. Joseph School.

I had turned eleven in the spring of '54 when my family made the move to 50 Daffodil Lane in the Dogwood Hollow section of Levittown, Pennsylvania. My sister Annie was six and my younger brother Skip was an infant. I was rather melancholy for having to break away from all I had known and valued as a youngster growing-up in an Italian agricultural community. I was extremely apprehensive about what to expect in my new social environment. At age ten I had concluded that some things in life just were not fair.

"Dogwood Hollow: 1954-'55"

New schools, changing environments, new towns and different friends can all be traumatic experiences for any kid struggling through maturation. From fifth grade through high school graduation I had attended six different schools and so like a Darwinian chameleon, I had learned to adapt to new situations as second nature. I had discovered plenty about human "social survival," which can sometimes be just as treacherous as battling for physical dominance in the animal kingdom.

Before 1954 my early youth was rather nondescript. At age ten I recall helping-out with chores at my grandparents' farm market on *Route 30* in Hammonton, New Jersey, playing *Little League* baseball for DiDonato's Bowling, and being very sad leaving childhood friends at St. Joseph School.

I had just turned eleven in 1954 when my family moved out of New Jersey to 50 Daffodil Lane in the Dogwood Hollow section of Levittown, Pennsylvania. My sister Annie was six and my younger brother Skip was an infant.

My parents became friendly with Jack and Stella Burns, who looked almost identical to Fred and Ethel Mertz on the popular *I Love Lucy Show*. The Burns' lived next door to Sal Palermo, his wife Carmella and their beautiful daughter, Angie. Mom and Dad would return home from the Burns' in the spring of '54 and report tales of yelling, cursing, bullying and general mayhem originating at 66 Daffodil Lane, the Palermo domicile, where Dad thought "the local Mafia" resided.

Levittown was designed to be a "middle-class community" but more specifically it was a "white middle-class community." Caucasian families moved there in quest of a better way of life free from the rampant social disorganization that existed in eastern U.S. cities. Levittown was an innovative experiment in suburban living where shopping centers, houses, highways, schools and recreation areas were engineered to mix together like a kitchen recipe to form a tranquil, harmonious physical environment. All in all it seemed like a great place to live.

In 1954 human interaction was stratified and compartmentalized in Levittown. The place was exclusively "white." I would come in contact with some black kids at St. Mark's School over in Bristol but most of them lived several miles away in that town and few blacks belonged to my Catholic faith. Blacks mostly interacted with blacks and whites stayed mostly with whites, and that brand of racial segregation was explained to young people as "separate but equal" by their parents.

"Ethnic and religious segregation" as well as racial separation was quite evident. The Kalens, who were Jewish, lived across the street from us on Daffodil Lane, and their neighbors, who were Irish and Scottish, wouldn't allow *their* kids to play with the Hebrew children. To avert neighborhood conflict Dad allowed Annie to play with the Kalen children on Monday, Wednesday and Friday and she was permitted to interact with the Irish and Scottish kids on the other four days of the week.

Divisions along nationality and Christian religious lines also existed. Protestants did not marry Catholics and Irish Catholics did not marry Italian Catholics, and Baptists did not marry Presbyterians, and Christians did not marry Jews, and Occidentals did not marry Orientals.

So to me, looking back, Levittown, Pennsylvania was like a giant Bingo card with horizontal and vertical lines drawn in orderly rows to demarcate race, religion, culture, nationality and a person's economic status. Levittown reflected the rigid norms and standards of America that had been established by the predominance of White Anglo-Saxon Protestantism.

Before I could even talk about a girl the elders wanted to know about her family's economic level, their religion, their nationality, her father's employment and the ancestral tree. People were imprisoned in rigid general classifications. At least that is the way I recollect American society as being constructed in the 1950s.

I don't remember too much about 1954 except that Mom would faithfully watch the *Arthur Godfrey Show* and Betty Furness would always say, "You can be sure if it's *Westinghouse*," and if I was well behaved I was allowed to stay up and watch *The Tonight Show* with Steve Allen. Everyone was afraid of someone calling him or her "a Communist." And an American adult's greatest dread was to be called a "Communist" or "a Communist Sympathizer" on national TV by Senator Joseph McCarthy of Wisconsin.

Twenty-nine million American households had television sets in the mid-fifties, or about sixty percent of the national population. The new media was already anchoring itself as a powerful force in the marketing of products and in the forging of a new set of contemporary values to challenge the practices supported by WASP America.

In 1954 the Cold War was mounting between the United States and Russia and on the domestic scene, racial segregation in public schools was being challenged in the judicial system, with rulings outlawing the practice of "separate but equal schools" in certain parts of the United States.

Jackie Robinson had recently broken the baseball color barrier with the *Brooklyn Dodgers*, and Little Richard, Fats Domino and Chuck Berry were about to do the same thing in the music world. The stage was set for massive and sweeping changes and Levittown was like a vast social test tube, ready to undergo cultural experimentation, upheaval and evolution.

In '54 at age eleven, like most starry-eyed boys, my aspiration was to become a professional baseball player. I loved athletics: baseball, football, basketball and running. In *Little League* I played second base for Meenan Oil and the coach was grooming me to be a pitcher for the team in 1955.

I was thrilled with Willie Mays' over-the-head catch off the bat of Cleveland's Vic Wertz at the Polo Grounds and being a National League fan, I was elated when the *New York Giants* beat the *Indians* four games to zip in the '54 *World Series*. That was done in spite of Cleveland's awesome pitching staff that included Bob Lemon, Bob Feller, Mike Garcia and Early Wynn.

I was greatly influenced by long distance runner Roger Bannister who had broken the four-minute-mile with a time of 3:58.8. The circumference of Dogwood Drive was approximately a mile long so I would imitate Roger Bannister's feat by dashing and sprinting as fast as my legs would carry me. If I could have improved my training methods and my conditioning, I might have been able to shave some time off of eight minutes and fifty-three seconds, my fastest lap.

The modest home at 50 Daffodil Lane cost Dad $10,000, a considerable sum in 1954. As a rule I use the "ten times principle" because most goods, items, products and services are at least ten times as expensive today as they were in the 1950s.

Deliverymen were always prowling the Daffodil Lane neighborhood. Milk was mostly brought to the door in glass bottles. We got ours from *Harbison's Dairies*, which competed with *Abbotts Dairy*. I remember what a change it was when *Harbison's* orange juice was suddenly packaged in a waxed carton as opposed to the standard glass bottle and how reluctant Mom was to try the new product.

And then there was the *Bond Bread* man, and the fruit and vegetable hucksters, and the three ice cream trucks that competed for business, *O'Boyle's, Jack and Jill* and *Good Humor*, all claiming to sell the best flavors in their mixtures.

When I think of the year 1955 my memory suddenly becomes more acute. I began to really enjoy music and when "Rock Around the Clock" hit the airwaves, that song by Bill Haley and the Comets became the new national anthem for young people. The lyrics said it all, a new generation with boundless energy, capable of partying all night, going far beyond the normal limits of fun. There was also a trace of rebellion in the song's words that was more than rhythm, that in fact was a statement of youth exploding out of *our* David Nelson stereotype and revealing to the world, "This is what we're really made of!"

"Rock Around the Clock" was without a doubt my generation's version of Patrick Henry's "Give me liberty or give me death!" It was also my generation's *Declaration of Independence* to the adult world, saying "We the Teens of the United States," and my generation's *Bill of Rights* and *United States Constitution* all compacted into one refrain, "We're gonna' rock, rock, rock till the broad daylight." Bill Haley and the Comets, a little-known Country and Western band from Chester, Pennsylvania performed summer gigs down at the Jersey Shore. But the group accomplished something magical when they bridged the gap between white country and western music and black rhythm and blues. Their hit song gained national attention in '55 when it was used as the theme for the motion picture *Blackboard Jungle* and it opened the floodgates for Elvis, Chuck Berry, Buddy Holly, Little Richard and the other founding fathers of rock and roll.

In the summer of '55 dances for teens in our area of Levittown were held in the outdoor basketball court, which was located in back of the Olympic-sized Brook Swimming Pool in the recreation area between the Farmbrook, Stonybrook and Greenbrook sections. I wore my standard attire of pegged pants with saddle stitching down each side and of course flaps on the back pockets were in vogue. A plain cotton short-sleeved shirt was worn and penny loafers and white socks completed the ensemble.

In 1955 I had a flattop haircut that was symbolic of being a jock as opposed to the James Dean greaser look of sideburns, long hair smeared with *Vaseline*, and engineer boots with rolled-up dungarees. And tough guys wore either a white or a black tee shirt, depending on whether one was a "good tuff greaser" or a "bad-ass greaser."

Other songs in 1955 were played on the radio like: "Moments To Remember" by the Four Lads, "The Yellow Rose of Texas" by Mitch Miller and his orchestra, "Love is a Many Splendored Thing" by the Four Aces, "Mr. Sandman" by the Chordettes and "Autumn Leaves" by Roger Williams. Although I spent time listening to those other artists, "Rock Around the Clock" was the song that captured my imagination, stirred my soul, activated my spirits and made me think about evolving into a greaser.

What Bill Haley had done to my ears, James Dean and *Rebel without a Cause* had done to my eyes and it was the synthesis of those two magnificent cultural forces that affected my choice to "switch" from an avid jock into a prospective greaser.

When I was twelve Mom took me to see *The Wizard of Oz* and a month later I painfully struggled through her favorite movie, *Gone with the Wind*, because Mom had almost memorized Margaret Mitchell's lengthy novel, which she had read so many times. And after I became really friendly with Carnie, we saw Walt Disney's *Twenty Thousand Leagues under the Sea* seven times, which was five less than we had seen *Rebel without a Cause*. Almost my entire allowance was spent on movies and theater popcorn.

Smoking was regarded as a glamorous activity in '55. Mom and Dad each smoked over a pack of cigarettes a day. Dad smoked *Pall Mall* and Mom puffed on the shorter *Lucky Strikes*. It's amazing that I don't presently have lung cancer from all of the passive smoking I had experienced.

One time, Dad drove us down to Baltimore to visit relatives and when we stopped at a traffic light on *Route 40, the Pulaski Highway*, I looked over to another kid, just like myself, traveling with *his* parents. The kid was enveloped in smoke and I was trapped in a thick cloud of tar and nicotine, and I truly sympathized with my unidentified colleague as we both endured our dense environments. I waved to the poor kid and he waved back in tacit acknowledgment of our mutual situations.

On the return trip from Baltimore I tried an experiment. I lit up a cigarette in the back seat and I signaled to Annie to remain quiet. I smoked the entire *Chesterfield* down to the bottom without my parents ever knowing, because the '55 Chevy was so saturated with fumes that my additional puffs spiraling upward went completely undetected. It was then that I seriously contemplated becoming a greaser.

The *Philadelphia Athletics* had left Connie Mack Stadium, moving to Kansas City, Missouri in 1955. My pal Tinker liked the *A's* and he and I got into countless arguments as to which was the better team, the *A's* or the *Phillies*, and which league was better, the *American* or the *National.*

Some of my friends thought that Bobby Shantz was a better pitcher than Robin Roberts, and that Gus Zernial was a better cleanup hitter than Del Ennis, and that Ferris Fain was a better first baseman on the

A's than Eddie Waitkus had been on the 1950 *Whiz Kids*. Tinker did make a concession when it came to center fielders. The *Phillies'* Richie Ashburn was easily the winner, hands down. Richie Ashburn was my baseball idol and hero.

I fondly recall the 1950s. The *Korean War* had ended, prosperity was flourishing, Suburbia was expanding, and with the *G.I. Bill* war veterans like my father were able to obtain low interest loans to purchase homes.

White families had evacuated the crowded cities in pursuit of a higher standard of living, cleaner air, better shopping centers, escape from urban crime, and most particularly, a brighter future for the baby boomer generation.

The '50s decade was a less complicated era than the present computer age. Interaction between human beings was direct and personal. There were no ATM Machines, no *Xerox* machines, no fax machines', no telephone answering devices', no cell phones, no compact discs, no video games, no personal computers, no databases, no *911*, and no cable television. Strangely enough my greaser gang "the Diablos" lived perfectly well without *McDonald's, Burger Kings, Pizza Huts, Denny's, Taco Bells, IHops* or *Boston Markets*. All we needed were places like our hangouts the Feed Bag and the Dairy DeLite to satisfy our lust for food.

Most stores and restaurants back then were mom and pop operations or were family run, like Luigi and Domenic managing the Feed Bag and Hal Irving overseeing Hal's Talk of the Town Delicatessen, where I was employed "under the table" at age thirteen as a teen kitchen laborer.

The '50s decade was a much simpler and less chaotic period before the deluge of giant franchises, corporate conglomerates and the perils of an impersonal Megalopolis. And we got along pretty well with only one public telephone company serving our needs.

I nostalgically cherish that very special time before Rap Music, before the Eagles, before Fleetwood Mac, before the Doors, before the Beach Boys, before ABBA, before the Rolling Stones, before the Supremes, before the Temptations, and yes, even before the Beatles.

Roller blades and skateboards were unheard of in Levittown, Pennsylvania in the '50s era. Hula-hoops, Davy Crockett coonskin hats, poodle skirts, saddle shoes, and black and white sneakers were "cool." Pegged pants, hangouts, saddle stitching, *Edsels*, white bucks, penny loafers, pedal pushers, sock hops, and *American Bandstand* were "boss." Passion pits, "submarine races," DA haircuts and multi-zipper black leather jackets were "not square." And finally, 3-D glasses, the jitterbug, and "cruisin" around the main drag in a sleek convertible were the "in things" to do.

There were friendly greetings like "Boogety-boogety-boogety-shoo" and "Ootie-ootie." There were fifteen-cent hamburgers, the Salk vaccine had been developed, roll-on deodorant was invented, *Disneyland* had opened in California and the *Hand Jive* had become a new dance sensation. And '50s teenagers were not haunted by the twin specters of drugs and AIDS. The '50s decade was a very special time for guys and gals to grow up', to share friendships, to fall in love and to experience life. The only real perils were neighborhood greaser gangs looking for vulnerable kids to pick on.

The a.m. dial dominated the radio waves, and in the Philadelphia metropolitan area, the "in" station was WIBG, Wibbage Radio' 99. The biggest name DJ was Joe Niagra, whose "Niagra Calls in Philly" was a battle cry for great rhythm and lyrics about to be spun. Later there was Hy Lit, another popular WIBG disc jockey whose immortal refrain "Hyski-O-Roonie-McVouty-O-Zoot" captivated the hearts of millions of teen fans. Other great radio personalities like Jerry Blavatt, the "Geator With the Heater," also known as "The Boss with the Hot Sauce," soon would also appear.

Every once in a while, my friends and I would tune in Cousin Brucie out of New York, or Alan Freed, a DJ transplant from Cleveland to Manhattan. Freed had coined the term "Rock and Roll" as a code name for "black rhythm and blues." But for the most part Philly' was where it was at, and "Wibbage" gave us Levittown kids our daily diet of Bill Haley and the Comets, Buddy Holly and the Crickets and Jerry Lee Lewis.

Many of my friends and I despised "cover versions" of black rhythm and blues performed by such lily-white artists as Pat Boone. We didn't mind Pat Boone's original "white" melodies like "Love Letters In the Sand" and "April Love" but when he did "white cover versions" of Fats Domino's "Ain't That A Shame" and Little Richard's "Tutti-Frutti," the nice guy with the "white bucks" turned the "Dogwood Hollow guys" off from the first note.

Yesterday I was riding through downtown Hammonton, New Jersey and my car stereo picked up the familiar baritone of a Philly' DJ, "Let's take a walk down Memory Lane." "Born Too Late" by the Poni-Tails was played and I felt a degree of remorse for all of those twenty-first century kids who were not interacting with their peers, sitting in their bedrooms playing video games on their computers, living a lonely isolated existence, and having machines as their best friends.

Today "virtual reality" allows kids to function in an artificial environment but back in the '50s, we had "actual reality" where we experienced firsthand thrills and chills, not through a machine or floppy disc but through minute-to-minute, face-to-face contact with other human beings. I'm so glad that I had the opportunity to grow up during the nifty fifties.

"Little League Baseball"

Kids' baseball is a really great American tradition. Fathers can relate to their children who play *Little League* because male adults remember the experience as something vital that taught them life-skills and socialization during *their* youth. *Little League* is as American as apple pie and now the rest of the world is finally wonderfully acclimated to enjoying everything American including baseball. That particular American sports' heritage was very special to me while growing-up in the 1950s and I will always have many fond recollections of *Little League Baseball*.

Even an institution as wonderful as *Little League* has its vocal critics. Some carpers complain that the sport emphasizes competition too much and that the lesser skilled kids sitting on the bench ought to get more playing time. Other grievers cite that the risk of injury is all-too-real.

I wholeheartedly believe that *Little League* is a terrific "coming of age" American growth experience. It teaches kids organizational skills, division of labor, cooperation and competition. By organization I mean nine kids have to function like one unit harmoniously working under one main coach. In division of labor those same nine kids must efficiently perform different tasks and responsibilities. The players must cooperate with each other in order to defeat the opposing team in fair and square competition. Dual Motors versus Kiwanis is actually a small-scale version of *Apple* going up against *IBM* or of *General Motors* taking on *Ford*. That's what makes *Little League* so uniquely American and why the inherent rivalries in sports help to perpetuate this country's unparalleled "free enterprise" value system.

For those critics who claim and insist that *LL* is dangerous, I should remind them that there is danger and risk everywhere. If every young boy or girl lived in a protective bubble, no kids would ever interact. Each one would be floating around in a separate vacuum. Those squeaky-gear *LL* critics should not cross streets, should not walk down crowded aisles in *Wal-Mart* having merchandise stacked up to the ceiling and should not mow their lawns or drive to Wildwood or Cape May on summer vacations because something threatening might unexpectedly happen.

Dangers exist and loom all around us and in *Little League* competition, injuries predominantly happen *by accident* and they are not deliberately or maliciously inflicted. I guess that's one particular reason I absolutely love *Little League Baseball*. I have always been quite fascinated by physical danger and by intense competition, especially in sports.

In 1953 I had played Hammonton *Little League* ball for the town team *DiDonato's Bowling.* My coach was Mr. Reid, and his son Bruce was also the shortstop on the team. Bruce's older brother Frank would come to the practices and help his dad work with the players and ironically, Frank's son Scott wound-up working for me in my boardwalk arcade in Ocean City, Maryland two decades later. From my own life experience, there's no doubt in my mind that *LL* promotes an appreciation of the American free-enterprise economic system. It made me love the thrill of competition on the field and later in my adult life in my business enterprises.

I remember how thrilled I was in '53 as a ten-year-old getting my first hit, a bunt single. I also recall playing in a game when an older kid on the Hammonton Dual Motors team hit a towering fly ball to me in left field. I anxiously backed up to the fence, looked up above the lights into the night sky, closed my eyes, and miraculously, the white ball plopped into my glove as my knees were clattering. I opened my lids when I heard the fans on both sides of the field cheering my stellar achievement. That adventure was a real confidence builder I could have never found living in a protective bubble.

In '53, I still recollect kids still leaving their mitts on the field between innings. I still think about the thrill of playing night baseball at Hammonton (New Jersey) Lake Park just like the *Phillies* and the *A's* had done under the lights at *Shibe Park* (later Connie Mack Stadium) and how terrific it felt proudly playing ball in a league that had won the coveted *Little League World Championship* just four years earlier in 1949.

The following year, my family moved to Levittown, Pennsylvania where I had to make new friends and then find a new baseball team on which to play. I was assigned to Meenan Oil in the spring of '54, and there were so many kids out for each position that I was becoming discouraged. I had to beat out eight rivals to be the starting second baseman. The intense "competition" brought out the best in me and with sheer determination I eventually won the starting job. I played for Coach Siegel, who like Coach Reid back in Hammonton derived satisfaction from working with kids. Both men (and most adults associated with *Little League*) were (and are) good concerned citizens volunteering their time and effort to help youngsters accomplish and grow.

In 1955, my good friend Mike Hunter and I were selected from Meenan Oil to play on the Levittown National League All-Star Team.

70

We went up against our bitter rivals, the American League squad and with an element of luck won the game. After another victory, my National League All-Star Team encountered Morrisville, which had two kids that stood six-feet-three. One was Dick Hart (who later in life was a lineman for the *Philadelphia Eagles*) and the other Tommy Kaczor, who was Morrisville's main pitcher. Both kids were very intimidating. It was a close contest but then in the fifth inning Hart hit a ball so high to the centerfielder that when it came down, it split the webbing in Jerry Friedrich's glove. Hart was already on third base when the ball finally hit the ground and then he trotted home with the go ahead run.

I was devastated because I believed that Levittown National had a better overall team. But then Morrisville went on to win the *Little League World Championship* at Williamsport, and I listened to every one of their games on the radio. I got to admit that I became a loyal Morrisville fan that summer of '55 after being very disappointed being defeated by them.

So in conclusion, I suppose that possibly the best things *Little League* experience teaches kids are how to handle failure and how to show good sportsmanship after being defeated. And then in 1960 I was elated when Levittown, Pa. went on to win the highly coveted *Little League World Series*.

And so, I came from a league (Hammonton, NJ) that had won the *Little League World Championship* in '49, played against an excellent Morrisville, Pennsylvania team that won it all in '55, and cheered for the old Levittown, PA (American) League squad that won it all in '60. Those three unforgettable fond memories will always remain with me as long as I shall live, and in 1954-'60, the remarkable events could only happen in America.

"Wacky College Professors"

I certainly had a cross section of diverse professor personalities during my four-year teacher college preparation. Some were austere and pompous, others were liberal charlatans and many of them were eccentric in his or her unique way. Most of my college professors certainly didn't appear as members of mainstream America.

After registering in the college's main building with its "Majestic Golden Dome," I noticed that only the professors' last names were provided on my weekly schedule so unless one knew a particular instructor by appearance, the freshman didn't know whether the teacher was a man or a woman.

A good former high school friend of mine attending the college had almost the same class schedule as I had. The first day of fall semester I had inadvertently left my schedule home in the rush of excitement to drive my father's blue pickup truck twenty miles southwest to the picturesque college campus. I managed to remember the time and place of my first 8 a.m. class and waved to my friend Tim Amoro sitting on the opposite side of the classroom. After the dismissal bell for "The Fundamentals of School Organization," I met my friend and started up a conversation.

"Where's the next class Tim?" I asked. "I left my schedule at home on my bedroom desk."

"English," my acquaintance answered.

I remembered that English was *my* second class of the day also. "Your schedule was almost identical to mine," I stated, "so I'll just tag along if you don't mind."

After seating ourselves in the crowded second period classroom, the professor took roll from his master list. I felt rather uneasy when I recognized that my name had not been called. I raised my hand after the distinguished mustached professor asked, "Is everyone present and accounted for?"

"Are you Professor Sankin?" I innocently inquired. "My name was not called!"

The class then broke out in raucous hysteria. The abashed male professor's thick eyebrows slanted down at almost forty-five-degree angles expressing his displeasure with my inquiry. "My good fellow," the chagrined sage began, "I certainly am not Professor Sankin. I am Professor Stevens. I happen to be a man the last time I checked. Professor Sankin happens to be a member of the opposite gender. Since you are not supposed to be in this room," Professor Stevens rankled, "I strongly suggest that it would be in everybody's best interest if you proceed immediately to Room 217!"

Boisterous laughter could be discerned as Professor Stevens terminated his deriding and stern dissertation. I recall thinking at the time that I wished some faster mode of transportation would be available other than that provided by my two lower appendages. I rushed out of Room 212 red-faced, slightly humiliated and almost sweating bullets.

I finally located Professor Sankin's class down the second-floor corridor and unfortunately my belated entrance interrupted her introductory lecture. The class remained hush as the austere elderly woman taciturnly surveyed the rude intruder's body from head to toe. The no-nonsense matronly gray-haired lady motioned for me to occupy the last remaining desk next to the window overlooking the main building's scenic "campus green."

Professor Sankin had the distinct habit of carefully enunciating every syllable of every word. Her small oval-shaped mouth exposed her very active tongue continuously lubricating a *Lifesaver* wedged underneath it. The old dame had a warty face that would make any non-blind frog leap with terror. Her voice was either shrill or squawky depending on her articulation and when Professor Sankin hit a high pitch, a clanging burglar alarm would have seemed more melodious and appealing to the ears.

While managing to get mostly B's and C's on Professor Sankin's labyrinth-length *objective* tests, I was baffled by the professor's harsh criticism of my writing style. She *subjectively* described my compositions as being too "wordy" and too "flowery" using "too many adjectives and adverbs," and I was assured of a D or an F on every essay and theme that I submitted, no matter how meticulously each one had been organized.

'I know I have some writing and language arts' talent,' I thought. 'Creative writing and journalism are my strong suits. Professor Sankin is trying to stifle my aspiration to become an author. She's deliberately breaking my testicles in this crazy 'Fundamentals of Communications' 101 class!' I concluded.

Professor Sankin's attacks on my themes were comparable to how the *U.S. Marine Corps* trains' its soldiers. First the recruit is harshly broken down to demoralize his confidence, and then he is built up according to standards practiced by the drill instructor. My creativity had to be sacrificed to allow for the rebuilding of my mastery of basic writing mechanics.

Coincidentally, the girls in the freshman English class were all receiving B's and C's on their compositions while all of the frustrated male peons were *earning* D's and F's. In fact it was the two freshman' year D's I had *earned* from Professor Sankin first and second semesters that compelled me to switch my college major from Teacher of English to Junior High School Teacher.

'Professor Sankin isn't the first teacher trying to destroy my future with her dumb little dictatorial power game!' I thought. 'Somehow I'm going to graduate from this place and defy both Mr. Andrews (my high school trigonometry instructor) and Professor Sankin!'

I mentally thanked Miss Sankin for introducing me to the unwritten rules of *student* survival on the perilous college frontier:

1. Never challenge the professor (even though he or she' insists that he or she likes it).
2. Be courteous (falsely if necessary) and nice to the professor (color your nose brown).
3. Pretend to copy down everything the professor utters (for he or she speaks a rare English dialect known as gospel).
4. Ask questions that compliment (not complement) the prof's knowledge. Don't make the professor think of more than he or she actually wants to contemplate.
5. Avoid using the pronouns *I, me,* and *my* when asking a question (be humble, submissive and *subordinate* at all times).

In addition to the above classroom commandments I soon discovered that other secondary understandings would enable me to "play the game" and get better grades (while I exploited the "*subjective* factor" in teacher evaluation).

1. Work or study with other students in the class and always be cooperative (learn to kiss-up and flatter the teacher and be genial to his or her favorite students).
2. Buy the college outline series to the course (authored by the professor) at the campus bookstore and make sure the professor observes you reading his or her "companion book" to the course.
3. Cheat whenever necessary or when it is expedient.

During my freshman year, in keeping with a Human Behavior and Development course requirement, I was assigned to visit a nearby elementary school and observe a "single unique *student*" (translation: discipline problem) and copy down every disruptive thing he or she did in the class. Then I had to write a case study term paper on what I had noted and attempt to explain the *child's* aberrant behavior and propose solutions demonstrating how I would rectify the misbehaviors if I were the *child's* teacher. "Choose a candidate whose deportment slightly deviates from the norm!" our erudite professor instructed.

I believed that such a selection would add color and variety to my report and make it more intriguing to compile. It was really hard choosing a targeted *student* since half the members of the class demonstrated a definite affinity for naughtiness. Three times a week for an entire semester I had watched fiendish public-school *students* perform their repertoire of juvenile pranks, and then I recorded the teacher's very apparent frustration for lack of an antidote to remedy the erratic idiotic antics.

The elementary school *children* were showing off to me by chewing gum, passing notes, being defiant and insolent to adult authority, name-calling, blaming each other for unruliness and squealing on one another instead of listening to the directions of the perplexed teacher. This was my first insight into classroom dynamics as an independent observer assessing the many behavioral adversities that seriously blight the modern American education process.

'Instead of we must understand the *child*,' I thought, 'the philosophy of education should be 'the *child* must understand'!' Teachers are often the prey of merciless adolescent predators that are protected by law, the school system's philosophy and the general society. The only defense the teacher has against young anarchists is "educational psychology," which is as effective as trying to down a charging rhinoceros with an empty water pistol.

'Education should be based on what a *child* needs to know and not on what a *child's* needs are, which vary from kid to kid and are not specifically identified!' I concluded. 'Serious consequences should await the *child* that refuses to understand and respect adult authority in a school building.'

First Period Gym' Class was probably my favorite freshman curricular activity. Coach Holmes seemed to fancy me because my personality stood out like a sore thumb and my overall lack of athletic coordination managed to always capture his keen attention.

I usually showed up during roll call several minutes tardy from the locker room. In late September I had not yet obtained my brown and yellow college gym suit and instead wore my old *Edgewood High* green and white outfit to class. When I finally bought a brown and yellow gym uniform and wore it to class Coach Holmes had my gym locker secretly opened, removed my green and white shirt and trunks and directed the class to leave the gym and assemble outside on an athletic field.

The imaginative coach ignited my high school uniform with a cigarette lighter and the class began to chant in response to the ritual "Up in smoke! Up in smoke!" The other freshmen sounded as if they were members of a primitive jungle tribe worshiping and extolling arson. Their dissonant medley then transformed into a ceremonial dance and the fellows hopped and skipped around my smoldering forest green *Edgewood High* gym apparel. Little incidents like the tribal dance, towel fights in the shower room and the overall congenial looseness of Coach Holmes' informal gym class made it my favorite curricular freshman enterprise.

Looking back on my college preparation, I envision an asylum of wacky liberal and eccentric professors trying to rearrange my mind. Mr. Rolphs taught sociology and anthropology. He was a restless neurotic speaker who oscillated from one side of the classroom to the other as if he was a person with diarrhea seeking entry into an already occupied lavatory stall. Professor Rolphs' speeches were saturated with vitriolic condemnations of traditional institutions and their' failure to solve the country's many domestic dilemmas. Rolphs made 'Blame America first' a common understanding forty years before the motto became popular on radio talk shows.

Most of Professor Rolphs lessons would envelop arguments questioning the existence of God, the limitations of our breast-oriented civilization, and the myriad inadequacies of *our* evil materialistic keeping-up-with-the-Jonses' culture. Rolphs and his vituperations wouldn't last a marking period in the average American public high school, but a liberal dissident endorsing a quasi-Communist ideology could easily thrive on most college campuses as a beneficial and a meritorious professor that promotes freedom of thought and freedom of speech.

I witnessed a half-dozen virtuous girls at various times storm out of Rolphs sociology class weeping after engaging in a bitter emotional debate with the professor over the virginity of Mary or the divine nature of Christ. Although Rolphs repetitiously indicated that his sole purpose was to stimulate open-mindedness, it was plainly obvious that his podium provided a convenient soapbox where the professor could (at liberty) perpetuate the doctrines of Marx, Engels, Lenin, Stalin and Rolphs.

I concluded in early 1962 that many frustrated thespians, actors and scriptwriters masqueraded as college professors under the guise of "academic freedom." The liberal lecturers experimented with *their* uninspiring rhetoric and used it on their captive audiences and as in the case of Professor Rolphs, many professors thoroughly enjoyed playing the role of "Devil's Advocate" while probing the minds and eroding away the traditional values of their insulted and/or fascinated listeners.

As long as *academic freedom* is the benchmark of liberal arts college courses professors feel quite comfortable incorporating *their* own radical liberal views and creeds into each lecture to challenge conventional (traditional) wisdom. And the majority of college *students* going through a rebellion against adult authority in their own personal lives find the bizarre and the extraordinaire "new forum approach" fascinating. The learners associate *bizarre* and *extraordinaire* with freedom of speech and with individual expression guaranteed under the auspices of the *First Amendment* to the *Constitution*. Any blitzkrieg of traditional moral or religious values is categorized as "intellectual investigation," and therefore those professorial assaults are tolerated by *students*, condoned by colleges and universities and perpetuated by professors.

So when someone like Professor Rolphs gets his or her jollies by blasting the maternal instincts of motherhood or the infallibility of the Pope, he or she is only executing his or her job description. The exposure to radical left-wing ideas will surely introduce *his* or her *students* to a vista of new perspectives that will undoubtedly widen their horizons and make them think and behave like avowed atheists and like loyal contemporary Communists and Socialists.

Dr. Peaferm was a strange Economics professor that appeared to be more interested in his private stock portfolio than in the balance of international trade, the guns-versus-butter debate, inflation or the rising cost-of-living index. His drowsy monotone (even during his most enthusiastic oral presentation) eventually sent the most avid *students* on one-way excursions to Slumberland. Dr. Peaferm's boring lecture method could never cut it in a public high school but a fellow of his unremarkable caliber could easily flourish in a college classroom environment.

The highlight of Peaferm's Economics seminar was a coed that Bob Abrams (a fraternity friend) had labeled and code-named Tokyo Rose. Bob and I would sit in Peaferm's crowded lecture hall and watch Tokyo Rose systematically squeeze the pus out of her facial and neck pimples. This daily ritual would make us revel because it added a new dimension to an otherwise very dull and dismal class.

In a way though, Dr. Peaferm's style was different and unique. Peaferm had no axes to grind or dragons to slay as Rolphs and Sankin had. Peaferm was more interested in *Standard and Poors* than he was in raising the standard of the poor by sharing and redistributing the limited wealth and resources of the average middle-class American. Despite his nauseating mediocrity Peaferm's course was refreshing in the sense that he wasn't riding a white charger looking for the *Holy Grail* or crusading for the downfall of selfish capitalism while simultaneously championing the pursuit of reconstructing and redistributing the world's wealth.

And then there was Dr. Su, a petite Chinese lady who dressed in 1962 as if *WWI* was still in progress. Dr. Su's class was titled Teaching Methods I, but it would have been more appropriately identified as The Evils of Mao Tse-tung. Dr. Su spoke with a heavy Oriental accent', despised Red Chinese Communism with a passion and she always mispronounced my last name Wiener (as in hot dog) instead of Wiessner.

One day before class a friend (during a moment of jocularity) scribbled on the front blackboard, "Do not erase-Dr. Wiener." Before I had a chance to remove the prosaic verse, Professor Su entered the room. She automatically grabbed an eraser and then momentarily hesitated as she somberly studied the message scrawled upon the black slate. She then innocently prattled, "Ah so, class! Dr. Wiener say I should not erase board, so I just lecture today and not write notes with chalk for you to copy." The class slipped into a minor state of pandemonium in response to her shallow perception and reaction to my friend's juvenile prank.

On another occasion I had cut Dr. Su's class to engage in an impromptu softball game on the baseball diamond adjacent to her corner second-floor classroom. Dr. Su stepped to the back of the room to open a window and observed me gallivanting on the baseball field below. "Wiener!" she imperatively bellowed. "You come up here this instant to my class!"

Although I had distinctly heard her piercing soprano voice I ignored the diminutive lady professor's command pretending not to hear the dictum. Dr. Su re-evaluated her impetuosity and exclaimed to the already hysterical class, "Maybe that isn't Wiener down there after all!" A thunderous burst of laughter blared down to the baseball field from the upstairs corner classroom window.

Dr. Attleburg taught the subject of Mental Health and had a gruff-looking square face that qualified her to enter and win any ferocious dog show as a female pit bull. Her wrinkled countenance was a portrait of emotional anguish and her tainted breath exuded an odor akin to a dried-up Manhattan. Her anomalous lectures sounded very much like humdrum epistles from the lips of a peevish tavern patron about to fall off of her bar-stool.

Dayton, a black *student* in Dr. Attleburg's nondescript seminar, sat in the fifth seat in the row to my right next to the sidewall. Dayton worked nights on the back of a garbage truck, was extremely fatigued during the day and would always lean his body against the wall and fall asleep during the climax of Dr. Attleburg's dissertation. During one particular lecture the lady professor was elaborating about the need for love, forgiveness and sympathy in *our* interpersonal relationships as if she was giving an examination of conscience testimony at an Alcoholics Anonymous meeting. I then quite mischievously removed and opened a safety pin from my pocket and next quite methodically pierced the sleeping Dayton's pants and leg with it.

Dayton howled as his reflexive reaction to instant pain sent both him' and his desk crashing onto the polished wooden floor. Dr. Attleburg continued her lazy lecture as if nothing at all had happened. I wondered how such a numb person could be an authority on the manifold operations of the human mind after she had been completely oblivious to reality transpiring in her midst. But people of her ilk thrive in education, especially at the college level. They draw *lush* salaries and help pollute the educational canal by supporting the advancement of non-learning.

Dr. Attleburg's favorite maxim was "There's a big difference between teaching thirty years and teaching one year thirty times!" The most lamentable aspect of her oratory was that Dr. Attleburg had been uttering the impressive proverb ever since her initial year of professoring.

Speech with Dr. Lane was another class I had to attend. On the first meeting of the September session of my junior year, I sedately sat in my desk awaiting the instructor's arrival. An older gentleman I had presumed was pursuing a teaching degree sat next to me. The self-proclaimed *Korean War* veteran initiated a conversation. I soon discovered that he was very critical of the speech professor who was to teach *our* course. The elderly man used the terms "lousy" and "hideous" in his depiction of Dr. Lane.

I explained that I hardly knew anything about Dr. Lane except that the speech teacher's behavior was rumored being "a bit on the eccentric side." Five minutes elapsed and then the distinguished-looking *Korean War* veteran sitting next to me arose and announced to the class that *he* was the inimitable Dr. Lane.

On the class's second session Dr. Lane made what he considered to be "a spectacular entrance." The nutcase had scaled the tall oak tree that had grown parallel to the main campus building, crawled out onto a sturdy limb and then clumsily swung his frame inside an opened second floor window.

Dr. Lane's interpretation of the meaning of the word *creativity* was doing something excessively peculiar or something unexpectedly sensational. His mannerisms were predictably unpredictable and one could only expect the unexpected from him. However, even climbing through opened second floor windows, standing and lecturing from atop the teacher's desk and shouting slanderous obscenities for no reason at all soon became tedious and unimpressive after becoming accustomed to their constant enactments.

Professor Flank taught History and Issues in United States Government. His lectures were as dull as an eight-inch-thick razor blade. Flank reveled in discussing American social disorganization, world chaos and the general frailness of the culturally retarded human species. Somehow, his "Blame America first" quips always seemed devoid of integrity, sincerity, honor and courage.

One winter day while delivering a vitriolic critique on American imperialistic military/economic institutions, Dr. Flank's nose began bleeding. Feeling the slight trickle, the critical professor dabbed his nostrils with a handkerchief, but the flow of scarlet became even more profuse.

Flank glanced down in horror at the quantity of blood in his handkerchief, and feeling exceedingly frightened and embarrassed, his face turned as white as a lily. The professor swiftly canceled the remainder of the pathetic lesson, dismissed the class and hastily departed the scene looking as if he was a wounded infantryman searching for the nearest Florence Nightingale.

Professor O'Connor was a very outspoken man that thought his essential destiny in life was to expose the numerous faults and weaknesses of our corrupt American social structure. The intellectual establishment (college deans) regarded O'Connor's attacks on U.S. institutions as productive and scholarly as long as the axe-to-grind crusader lectured his way through issues like American racial prejudice and evil capitalistic exploitation both on the domestic scene and abroad.

But Professor O'Connor began skating on thin ice when *his* research investigations revealed instances of homosexuality among other notable members of the college faculty. Although he was one of the *students*' favorite professors O'Connor soon became the object of detestation (of his envenomed colleagues on the faculty). In an incredibly short time, Professor O'Connor earned the disfavor of the college administration that suddenly abhorred *his* inquiries into his fellow instructors' bedfellows' habits rather than focusing his attention upon what was diabolically wrong with America.

O'Connor's bold muckraking and whistle blowing activities drew newspaper attention to the local college campus, thus casting a dusky pall that immediately eclipsed all of the favorable publicity that the school's deans so sanctimoniously had labored to build. O' Connor's flirtations with attempting to right all wrongs (including social injustices and sexual perversions) became an uncontrollable obsession and the maverick professor did not heed the admonitions of the school's executives about what *he* had deemed immoral on the college campus. O'Connor was no longer an outspoken iconoclast! He was now perceived as a threat to the college!

Professor O'Connor could best be described as a combination of Upton Sinclair and *Don Quixote* and he appeared quite oblivious to the hatchet of doom being held over his head. His obsessive determination to expose all evil ruined his career. O'Connor was denied tenure, not because of his incompetence but because his mouth had oracled bad publicity about the school.

It was perfectly all right for O'Connor to subvert and indict the *United States of America*, but when he made it too personal by demonizing the college's good reputation then he was abruptly dismissed from academic service. The image of the school was much more important than the necessary criticisms prolifically directed at corrupt America.

Professor McIntire was an English prof' and a scholarly expert on William Shakespeare's work and life. McIntire relished several of my literary contributions that appeared in the campus newspaper and in the school's literary magazine. The fellow was a jolly sort of man who seemed to be knowledgeable and conversant in almost every subject. McIntire was rumored to be a "gay instructor" and to listen to his unique speech patterns, which featured a distinct effeminate twinge, I had good reason to place credence in the hearsay. On one occasion inside the *Student Union*, Dr. McIntire politely invited me over to his abode for cocktails to discuss *romance* in British literature, but I took a rain check when he intimated that only the two of us would be "romanticizing."

82

In all fairness to my college education, I had several dozen other dedicated professors that contributed positively to my professional development. To them, I will be eternally grateful. But decades later, the professors I have just described somehow seem to stand out in my mind for several very obvious reasons. The most discernible explanation is that instructors of their kind still populate virtually every college and university faculty in America. But Miss Sankin's skeleton is probably spinning around and gyrating in her grave with her "D Average" mediocre talent-less *student* evolving into an author of sorts.

"Reminiscing Glassboro State College"

The lucky *thirteen*-mile April 1, 2004 drive from Hammonton to Glassboro, New Jersey was pleasant and almost inspirational. As my merlot-colored *Nissan Maxima* passed through downtown Williamstown and onto *Route 322*, I pondered the four years I had spent at *Glassboro State College* preparing to become an idealistic New Jersey public school teacher, a difficult career which I had diligently pursued for thirty-four years until my very happy retirement in June of 1999.

But many important fragments of my past have been erased by circumstances beyond my control, further adding to my general quandary that often hypothesizes whether those four incredible years between ages nineteen and twenty-three had really occurred or not, for my entire life has been dangerously lived "on the cusp." Let me explain the basis for my current rumination.

I had attended Bishop Egan High in Levittown, Pennsylvania from 1957-'59 but now the former parochial school is boarded up and its identity no longer exists. And then in 1960 I managed to finally evolve out of Edgewood Regional High School in Atco, New Jersey, but the name of that institution is now Winslow Township High School. And consistent with *that* strange coincidence of my educational past being eradicated, the *Glassboro State Teachers College* of 1965 I had known and often reflect upon has now been transformed into *Rowan University*.

But for some remote inexplicable reason, I seldom revisited my former *Glassboro State* Alma Mater, but now I felt driven by a strong compulsion to re-connect with my past escapades. Perhaps it was pure nostalgia, or maybe I was motivated by fanciful memories that still haunted my delicate psyche, or perhaps my impulse to visit Glassboro was a desperate measure to recapture the essence of my youth. 'April is symbolic of the rebirth of nature and plant life in the *Northern Hemisphere*,' I rationally considered, 'and just like daffodils sprouting out of the ground and deciduous trees miraculously forming new green spring foliage, my soul too is being rejuvenated this *April Fool's Day* by the wonderful annual spring regeneration.'

Upon crossing two-lane *Delsea Drive*, which also masquerades as *Route 47*, I ambitiously entered the small college town. I figured I would tour some exclusive sites to determine if any of my old haunts were still around and viably functioning. My eyes instantly recognized that Mazzeo's Bar and Lounge on High Street on my right was now the Study Hall Coffee House, a defunct boarded-up business that obviously had seen more prosperous times. Across the street and a block west was the former splendid Glassboro Movie Theater, now a mere empty bankrupt business with a huge "For Sale" sign hung in its ancient window, but back in 1964 the cinema was the site of a raucous fraternity shindig. That particular violation along with other high jinks almost got my Greek brothers and me expelled from the school of higher learning for the final time, our fifth ultimatum from the college's beleaguered administration.

Joe's Sub Shop further down on High Street now had the creative appellation Little Beef's Hoagie Shop, a true indication that nothing is really permanent in this ephemeral life in an ever-changing world. I recalled that the Glassboro Police Station had formerly occupied the space behind the town bank situated at the central intersection of High and Main Streets, but now I observed that a new police building occupies the corner opposite the prestigious financial institution. The town's gendarmes had moved a fantastic hundred feet away from the address where I had known them to operate and practice their brand of law enforcement back in the early '60s.

I felt my heart pound a little more robustly when I stopped my vehicle to study the upstairs rooms of 38 South Main Street, where my roommates and I had hibernated for three fabulous coming-of-age years. Our sophomore-to-senior residence was located right next to a funeral home, which no longer exists as a family business. 38 South Main now appeared old with its light green siding fading as a result of four decades of wear and tear and exposure to Mother Nature's indiscriminate cruelty, but nevertheless the aging house still represented the space I had shared, a little smaller than I appropriately remembered it being as my "home away from home" from September of 1964 to June of '65.

Back in the early-to-mid '60s Seedy's Bar was a popular hangout for my unauthorized non-sanctioned off-campus fraternity, the Lambda Phi Sigmas, a social group of Greek wannabes' more interested in chugging *Budweiser* and hustling pretty girls than becoming engrossed in the actual pursuit of academic excellence. Ironically Seedy's suds and sandwich hangout was just down the street from St. Bridget's Catholic Church, which predictably held its Sunday services on Church Street. But now the site where Seedy's was situated back in 1965 is presently a barren vacant lot.

I slowly navigated my *Maxima* west down Oakwood Avenue, which I had often used as a back approach to the rustic and still handsome college campus, and while passing over the familiar railroad tracks, I noticed the old Glassboro Train Station and Depot, empty, boarded up and depressingly decrepit-looking. That ramshackle edifice also brought back several sentimental memories that I'll never forget as long as Alzheimer's disease doesn't completely evaporate my recollections. But the dilapidated condition of the once vibrant train station made my heart feel melancholy and had my sixty-two-year-old body suddenly feeling worn out and tired too, for both the train station and I had seen better days.

I took Whitney Avenue past #501, Hollybush, the *Glassboro State College* President's residence back in 1965, but today the structure proudly stands as a historic building dedicated to commemorate the famous 1967 *Summit Meeting* between President Lyndon Baines Johnson and the U.S.S.R. Premier Alexei B. Kosygin, which coincidentally had transpired on the *Glassboro State College Campus,* and the great international conference remains today the venerable Jersey sandstone college mansion's greatest claim to fame.

I made a right on *322* wanting to view the historic Franklin House, which was an inn dating back to the aristocratic fox-hunting days of the early 1790s, but I was disappointed in discovering that the building had been renovated and converted into the Landmark Americana Tap, Grill and Liquor Mart. Across from the former Franklin House was State Street, which formed a Y two blocks down at New Street where Academy Street began. So being a little sad and disappointed at the Franklin House's demise, I turned around in the Landmark Americana's parking lot and returned west on *322*, which now divides the old campus from the new building additions, most of which have been constructed since my graduation in '65.

Only *Bosshart Hall, Winans Dining Hall* and the *Esbjornson Gymnasium* were situated on the north side of *322* my senior year, but now a grand *Student Union Building, Robinson Hall, Mimosa Hall, Rowan Hall, Wilson Hall,* the new *Savitz Library* along with six massive co-ed dormitories have been added to the north *322* campus scenario. *Winans Cafeteria* has been renovated and ingeniously converted into *Winans College Bookstore,* and so the *Glassboro State College* campus (now *Rowan University*) like the rest of the universities on the planet continues its new growth and its unique chameleon retooling of older facilities.

Glassboro's residential streets west of *Rowan University* (*Glassboro State*) attempt to confirm and promote a college-town atmosphere theme. Girard Road parallels the railroad tracks that happen to form the campus's western perimeter, and the remembrance of *our* Lambda Phi Sigma initiation along the railroad tracks immediately surfaced from my subconscious and managed to rekindle my flagging spirit. Princeton, Pennsylvania, Columbia, Yale, Harvard and Lehigh Roads horizontally followed in succession to the west after Girard, and then Georgetown, Dickinson, Villanova and Swarthmore Roads run vertically west forming a characteristic lattice pattern with the aforementioned west-layered streets, which traditionally have housed many off-campus students from back in the '60s up to the present time.

University Road is the main residential thoroughfare that parallels Dickinson and Villanova in the well-conceived interlacing pattern. Many of the University Road homes that I had considered mansions back in the '60s now appear in need of repair and rather mediocre in appearance. But it was not University Road's stately oak and elm trees nor the architectural grandeur of its aging palaces that prompted me to nostalgically desire re-exploring the remainder of the serene boulevard.

At the very end of the avenue was Peaks Horse, Apple and Peach Farm', which is now fenced in and designated off limits to strangers. But despite the three prominent "No Trespassing" signs, I felt a need to exit my *Maxima* and traverse down a familiar rural trail a hundred feet into the woods where I intended to re-discover a shallow stream. I rushed along the still-secluded path, now tangled in dense brush until I came to the "Sacred Oak," majestically towering above me and deeply rooted amidst the woods' briars, thick brambles and wild vegetation.

The old severed "Tarzan jungle vine" still dangled from around the still-dignified oak's third revered limb and the fallen-but-decomposing elm tree footbridge still spanned over the fifteen-foot-wide brook that remains today a rather imposing sight, but absolutely ravaged by time, rotted through its decayed bark and trunk and in its present flimsy condition, totally incapable of holding a sixty-two-year-old male of average weight. 'That's the third of nine major memorable scenes I want to see besides the railroad tracks and 38 South Main,' I evaluated. 'The fourth through seventh items of interest are on the old-side of the college campus and the eighth and ninth can be found two miles south of Glassboro in rural Aura.'

I then carefully ambled back to my *Nissan*', gingerly entered the vehicle, cautiously backed up, turned around and drove the mile-distance to the still-attractive countryside campus. 'I wish I had phoned a classmate fellow graduate friend of mine to accompany me on this ramble,' I thought. 'My Buddy Tim Amoro would relish this nostalgia as much as I am fondly recalling it right now.'

88

I halted my auto in the makeshift parking lot owned by the Pennsylvania Railroad. 'It's safe during the daytime,' I reckoned while recalling that once I was taking a graduate night course at the college, arrived at the campus a bit behind schedule, hastily parked my wife's green *Pontiac* in the same lot and returned from class finding the car's battery stolen. 'My brother-in-law was not too keen on driving from Hammonton to Glassboro with a replacement battery in the middle of a wicked January snowstorm,' I recollected with a naughty grin.

Although it was an early spring day, fallen leaves cushioned my steps to the old campus buildings I wished to observe. The bright golden dome still formed a cupola above the main academic building erected in 1923, then *College Hall* up until '65 but now renamed *Bunce Hall* after a revered college dean. I stopped to marvel at the majestic spectacle as students less impressed with its essential existence chatted and rushed to their next scheduled classes.

I detoured to where the Student Co-op snack bar used to be, a unique 1960s malt-shop carryover from the previous less hostile '50s decade. The mammoth *Student Union* across *Route 322* had replaced the Co-op (and its attendant lounges in nearby *Memorial Hall*) as the campus nerve center, and the entire *Memorial Hall* complex was now a suite of specialized offices being utilized for student organizations, clubs, the *Whit* newspaper, the *Avant Literary Magazine*, and for individual student counseling.

I passed by several groups of garrulous preoccupied students, oblivious to my intense scrutiny of their taken-for-granted physical environment. The walkers were laughing and exchanging gossip en route to their next destinations. Four decades before I had shared their youthful vim and vigor, their enterprise, their great expectations for individual accomplishments and their vision for a more peaceful world, along with *their* rosy hopes and dreams for prosperous futures, but then I felt myself' being quite out of place standing there, a realist and modern-day cynic among those that were still vulnerable to professors' unbridled entreaties and idealistic optimisms. Forty years separated their same enterprise from mine (as a student trekking down that same well-worn asphalt path), and my skeptical mind appreciated and rehashed the salient fact that I did not have to relive those forty years from 1965 to 2004 over again.

I next casually strolled to the old magnificent dorm' Quadrangle consisting of *Laurel Hall* and *Oak Hall*, originally constructed parallel to each other in the 1920s to accommodate the women attending the two-year "Normal School" to earn teaching certification, and to the far end of *that* most beautiful sector of the scenic campus was *Linden*

Hall, built in the late 1950s to complement the more distinguished twin dormitories. *Oak Hall* was just a short saunter from Hollybush, where several asphalt paths lead to *Evergreen Hall*, where Joanne (my future wife) once cheerfully resided. And next to *Evergreen* is *Mullica Hall*, a men's dormitory back in '65.

I peered across *Route 322* at the numerous building additions supplementing what I had known in '65, and the edifices now stretched all the way to Carpenter Street, which in my senior year seemed to be in another county. Behind the new dormitories and brick-faced academic buildings are numerous parking lots, tennis courts, softball, hockey, la-crosse and soccer fields, intramural fields, and finally the rather outstanding *Rowan University Football Stadium.*

I cut back across the area next to *Memorial Hall* and jaunted through a nice clean pristine-looking park that was once a student parking lot for "commuters." *Hawthorn Hall* was now altered into an administrative office building and no longer was the men's dorm' I had recalled from '65. The *Campus School*, where many of my colleagues had completed their Student Teaching and fundamental Practicum experiences was now called *Bozarth Hall*, named after another college dean of my era. Next to the former *Campus School* was the old baseball field where Ralph Crenshaw and I used to broadcast the games for *WGLS-FM*, the college radio station, which was now housed in *Bozarth Hall* and no longer was situated above the old *Savitz Library* building (now an administrative building) on the entrance oval next to what is now *Bunce Hall.*

I stood gazing at *"College Hall"* for a full minute on the pitcher's mound as the April 1st wind swirled dust and the remains of the autumn leaves about my black leather shoes. Forty-five years had elapsed since I had played gym-class soccer for Coach Holmes on that same verdant field, and only the passage of time separated my present memories from those past happy experiences that had occurred in that exact same place.

'Now that I've seen the railroad tracks, the vine, the elm tree bridge and the creek, the *College Hall Golden Dome*, the *Quadrangle*, the former Co-op, and *Evergreen Hall* there's only two more essential memories to see on my *April Fools Day Glassboro State* excursion,' I pondered as I slowly stepped around the corner of *Bunce Hall* (College Hall) to the oval drive before it, now blocked off to local traffic. Arriving at my parked automobile in the dirt and stone railroad parking lot, I decided to motor south two miles to Aura to complete my day's personal itinerary.

I anxiously drove through downtown Glassboro on High to Main Street, looked left and smiled upon seeing that all-too-familiar Angelo's Diner was still in business, and then traveled south until Main became *Gloucester County Road 533*. Soon I crossed the railroad tracks a mile from the college town and then crossed *County 610*. Another mile or so on *County 533* I arrived at good old *Gloucester County Road 608*. After turning left, my right foot stepped more heavily on the accelerator as I wondered whether or not my fraternity's old original Lambda Phi Sigma party place was still standing.

I halted my *Nissan* to obtain a closer inspection of the structure that I had been so anxious to see. Yes, there it now stood, painted red, but still in the exact shape I had remembered it being. The ultimate objective of my Hammonton-to-Glassboro excursion was Steve "Hoppy" Cassidy's chicken coop, but in 1962 the commonplace building had been imaginatively converted to a swinging college student attraction, the infamous Lambda Phi Sigma fraternity house.

On the way back to *Delsea Drive* following *County 608* I passed by another landmark from my past, the picturesque *Academy Street Lake* in the rural town of Clayton. Feeling satisfied and renewed from my morning excursion, I then motored back to Hammonton.

"School Assemblies"

The Teachers Handbook prepared by the school administration explicitly states, "All school assemblies are scheduled by the main office and the meetings constitute an integral part of the total school program. Assemblies provide opportunities for the *cultural* and *intellectual* growth of *students* and they contribute significantly to the development of school spirit and school morale."

I have attended in the neighborhood of three hundred school assembles in my thirty-four-year teaching career ranging from pep' assemblies and science demonstrations to boring lectures, spelling bees and popular "G-Rated" movies shown before major holidays to "Keep the lid on."

Recently the tone of assembly subjects has turned from *cultural* and *intellectual* to *bleak* and almost *macabre* themes such as drugs, teen pregnancies and question and answer sessions with convicted prisoners with the convicts showing up on stage (with prison guards) in their official orange uniforms. However, several extraordinary assemblies that I had the misfortune of attending stand out in my mind.

Once I had the displeasure of attending a junior-high school assembly in the high school auditorium. A circus clown wearing oversized shoes walked onto the front stage from behind the curtain and began doing magic tricks that were about as complicated as a basal reader. The *students* became quite restive and soon were hooting and shouting like a pack of vitriolic hyenas.

It is embarrassing to have to stand during the entire assembly and play Gestapo when the teacher himself' wished he had an old vaudeville cane to yank the idiot off the stage. 'A profit-minded huckster could amass a small fortune vending soft rotten tomatoes for the *children* to hurl at the zany entertainer,' I thought. That particular assembly definitely contributed to the "cultural and intellectual growth of the *students*."

The intellectually gifted *student* is often stifled spending thirteen years in a public-school system that promoted *democracy in education* within the comprehensive high school. Ben Locanta was a gifted *child* whose public-school preparation was about as useful as a bamboo paperweight during a tornado. The gifted *student* possessed admirable resourcefulness.

Whenever the school videotape machine went haywire or whenever the intercom went amuck, Ben was summoned to the office before any outside repairman was contacted. The young genius's knowledge of physics, electricity and chemistry was praiseworthy indeed. Regrettably Ben Locanta was so advanced that his mental needs were sadly neglected by the school curriculum. In the early '70s the high school had no modus operandi to effectively deal with the exceptionally talented *student.*

Usually in high school education the intellectually precocious *child* gets the short end of the stick since the entire system is geared to raising the mentally downtrodden up to "academic mediocrity." When schools have all-gifted sagacious *students* like Ben Locanta that is when they need the "laboratory approach to learning," "independent study" and "the *student*-oriented curriculum."

As it is according to the mandates of *democratic education,* those three splendid programs apply to the masses and not exclusively to the gifted *student.* Ben was the *child* that really needed to explore, create, invent, discover, synthesize and push his intelligence to the max'. But in American education *those* marvelous terms were and still are harnessed mostly to *students* that didn't (and don't) know a Bunsen burner from a Franklin stove and who' don't care to know.

One afternoon an opera company visited the school to give two assembly performances for the *student* body. Ben Locanta assisted the troupe with the stage arrangements, stationing the props', positioning and focusing the spotlights and overheads, and operating the backstage electrical controls.

One of the more-cocky thespians who had been traveling with the opera production bent down to adjust a spotlight that would be shining on him during the first scene. The light had been turned on for only a minute and Ben cautioned the fellow, "You'd better not touch that right now or your hands will get scorched!"

The middle-aged fellow, who was wearing a medieval costume with leotards, felt more than slightly chagrined at being admonished by a young high school *student.* The actor snorted back to Ben "I've been in show business all my life!" he boasted. "Do you think I'm some kind of greenhorn when it comes to simple high school stage lighting!"

The enraged actor/baritone bent down and grabbed the spotlight with both hands, and then an instant expression of agony beamed from his facial features. The fellow howled so loudly that I thought he was going to turn himself inside out and the heat from his sizzling hands almost triggered the school's fire alarm. Ben was gracious enough to escort the anguishing singer/actor down to the nurse's office where his seriously blistered fingers were professionally bandaged.

The assembly opera program did commence an hour later and the distressed fellow with the gauze around his hands didn't even have to wear white gloves. "That guy was punished by fate for being so nasty to Ben," history teacher Bob Gordon confided to me. "He deserved to get roasted because the nurse told me he's about as sociable as the Abominable Snowman."

That same year I was the adviser to the high school's chapter of the *National Honor Society*. Ben Locanta was president of the *NHS* and as usual, the week before the induction assembly the entire ceremony program was rehearsed. This was in the early '70s during the *Vietnam War* era, and most of the male *students* in the school had long hair, sideburns, mustaches, and they wore bell-bottom denim-jeans. I soon found out that there was a degree of rebelliousness and anti-war sentiments even among the school's most honorable *students*.

Towards the end of the *NHS* induction assembly there was always a segment where the *students* broke away from formal decorum and did a "Have You Heard" routine where high school gossip was done between two *students* over two separate microphones. Of course, Ben and another *NHS* officer stepped over the line and announced that *students* with certain initials were having casual sex with *students* with certain other initials. Before the principal could run onto the stage and terminate the assembly the *NHS* officers gave the familiar '70s peace sign and all of the *students* in attendance stood up, cheered and gave reciprocal peace signs to their honorary academic leaders on the stage.

"That assembly was a disgrace to this school!" the principal screamed at me in his office.

"Look, *we* rehearsed the whole program last week and none of that sex stuff at the end was in the rehearsal!" I defended myself by yelling back. "Those *students* inserted that dialogue at the end without my knowledge or permission!"

"You're through as *NHS* adviser!" the head honcho bellowed. "And this disgrace will definitely go into your personal folder!" he added.

And so that's the way it often goes in American education. Botch up either unintentionally or deliberately and by a stroke of luck the teacher is suddenly and fortuitously freed of an important responsibility like being *NHS* adviser.

At another school assembly the faculty and *students* were honored to have an inspirational guest speaker whom John Rizzotte had heard address the local Kiwanis Club. The driver education teacher was very impressed with the hard life and tough approach of the self-made businessman so he convinced the administration to schedule the fellow to be an assembly speaker.

The assembly was slated for eighth period, the final time slot of the school day. John Rizzotte introduced the self-made man and a distinct hush followed by light applause filled the six-hundred-seat chamber. The fellow approached the podium and then began speaking didactically into the microphone. The man's "talking down to his audience" style completely turned off his youthful listeners after the first three minutes of his biographical presentation.

At first I felt a degree of compassion for the silver-haired Pericles. I got up from my seat like a dozen other teachers and patrolled the aisles chastising snickering wise guys. But then the speaker used an excessive amount of *selfish* personal pronouns like *I, me, my, myself* and *mine.*

The *students* were becoming more neurotic, impolite, obnoxious and unruly as the man's rigid speech continued. Again, I rebuked several young punks by saying, "This fellow is a self-made millionaire. He has gone from rags to riches!" I clearly lectured. "Maybe you can learn something from him about success by paying this man the respect he deserves!"

But most of the *students* (who were used to being entertained at assemblies and not *lectured* to) were as interested in Horatio Alger stories as they were in quadratic equations. The elderly gent then sanctimoniously spoke with a heavy Polish accent about the need for patriotism, nationalism, free enterprise and loyalty to flag and country. By then nine-tenths of the *children* in the jam-packed audience were becoming quite antsy. The undercurrent of muffled *student* conversations could be heard throughout the auditorium when the entire assembly became less and less receptive to the self-made Polish immigrant millionaire's speech. Civil peace was rapidly reaching the danger level.

'This guy is completely turning these spoiled *students* off!' I thought. 'What was John Rizzotte possibly thinking when he invited this man to speak? What works great at the Kiwanis Club might bomb when immature *students* are asked to sit still and listen for forty-five minutes!'

The end of the period arrived on the clock and the dismissal bell finally sounded. But the self-appointed Polish Demosthenes at the podium microphone disregarded the bell and kept on addressing the totally bored *students.* The guy just wouldn't shut up!

The assistant principal and John Rizzotte motioned and waved their hands for the man to finish his presentation but the undaunted speaker simply waved back responding to what he thought was a supportive salutation and kept talking to his lost audience.

The old fellow then sensed the restlessness that existed in the auditorium so he demonstrated his dexterity. The former circus acrobat did three consecutive cartwheels on the stage for the benefit of his audience. The *students* then went crazy and gave the old gentleman a standing mock round-of-applause as the principal, vice principal and John Rizzotte first gesticulated with their hands and then wildly and frantically signaled with both arms for the *students* to be seated so that an orderly dismissal could be initiated.

The hapless old gent started speaking again since he interpreted the *students'* reaction as a relishing of his work-ethic philosophy. Ben Locanta came out on stage with a plaque to present to the speaker to terminate the bizarre assembly program. By then the school day was over by a full ten minutes and all of the bus routes to the elementary school were already messed up and off schedule.

The now-enthusiastic *students* again swiftly stood up after the brief plaque presentation and the assembled *children* gave the oblivious speaker a second mock ovation. The old man left the school five minutes later thinking that his talk had been well' received and he told John Rizzotte on his way out of the building's front entrance that he "has faith in the future of America based on the fine *students* in your high school."

At another daft assembly just before the *Easter* holiday break the *students* were slated to view an hour and a half Hollywood motion picture entitled *A Man Called Horse*. The *children* silently filed into the auditorium by homerooms, sat in their prearranged seating sections, the lights were dimmed and the projector began flickering the film frames upon the stage's white screen.

The movie's opening scenes was a real eye-catcher. Richard Harris had been stripped of his attire and was running naked through prairie grasslands while being chased by a virulent Indian tribe. Any teacher seated in the auditorium could hear a pin drop. The silent *students* were amazed that their high school (a bastion of Victorian middle-class morality) auditorium would suddenly be converted into a bawdy X-rated movie house.

The abashed school czars scurried to the back of the auditorium and had the head of the *student* audiovisual crew (now a prominent town councilman) place a flimsy piece of cardboard in front of the projector lens every time a bare pair of buttocks flashed onto the white screen. The unhappy *students* booed, jeered and chanted every time their innocent eyes were denied the opportunity to view what they considered carnal pleasure.

A later scene in the film *A Man Called Horse* was one of the goriest and most gruesome spectacles I had ever seen in a movie. The pursued cowpoke (Richard Harris) had been captured by the Indians and was about to be accepted as a leader in the tribe after winning the clan's approval by demonstrating extraordinary bravery. His acceptance as honorary chief was accompanied by a most bizarre and sadistic Indian' initiation rite.

Two gaping incisions were made into the paleface's chest, one into each *breast* (if this were a woman being initiated into the tribe then obviously the audiovisual crew would have to cover the projector lens with the piece of cardboard as commanded by the nervous school principal standing nearby). Two meat hooks were tethered to ropes that had been suspended from a rafter and then the hooks were inserted inside Richard Harris's chest.

The white man' honorary chief was next hoisted up into the air, hanging and suspended in a vertical position from the ropes with the inserted meat hooks being on either side of his sternum. The actor's body was then spun around so fast that, as his form assumed a horizontal plane, the honorary white chief resembled a gyroscope whirling around.

The scene was so hideous that even the most daring pugnacious *students* had to turn their heads on lower their eyes. Not even the worst behaved *students* that were always *suspended* themselves' could watch the climax to the ugly Indian initiation exhibition.

But the entire *A Man Called Horse* movie assembly was quite indicative of our Neo-Victorian American Puritanical society. It's all right to show bloodshed, murder, death, suicide, homicide and shootings, so gore and violence are generally regarded as acceptable and almost commendable. But to show a man's buttocks, a woman's breast or a pubic hair required a rectangular piece of cardboard in front of the movie projector's lens. The elite *student* audiovisual crew however was able to focus the forbidden images on their side of the piece of cardboard and had a few visual treats all to their own.

The week after *Easter* break, I saw Mr. Bill W., the assembly program adviser in the hall. "What happened with the administration after you showed that movie before the Easter break?" I asked.

"I was really chewed out!" the adviser confessed. "I guess they'll now get somebody else to order and show the films."

"Don't feel bad!" I empathized. "I was fired as *NHS* adviser after the honor *students* pulled a fast one on me and changed the ending of the assembly."

"Good, you can have my former job as assembly film organizer!" my colleague joked. "If the boss doesn't formally fire me I'll quit!"

"No thanks," I replied. "I think I'd rather go into alligator mud-wrestling or wild elephant training!"

Another pretty interesting assembly was of the school spirit-pep' variety type and this one particular event happened in the late 1990s. The middle school *football team* ran out onto the school gymnasium *basketball court*. The last *student* football player carried a manikin's faceless head with a woman's wig on top. He was enacting an imitation of a famous and popular *World Wrestling Federation* professional wrestler at the time, Al Snow. Just like *WWF* fans had done on television many times in response to the appearance of the manikin's head, the energized *students* in the gallery wildly chanted, "We want head! We want head!"

The next morning the beleaguered principal called the *student* that had held the manikin's head down to the office and the *child* claimed that he was unaware that the chant "We want head!" involved any sexual connotation. "And besides if it did," the *student* argued to the principal, "the kids in the stands were yelling the dirty words and not me! I was only holding the fake head up in the air!"

The clever *student* got away with murder conducting his little "inappropriate" charade and received only two days of Office Detention for causing widespread chaos and instigating the ultimate in bad taste during a school spirit pep' assembly.

And finally, schools also have quasi-assemblies where films are shown on rainy days to fill the second half of a forty-five-minute lunch period. I usually stepped into the main office just before lunch duty and asked the principal what films might be available to show to the eighth graders in the auditorium after they had eaten their lunches in the cafeteria.

"Here, try this one!" the busy principal confidently suggested. "It came from the county film library."

"*Code Blue*!" I exclaimed with surprise. "Have you screened or previewed it to make sure it's safe to show to eighth graders?"

"I just told you it came from the county film library," the school executive insisted, "so it's probably something like *Blue Hawaii* or something like that!"

"Okay, you're the boss!" I sarcastically complimented and then left the main office to set up the film for viewing.

The *students* were expertly transferred from the cafeteria to the auditorium and after settling down, I dimmed the lights while the other teacher on duty started up the projector. Neither Joe Sacci nor I had realized at the time that *Code Blue* was hospital terminology for "Emergency Operating Room."

The first bloody scene showed a man with a bashed up head being assiduously stitched-up by a very skilled surgeon. The second scene showed a huge Afro-American woman giving birth. The corpulent lady's legs were wide open and all of her femininity was right there for the absolutely captivated audience of fourteen-year-olds to inspect and evaluate.

The other teacher on duty and I rushed to the projector to shut the questionable film off when suddenly the hospital scene shifted to two unconscious automobile accident victims in need of immediate surgery being wheeled on gurneys into the very busy emergency area operating suite. The scene continued and showed the men being attended to and resuscitated by qualified and competent hospital nurses and doctors.

Then suddenly the medical film shifted back to the black Afro-American woman giving birth to her second and third babies. Joe Sacci and I made a beeline to the film projector and shut it off just as the second part of the lunch period came to an end. A deluge of boos generated from the disappointed *students* engulfed my embarrassed colleague and myself.

"I think I'll stay home after living through *that* fiasco," my friend related. "I need a mental health day!"

"Me too Joe!" I concurred. "There's bound to be a ton of parent flack after this farce, that's for sure!"

The next day was Friday and Joe Sacci and I both took a "mental health" or "stay alive" day off from school. The following Monday we both showed up and were amazed to find out that not one irate parent phone call had been received in the main office about multiple birth scenes shown in the second half of the previous Thursday's eighth grade lunch period.

"The High School Faculty"

Tim Carley and Bob Gordon were close friends and almost inseparable amigos on the high school faculty. Tim taught both U.S. and Ancient History courses in a room that had been originally designed as part of a larger family living classroom. A toilet that was once in the family living room had been partitioned off and soon became a part of Tim's social studies' office. An entrance door to the office and toilet separated the porcelain fixture from Tim's history classroom.

The availability of the toilet proved very *commod*ious to Tim. Whenever a *student* with weak kidneys asked the history teacher if he or she could visit the lavatory Tim would open the door to *his* office and say, "Sure! Use the facilities right in here!" The history mentor would then proudly open the door to his *office* exposing the glistening hopper to the view of the appreciative class.

The *student* seeking relief would consider the thought of embarra*ss*ing noises emanating from *the office* into the classroom and then become discouraged from attempting to conveniently answer nature's call. Tim Carley was seldom plagued with continuous annoying *student* requests to leave the room and use the bathroom facilities.

One day when Tim was enlightening his second period World Civilizations advanced *students* on the brilliant attainments of the ancient Mesopotamian culture, a temporary classroom silence was created when everyone in the room heard a distinct gurgling reverberation. All heads turned left as the office door opened and then out stepped the unabashed Bob Gordon. He casually waved a cute salutation to Tim and *his* World Civilizations class, acting totally nonchalant about the impropriety of *his* "unprofessional toilet flushing conduct." Tim Carley's face turned redder than a beet as the mixed class snickered and chuckled for a full five minutes.

On another memorable occasion Tim Carley and Bob Gordon were chaperones on the senior class Washington Trip. The two teachers supervised rooms and randomly searched *student* luggage for booze that might have illegally been smuggled into the motel. After confiscating six pints of alcohol in true Eliot Ness fashion Bob and Tim generously re-distributed their plunder to the ten faculty chaperones on duty as a well' deserved "Washington Trip fringe benefit." And so, the grateful teachers had a small all-night party at the expense of some irascible-minded *students* trying to pull a fast one.

On that same Washington Trip, Tim and Bob had a photo taken of them sitting with a manikin of Lyndon B. Johnson at a District of Columbia wax museum. A mock newspaper headline along with the photo' was published at a novelty store and it read, "Local Teachers Confer with President Johnson." The front page of the mock newspaper was conspicuously hung on a central bulletin board in the main high school corridor. The unique piece of journalism lingered there for two whole months without it ever being noticed or scrutinized by *students* changing classes. Then I decided to bring the unique newspaper item to a talkative *student's* attention and it wasn't long before the thumb' tacked poster became one of the featured points of *student* interest while *they* were passing and then stopping to gander at the newspaper headline spectacle between classes.

Bob Gordon was notorious for playing pranks at teacher parties. Once while Mr. Gordon was attending a rollicking Friday night affair hosted by math' teacher Jim Kyle, Bob tested the alcoholic capacity of seven fish swimming about in Jim's aquarium. When no one was looking Mr. Gordon poured a large quantity of vodka into the fish tank to scientifically study how the intoxicant would influence the swimming patterns of the victimized marine-life.

The next morning the teacher that had thrown the big shindig the night before discovered his seven fish floating on top of the water instead of in it. The following Monday at school I consoled the depressed party host by saying, "Well Jim, I guess there isn't too much validity to the statement *he drinks like a fish*! I believe someone with unscrupulous intentions must have poured vodka or gin into your aquarium! What a way to get *tanked*!"

"Thanks a lot!" the despondent teacher disgustedly answered. "Your kindness *underwhelms* me!"

At another wild faculty party given by Jim Kyle, Bob Gordon raided the bathroom medicine chest. He secretly confiscated our host's razor blades leaving only one behind, which the trickster mercilessly warped out of shape and then somehow managed to insert the twisted shaving blade into Jim Kyle's razor. On Monday morning the aggravated teacher that had just lost seven aquarium fish the week before showed up at school with a face that appeared as if it had been shaven by a power lawnmower.

"Well there Jim, at least you don't have a five o'clock shadow! Anyway that was a great happening at your place Sunday night!" I commented as I stared at the nicks and gashes that gutted Mr. Kyle's countenance.

"Somebody else is gonna' throw the next damned teacher party," Jim glumly answered. "I've just about had it hosting this damned unappreciative faculty!"

Bob Gordon always had a prank or two up his sleeve. The main corridor of the high school had two attractive planters attached to a wall with neatly arranged displays of artificial plants and flowers inside them. Bob surreptitiously noticed that certain overhead spotlights ideally beamed shafts of light directly into the flower-boxes.

In January of '68 early each morning Mr. Bob Gordon would clandestinely deposit several pounds of dirt into the flower-boxes before any administrators were in the building. After two weeks passed Bob was ready to initiate phase two of his devious scheme. He planted pumpkin and sunflower seeds into the freshly transferred soil. Several weeks' later *student* passers-by stopped and incredulously peered at the remarkable planter, which had a splendid array of real natural vegetation and then huge vines growing above the dwarfed synthetic greenery.

In conjunction with the late '60s ecology fad, Bob Gordon and Ron LeFey took two conservation-minded biology classes on a school-sponsored three-day camping trip to a lake located twenty miles from the high school. Tim Carley and I drove out to the lake the second night to see how the contemporary Thoreaus were doing. When we arrived at our destination larking *students* were chasing each other through the briars while others were already paired off and passionately necking under tall pine trees. Tim noticed a mixed group' of *children* dash into the woods and the errant *students* immediately vanished to avoid the detection of the two old-fashioned newly arrived conservative visitors.

"I hope those *students* don't eat any poisonous mushrooms!" Tim exclaimed after witnessing the sudden exodus into the forest.

"I think the *students* are more interested in basic biological pursuits than in honest intellectual ecological inquiry!" I replied.

About the only souls in the immediate environment that Tim and I could locate were Bob Gordon and Ron LeFey, the organizers of the frolicking nature study junket. The curfew was supposed to be ten' o clock, but the dials of my trusty *Timex* accurately read 11:30.

"The *students* are really infected with the pioneering spirit now," I jested to Bob and Ron as Tim laughed his rear end off. "What happened to the Conestoga wagons?" I joked as I watched silhouettes darting in and out of the distant foliage.

"It looks like a screwed-up primitive Sadie Hawkins Day with a surplus of Little Abners and Daisy Mays," Tim Carley added while still laughing. "But it's about equal the number of boys chasing after girls and the number of girls chasing boys!"

Bob Gordon was more optimistic than we were and attributed the excessive chaos we were witnessing to something else. "Guys, it's just the first time these *students* have had any freedom on their own," he generalized. "They simply don't know to act when not under their parents' domination!"

"I'm glad I'm only a social studies teacher and don't have to teach *wild life!*" Tim amusingly interrupted his favorite faculty pal.

"Actually, these sensational *student* shenanigans do look a little Saturnalian to the, pardon the expression, to the *naked* eye!" I calmly stated to the two embarrassed and slightly chagrined chaperones.

With two reinforcements from the high school faculty on hand, Bob and Ron (with the assistance of Tim and myself) rounded up the revelers and herded them back into their respective gender-separated designated cabins.

But before the *students* had been officially returned to their particular corrals Bob Gordon had taken the time to smear butter on all the bunk bed sheets in the four *student* cabins of the kids that had been assigned to *his* custody. After his *students* tramped into their cabins for the night devilish Bob sternly entered each logged building and reprimanded his underlings a cabin at a time for their aberrant conduct cavorting around in the pine-barrens forest. "I didn't appreciate your Pan-like goofing off one bit!" he yelled out in relation to the *students'* wild gamboling. "Now get to bed in a hurry and I don't want to hear one peep outa' any of ya' for the rest of the night!" he vehemently snarled.

The *students* under Bob's care washed up and when they slid under their bed-covers, a low chatter could be discerned outside the cabins as the victimized *students* accused each other of skullduggery. Bob Gordon pretended to be angry after hearing the recriminations being volleyed back and forth. He opened the cabin door and rebuked the chatterers, "What's wrong with you imbeciles!" he boomed. "I just yelled at ya' for foolin' around like a pack of imbeciles in the woods! Don't you kids have any sense of shame?" Bob screamed at his doubly startled prodigies.

When Bob left the third cabin after hollering at his *students* Tim Carley said, "Well Bob, I'm sure glad to see that you know how to *butter up* your advanced learners!"

"You leave little *margarine* for error!" I added referring to the butter *spread* in the bed sheets.

"Those obnoxious kids will blame each other all night long and never suspect that Mr. Gordon would play such a dastardly prank!" Ron LeFey laughed.

"Yeah, it's almost like Smokey the Bear moonlighting as an arsonist or George Washington turning turncoat for the redcoats!" the amused sophomore history teacher stated. "Somebody's got to get back at these kids for all the crap they pull on us!" Bob Gordon summarized. "So, I've deputized myself a one-man vigilante committee!"

Being an accomplished prankster sometimes has its pitfalls as Bob Gordon once found out. Every *Halloween* the sophomore social studies' teacher would unexpectedly dart into a classroom where I would be permanent subbing and Mr. Gordon would be wearing a dreadful-looking Dracula mask. The unexpected intrusion would startle the wits out of even the most bored *students*.

I thought that Bob's *Halloween* caper was amusing so I always kept a Frankenstein mask in the desk of the room where I was instructing. And towards the end of October when the *students* would be busy taking a test or doing a worksheet. I would get the mask out of the desk and hide it under my sport jacket. Then I would put the mask over my face in the back of the room and walk around until the first *student* (usually a female) would see me, become frightened and then let out a shrill shriek. So when Bob Gordon would unexpectedly enter the same classroom a day later wearing the grotesque Dracula mask the *students* believed that the entire faculty was going off the deep end.

The laws of karma however have a way of boomeranging when one' least expects a negative consequence to happen. One *Halloween* afternoon Bob Gordon was driving his red *Volkswagen* home from the high school. The sophomore social studies teacher had the bad habit of attempting to scare adults he knew with his hideous Dracula mask (besides startling his *students*).

Bob's red *Volkswagen* was approaching a very friendly school-crossing guard that always enjoyed waving greetings at motorists and exchanging pleasantries with pedestrians. When the red foreign car neared the woman traffic director Mr. Gordon donned his frightening mask.

As the red *Volkswagen* slowly passed by the pleasant crossing-guard Bob let out a ferocious growl that immediately stunned the woman. However, as Bob removed his mask to reveal his true identity to the shocked guard his small vehicle was still advancing forward keeping pace with the slow-moving road traffic. A town garbage truck turned the intersection corner and Bob's red *Volkswagen* plowed into it as Gordon was exposing his true identity to the amiable crossing-guard. The total damage amounted to four-hundred-dollars and ironically, the next day at school Mr. Gordon told everyone in the faculty room that his costly impractical joke turned out to be a "smashing success."

Jim Kyle wanted to get even with Bob Gordon for drowning *his* seven tropical fish and for warping his only remaining razor blade. Bob was a big citizen-band-radio operator and would talk incessantly over his *CB* with big-rig truckers and other radio-talking enthusiasts.

Tim Carley, Jim Kyle and I pulled up in front of Bob's condominium with a walkie-talkie that was electronically set to communicate with Bob's *CB*. We sat in Tim's car and Jim disguised his voice with a handkerchief while conversing with Bob. But Mr. Gordon was slightly paranoid and thought that other *CB*ers and the *FCC* might be monitoring his transmissions so *he* practiced keeping all his conversations over the airwaves clean and free of foul language.

Jim's walkie-talkie in the car could send and receive to Bob's *CB* in his condo', but no one else could hear Jim's transmissions except Gordon on *his* receiver. All other *CB*s were out of range and could only hear Bob Gordon speaking, but talking to no one that (apparently) was communicating back.

"Well Bob," Jim said over his walkie-talkie, "how the hell are ya'!"

"Hey, who is this anyway?" Bob barked into his *CB* microphone. "Watch your language!"

"I've been listening to your bullshit over the *CB* for years," Jim indicted, "and everyone I know thinks you're totally full of crap. Why don't ya' just piss off and leave everybody the hell alone!"

"Hey, what's your handle?" Bob demanded to his entire *CB* audience. "Who are you?"

"Do I sound like a pot? I don't need a damned handle! And I don't like talkin' to stupid assholes," Jim enunciated into the speaker through his handkerchief while Tim and I were biting our tongues to avoid splitting our guts. "I thought you had balls Gordon! You're probably even friggin' scared of the damned *FCC!*"

"You can lose your license talking foul language like that!" Bob yelled to everyone out there operating a *CB* on or near his popular frequency. "Stop with the obscene language already!"

The three of us sat in Tim Carley's car and laughed our rear ends off as we watched Bob Gordon's silhouette pacing back and forth in front of his sheer drapes. After a few minutes other *CB*ers were calling

Bob and asking him why he had been talking to himself. Tim backed his auto' up and after we left the condominiums' asphalt driveway the navigator put his headlights on and drove Jim and me to the nearest tavern to enjoy some great conversation, a few really good roast-beef sandwiches and several cold mugs of tasty brew.

A guidance counselor with curly hair named Mark Singleton looked just like a junior *student* Ken Tomasini. So, every time Mark would come into the faculty lounge and sit in a chair Bob Gordon would sit down right next to the guidance counselor and say to me, "Hey J.W., do you know a *student* named Ken Tomasini!"

I knew that Bob was actually referring to the physical similarity between Mark Singleton and Ken Tomasini, but Mark thought that Mr. Gordon was simply engaging in *his* typical zany frivolity.

"No Bob," I would say with a stoical look on my face, "tell me more about this *student* Ken Tomasini!"

Bob Gordon would always talk about imaginary places whose names *he* would creatively make up. "Well J.W., for your information Ken Tomasini has been accepted at the Driftwood Naval Academy up in East Squirrelsneck, Pennsylvania." Then Bob Gordon turned to Singleton and said to the look-alike guidance counselor, "Say Mark, do you know a kid named Ken Tomasini!"

"No, I don't!" Mark honestly answered while holding a morning newspaper in front of his face. "I'm in charge of all the *students* whose last names range from A to G!"

"Oh, okay!" Bob solemnly answered. "I meant to tell ya' that Ken Tomasini's been accepted at the Driftwood Naval Academy up in Squirrelsneck, Pennsylvania!"

"Ya' don't say!" Mark Singleton reflexively replied.

I was holding back laughing so hard that I thought my kidneys were both going to burst. I got up from my chair and made a beeline for the Men's Lavatory just in time to make it to the urinal.

Dean Miles was an affable general science and environmental science teacher on the high school faculty. Miles possessed an abundance of trust in his *students* and was always optimistic with the glass being half-full all of the time instead of always half empty. Mr. Miles strongly believed in a permissive classroom atmosphere where *students* could ramble around from experiment to experiment giving their input and advice to their comrades. "*Student* freedom is necessary for kids to grow up becoming mature thinkers and eventually realizing their own potential and also achieving their own destinies," Dean once preached to me in the faculty room.

"That approach works with small classes with honor *students*," I answered, "but I don't think it would be too practical trying it with unmotivated general *students*. Say Dean, what college department are you in charge of anyway?"

A narrow creek ran parallel to the high school property and the recent ecology trend in late '60s education promoted the preservation of the natural environment. Dean Miles ambitiously organized a *student* cleanup program that would purge the stream of litter and debris. Assisted by a crew of conscientious select science *students*, Miles and his loyal disciples diligently converted the half-mile-long murky creek and its bramble banks into an attractive brook-like setting.

"Do you now see what a team of motivated *students* can accomplish?" Dean Miles informed me at lunchtime in the faculty room. "All I had to do was establish the goal and then set *them* free to attain it any way they wanted!"

"I don't trust human nature quite as much as you do," I suspiciously maintained. "Over the summer the stream will again become polluted with litter despite the fact that your environmental *students* have wonderfully cleaned up the place three times each week."

"I'm even having trash barrels installed every hundred feet to cut down on the random litter!" Mr. Miles related.

Three days later before school some of the more humanitarian *students* had transported six full-barrel-waste cans from the sides of the creek and then maliciously hurled the metal cylinders loaded with debris into the formerly pristine stream.

Tim Carley and I parked our cars in the teachers' lot between the high school and the creek and then walked over to talk with Dean Miles, who suddenly appeared quite disillusioned. The metal trash receptacles were bobbing up and down in the water. I suggested to Mr. Miles, "Maybe the *students* are studying Virginia Woolf's *Stream of Consciousness* literary technique in senior English."

"Yeah Dean," Tim Carley pitched in. "The *students* might be integrating English with ecology!" he offered. "Whoever did this to *your* stream has really gotten *into the swim of things*, wouldn't you say?"

Dean Miles did not savor Tim's remarks or my comment very much. The stealthy *student* vandalism triggered off a good deal of faculty banter that Mr. Dean Miles had to suffer. Poor Mr. Miles had to endure incessant jesting from his peers about *his* major twentieth century contribution to American education, "The Barrel-Stream Concept of Learning and Talking Trash!"

Tim Carley had a reputation for being a fair-but-tough history teacher that did not tolerate *student* dereliction. One fine morning he stepped from his home to his car to find several gallons of paint splattered on the hood and trunk. By coincidence the history instructor had failed several *students* the previous marking period and Tim interpreted that the ugly vandalism had been deliberately targeted at him. The school administration didn't want to get involved in the case because the destruction had not occurred on school property. So Mr. Carley had a good idea who had performed the acts but the suspected perpetrators had influential parents and relatives in the community and also connections with school board members.

Miss Presti was another victim of *student* retribution. The English instructor had made the mistake of not locking her car in the B-Wing parking lot. When she returned to the parking lot after school she found a dozen egg-yolks staining the upholstery of her new sedan. Another time Miss Presti was having nighttime conferences with concerned parents on Teacher/Parent Conference Night. When she returned to her car after thirty exhausting ten-minute conferences all four tires on her auto' were deflated. Destructive *students* ought to find more constructive ways to *air* their opinions and frustrations.

John Taylor taught math' and had the displeasure of walking out to the parking lot after school one Wednesday only to find a gaping hole in his car's rear window. Another time John's auto' wouldn't start because a number of wires in his engine had been mysteriously disconnected and severed.

Phil Tweston was a well' mannered man that demanded strict self-discipline from his *students*. The *students* mischievously called him "Stone Face" after some of Phil's literature classes had read Nathaniel Hawthorne's classic tale "The Great Stone Face."

One Saturday night Phil was sitting in his living room with his wife when the town rescue squad burst into his house with a stretcher and respiratory apparatus. The paramedics were very seriously responding to a crank phone call about an emergency heart attack victim at Phil's residence. After the incident Mr. Tweston confided that "Someone should never live in the town in which he or she teaches." Phil along with other teachers also frequently complained about anonymous phone calls at all hours in the morning. And this was in the early '70s before American society became even more dysfunctional than it is today.

All-too-serious Jack DeCicco was really revered by other faculty members mostly because he had taught most of them or at least one of their parents through rough times during the '40s and '50s. The French and Spanish instructor was a carryover from the past who' had instructed his foreign language *students* on the same staff as veteran teachers Bill Catello and Charles B. Sipley. I always enjoyed listening to Jack DeCicco's stories that focused on the past.

One time, Jack related that he was on his way home from teaching at the old high school in the 1940s when he was stopped on the highway by state policemen and told to get out of his car and help firefighters combat a raging forest fire.

"Didn't you have a choice in the matter?" I asked Jack. "I don't think that today the state police could get away with making someone involuntarily do something against his will!"

"Back in those days it was part of a citizen's civic responsibility to chip in and help whenever requested to do so by someone in authority!" Jack respectfully replied. "And that's the way it was in the old days! People respected and obeyed authority and gladly assumed responsibility when asked to help out!"

I always regarded Jack as a noble and distinguished man and it was sad that he was close to retirement in 1968. He still possessed a great fervency for his foreign language subjects and for the art of teaching. But unfortunately for Mr. DeCicco in 1968, times were changing and *students* were changing too with the *Vietnam War* protest movement gaining momentum. In addition to being gray-haired and elderly in appearance Jack was short in stature and a trifle bulging around his waist.

When Jack was assigned to the doom of cafeteria mass study hall patrol, several of the more fiendish male demons hibernating in the mass educational study hall wasteland showed little homage for either age or decency. They would deliberately call Jack "meatball" and "old geezer" whenever he walked by the *students*' tables.

When I was assigned to permanent sub' on cafeteria mass study hall duty with Jack, I would shudder upon hearing the ugly adolescent disrespect being mumbled and muttered in *his* direction. The man had dedicated his entire adult life to the education of youth and some of those audacious imbeciles in the mass cafeteria study hall (around eighty kids) were brazenly ridiculing the fine teacher that had devoted *his* entire professional energy to *student* betterment.

I had to control myself and show cool self-restraint because my first instinct was to grab one or two of the juvenile fools and bash their skulls against the cafeteria's tan-painted cinder-block walls.

110

Either Jack or I would eventually escort two or three of the impudent clowns down to the vice-principal's office and write out Discipline Referral Cards on the uncivilized renegades. The punks would then receive two or three days of Office Detention and of course some unfortunate teachers would have to be punished after school sitting in the atonement room for forty-five minutes with them.

Jack DeCicco despised both cafeteria duty and the mass study halls because he only wanted to teach good kids in French and Spanish classes of fifteen or so *students*. He even requested an extra teaching period to avoid the horrendous "mass duty periods" and the administration finally granted Jack's wish the last two years of his teaching career.

Jack once told me something during a teacher lunch period that has stuck in my mind. "Years ago the teachers didn't have community respect back in the '40s and the '50s," he began, "but at least the *kids* respected *us*. They saw the value of education while their parents mostly worked with their hands in local factories and resented teachers since they thought *we* never got our hands dirty," Mr. DeCicco noted. "Today teachers neither have community respect nor *student* respect either! That's the big difference between 1948 and 1968!"

Jack then told me that even in the "good old days" a teacher's life was never peaches' and cream. He had been assigned *to volunteer* and collect gate money for high school football games without pay as part of *his* professional *duty* as a teacher. Cash wasn't too readily available in the late '30s and early '40s. And when Jack first started teaching, the board of education paid him and his colleagues in *script*, which was a promise of salary that was honored by town pharmacists, barbers, doctors, retail stores and other businesses and services during the tough times before and during *World War II.*

Mrs. Finnian was another teacher on the high school faculty who was ready to retire. Her starting salary was $1,200.00 and was paid in *script*, a board of education "I owe you!" as she called it. To secure a teaching position in the system, Mrs. Finnian had to orally agree to purchase a new automobile from a school board member that also coincidentally owned a local retail car dealership. The acquisition had cost Mrs. Finnian an entire year's salary, but that's the way educational politics worked in small towns during and right after the 1930s' *Great Depression.*

In 1968 Mrs. Finnian had failed several *students* second marking period in Math' and in Algebra. Upon entering her B-Wing class-room between the changing of classes, the elderly woman noticed that her grade book and her attendance record book had been pilfered. And upon going to the teacher parking lot after school Mrs. Finnian's car would not start. It was soon towed to a town garage and the mechanics found a mixture of sand and sugar in the gas line.

The administration did not want to get the town police involved because of the bad publicity a police report would generate in local newspapers. So Mrs. Finnian had to quietly absorb the expense for the damage to her car's engine herself' and re-do her roll book and her attendance record journal for the reticent-but-authoritative administration.

European *students* that immigrated to America were amazed at the amount of irreverence directed toward teachers by rebellious and obnoxious kids that had grown up in this country. Bill Catello summed it all up rather nicely. "J.W.", he said, "we can thank the community for the remnants of teacher serfdom that we now experience daily, and we can thank educational psychology for the disrespect *we* get from *students*. The rules of the game have changed since when I started out in this *profession*," Bill articulated. "Teachers must respect and must be courteous to all kids but all kids don't have to reciprocate! It's no longer a level playing field!"

Over the past forty years, school authority has been transferred from teachers to school *specialists* like principals, vice-principals and guidance counselors. The teacher is still a *generalist* as he or she was back in the 1930s. But now teachers are the vulnerable prey of certain nasty *students,* of certain irate parents of nasty *students,* of cloud-nine college professors, of amateur school board members and of bungling/public-relations-minded school administrators. Some may consider my position on this matter as being "cynical or unprofessional," but I maintain that teachers (in the taxpayers' eyes) have never been professional people during the last century.

The daily activity of being permanent subs' was a challenge to Bill Catello and me. We both preferred the euphemism "special assignment teacher," only because it sounded more professional than the appellation "permanent substitute" did. Bill was getting weaker with each passing day so he decided to call it quits and retire before cancer made him "die on the job" as he put it. In June of 1970 the frugal-minded board of education and the administration agreed to eliminate two of the four permanent substitute positions in the school district. "One from the elementary school and one from the high school *must* go!" the principal told me.

I saw the writing on the wall that soon all four permanent sub' teaching positions would be eliminated. 'It was a real innovation of this school system having four certified teachers as subs and now it's being junked for the sake of saving taxpayers' dollars!' I realized and concluded.

I also finally surmised that teachers were regarded as expendable entities regardless of one's worth to the system, one's personal dedication or one's total contributions. The administration and the board of education believed that replacing any teacher was as easy as removing a dead light bulb and then twisting a replacement in the temporarily empty electrical socket. 'No matter how a person looks at it, in the end the teacher will get *screwed* (or unscrewed),' I concluded.

"The MEATs"

The teachers on the high school faculty felt a great deal of anxiety and stress from always having to be perfect role models and knowing that at any time a parent or a *student* or a *student* conspiracy could fabricate some outlandish lie and get an instructor suspended. The men teachers had our own fraternity, which met (usually at bars) several times a year both in our town and out of our community. The MEATs was our unprofessional organization, and the acronym stood for "Men's Epicurean Association of Teachers." The MEATs was a convenient safety valve where the male faculty members could let off steam and the bizarre social organization was a terrific escape mechanism from the rigors of teaching.

The acronym MEATs had nothing to do with the local teachers' association, the *New Jersey Educational Association* or the *NEA*. The loosely configured "teachers' fraternity" was an appropriate emotional outlet because it afforded the men teachers a chance to have male bonding, to commiserate with one another and also to get away from the mental anguish associated with educational pressure. Our beer and venison bashes unveiled our hidden carnivorous natures and gave us a way of basically thinking and behaving like primitive *Neanderthal Men*. Some of the guys on the high school faculty were accomplished hunters so boar, deer and bear meat were often on the dinner menu.

In 1972-'73 I was President of the MEATs and conducted the general meetings. I was also the vice-president of the district's teachers' association at the time and the one thing I didn't like about the MEATs was the fact that the school administrators had helped found the organization before I had commenced my teaching career in September of 1965. I had always been suspicious of school administrators "in the organization" fearing that their' motive for membership was a means of intelligence gathering about male faculty members. Some town school board members didn't exactly savor *my* opposition to their directives during teacher contract negotiations and I really didn't need any principal or superintendent spouting off about how I had acted "unprofessionally" at the MEATs' unprofessional dinner meetings.

New male teachers in the district had to be accepted into *our* social rank by initiation. The men teachers all recognized that we needed such an ignoble organization to temporarily lose our identities, get plastered and behave unprofessionally just like the community attitudes had always perceived us as being and doing.

Each prospective first year teacher was given a topic for a "ten-minute formal induction speech" that had to be presented to the group of eighty-or-so educators in attendance at the first of two annual MEATs' feasts. Each new male teacher had a sponsor, who would lead the candidate from the restaurant's bar area to the secretive meeting room. The Board of Directors and Officers had carefully constructed and distributed speech assignments for the novices' final acceptance into the prestigious brotherhood. Here is a typical speech topic for a junior high school English teacher.

"Your subject is as follows: An intensive dissertation on the relevancy of subjects and predicates (as opposed to nouns and verbs) in this age of technological transformation and cultural upheaval."

A social studies teacher might be given the subject: "The need for non-tenure teachers to get directly involved in national and local social and educational controversial issues."

A science teacher might draw the speech premise: "The necessity of permissiveness in an unstructured high school laboratory classroom to teach *students* independence, responsibility, rebellion and anarchy."

A new high school literature teacher might have the speech topic: "The significance of the development of thespian and lesbian appreciation in education ranging from the gay nineties to the modern gay community."

Each new male teacher received a letter of invitation outlining his prescribed oratory. Here was the official cover letter sent to all candidates. "The MEATs speech committee, after contemplative investigation has agreed upon the subject appearing at the bottom of this page as the most applicable to your ten-minute formal presentation to our noble organization.

"Your monologue must not exceed fifteen minutes nor should it constitute a mere nine-minute rhetorical utterance. All fledglings seeking membership into this esteemed organization should pay particular attention to your poise, dignity, confidence and mastery of content during your presentation along with other pertinent ramifications. We suggest that you practice as Demosthenes had done by putting pebbles in your mouth to improve your elocution and your enunciation.

"You will be addressing knowledgeable professionals having eminent and distinguished reputations. Our organization is comprised mostly of dedicated educators that have proven themselves worthy of the title of public-school teacher. Be prepared to defend awkward intellectual positions that you might inadvertently propose or maintain, and above all else, don't act like an arrogant asshole. Your social acceptance into our most reputable association depends almost exclusively on your competency at defending your generalizations and hypotheses on your assigned topic. Be prepared to answer questions advanced by the MEATs' Officers and by the Board of Directors after you deliver your speech. Any hint of frivolity on your part will not be tolerated and might result in you being ostracized from the faculty."

An incoming Spanish teacher was given this speech topic. "You are to present a provocative comparison and contrast report on the structural analysis, etymology and evolution of frequently used Spanish and English expletives and exclamatory obscene nomenclature. Your fundamental focus should be on past history, current trends, phonetic patterns and tonal accents as opposed to traditional English and Spanish vernacular.

"Also Gentlemen, come to the meeting prepared to attack and critique all new innovations in the teaching of Spanish in the curriculum that have surfaced in the last twenty years. Finally, you should include in your presentation a justification of the need to teach Spanish to *students* in a community that espouses a WASPish Anglo-Saxon tradition and heritage."

The greenhorn teachers literally spent hours of honest research and mirror-practice perfecting their dissertations. At the initiation meeting each candidate's sponsor (at twenty-minute intervals) escorted *his* novice instructor from the bar into the stone-silent general meeting/banquet room. After the department area sponsor introduced the novice to the assembled MEATs' conclave, the newcomer to the district would initiate his lecture.

Naturally all MEATs' members would politely sit attentively and pensively listen to the novice's articulation for the first five minutes. But then the MEATs' members would begin talking among themselves' while the new teacher was struggling through his oral presentation. Soon everyone seated in the room was ignoring the standing speaker's sincere words.

As the stunned newcomer labored on with his oration intermittent burps and belches and also occasional loud farting interrupted *his* sentences. Despite the chafing distractions most of the shocked neophytes would persevere on until the conclusion of *their* discourses. Then heckling and jeering would ensue and several of the more muscular MEATs' members would rise from their chairs, grab the new candidate and threaten to pulverize the pledge, much to the elation of the membership.

Once the MEATs even had two local uniformed policemen enter the meeting during a speech presentation with a barking German shepherd baring sharp fangs and the cops then put the candidate in handcuffs, made a pretend arrest and finally the serious-looking patrolmen conducted the shocked rejected speech giver out of the smoky meeting room.

After a speech was finally delivered the rookie was shown a large hypodermic needle, which the President had earlier told "the candidate" would be used to inject a potent stimulant into *his* buttocks. He was also shown a large club and had been told that the awesome weapon would be used against him if *he* did not fully cooperate and give a professional presentation. The pledge would then be blindfolded and instructed to bend over holding the seat of a restaurant chair. He would then be stuck in the buttocks with a safety pin, which the anxious pledge naturally suspected was the giant hypodermic needle.

Next came the highlight of the MEATs' initiation ceremony. Bob Gordon and Tim Carley poured red food coloring onto a feminine sanitary napkin and then placed the wet fabric into the blindfolded pledge's mouth. Jack DeCicco (the smallest MEAT member) next lifted and held the aforementioned giant club above *his* head. The blindfolded candidate was told to again bend over.

As the assembled male teachers all yelled "One, two,..." sweat beads would be cascading down the pledge's forehead during the extended hesitation. On the count of "three," Jack then slammed the huge shillelagh against the leather seat of another chair other than the one the anxious blindfolded candidate had been gripping.

Usually the most laughter was derived when the newcomer was instructed to "take the blindfold off and also remove the *handkerchief* out of your mouth." The staggered first-year teacher would incredulously gape at the red-stained feminine napkin being held in the palm of his hand. The newly accepted fully initiated teacher would then join his colleagues in harassing the next incoming prospect, who would soon be escorted into the room by *his* department sponsor.

As President of the MEATs I had the distinct honor and the unenviable task of controlling the avid half-inebriated beer guzzlers while attempting to preside over the meetings. My concluding remarks to the membership had been designed to make absolutely no sense at all. It was well' received and went like this:

My fellow processionals:

I would like to extonate to you', my trulifinated colleagues the salutrified experience it has been for me to be enulbed as el presidente of this trankanimous organization. This sobravenous group behoones me to be very podulent and pedistic about our civic troduncidies.

While you hornts and you cubinators have been blitumated in *men*struation, I have been sedunting about the future mentronals of tomorrow, which will certainly allutinate our present circumcisions.

With such a relantrified faculty, ajending in consulfinating challenges, I am confident that the hermotudes of our civilization will certainly be donafied.

The ventrunal nature between teacher and *student* couldn't be more robundant and reperdidified. It can almost be vernificated that without being fully kakrinated into our produngeous society the citizens of tomorrow might be doomed to being ad-hutinrotted. I thank the MEATs for your gruntudinous attention and I hope I have merited your metronical conjuence.

I'll never forget the time I organized a Saturday noontime spring MEATs' fishing expedition to a salt-river-inlet that was fed by the *Atlantic Ocean*. The fellows showed up en masse, many of them not knowing a fishing rod from a lightning rod. After the six dozen of us consumed gallons of homemade Dago' wine and cases of *Budweiser* along with other potent intoxicants, the male teachers were more prepared to lampoon than to harpoon.

Several of *our* aberrant fishing lines became entangled with those of three more skilled and serious-minded fishermen that frequented the isolated beach every day. Then one of the more extroverted MEATs' members demonstrated his casting prowess and suddenly his line intersected with those of the three serious regular anglers right after they had spent fifteen minutes unscrambling their lines from the first major entanglement. After *they* finished unwinding and unraveling the incredible knots the three disgruntled fishermen evacuated the sandy beach and left the MEATs stranded there to contend with each other's obnoxious high jinks. The MEATs continued our merriment, drank some more intoxicants, and a few of us even danced around on the hot sand to accordion music provided by one of our newest inductees, which incidentally scared every fish within a five-mile radius far out to sea.

The MEATs' activities provided the men teachers the opportunity to abandon the tensions associated with the demanding role of being school teachers and gave us a license to act imperfectly and unprofessionally in secluded places far from our base of employment. It was a way for us to have some connection with the manner in which "regular civilian people" enjoyed themselves.

I recall a minor vendetta brewing between two members of the MEATs' fraternal order. Many of the fellows took sides in the friendly quarrel, which soon escalated into intense one-upmanship between the two competing camps.

Cars in the school parking lots were found stuffed with crinkled-up papers, which at first some instructors suspected had been done by naughty *students*. Bob Gordon was getting long-distance phone calls to buy swampland Florida real estate and defunct alligator farms. Tim Carley received inquiries at his home phone over falsified newspaper want ads published in *his* name advertising to sell "pedigree dogs', thoroughbred horses and collectible skunks."

The escapade expanded and more faculty members were soon affected by the imaginative pranks. I was summoned by a secretary over the intercom to the main office to answer a phone call before my lunch period. A man from Colorado wanted to sell me a bulldozer and a steam shovel and became rather angry when I informed the long-distance caller that *we* were being "innocent victims in a mass practical joke." Joe Sacci (a music teacher) woke up one morning and found over a hundred dead blackbirds and sparrows strewn all over his front lawn.

But the issuance of junk mail was perhaps the biggest craze. Men teachers were scanning every available magazine and newspaper and clipping out coupons guaranteeing free information on any product "with no obligation." Then *we* would print another staff' member's name and address in the information blanks instead of our own.

Some days I would go to my teacher mailbox and discover forty pieces of junk mail and then go home and find forty more waiting for me in my driveway mailbox. And the problem was growing to monster-proportions because all our names were being placed on other mailing lists all the time.

Teachers were getting mail addressed to crazy names like Sir Loin' Kyle and Missed Her Carley. And the junk mail was coming from unknown hamburger franchises, from taxidermy schools, from locksmith institutes of higher learning and from butchering academies.

120

Jack DeCicco (a diminutive man) received at least five "Big and Tall Men's Catalogs" every week. Ron LeFey drove home from school one fine afternoon and found that a "test-drive camper" had been left in his driveway for a "free week's trial demonstration." And three years after the height of the junk mail deluge I was still receiving vestiges of the wild male faculty members' royal caper.

John Rizzotte was a personable driver education teacher. John and I were appointed by the MEATs' executive committee to go to a local slaughterhouse and pick up a hog for the next annual end-of-year pig roast. John and I were standing in the meat house's receiving area and talking about what kind of hog we would be getting when a trap door opened behind Rizzotte and a tremendous pork belly (slit down the middle) came rolling upside down toward us on a chain rotary.

The fresh out-of-the-freezer recently severed pig was speeding directly toward Rizzotte. John turned around, saw the suspended animal heading his way and let out a scream that scared the heck out of me. The gigantic moving pig had blood oozing out of its nostrils and had just been carved open by skilled butchers.

At the end-of-year pig roast Zeke Shullmon, a junior high science teacher entertained the assembled MEATs. Zeke showed us images from a slide projector of past MEATs' banquets with certain members vomiting in toilet bowls or having simulated sex with a rubberized woman dummy used in health classes to demonstrate artificial respiration. That particular meeting was perhaps the most raucous one ever for our illustrious organization.

The high school vice-principal tied one on good that afternoon. First he mixed the salad by putting all of the chopped-up lettuce, radishes, pickles, green peppers and onions into a new clean waist-high trashcan. Then he liberally poured a gallon of oil and a gallon of vinegar into the mix, put the trashcan lid down onto the container, lifted the metal can upside-down over his head and blended all of the delicious salad ingredients together. Actually that was the best salad I had ever tasted.

Next the feeling-no-pain vice-principal put the decapitated pig's head on his own crown and stuck bones in his nose and mouth, looking very much like a cannibal out of *Robinson Crusoe*. The school administrator and I soon got into a heated argument over "teachers' rights" and "educational philosophy" and the school executive stood up and wildly took a swing at me. I ducked down and his fist penetrated a wall of the club we had rented for the *MEATs'* party. The fellows then moved a piano over from an adjacent wall to cover up the hole that had recently been formed.

The following Monday morning the high school principal called me into his office. I thought I was going to be interrogated about the hole in the clubhouse wall incident. Instead the principal was upset that I was violating the school's teacher dress code by wearing a '70s leisure suit with an open collar and no tie.

"I want to see you wearing a tie to school," the straight-laced principal (who was not at the most recent *MEATs'* feast) insisted.

"Leisure suits are now in style," I argued, "and ties aren't worn with them. Check any men's fashion catalog to see what I mean."

"I still want *you* to wear a tie at all times," the principal rankled. "I have nothing against leisure suits, but if you want to wear one then you must wear a tie too!"

"Ties strangulate blood circulation to the brain," I replied. "Do you want me to suffer a massive stroke?"

"Wear ties!" he maintained. "If you don't, you'll be regarded and treated as being *insubordinate*!"

"Ties *are* symbols of *subordination*!" I fired back. "And besides, the women teachers don't have to wear ties when *they* wear suits! It's gender discrimination against male teachers!" I shouted. "Yes, that's what you're advocating with this stupid tie thing! You're playing a silly power game, that's all you're doing!"

"Wear ties!" the principal yelled as his face turned red. "*Wear ties* I said!" he repeated in a maniacal tone of voice.

"I can only wear one tie at a time," I laughed in response to *his* crazy and animated anger.

"Why are you so stubborn!" he challenged. "Why can't you just wear a tie as a favor to me instead of being so obstinate!"

"Do you see this gold necklace?" I exclaimed to the uptight principal while pointing to an expensive piece of jewelry hanging down from my neck. "This golden necklace cost as much as fifty ties, so the next time *you* see me wearing a leisure suit with this golden necklace around my throat just pretend you're looking at me wearing fifty ties!"

"Very well then, you can leave now!" the principal ordered. "I only wish that you were more cooperative!"

"You mean more subordinate!" I answered as I rose from my chair and then left *his* comfortable beautifully decorated office.

The *MEATs* to the male teachers was like a twice a year *New Year's Eve* party where everyone (except the high school principal) could deviate from stiff rigid "professional behavior," discard our inflexible public' image and then explore the suppressed *Mr. Hydes* that dwelled deep inside of us. Over the years our membership has gotten older and has mellowed. The members from the early 1970s are mostly now married, have wives and families or are retired or dead. The '70s *MEATs*' camaraderie has lost much of its former momentum, zaniness and spunk, and by 2003 it is but a faint memory of a happy bygone era.

Short-in-stature rather amiable John Magliari had been inducted as a new member into the *MEATs*. But I remember John (who was actually shorter than Jack DeCicco) from the first day of school in September of '69. I was in the main office seeing if any teacher had been absent when Magliari entered to put a check next to his name on the teacher attendance sheet.

"Are you an administrator?" John asked seeing that I was hanging around in the main office.

Before I had a chance to answer or even introduce myself as a permanent sub', the principal came out of his office and said, "Mr. Magliari, I'd like to talk with you a minute!"

That early September day I had little to do and was becoming bored. No teachers were absent so Bill Catello and I walked around the building and gave teachers on cafeteria or on study hall duty fifteen minute breaks to freshen up or to use the facilities. When I stepped into an A-Wing classroom, I was about to formally introduce myself to John Magliari but he beat me to the punch.

"Oh, you administration!" he exclaimed in his broken Argentine Spanish accent. "Just sit in back of room and observe my lesson if you'd like!"

I stepped to the back of the room, watched John's entire lesson and then told him *he* had done a "satisfactory and almost excellent job." He thanked me for my compliment and still thinking that I was an administrator, John invited me (the permanent sub') to come in anytime I needed to write up an official lesson observation report.

A month later Bob Gordon told John Magliari that he had heard that the principal was going to observe the jittery teacher the next period, which was only five minutes away. "You'd better use the bathroom now. I know I would if I were you!" Bob told the recently hired English-As-A-Second-Language teacher.

"That's a very good idea!" the new *ESL* teacher acknowledged.

After John Magliari entered the Men's Room (which was really part of the faculty lounge), Bob Gordon, Tim Carley and I slid the *Coke* machine from a side area to the lavatory door, which needed to open outwards for someone to exit.

After John had finished doing his business, he attempted to open the bathroom door but couldn't because of the huge heavy obstacle in the way. He began pounding on the door and screaming and begging, "I need to keep my job! Let me out of here! I have to be observed by the principal!" John was screaming.

I had the next period off so I walked down to the A-Wing to get John's next class settled. Two minutes later Bob and Tim moved the heavy *Coke* machine back to where it belonged. Magliari rushed out of the Men's Room and sprinted like a wild man down the C-Wing to the A-Wing. He entered the classroom and was very relieved to see no principal seated in the rear. Then he thanked me for "watching my class!" John did not realize that I had been one of the conspirators and perpetrators who had blocked the Men's Room door with the bulky soda machine.

The following fall I organized a little MEATs' hunting trip to a small game preserve not far from Gettysburg, Pennsylvania. Bob Gordon was a skilled taxidermist' who promised to stuff any animal that one of us might bag. John Magliari came along on the hunting expedition, and my brother-in-law was a guest member of the hunting excursion.

I had shot a white ram on the expedition, which Bob Gordon later mounted onto a large plaque that now hangs from a wall in my den. My brother-in-law was on the other side of a hill. He fired several shots from his rifle, and before John Magliari or I knew what was happening a wild boar with sharp tusks came snorting over the crest heading right towards Magliari and me.

John and I dropped our rifles, dashed to the nearest tree and then started scaling the oak as fast as we could. The ferocious wounded beast slammed its head into the base of the oak, nearly knocking John and me off our limbs. When the MEATs' hunting trip had ended I had shot the ram, my brother-in-law had killed the boar, Bob Gordon had gotten a deer head trophy and John Magliari had killed three blackbirds while frantically shooting at a wild turkey.

I had always liked John Magliari. He often came over to my home along with math' teachers Jim Smythe and John Senna and we played cards in my carpeted basement and enjoyed more than a few beers together. John would even accompany me down to Ocean City, Maryland on April weekends and help me set up the arcade prizes at 410 South Boardwalk.

Being an *ESL* teacher, John Magliari always had small classes with around *ten* or less *students* in each one. Then the administration assigned the shy young man cafeteria duty and a difficult study hall loaded with eighth grade hellions that John had trouble disciplining. "I can't control those crazy kids!" John openly cried one evening at my house. "In Argentina the *students* always respected the *teachers.* Here the kids try crucifying me every day!"

John went to the administration and asked for small classes to teach rather than be abused in the cafeteria or having rolled-up paper balls hitting him in the back of the head when he was facing the opposite direction in the hard-to-handle eighth grade *study hall.* John Magliari was never re-assigned and subsequently went into a deep state of depression. "Learn how to keep the lid on!" he was told. "You're a teacher and you have to be able to control *students* in all situations!" was *his* advice received from the administration.

John's unfortunate fate was chronicled in the local newspaper with a headline: "Local Teacher Shot to Death." The article described John and his exemplary teaching record. Administrators stated that his work was most satisfactory. The newspaper never reported the truth that John Magliari had shot and killed himself because he was despondent about not knowing how to cope with or how to control the malicious non-*ESL students* he had encountered both in the cafeteria and in the very challenging eighth grade study hall.

"Catty Cat Catching"

In the spring of 2005 a neighborhood mother cat gave birth to four adorable kittens. In May the mother cat brought her litter of four to my back yard to show them off and introduce the new brood to some friendly surroundings where future food and an accommodating environment would be provided. My wife named the four kittens Fluffy (an orange-furred critter with an attractive broad bushy tail), Midge (an orange and white striped animal), Calico (a patched offspring) and Smarty, a smarty-cat tabby that was always first to spot and eat available cat food conveniently placed outside in clear plastic bowls.

Joanne and I took immense pleasure in watching the four daily visitors grow and mature to where they were establishing their independence and developing different personality traits while playing and amusingly wrestling on the backyard grass, honing their individual hunting skills and at the same time creating a pecking order and instinctively determining dominance and subordination within the group. The quartet would entertain us by sparring one another around the black capped pipe that led to the septic tank, accidentally knocking the round lid off at least once a week, would advantageously jump and ambush each other at every opportunity and would chase squirrels and attempt to hijack birds whenever bored with each other's rambunctious company.

In August Midge and Calico disappeared, presumably in search of "greener pastures" or more generous humans with unlimited cat food supplies. At least that supposition is what my wife and I had suspected.

"Perhaps Calico and Midge are following their innate drives and contemplating starting new families," I suggested to my wife. "Maybe we didn't feed them as often as they were demanding. I would feel guilty if I found one or both of their carcasses as road kill on the busy White Horse Pike!"

"Whatever will be will be!" Joanne answered sounding a lot like a contemporary Doris Day. "I think that Fluffy and Smarty will probably be our permanent local back yard residents. Although I'm no cat authority I do believe Fluffy to be a male and Smarty a soon-to-be-fertile female!"

"We won't have to buy as many twenty-five-pound bags of fish-flavored cat food at Wal-Mart," I stated. "Those four kittens were becoming mighty expensive with their discriminating gourmet culinary preferences! I'm sort of glad that our cat population has now diminished to two persistent beggars!"

"Yes, my frugal husband," Joanne concurred. "Now we're down to two bowls of leftovers and cat food instead of four. The absence of Midge and Calico has definitely allowed us to be more economical in the cat food acquisition department!"

But then in the spring of '06 Smarty gave birth to a liter of five and a mere month later brought her new obedient disciples over to our back lawn to be proudly exhibited. Joanne and I were immediately concerned about overpopulation regarding the new animal influx.

"I've decided I'm going to call the black one with the attractive brown markings Tiger," Joanne declared. "And the small gray and white striped one will have the name Tiny. And the aggressive solid gray kitten ought to be dubbed Knight and the pitch-black beauty will be referred to as Midnight. And the totally weak-looking little orange kitten should be...."

"Runt!" I confidently replied. "That poor creature seems to be partially blind and will have a difficult time surviving on its own. It's just the type of weak slow kitty that preying hawks look for to swoop down from the sky and capture!"

"But Runt is so cute standing in the middle of the plastic bowl and eating its kitty food!" my wife humorously noted. "I hope that Smarty protects it! The poor thing is too small and too slow to adequately fend for itself!"

Soon two additional strays joined the enclave and Joanne designated the two "freeloading guests" as Silver and Renegade. Now we had nine mooching cats hanging around our property and at nighttime taking residence in various flowerbeds and bushes situated around our house's perimeter. My wife cleverly used a play-on-words and genially referred to the thriving throng as "the whole *kitten*-kaboodle!"

"At least we won't have any mice pesterin' us!" I said putting a positive spin on our invasion dilemma. "We now have a decent rodent patrol!"

"This whole scenario is intolerable!" Joanne remarked and exclaimed. "Next year there'll be eighteen hungry cats and the following summer thirty-six! Something drastic has to be done or else we'll have to turn our mortgage over to Smarty and Fluffy!"

"Okay!" I admitted and agreed. "And now the venerable elder Gramps is coming around too! I presume that he's a patriarch in the clan because the others all lower their heads in submission every time *he* makes his regal grand appearance! Even Renegade shows Gramps exceptional respect!"

"I think that you and J.T. should catch the four youngsters and take them to an animal refuge," Joanne candidly recommended. "Perhaps the staff there can locate the kittens into people's homes! They're still young enough to be domesticated!"

"My brother Skip has a cage we can borrow!" I recollected and offered. "If our son and I can lure the kittens onto the side porch, then J.T. and I can deftly apprehend the little varmints! I had read in a magazine where a frightened wild cat can be tricked, cornered and taken into custody by throwing a towel on top of its head! I'll assign J.T. the task of performing that very complicated duty! Obviously, he's less likely to get a coronary than I am!"

"It's too bad that Runt no longer is coming around!" my devoted spouse indicated with an element of regret. "But still, Tiger, Tiny, Knight and Midnight should all prove to be formidable challenges to catch!"

"I wish there was a way to get the four into a *cat*atonic state!" I awkwardly joked. "That method would be a sure way to avoid any impending *cat*astrophe during the ongoing search-and-seizure operation!"

"You make a terrible stand-up comedian! It's amazing that you haven't been hit by any red-ripe juicy tomatoes in your lifetime!" Joanne mockingly jested. "On second thought, a few pounds of messy ketchup on your face might actually improve your overall appearance!"

Joanne contacted the Delaware Valley Animal Clinic over the telephone, a facility located thirty miles southwest of Hammonton in Mullica Hill, New Jersey. The courteous receptionist said that the clinic would take all four of the cantankerous kittens and promised to find caring keepers for them for a donation of fifteen dollars each. Reluctantly my wife and I acceded to those simple conditions to eliminate the proliferating and potentially unbearable "cat dilemma."

On a Wednesday morning in mid-October J.T. and I planned to collar the four impetuous but still-gullible fast-growing kittens. After obtaining the aforementioned large cage from Skip, my son and I cunningly initiated our well-rehearsed deception. First we strategically placed the heavy cage on the side screened-in porch. Then we placed several bowls of tempting cat food inside the enclosure and next opened the porch door to allow our targeted kittens to enter. Much to our surprise Smarty (the mother), Fluffy, and Silver stepped into the area followed by the four intended victims: Tiger, Tiny, Knight and

Midnight. But only Tiger had the appetite to cautiously go inside the cage.

I swiftly and courageously closed the cage door and managed to quickly lock Tiger inside. The alarmed kitten freaked-out and leaped and jumped about inside, almost knocking itself unconscious from banging its head. A wild scramble ensued as Smarty, Fluffy and Silver darted around various chairs and obstacles on the side porch before finally exiting via the screen door. Joanne stepped onto the porch to inspect *our* progress but panic-stricken Tiny squeezed through the opening between the dining room door and its frame and escaped into our two-story colonial home. During the ongoing mayhem J.T. shut the porch screen door just after Midnight had escaped, leaving only scared-to-death Knight trapped on the cement floor with the still-frantic Tiger confined to its all-too-certain incarceration.

J.T. and I then entered the house, closed the dining room door and initiated our search to discover Tiny's hiding spot. My son observed the neurotic gray and white-striped kitten furtively lying under the dining room table and we simultaneously exclaimed, "There it is!" No sooner had that declaration been loudly articulated that the intimidated kitten scurried around the polished hardwood floor, spinning its wheels (paws) and unable to generate any needed traction. The small animal then bolted across the dining room and leaped up to clamber onto a serving tray. Next, the ornery-but-nimble critter appeared to perform four consecutive chin-ups attempting to elevate its torso onto the expensive two and a half-foot high serving tray. After realizing the futility of its endeavor, the frustrated two-toned kitten plummeted to the floor and then skittered behind a statue of a Roman maiden pouring water from a jug. And before either J.T. or I could throw a towel over the bewildered terrified kitty, it zipped across the room and soon totally evaded our scrutiny.

"Great!" I shouted in utter aggravation. "Now Tiny's hiding somewhere in the house! We have to search every nook and cranny as if this home is one of those infamous English muffins you see advertised on TV!"

"It could've rambled and scrambled off to anywhere!" J.T. inadvertently rhymed and added. "Let's search the entire place before Tiny makes a mess somewhere like under the sofa. Then I'll never hear the end of Mother's protesting!"

The three of us looked everywhere inside the dwelling. We peeked under every chair, beneath every table and behind every desk and television. The frantic expedition required a full forty-five minutes to complete but nevertheless our efforts were in vain. The wily gray and white kitten had the wherewithal not to make a sound as J.T. and I maneuvered furniture and used flashlights to examine underneath every bed and behind every end table.

"It's a good thing that Smarty didn't become too overprotective and attack in defense of her young!" I noted as I wiped sweat from my brow. "She was hissing when I chased her off the porch with the broom! That cat can be vicious!"

"I have an idea!" my wife constructively said. "Why don't you two heroes venture out onto the porch and retrieve Knight and put him in the cage with Tiger. In the meantime, everything will be sufficiently quiet in the house and perhaps I'll be able to hear Tiny whimpering for its mother."

Catching Knight on the side porch proved to be a Herculean task. J.T. seemed quite comical chasing the nervous kitten around the cement floor in all directions and throwing the towel and missing its head over and over again, looking like a crazy matador going amuck with his cape. Finally, Knight leaped up onto the side ledge and tried climbing up the screen, but then J.T. managed to hurl the blue towel over its head and next grasped the cat, the creature making my son fumble the loaded towel against his chest as if the round mass curled-up inside the towel was a slippery greased pigskin.

"What tremendous excitement! That combative kitten is a real *wild cat*!" I bellowed all out of breath from observing J.T.'s frenetic ordeal.

"Yeah Dad! Maybe it plans attending either Villanova or the University of Kentucky!" my son cynically panted. "I definitely need to be in better shape and intend to spend more time exercising at the gym! But thanks for helping me pursue and isolate this extremely evasive animal! That dependable broom you're holding sure came in handy as a persuasion device."

After J.T. gingerly inserted the disoriented Knight inside the cage to accompany Tiger, my wife abruptly opened the dining room door and anxiously announced, "Tiny's definitely hiding behind the dining room breakfront! I just heard it meowing after I had opened a can of tuna fish and placed it on the dining room floor!"

"Let's be as gentle as possible!" I related to J.T. "We don't want this furry creature arrest to be a harrowing experience for us and a traumatic one for poor Tiny."

"Maybe Mom can film the adventure and send it to *Animal Planet*!" my son laughed. "On second thought, maybe she should just destroy the evidence!"

The credenza/breakfront must have weighed over five hundred pounds but J.T. and I gradually maneuvered it back and forth until we budged the heavy object an additional foot away from the wall. The back panel was around three inches above the floor and it had allowed just enough room for Tiny to wriggle underneath. Soon the petrified kitten emerged from the crevice and reflexively tried making its desperate escape. It fiercely scampered upon the polished hardwood floor (next to the wall) in my direction and upon detecting my' illustrious presence, Tiny accomplished a full backward somersault in mid-air, thumped against the wall and then rapidly headed toward J.T.'s position. Two seconds later the acrobatic phenom performed a similar mid-air act of dexterity and next again proceeded fleeing toward me. Tiny remarkably launched itself to a knee-high level and its all-or-nothing lunge resulted in the animal being contained between my thick winter gloves.

The terrified kitten clawed and wiggled around and then temporarily eluded my grasp by wriggling free and then flipping itself around as I incompetently fumbled to regain its control. Tiny scratched away (at my heavy coat at greased-lightning speed) while simultaneously executing its super-impressive circus-like gyrations. Much to my relief J.T. was successful at putting his familiar blue towel over the animal's head, thus preventing it from engaging in any more hectic havoc. And then demonstrating marvelous precision, my son skillfully deposited Tiny into the cage so that the hard-to-catch kitten could be reunited with Tiger and Knight.

Accompanied by my wife and my son I drove the three stubborn prisoners to the Delaware Valley Animal Clinic over in Mullica Hill where we presented the brood along with the forty-five dollar contribution.

"I thought you had said that you had four kittens," the alert receptionist mentioned. "Where's the fourth little guy?"

"Midnight had shrewdly escaped our entrapment scheme!" I solemnly confessed. "If we ever catch the little savvy imp I promise to bring it right over!"

Upon completing our important mission and then arriving back in Hammonton, the three of us immediately spotted Smarty and Midnight prowling around in our backyard. We automatically explained to each other that the two wanderers were searching for the whereabouts of their beloved missing companions. But we humans were in for a rather shocking surprise.

Amazingly three carefree itinerant kittens came ambling around the corner of our home's "Great Room" and the newly arrived trio appeared to be identical reproductions of recently conveyed Tiger, Knight and Tiny. 'Is this some sort of weird paranormal mirage or illusion?' I conjectured. And next a fourth kitten having jet-black fur made its backyard debut. 'How could this be? Midnight astoundingly has an identical twin!'

Then I perceptively noticed that long-lost Midge rounded the corner and appeared on the scene and I finally understood exactly what had happened. Midge was indeed a female and had returned home after giving birth to a litter that was almost a facsimile to Smarty's. And my wife and J.T. speculated (and subsequently believed) that amorous Gramps had proudly fathered both families. At least *their* theory did make some sense out of what at first had been a rather confusing riddle.

"The cycle's being repeated!" my wife moaned. "We'll have to collar the new ones while they're still naïve and easy to catch! "Apparently Skip's cage won't stay empty for long!"

A week later my wife, J.T. and I re-did our thirty-mile excursion to Mullica Hill but this time with "five furry inmates." J.T. humorously joked about how we had admirably completed our splendid roundup without ever being reported for animal cruelty to the local *SPCA*. All throughout the forty-five-minute trip the five imprisoned cats sat mum in Skip's huge cage resigned to their fate and feeling quite comfortable resting and traveling with their familiar companions. Upon returning to our Hammonton home J.T. had a pleasant surprise in store for Joanne and myself.

"Here's a little token to fondly remember our spectacular cat escapade!" J.T. said as he very deliberately handed me a sealed envelope.

"Can you give me a vague clue as to its contents?" I genuinely requested.

"Yes, just think of a series of poems written by T.S. Eliot!" our son (who was pursuing a Master's Degree in Creative Writing at *Rowan University*) uttered just to intentionally prolong the suspense.

I hastily opened the envelope and much to my elation discovered a rather appropriate gift. "Look Joanne, tickets for two to see the play *Cats* now being presented at Philadelphia's Forrest Theater!"

"Life on the Blueberry Farm"

Being a New Jersey public school teacher for thirty-four years meant that I had to find summer employment to supplement my mediocre yearly income. Since schoolteachers are "contracted" employees they're not eligible to collect unemployment benefits during their ten-week unpaid summer vacations. And in fact teachers don't receive paid vacations or paid holidays at all since they're contracted to work a hundred and eighty school days! My job predicament allowed me to find and explore many different alternative occupations during the summertime that I wouldn't have ordinarily dabbled-in if I had been employed in a profession that demanded a twelve-month-commitment and a corresponding twelve-month-remuneration.

In the summers of 1965 through 1967 I worked on my father-in-law's four hundred-acre fruit and vegetable farm on the White Horse Pike (*Route 30*) in Elm just outside Hammonton, New Jersey. I drove a forklift, loaded tractor-trailers, spent many hours in the packinghouse's cold storage and generally helped manage the growing, harvesting and shipment of peaches, nectarines, apples, sugar plums, zucchini squash, corn, peppers and tomatoes, for those were the principal crops raised on White Horse Farm. My father-in-law was a tough Sicilian taskmaster and we often didn't see eye-to-eye in regard to personnel management and our colliding philosophies pertaining to regular day-to-day operations were often at different ends of the thought spectrum.

From 1968 to 1981 I co-owned and operated Dealers Choice, an amusement arcade doing summer business under the Atlantic Hotel at 410 South Boardwalk in Ocean City, Maryland. People (mostly tourists with money to burn) would come into the establishment and play poker machines that were activated upon the dropping of dimes into slots, and if the players obtained hands of "Jacks or Better" the customers received coupons of different values depending on whether the hand was a pair, two pair, three of a kind, a straight, a flush, a full house, four of a kind or a fabulous straight flush. If a rare Royal Flush occurred the player was entitled to "Choice of the House," which constituted the top-value-prizes ranging from a giant stuffed animal to a blender, a roaster oven, a desk radio or an electric frying skillet. The boardwalk arcade also featured "money pushing games" like Flip-A-Winna', Splash Down and Pot of Gold where the player would insert a dime or a quarter and moving arms and ledges would push the inserted

135

coin against a pile of similar coins. The object of the "Money Pushing Games" was to force coins to accumulate and then fall down a chute. Let's say if seven coins plummeted down the appropriate opening, then seven tokens would be won and would be ejected into the winning tray situated below where the player was standing. Each token was equal in value to a ten-cent coupon won on the poker machines, thus making the coupons and the tokens wholly compatible in terms of monetary exchange.

From 1972 to 1981 I also co-owned the New Horizon Gift Shop on the boardwalk in Rehoboth Beach, Delaware where the enterprise specialized in applying decals to tee shirts using special heat transfer machines. And for four summers I was also a partner in an arcade business called Wheel and Deal on the Atlantic City Boardwalk near Missouri Avenue that was similar to the Ocean City, Maryland operation. Wheel and Deal lasted until legalized gambling was passed to salvage the famous-but-declining New Jersey resort. My two partners and I lost our lease as competition for boardwalk space heated-up when prospective casinos began buying-up strategic real estate all over the *Queen of Resorts*. So from 1977 to 1981 I was frantically hopping back and forth like a neurotic jackrabbit from New Jersey to Delaware to Maryland riding the *Cape May-Lewes Ferry* delivering and shuttling around merchandise for the three independent summer operations.

In the sweltering summers of 1982 and '83 I returned to White Horse Farm to give the place (and my obstinate Sicilian father-in-law) a second chance but the aging man stubbornly refused to relinquish any authority so I again bolted from that Hammonton, New Jersey business and began managing an almost defunct farm market a mile west down *Route 30*. Much to my father-in-law's chagrin in three short summers Pastore Orchards Farm Market had been miraculously transformed into the busiest and best retail produce outlet on the busy highway.

From 1987 to 2004, I diligently worked the hot summers as a field manager for Atlantic Blueberry Company, the largest cultivated blueberry farm in the world. The farm owned by the Galletta Brothers and Sons actually consisted of two pretty massive plantations. The main farm called the Weymouth Division was located just southeast of Hammonton and was comprised of eight hundred and fifty acres growing the luscious blue fruit and eight miles away on *Route 322* (the Black Horse Pike) the Mays Landing Division of Atlantic Blueberry sported five-hundred and fifty acres. All the berries harvested on the smaller New Jersey farm were transported by large company trucks from the Mays Landing plantation to the Weymouth Farm to be packed and then shipped via tractor-trailers all over continental United States and Canada.

Atlantic Blueberry was a massive operation growing anywhere from twelve to fifteen million pounds of the blue fruit (depending on seasonal crop volume) in what constituted an eight week harvest season. The biggest problem with blueberries is that the crop is very labor intensive. A hundred men could operate a fourteen-hundred-acre peach farm but a fourteen-hundred-acre blueberry operation required anywhere from fifteen hundred to two thousand pickers a day during the height of the season. It was impossible for the owners of Atlantic Blueberry Company to house that many workers on their two properties.

The Weymouth Road camp accommodated three hundred Mexicans, a hundred of whom worked in the packinghouse and in the bulk house next door while the remaining two hundred men picked with the "Home Gang," which was supervised by brothers Mike and George Estrada, Puerto Ricans that had started as pickers back in the '60s and who had eventually been promoted to lower management positions. Mike and George each have small houses situated on Farm #1 and they and their families live rent-free as permanent year-round employees. And the smaller Mays Landing camp houses approximately two hundred and fifty men, all of whom' pick berries on that very scenic plantation. Juan Lopez (Lopey) and Ephraim Torres, long-time Puerto Rican employees, had the chore of overseeing the "Home Crew" and the prodigious harvests at the Mays Landing Division.

Because the combined farms only housed four hundred and fifty pickers in their respective camps Atlantic Blueberry had to contract with "Day Haul" crewleaders that could provide additional farm labor. Modesto Flores (a mild-mannered long-time Puerto Rican employee) and I managed the "Day Haul" pickers at Plantation #1 and I was the Weymouth Road farm's liaison to the "outside crewleaders" and in the process had authority over their respective gangs.

In the mid-1980s the outside gangs were mostly Orientals with pickers (commuting from Philadelphia in vans and Farm Labor Transport buses) of Laotian, Cambodian and Vietnamese origins all possessing "green cards" showing that they were "legal resident aliens." The Oriental crewleaders had hard-to-remember names like Bunyan Yang, Lu Vang, Vang Kusanni, Inxay Pathatogong, Chia Lin, Muoa Lo, Khammy Pathong and Yang Lo. One black gang at the Mays Landing Farm still remained from the 1950s and it was commandeered by a woman crewleader, Frances Dantzler, also respectfully called "Miss Frances" by her obedient underlings. But in the mid-1970s area Puerto Ricans that had started-out working on the local South Jersey peach and blueberry farms had found employment and more lucrative paying occupations in other industries and *that* job migration left a giant agricultural workforce vacuum that needed to be filled.

Soon an abundance of Mexican crewleaders and their followers began appearing in the early 1990s and these new groups rapidly replaced the Oriental gangs that had previously fulfilled the farms' labor needs. The Laotians, the Cambodians and the Vietnamese pickers had been sponsored by their crewleaders, who in effect practiced a modern type of indenture system. The employees loyally toiled for their crewleaders for seven or so years and then migrated to and assimilated into performing various factory jobs, construction work, laboring in fish canneries, engaging in lawn care services and toiling in tree and plant nurseries. Most of the Oriental blueberry pickers had traveled early each morning in "Farm Labor Transport" buses and in vans thirty miles from Philadelphia to begin work on the New Jersey blueberry farms at 6 a.m.

The Mexican crewleaders that replaced the Orientals in the 1990s had names like Hermann Castro, Juan Bravo, Mario Valesquez, Francisco Fuentes, Tomas Agguire, Margarito Gonzalez, Marco Rodriquez, Carlos Lopez, Olegario Garcia and Marco Sanchez. Most of the Mexican pickers now come to Atlantic Blueberry on yellow school buses hired by the company to transport them up to the Weymouth and Mays Landing farms from Bridgeton and Vineland, New Jersey, communities where most of the Mexican pickers temporarily reside during the summer harvest season. This is a win-win situation for all parties involved. The farm benefits because the workers now arrive safely to work on state inspected school buses that have the proper insurance coverage. The school bus company benefits because their drivers now have summer employment and the bus owners can generate additional revenue when area schools are not in session. The "outside Day Haul" crewleaders like the new school bus transportation method because they save the expense of having to own and operate their own "Farm Labor Transport" buses that in the past had required costly gas, maintenance and high insurance and inspection expenses.

My responsibilities at Atlantic Blueberry were manifold and the farm owners had amusingly dubbed me "the Director of Documentation." Each "Day Haul" picker had to fill-out a federal I-9

Form (Immigration Paper) proving that he or she was legally eligible to work in the United States. Many of the older Orientals and Mexicans were illiterate and could not read or write so the crewleaders would fill-out the I-9 for them and I would check the forms to make sure that the information was correct before approving and collecting them. For example, a social security number on the I-9 would have to have nine numbers and an alien green card cited as an official credential contained either eight or nine digits. For pickers that were U.S. citizens, a bona fide state driver's license and a valid school I.D. or a recently updated voter registration card or a government-issued welfare card had to also be presented for me to check.

The federal I-9 forms were a real challenge to keep track of because pickers would often get on different yellow school buses and travel to different South Jersey farms and work for other crewleaders from day to day so the daily work force was continually changing. The Weymouth Farm would have anywhere between five hundred and a thousand "Day Haul" pickers show-up at the south-end dirt parking lot every morning and the Mays Landing Farm would have anywhere between three and eight hundred prospective day workers waiting in line at the front gate to hook-up with a crewleader and then be admitted onto the property at 6 a.m. A crewleader would usually have anywhere from fifty to one-hundred-and-fifty workers that he or she would bring (or have transported) every morning to Atlantic Blueberry.

Another farm duty I had besides keeping track of the ever-challenging I-9 forms was monitoring and collecting daily pay slips. Every "Day Haul" picker was paid cash by his boss (the subcontracted crewleader) in the farm's parking lot after the workday had been completed. At the end of each afternoon every crewleader had to fill-out a pay slip contract (on color-coded triplicate forms) for each worker with the worker's name, social security number, home address, date, hours worked, time in and time out, units picked and total daily wage jotted-down. The white copy went to the field worker', the yellow copy to the farm's main office and the pink copy was kept by the crewleader. The following morning or afternoon I would drive my pickup truck to the crewleaders' fields (Atlantic Blueberry Company had over a hundred and twenty separate fields) and check each worker's yellow form to ascertain that everyone had made more than minimum wage the day before. Then I would drop off the crewleaders' yellow copies to the farm's main office on Weymouth Road, *County Route 559* for Farm #1 or to the Mays Landing Division Farm office located off of *Route 322*.

Checking each Day Haul worker's yellow pay slip was necessary because the pickers were all paid by piecework or "units picked" and not by hourly minimum wage (the "home gang pickers" that lived in the camps on the two farms were paid weekly by Atlantic Blueberry checks). The piecework system was good for all parties concerned because it provided incentive for the Day Haul workers to fill flats fast since they were not paid by the hour and thus, they could make much more than minimum wage if they hustled (around forty-two dollars for an eight-hour work day would have been the minimum wage daily salary). Most pickers earned between fifty and a hundred dollars a day on piecework being able to fill thirty-three trays to make a hundred dollars. Some conscientious swift-handed pickers earned over a hundred and thirty dollars a day.

Each picker was distributed a plastic picking basket attached to a cord, which the field worker was required to wear around his or her waist. Usually two full picking baskets would constitute a "full red picking tray," which was equivalent to a "flat" of twelve pints when brought to the packing house by one of the crewleader's drivers. When two red picking trays were completed the picker would carry the "two flats" to the crewleader's company owned field truck and then the worker was given a ticket for each flat by the driver. Each "movie ticket" (with the crewleader's color code and name printed on it) represented one flat' picked and the worker was later paid three dollars and twenty-five cents for each tray filled. The farm would pay the crewleaders three seventy-five for each tray picked so each "gang master" made on-the-average fifty cents a tray, with some of the bigger crews during the height of the season picking over two thousand flats a day for their ambitious bosses.

The crewleaders were also accountable for maintaining quality control in their assigned fields. The blueberries on their trucks destined for the packinghouse had to be hard and not green. Each flat when brought to the field truck had to be inspected by the driver and/or by his loader to make sure it was acceptable to take to the packinghouse. After that quality standard had been met a picking ticket for each red tray was then handed to the worker, who would redeem his or her total tickets at the end of the day for cash in the dirt parking lot, the earned money (according to New Jersey Labor Law) being strictly disseminated by the employee's crewleader.

The farm provided each "outside Day Haul crewleader" with two box trucks. The crewleaders' drivers would circle their fields until four skids of forty-nine trays on each had been loaded onto one of the two assigned farm trucks. Then the berries were carefully driven to the packinghouse where each skid would be picked-up by forklift operators and separately put on a scale for weighing. If the weight did not conform to a specified standard then the crewleader would be "docked" (deducted) trays from his percentage of making fifty cents a tray, so the workers were constantly reminded to pick hard berries and to sufficiently fill their red trays so that their bosses made a decent profit.

At the packinghouse each skid was labeled with the crewleader's name, Field Number and Blueberry Variety and then the berries were transported and temporarily held in the farm's cold storage, which for blueberries had to be maintained at forty-two degrees (conversely a peach farm's cold storage would be set for thirty-two degrees). When the packinghouse production crew was ready to pack the berries from the cold storage, a forklift driver would transport the skid of forty-nine red trays (neatly stacked seven flat by seven high) to one of ten conveyor belts on production lines. Next each red tray was carefully dumped onto a slow-moving belt.

Four sorters on each working line would take out the soft berries and the green ones to again ensure quality control. A weighing device would then insert the exact number of berries to make a standard satisfactory weight for each filled plastic pint. Another machine would then automatically close each lid on each plastic pint. Next the pints were trafficked to one of ten rotary tables at the end of each packing line and finally the finished product was hand inserted into a handsome company shipping flat neatly containing twelve pints each. The flats were then neatly stacked on skids and immediately loaded onto tractor-trailer refrigeration trucks to be shipped and transported all over continental United States and to destinations in Canada.

When the berries arrive from the field to the packinghouse's un-loading dock and accepted in terms of weight for each skid, the packinghouse manager gives the crewleader's driver a yellow receipt for four skids (usually 196 red tray flats). Late in the afternoon the crewleader takes all of his "yellow slips" to the farm's main office and a secretary adds up all the receipts and then issues a farm check to the crewleader. The field boss then goes to either the Hammonton or Mays Landing bank and cashes the farm check, getting the money to pay his or her people at the end of the day in the farm parking lot. Of course the following morning or afternoon I would visit each crewleader in his assigned field and check and collect the yellow copies of the pickers' previous workday contracts.

Another important duty I had as a field manager was filling-out and checking working papers for children between the ages of twelve and sixteen that had shown-up on the farms each morning as part of a crew. These kids were sorted-out each morning and not allowed to pick until proof of proper work-eligible documentation had been obtained. Even if Asian kids had Pennsylvania working papers or if Mexican children had working papers from another state, those substantiating documents were not valid in New Jersey. I had to make sure that each new arrival had an authentic birth certificate or alien card along with a social security card and an available parent to sign the working papers. Then I would transport the kids to either Hammonton High School for the Weymouth Farm or to Oakcrest High School for the Mays Landing Farm to get their credentials officially certified. Since the schools' main offices weren't open on weekends kids that came with working papers completed and registered with the farm on Saturday or Sunday could not go into the fields to pick. And kids under the age of twelve were ineligible to perform labor for wages and were not allowed to work at all and had to remain in the parking lot until quitting time.

I also drove a bus for the Weymouth Farm. Modesto Flores and his son Willie (the farm's parking lot guard) would have each crewleader line his or her people up in single file at 6 a.m. each morning and four buses would transfer each of the "gangs" to their designated picking fields. First the "Home Gang" had to be transported from the camp to their field and I would assist Mike Estrada driving his bus accompanied by my bus, good old faithful "Number 74." After the two hundred home crew pickers had been efficiently deployed to their assigned field, I then drove white Bus Number 74 to the dirt parking lot where I joined the other three buses in transporting the eight hundred or so "Day Haul" pickers to their respective fields. A crew could not go into a field without its crewleader present or a state registered crewleader's agent wearing an appropriate state-issued badge. Usually I would make six or seven bus excursions each morning.

The crewleader would assign two pickers to each row in a particular field. The two workers would stand on either side of the row and together pick each bush thoroughly. When a crew had finished picking a field I ("Unit 13") would be called on my radio and I would quickly transport the workers by bus from (let's say) Field #14 to Field #48, which might be over a mile away. Then at the end of the work day I would again drive white Bus Number 74 around the distant fields and pick-up tired workers at various waiting stations near irrigation pumps on the main gravel roads and courteously return them to the parking lot where they would eventually be paid by their bosses.

Usually each field was picked three times by hand at eight-day intervals. These are the berries that are sorted and packed in the packinghouse and then sold to the "fresh market" grocery and chain stores. After the third handpicking by the crews, large farm machines are deployed to do the fourth picking. The machine-picked berries are generally smaller and of lesser quality and they are taken to the farm's bulk house where the fruit is graded by hand sorters and then frozen and packed in either ten or twenty-pound boxes (for the better grade) or in fifty-gallon steel drums for the lesser grade "fourth picking fruit." The frozen machine-picked blueberries are ordinarily sold to large food processors and subsequently used for mass-produced pies, muffins and jams.

My final responsibility (as the Atlantic Blueberry Company field manager in charge of crewleaders) was to represent them if they received citations for alleged violations from Inspectors from the New Jersey Department of Labor. Citations received might involve an under-aged child working in the field, a child found in the fields between the ages of twelve and sixteen without working papers, a pay slip discovered with a stated salary that did not conform with minimum wage laws, or a crewleader without a badged agent in his field or inadequate insurance on a privately-owned van taking workers to the farm. Usually the *New Jersey state inspectors* would visit each farm three times a summer and twice each summer they would stop the yellow school buses carrying workers to or from the farms at certain checkpoints on the area highways to look for violations. *The federal labor inspectors* would check the workers' I-9 Forms along with other requirements (including field portable toilets) and would visit the two farms once each summer.

A crewleader's day might have some significant downsides too. On rainy days the people could not work in the fields and all must go home disappointed without earning any pay. Sometimes it rains at noon and the workers only make a half-day's wages. But some gang bosses manage to compensate for their rainy day losses by running food businesses that sell meals to their workers from their own food trucks constantly roaming around out in the fields.

The Weymouth Road Farm's parking lot at the end of the day seemed like a combination of a carnival food bizarre and an amateur sporting event in progress. Tomas Agguire's wife and brother and Francisco Fuentes' wife would sell tacos and burritos from their enclosed food trucks, Ricky's Tacos and Franco's Tacos respectively. Other relatives of crewleader's would set-up shop and vend food, chicken, cold soda, snacks and clothes from various homemade stalls or improvised benches and tables set-up along the dirt parking lot's perimeter.

In the meantime children would play impromptu games of touch football and soccer in the center of the huge dirt parking lot until the crewleaders finally arrived with their cash payrolls. Then everyone would quit their preoccupations and get in line to receive their daily wages. In 2004 (my last year at Atlantic Blueberry) the Weymouth Farm had an empty field next to the parking lot seeded and management installed soccer nets to allow for crews to compete against each other in friendly competition. And a baseball field still existed on the Weymouth plantation where Puerto Ricans from visiting Farm #2 would play softball (and sometimes hardball) against its rival Farm #1 home field opponents.

I had witnessed and experienced some rather amusing and crazy things during my eighteen-year-tenure at Atlantic Blueberry Company. One July morning in the mid-1970s a black man and woman pulled up to Field 29 on Weymouth Road where a Mexican crew was picking. The gentleman asked me if any black crews were on the farm.

"No!" I politely answered. "The only black crew belongs to Frances Dantzler over at the May Landing Division. Her pickers call her Miss Frances."

"What's your name?" the man requested.

"John!" I stated. "I'm the field manager in charge of crewleaders here!" I proudly added.

"Well John, could you give me directions to the other farm you mentioned?" the concerned fellow asked. "This woman wants to work."

I provided accurate directions to the Black Horse Pike Farm and later that afternoon when I arrived there to pick-up the yellow pay slips Miss Frances, a *Bible* toting chapter and verse quoter and a notorious stern disciplinarian accosted me at the guard's gate, which was situated between the dirt parking lot and the sprawling plantation.

"John, what's the big idea of you sending that woman over here to my field this mornin'?" Miss Frances demanded.

"The man she was with asked me if I knew of any black crews working and yours was the only one," I innocently and defensively replied, "so naturally I explained to the guy how to get to the Mays Landing Farm."

"Well John, for your information that black man was a lousy pimp and the lady that wanted work was a prostitute!" Miss Frances chastised. "The next time someone wants to work for me please call Lopez on the radio so that I can meet that person at the parking lot gate. I'm a faithful churchwoman John! I'm sure you know that! I don't tolerate no guff, drinking, drugs or sex in my field from anyone! Ya' hear what I'm sayin'!"

"Yes Miss Frances!" I answered with embarrassment and regret showing all over my crimson face.

Once I was driving a Federal Inspector around the enormous Weymouth Farm to show him that portable bathrooms had been specifically placed next to all fields being picked that day. No sooner did I finish boasting to the examiner how organized and efficient the farm was, that is, having six portable toilets on six different wagons that Modesto Flores would frequently move around the mammoth plantation to accommodate the workers in new fields being picked. Soon the Federal Inspector and I observed something that rendered itself as being rather humiliating to me. An old Mexican was washing his arms and face splashing murky water onto himself from an irrigation canal while a companion was urinating into the same canal only three feet from the first farm laborer.

"That's a serious violation!" the Inspector yelled as he began intensively jotting-down notes thoroughly describing the reprehensible incident.

"But both men are only ten feet away from the portable toilets!" I angrily hollered back in defense of Atlantic Blueberry's integrity. "It's not *our* fault if these uneducated workers don't have or use common sense!"

"Regardless John!" the angry Inspector maintained in an austere tone of voice. "All your workers must be advised of the law and how it applies to them. That's why *we* require sanitary facilities with sinks and toilets stationed in the fields. And no worker can be more than a quarter of a mile away from the portable facilities or it's a serious violation!"

"Those two men were only ten feet away from the portable bathroom!" I vigorously argued. "How can the farm be responsible for individual irresponsible behavior?"

"That's for you, Modesto and the Galletta family to figure out!" the incensed Inspector shot back. "I won't give the farm a citation this time but I assure you next time I will! A warning letter will definitely be issued!"

Another time I got into a heated argument with a young New Jersey State Inspector in a field at the Mays Landing Farm. The over-aggressive labor law examiner had found fault with a Cambodian kid's working papers and brought the matter to my attention.

145

"The school principal did not sign on the line at the bottom!" the overly conscientious inspector insisted. "The kid has an invalid working paper."

"Look!" I snapped back demonstrating a degree of hostility. "There are two kinds of working papers. The first kind is for kids from ages twelve to sixteen that pick berries out in the field. The second kind like the one you have in your hand is for kids sixteen to eighteen that work near machinery, like any kid working up in the packing house. Obviously, the school made a mistake by issuing the wrong working paper to this boy. He needed to be given the field working paper that does not require the principal's signature and not the packinghouse working paper that does."

The young state inspector became quite perturbed that I knew something about his job that he didn't. He pointed to his New Jersey Department of Labor badge hanging around his neck, which looked exactly like a regular policeman's shield. "I'm the authority out in this field!" he boisterously and sanctimoniously hollered in my face. "And I know exactly what I'm doing!"

'This guy is trying to *badger* me!' I sarcastically concluded. As the callow inspector was busily writing out the (crewleader's) citation (for having a kid with an incomplete working paper) a nasty fistfight broke out around fifty feet away. Two Cambodian roughnecks began brawling and then wildly thrashing-around in the bushes.

"Aren't you going to break up the fight?" I yelled at the already rattled inspector. "Now's the time to use your' badge and exercise your authority!"

"That's your job and not mine!" the perplexed fellow volleyed back. "You're supposed to be the field boss here!"

I shook my head in disgust and called over the radio for emergency backup. Lopez showed up with six burly Puerto Rican associates and thanks to farm security, order finally was restored and civil behavior prevailed.

On another very interesting occasion I was driving past "the Aqueduct" (also called "the Artesian Well") that fed water into the Weymouth Farm's main "grand canal." Laotian young men had killed a twenty-foot-long black snake and were standing on opposite sides of a smaller irrigation ditch using the dead serpent as a rope in a weird game of tug-of-war. Suddenly four vernal Laotians on the losing side of the deceased snake lost their equilibrium and then plunged into the shallow-water irrigation ditch below.

Another time I had come across a group of Cambodians that were roasting a small animal on a makeshift rotisserie. Out of sheer curiosity I decided to stop my truck and chat with them for a moment.

"What's that you're cooking?" I casually asked. "Looks pretty delicious!"

"Raccoon!" a young fellow answered. "Want some?"

"Not really!" I laughed in total disbelief as I suddenly lost my appetite. "Where did you get it?"

"Up on the highway!" a second kid replied while pointing out to Weymouth Road. "Probably run over by a truck!"

"That animal might have rabies," I warned. "Be careful! You are what you eat! Rabies is dangerous!"

"What's *that*?" the first Cambodian kid asked.

"It's a bad disease!" I cautioned. "Make sure you roast that animal really good before you decide to eat it!"

Then one day in July of 2000 I received a call on my radio from Modesto Flores to drive out to Field 39 (Blue Crop variety) and transport a Cambodian to the dirt parking lot.

"Is he sick?" I inquired over the radio.

"No," Modesto answered. "Willie just called me over the radio and said that the guy ya' gotta' take to the gate is the owner of a car that just turned over in the parking lot."

"How did it turn over?" I inquired.

"According to Willie the driver had borrowed the car from the guy you're taking from Field 39," Modesto explained. "The guy was drunk and my son Willie wouldn't let him drive the car into the fields, which isn't allowed anyway! And then to harass Willie, the crazy guy started drivin' the car in circles real fast and then hit some soft sand and turned over! Serves him' right!"

"Does the guy I'm gonna' take to the parking lot know any English?" I asked.

"No!" Modesto yelled into his receiver. "And don't try tellin' him anything either! We're gonna' kick them both off the farm as soon as I get down to the parking lot myself!"

I picked up the puzzled owner of the aforementioned car along with a friend and taxied them one mile down main elevated gravel roads to the dirt parking lot. During the lengthy ride the two Cambodians were conversing with each other in their native tongue and I could tell by their expressions and by their gestures that they were wondering what the present in-progress excursion was all about. A funny thing happened on the way to the parking lot (sic, forum). When we finally reached our destination the owner of the white

147

Toyota automobile noticed his vehicle resting upside down in the white sand and much to my astonishment the owner loudly yelled at the top of his lungs, "What the hell! Oh shit!" 'At least he knows five words of English!' I thought with a smile decorating my facial features.

When I first began working at Atlantic Blueberry in 1986 I was basically unfamiliar with the various fields and their immediate environments. High reeds, weeds and grass grew between certain fields and several times I assumed that roads continued from one field to another and then suddenly (on at least six occasions) I found my pickup plunging into small canals or into irrigation ditches. Then I would call Modesto on Farm #1 or Lopez (Lopey) on Farm #2 over the radio to come by and drag me out of my entrapment using sturdy chains as towlines attached to their trucks.

But one time in the early eighties I had a really close call. I confidently and nonchalantly drove my empty bus #74 up Puerto Rican Avenue (local farm reference) on Farm #1 to "the Columbian Highway" (another local farm jargon term) that wended its path through a woods'. The dirt and gravel trail led to seven distant and remote blueberry fields (located above Creek Road) that bordered on the *Atlantic City Expressway*. I had been directed to help Mike Estrada deliver the "Home Gang" to Field Number 14 (The Funny Field). Two buses doing the job could make the transportation of two hundred men a lot easier with fewer trips back and forth for the Home Gang foreman.

At the end of "the Columbian Highway" was a wicked right-angle curve that only a very skilled bus driver could negotiate. I cautiously and slowly approached "Deadman's Curve" in my white #74 bus and after getting halfway around I feared that I had not sufficiently cut the angle. I panicked and then gingerly backed-up, not realizing that my right front wheel was passing over soft sand. The bus began sliding to the right and I feared that my vehicle was going to topple over and plunge into a large canal. Luckily the bus stopped its slide down the rugged treacherous slope but then the front door couldn't be opened because it had become embedded in sand. Furthermore, the bus's hood and engine had tilted sideways and motor oil had leaked-out and gotten onto the hot engine causing fire and smoke to escape. "I'm trapped inside!" I distressfully yelled to Mike and George Estrada over the radio.

I attempted squeezing out one of the side windows of the old refurbished school bus but my body was too big and bulky. I tried escaping out the back door but it was rusty and would not open.

148

Meanwhile smoke billowed and fire raged out from the bus's very hot motor. Then I remembered that there was an axe under the driver's seat and I was about to smash my way out of the back door when an alert Mexican managed to open the hood and throw handfuls of sand inside, thus effectively smothering the engine fire. A farm front-end-loader was summoned and it dragged the bus out of its precarious entrapment. Once back on level ground I finally was able to open the door and personally thank my rescuers. 'Thank heaven that the bus wasn't jammed with fifty screaming hysterical Mexicans!' I solemnly thought.

In the summer of '99 a tremendous-sized septic truck came rumbling onto Farm #1 to empty and service the several dozen portable toilets strategically stationed between various fields being picked. Apparently the in-a-hurry driver was behind schedule and he was speeding (in the monster vehicle) down the parking lot entrance road, which was elevated eight feet or so above parallel canals that existed alongside the hard gravel thoroughfare. All of a sudden, the immense truck's right front wheel hit a soft spot and before the speeding driver could steer the out-of-control "Honey Wagon" in the opposite direction the vehicle's great weight made it skid and then wildly flip sideways down into the right-side canal. I was the first responder on the scene and I stopped my vehicle on the gravel road, fearing that the septic truck driver had been killed, seriously injured or perhaps was unconscious.

"Hey there, are you okay?" I yelled down into the canal. "Please answer me!" No response was forthcoming so I figured I should radio for help. After a third holler I noticed a hand and then a body slowing emerging from the driver's side of the cab, which was partially submerged in water (so to my imagination the fellow appeared to be exiting from a submarine hatch). The disoriented-but-unscathed driver climbed sideways out of the vehicle's open window and a half hour later two large farm bulldozer operators collaborated to extricate the massive septic truck from the brackish-water canal. Luckily (for the truck's navigator on that particular morning) the ditch was not filled to its seven-foot-deep capacity.

On the Fourth of July in 2002 Modesto Flores summoned me over the radio to come to Field Number 23 (Duke Variety) in a hurry and to bring several large sheets of cardboard and a blanket from the office "pronto." I immediately sped my truck towards the packinghouse.

"What's wrong?" I nervously asked into my radio. "What's going on Mo?"

"A Mexican lady is having a baby and you and me are gonna' be the doctors until an ambulance arrives!" Modesto screamed in a panic-oriented voice.

I rushed to the office, obtained the requested blanket, threw two sheets of cardboard onto the back of my company truck and frenetically raced out to Field Number 23. Dr. Modesto was in the process of delivering the baby and its head was already sticking-out of the woman's womb. I laid the cardboard down and handed Modesto the blue blanket.

"Quick John!" Modesto ordered as I gazed in amazement at the spectacle before me. "Go out on Weymouth Road in front of the packinghouse and wave down the ambulance that's been called. Have them follow you to this field!"

I did as I had been instructed, and when the Hamilton Township emergency paramedics arrived, I dutifully led them to the scene of confusion. When the rescue squad unit's vehicle came to a halt I noticed that the baby had already been delivered by Dr. Modesto' and that the infant was being cuddled in its mother's arms with the umbilical cord still attached. The woman and her newborn were immediately conducted to a nearby hospital to receive professional care.

'Thank God that there weren't any complications!' I thought. "Modesto, you've performed a minor miracle!" I commended.

* * * * * * * * * * * *

My daily routines with Atlantic Blueberry Company were conducted from mid-June to August 1, the length of the main blueberry harvest. The company raised over twenty varieties of berries with Dukes, Bluetteas and Blue Crop being the most popular and abundant varieties. Many of the varieties were developed on Farm #1 under the supervision of the Agricultural Department of *Rutgers University*, New Brunswick. In fact, the Duke variety name originated from Arthur "Duke" Galletta, one of Atlantic Blueberry's founders. The large sweet Dukes had replaced the early-season Weymouth and Collins varieties that were popular and prevalent in the 1950s, '60s and early '70s. The last variety of the season was the Elliotts, a tart berry used mostly for making pies and jellies. The Elliotts were handpicked a second time around August 10th and then machine-picked a third and a final fourth time thereafter.

My workday started at around 5:30 a.m. and lasted until 5:30 p.m. seven days a week for eight action-packed consecutive weeks. I only had off when it rained since the pickers couldn't work in the fields, which in total amounted to around six days each summer. And I drove my white company truck between the two farms and through dirt fields with dusty roads putting on an average of eighty miles on the odometer each and every day.

The crews of various nationalities had to be kept in separate fields far apart from each other in order to avoid conflicts. The Laotians didn't mix too well with the Vietnamese, who also had problems with the Cambodians. And the Mexicans didn't get along too well with the Guatemalans, and several times while driving around "troubleshooting" I had to send out a "Mayday" for help to break-up altercations that would instantly flare-up. In a matter of five minutes twenty farm trucks would converge on the scene of alarm to calm matters down.

Two crewleaders that hated each other were Laotians Inxay Pathatogong and Khammy Pathong, who both claimed to speak ten languages including Chinese, English and Cambodian. Inxay (pronounced "In-sigh") claimed to be a tank gunner in Laos during the time of the *Vietnam War* and Khammy (pronounced Ka-my) claimed that Inxay was nothing more than a flunky foot soldier and jeep driver working for him when Pathong was a respectable prestigious Captain in the Laotian Army. I tended to believe Khammy's version of their Southeast Asian relationship because I knew that Inxay had started-out at Atlantic Blueberry as a field driver and loader for Khammy and then after gaining experience the maverick demonstrated his propensity for free enterprise and started his own crew and became a "gang leader" on his own initiative. That background (for all intent and purpose) explains the tremendous rift and fundamental animosity existing between the two strong-minded individuals.

Both Khammy and Inxay always wore paramilitary clothing and heavy combat boots and had gold-framed front teeth showing in their mouths. The two carried knives concealed inside sheaths that dangled from their waist belts. And with the strange farm environments having plenty of canals, ditches, high reeds, thousands of blueberry bushes and accompanying military jets flying overhead from the nearby Pomona National Guard Air Base (located right next to *Atlantic City Airport*) practicing flight maneuvers above and around Atlantic Blueberry (with all of the Oriental and Mexican pickers peering-up at the A-10 Warthog jets), the immense place actually at times seemed like a foreign country to me.

The Galletta family made sure that they assigned Inxay to Farm #1 and Khammy to the *Route 322* Mays Landing Division to keep the two

151

dedicated enemies eight miles apart from one another. Inxay would often hop up on the back of a pickup truck in Farm #1's dirt parking lot and violently yell out instructions to his scared workers in his native language as if he were Pol Pot or a formidable Asian military general laying-out battle plans to *his* hundred intimidated troops grouped below and around him. But Khammy once told me that *he* had worked closely with the *CIA* in Laos during the *Vietnam War* and that Inxay had never had the opportunity or the courage to shoot or kill anyone.

"Did you ever kill anyone?" I respectfully and warily asked Khammy.

"Yes John, I kill many, many people!" Khammy tersely and matter-of-factly answered.

"Did you shoot them with a rifle or pistol?" I sincerely inquired.

"No!" Khammy curtly replied. "I kill at least a hundred people with my knife!" the maniac indicated as he removed his sharp weapon from his belt sheath and boldly exhibited it to me. "I cut their throat like this!" the fanatic exclaimed as he gestured menacingly while wielding his knife.

"Okay Khammy, I believe you!" I remarked with great apprehension and feigned admiration. "Now you're peacefully living in the United States of America so please put your knife away."

Khammy had at least twenty-five red-bandanna Bloods working in his crew, which consisted mostly of a South Philly' Oriental street gang whose tattooed members looked both fearsome and gruesome. One day at around 5 p.m. a New Jersey State Trooper followed a gang member off of *Route 322* into Farm #2's parking lot with his patrol car's overhead red lights flashing. No sooner did the trooper come to a halt when twenty or so Blood' Cambodians surrounded his patrol vehicle and the thugs began throwing cherry bombs and firecrackers onto and underneath the cop's car. The young trooper panicked and called for backup and in a matter of three minutes at least twenty State Trooper and Hamilton Township Police cars converged on the parking lot and the responding officers managed to successfully quell the disturbance.

One day vindictive Khammy surprisingly showed up on Farm #1 and drove out to Inxay's field, took out a rifle and hostilely began shooting at his prime foe. Inxay instinctively fled for cover inside a field of tall blueberry bushes. The State Labor Inspectors had heard about the bizarre incident and issued five citations to Khammy citing the rifle confrontation along with other more minor outstanding labor-related violations that the wily Laotian crewleader had committed and accumulated.

"Look here Frank," I told the Chief Inspector before Khammy's hearing inside *his* partitioned office in the State of New Jersey's Hammonton Labor Building, "this crazy guy Khammy is not wrapped too tight. Don't trigger him off or else he might have a flashback to Laos during the *Vietnam War* and then become volatile and uncontrollable! In fact," I elaborated, "Khammy confided to me that he had personally slit at least a hundred people's throats back in Laos and had mercilessly killed them without showing any conscience or remorse!"

"Look John," the Chief Inspector calmly answered, "he's in the United States of America now and the rule of law prevails here. And besides," the Chief Inspector bragged, "I myself was in the *U.S. Army* and I know how to defend myself if it becomes necessary!"

The scheduled hearing commenced in a placid manner for the first ten minutes but when Khammy learned that the State of New Jersey was going to fine him five hundred dollars and revoke his Crewleader's License, the dysfunctional Laotian felt threatened and was suddenly provoked to take defensive action. Khammy stood-up and much to the Chief Inspector's astonishment and consternation removed his sharp knife from his belt sheath and then almost instantaneously lunged at the Chief Inspector, who spontaneously fled the room as if he were a rattled rabbit (while I stupidly and foolishly wrapped my arms around Khammy's shoulders to prevent him from pursuing after his newly-declared adversary).

But in the final analysis I must confess that Khammy maintained excellent discipline over his crew of Bloods, who all feared him worse than they feared either a hundred' Los Angeles or South Philly' blue bandanna Crips. His pickers always sent quality berries to the loading dock and the intimidating Laotian's pay slips were always done correctly with hardly ever an error to be found. Khammy was organized and meticulous and I must confess that he conducted his field operations as if his assigned turf was a sophisticated military staging area, but the State of New Jersey and its Labor Department Inspectors viewed the dangerous and unpredictable cold-eyed surreptitious Pathong as if he were an *FBI* "Most Wanted Criminal."

In the winter of 2001 Khammy and three henchmen slipped into a Philadelphia factory where Inxay was managing a work crew and the culprit maliciously jumped his avowed rival, wantonly beating Pathatogong up badly. Police warrants were issued for Khammy's arrest and the last I had heard about him was that the itinerant maverick had been reported to be a fugitive from justice hiding-out in either Alabama or Mississippi and operating a fish store.

The following summer Inxay (with his characteristic mercurial temper) had a disagreement with one of the owners of Atlantic Blueberry Company and the temperamental crewleader was promptly dismissed from the farm. Rumor has it that the Laotian now is the proprietor of an Oriental food store in West Philadelphia and his somewhat reputable new business caters to former Laotian, Thai, Vietnamese and Cambodian Jersey blueberry pickers. I presume (with a degree of certainty) that Khammy Pathong is not one of Inxay Pathatogong's current steady customers.

Part II:
33 Essays

"There's a Lot to Being a Teacher"

Teachers are supposed to be dedicated individuals, devoted to giving more than they receive monetarily. Teaching is indeed an unsung "profession." "Public servants" are expected to go the extra yard, tutor "students" after school to prep them to pass challenging standardized tests, and "voluntarily" agree to do other activities like chaperone a school dance, organize a school assembly, sponsor, oversee and advise a club, give an in-school workshop or plan and moderate a spelling bee for gratis.

Twenty-eight times during my teaching career I accompanied eighth grade classes to Washington DC, to Williamsburg and to Luray Caverns, Virginia working two eighteen-hour days without receiving any additional remuneration. These "professional" extras come with the territory and they are expectations assigned by school administrators.

Teachers are expected to go above and beyond the call of duty. That means beyond the "unprofessional" responsibilities of cafeteria duty, early morning duty, office detention duty and monitoring the halls and bathrooms between classes duty. In American public-school education, the term "duty" means teacher exploitation by administrations and boards of education. "Duties" have little or nothing to do with education and they are things that aides or parent volunteers could easily perform with little on-the-job training. *Duties* require little *professional* ability or teaching skill, and they are a major factor in keeping today's teachers *unprofessional* and subordinate to administrative fiat. Duties make teachers generalists instead of being what they need to be, specialists.

Faculty members must set good examples for the students they teach by demonstrating the spirit of self-sacrifice for the good of the school and the betterment of the community. Administrators always emphasize to teachers, "Doing extra is part of your *professional* responsibility," they sanctimoniously lecture at faculty meetings. "Now we still need three more teachers to volunteer for the Six-Flags' Great Adventure trip. You'll be getting back at eight p.m. Friday night. That's not too bad. And also, we need another volunteer for the after-school volleyball program and two more chaperones for the Halloween Dance."

First of all, let's get the record straight. Teachers are *not* professional people. They are school employees who are usually only told by administrators that they are *professional* when something *extra* or something *unprofessional* (a duty) needs to be done. Public School instructors follow administrative orders just like janitors, school secretaries, cafeteria workers and classroom aides do. Faculty members have little choice in matters when assigned to extra non-paying unprofessional duties or administratively arranged professional expectations (Parent Conference Nights, before and after school boring faculty meetings and grade-level or department meetings, curriculum revision meetings, etc.). Teachers are generally treated like employees and not like they genuinely are "professional" people.

Let's cut to the chase here. A real *professional* person like a good doctor or a successful lawyer makes over a hundred and fifty thousand dollars a year. By that economic standard, not even school administrators are *professional* people in the real economic world. True professional people like physicians and attorneys are autonomous. They answer to their own consciences and to nothing else. They work for themselves in their own medical, law and pharmacy practices. They are independent of administrative fiat. They don't have nor need administrators, superintendents and supervisors telling them what to do or how to do it. But in public schools all across America teachers must always be above and beyond the call of *unprofessional* "duty."

When teachers openly challenge administrative edicts, they are immediately labeled *insubordinate*. Someone please explain to me how a true *professional* person could be insubordinate! Is there a doctor in the house? Are our public-schools individual military bases where instructors have to salute their superiors?

What has always staggered me the most about being a teacher is that almost every citizen in the community happens to think that he or she is an expert on what a teacher does for a living. Most everyone out there thinks he or she is your boss. And when a teacher happens to talk with members of the community, people instinctively know exactly how you must execute your *professional* life and they fill your ears with precisely what is wrong with today's public schools. The taxpayer (in his or her mind) is right because he or she pays the freight for public education.

Teachers are *unprofessional* because their vital missions are subordinated to school board members, to administrators, to parents and to the court of public opinion (the frugal taxpayers, many who are also parents and many other opinionated adults who are not). These disappointing circumstances do not alleviate teachers' lives.

Why don't the educational "community experts" (taxpayers) prescribe their own medicines, formulate their own pills, file their own legal briefs, defend himself or herself against the *IRS*, operate on each other, or perform brain surgery on other citizens in the community? I'll tell you why! It is because true professional people do those special services for them. *Employees* (teachers) must enact what their bosses (administrators) say they should do. Teachers are like administrative puppets and stringed marionettes.

So, in the final analysis, the teacher must try to please everyone. It is very difficult to be an independent *professional* having strong convictions that reflect individuality when one is a mere chessboard pawn. A teacher possessing qualities of leadership and autonomy stands out from everyone else on the faculty if his or her ideas are distinct and quite contrary to dictatorial administrative directives.

A teacher that is tough on kids and makes them work hard, or one who bluntly answers parental grievances about how he or she handled a "student" in a given situation, is not supposed to vigorously defend himself or herself during a *parent requested'* conference. Administrators want teachers to placate hostile parents and concede to *their* demands and concerns. But smart teachers realize that when the boat rocks, the officers up on the bridge (the administrators) feel the most swaying.

The irate parent often comes into the building fuming about something "insensitive" *you* had said to his or her "child." He or she does not want to discuss the "student's" performance in class or the "student's" academic progress (or lack of) in school. That parent will magnify one event (let's say sternly disciplining his or her offspring) and wants *the teacher disciplined* by the administrators, who often wind-up doing exactly what the petulant parent desires. Some parents are so blinded by philoprogenitiveness that they will attempt to vilify, indict and insist that a teacher be "fired" in order to protect the errant behavior their precious son or daughter habitually exhibits in class.

These over-concerned "parents" and "taxpayers" really don't care about the ten thousand wonderful things a teacher has done in his or her career. That teacher being attacked is only as good as the last thing he or she has done to upset the "student" and his or her aggrieved parent.

The customer (the boss, the parent, the expert taxpayer) is generally usually right in American education, and the teacher is usually wrong if he or she defends himself or herself too aggressively against the accusations of belligerent parents who appeal their grievances to accommodating school administrators.

Administrators are like water; they generally take the path of least resistance. If a conflict arises between a parent and a teacher the professional person (teacher) must soothe, pacify and satisfy the irate complainer. Administrators are quite aware that teachers are mere employees that can be manipulated or coerced into concession out of fear of job loss, out of anxiety about being punished by teaching different and unfamiliar subjects, or out of dread of having salary increments withheld because of *insubordination.*

I certainly don't believe or think that real *professionals* have to worry about losing their *employment* or their salary increments. This is another reason why teachers are not bona fide professionals. Again, do doctors or lawyers have to worry about being insubordinate? School authorities and the omnipotent Teacher Handbook indoctrinate instructors into thinking that administrative orders must be obeyed and that friction with bad-tempered parents must be avoided for the sake of school tranquility and community harmony. If any faculty member fails to follow management's mandates, then that individual is acting "unprofessionally."

Does authentic academic freedom exist today in public schools? I don't think so. That evasive reality will not happen until teachers become true professionals, not in terms of professional incomes, but in terms of professional autonomy. Faculties must escape the obsolete factory-manufacturing model of the nineteenth century smokestack economy: the management (administrators), employee- (teachers), and products (students) mentality that has dominated public school education for the past hundred years ever since the introduction of the Industrial Revolution. That archaic "factory business model" must be dismantled, redesigned and renovated. Teachers need more voice and power in school management to finally ascend to the distinction of being *professional persons.*

How can the public assist in making teachers feel as if they are appreciated professionals? That's an easy answer. Respect what teachers do in the classroom. Don't base your opinion of a teacher on one unfavorable incident and ignore five hundred positive experiences a particular child had in an instructor's classroom. Parents must learn to be more tolerant and supportive.

Teachers have bad days, too. Parents should not treat classroom educators as if they are *their employees* because property owners happen to pay taxes just like teachers do. And finally, taxpayers and parents should not act like they know more about education than teachers do. In no uncertain terms, the job is not half as easy as the public thinks. Sometimes I wish that I had done something different for an adult-life occupation, but once you're married with children and real responsibilities, it's often hard changing horses in midstream. And since I didn't like the role of School Administration, I never desired ever being one. I always believed that the teachers were the only true educators in the school because teaching was beneath the dignity of a sanctimonious school administrator.

"Rap Music Is Not Music"

"Rap Music" is not music but the phenomenon is a cleverly marketed euphemism deliberately disguised to give the obnoxious noise societal legitimacy. Describing the (disenchanting) chanting of "Rap Music" as "singing" or as "music" is indeed (in either case) a capital misnomer. Real Music is the careful arrangement of organized sounds in the form of notes that then result in a smooth blend of rhythm, tone, and pitch that when united, is quite pleasing to the ear. Rap is none of the above and therefore it is not music.

The unpleasant-sounding horror known as "Rap" is chaotic dissonance and certainly not elegant consonance. Rap is veritable noise pollution that is tastelessly amplified from a cumbersome boom box. Generally speaking, unlike black soul music and traditional black rhythm and blues, Rap is both heartless and soulless. Standard love songs show respect and consideration for a member of the opposite gender but most contemporary Rap lyrics promote a hedonistic "me first" ghetto survival theme that is cruelly perpetuated upon its afflicted listening audience. "Rap" ought to be spelled with an "e" at the end because it "rapes" what good music is expected to provide, beauty and harmony.

When Rap songs first appeared on the radio waves I believed that the clamorous nonsense would be just another flash-in-the-pan fad-phenomenon that would gradually vanish from the contemporary scene like '70s disco music had slowly-but-surely lost its clout (along with *our* attendant intrigue and curiosity about it). But unfortunately, the dunce-like inner-city-garbage-talk Rap lyrics herald the worst elements of society and the brazen inflammatory words glamorize sex, drugs, random and deliberate violence' and gang intimidation themes that through-and-through reek with sexism, racism and the glorification of the ghetto mentality.

In most Rap song themes, the dysfunctional dregs of the inner city are elevated to hero status while the "entertainers" sound like disgruntled grunting angry contemporary cavemen' who are advocating the downfall of "white America" with vitriolic words expressing rage, rebellion and social revolution. This expansion of the "easy-money anti-establishment ghetto mentality" is fueling resentment and hostility among "disenfranchised" inner city youth as well as contaminating the gullible and vulnerable minds of many suburban teens. But the entire reprehensible in-progress-brainwashing technique that "Rap Music" demonstrably utilizes is both a sham and a canard that is trafficking numerous affected teens down a treacherous One-Way-Street that leads only to a permanent lackluster socio-economic cul-de-sac. What a pathetic and ignoble social disaster that is now in progress!

In the '50s and early '60s black rhythm and blues imaginatively captured the hopes, the dreams, the ideals and the aspirations of both white and black teens as portrayed in the quality music of Chuck Berry and Fats Domino. Black music was a constructive factor in American society. White and black teens were on parallel wavelengths in terms of music preferences. Early '60s black music was definitely a unifying force in America. True, Little Richard's late '50s music was a tad rebellious but it was not downright dirty, immoral, divisive' or degrading like modern Rap is. The early '60s black artists' songs were socially appropriate and consistent with the dreams of both white and black America, and the entire country was basically on the same musical experience with rock and roll and Motown harmoniously co-existing.

And then this constructive and positive racial parallelism continued into the mid-'60s with the evolution of Detroit Motown where both black and white Americans continued to share a common interest in radio renditions of the ideal boyfriend, the ideal girlfriend, the ideal teen relationship and the quality music of that era beneficially emphasized the stability and the respect that typical teenage romance provided. The Temptations, the Supremes, the Shirelles, the Marvelettes, Stevie Wonder, Lionel Richie, Mary Wells, Smokey Robinson, The Four Tops and Martha and the Vandellas all espoused "civilized relationships" between males and females and their songs genuinely advanced the perpetuation of commonalities in our great American culture.

Ironically, several white performers were very instrumental in contributing to the origins of "Rap Music." Certainly Blondie's Debbie Harry's classic rendition of "Rapture" and the Beastie Boys' amusing "Fight For the Right To Party" preceded the appearance of more radical white rappers like Vanilla Ice and Eminem. And M.C. Hammer's unique song "Can't Touch This!" gave Rap a happy moniker and the lively tune showed both versatility and great potential for the development of new sounds in the recording industry. But then Run DMC, Public Enemy, Ludacris (Whatever happened to standard spelling?), 50 Cent (Whatever happened to the idea of plural usage in English grammar? I mean, I've heard of one cent!) and oh yes, Eminem and other leading rappers gradually emerged and began shouting and ranting words that featured intimidation, class conflict, hatred of authority (including police, parents and teachers), defiance, insolence, animosity, conflict and racial divisiveness.

"Rap Music" is both uninspiring and generally counterproductive to the "good of the order." The scurrilous pox lionizes a sub-mediocre ghetto/barrio existence as the epitome of human pursuit. "Rap Music" is essentially non-creative no matter how creative its performers think they are in writing it or in presenting it. And the rappers have the unmitigated audacity to describe themselves as "artists." Well I must state that Michelangelos, Leonardo Da Vincis, Picassos and Rembrandts most of those arrogant hedonistic buffoons are not. And few rappers can actually sing a strong note like Elvis Presley, Johnny Mathis, Jay Black and Ray Charles could! Most rappers can just robotically shout, yell, holler, drivel, rant, slobber, snort, prattle and babble in rubbish junkish mechanical non-poetic lyrics that are devoid of imagination, inspiration, heart and rhetorical quality. And the egocentric rappers' amoral anthems are designed to corrupt American society and tear it down to the dangerous and literal "dog-eat-dog" human condition that realistically exists and flourishes in American slums.

Why isn't "Rap Music" genuine music? Because Real Music possesses two authentic characteristics: it has grace and beauty, dual marvelous components that "Rap" sadly lacks. Rap tunes usually are nothing more than one monotonous beat accompanied by certain anti-social mantras repeated over and over again.

Real Music usually has pleasant-sounding singing (harmony and melody) associated with it but Rap only pretends to be music with relentless "in your face" threatening lyrics and assorted menacing hand and face gestures. Real Music has a variety of instruments while Rap is ordinarily arranged with only a hypnotic drumbeat and perhaps a guitar accompanied by some hyperactive dolt wildly scratching a record surface. Standard Real Music songs are generally arranged in a clever A-B-A verse pattern or rhythm format and most "Rap Music" just sounds like a flat tire riding and rumbling over a series of bumpy dirt roads. There are few chords (piano, guitar or otherwise) exhibited in "Rap Music" and the dictatorial didactical tone of voice that is exhibited (a pathetic substitute for real singing in Real Music) is quite deficient in acceptable harmony and melody and consonance. In short, "Rap Music" is a one-dimensional medium and is deficient in both width and breadth. It is shallow and hollow linguistic jargonized anger-oriented ghetto garbage. "Rap Music" is analogous to looking at a rainbow having only one dull color.

High-profile black leaders like Jesse Jackson and Al Sharpton should demonstrate the courage to condemn and denounce "Rap Music" that ostentatiously promotes negative and pessimistic views of American culture along with perpetuating an abundance of anti-social attitudes. For the most part (with few exceptions) Rap is quite detrimental and deleterious, and the repugnant curse is the antithesis of all that is good for the betterment of America. "Rap Music" extols and glorifies a subversive counter-culture that undermines all that is advantageous about the USA. The scourge is an adverse divisive force that pits parents against their children, rich against poor and teens against authority. Certainly, it doesn't take much of a genius to concoct lyrics that come up with diabolical rhyming words for "ditch and witch," for "lock and clock," for "pick and sick" and for "duck and luck!"

Of course, the self-indulgent rappers insist that they are fine examples teaching inner city kids the value of free enterprise and becoming successful junior entrepreneurs in a robust capitalistic economy by having the impressionable juveniles tailor *their* activities after *their* role-model mentors'. But the stark truth is that less than one percent of prospective rappers ever hit the jackpot with the remainder of aspirants finding a dismal crock of fools' gold at the end of their fanciful-but bankrupt rainbows. Like everything else from publishing to professional sports and from Wall Street to Main Street, only the top three percent of the participants wind-up making the big bucks while the remainder of the wannabes' in any given profession founder and flounder in defeat and mediocrity. This Dead End Street is the future of the bulk of aspiring rappers and of those adherents that advocate that type of repugnant degrading monologue.

In conclusion, the "Rap Music Industry" is no different than the rest of capitalistic America is in terms of its low percentage of success stories. Most of Rap's juvenile disciples are doomed to mediocre futures with going nowhere minimum wage jobs at best (if they don't become criminals in the meantime) and if the confused kids actively espouse the ghetto lifestyle as indicated in rap song lyrics, then those youngsters are truly heading in the wrong direction, a path that will guarantee them honor-less lives fraught with conflict with society, with adult authority and the with the law. There is no doubt in my mind that the Rap Record Industry exploits and corrupts both the consciences and the hearts and souls of inner city and suburban kids that gravitate to "the sound" and addictively revel in listening to it.

"Rap Music" is a toxic influence in American society. The pestilence haughtily praises the "ghetto mentality model" as an

166

example worthy of imitation and the cultural epidemic (that the rampant social cancer is) has up-to-now generated little redeeming value. "Rap Music" mercilessly reduces mankind to a base biological existence and it insidiously subverts the spiritual and the intellectual aspects of one's mental and emotional composition.

If human life could be expressed as a mathematical division problem, then according to the rappers' persistent messages, the lowest common denominators of all human relationships are sex, drugs, anger, contempt, survival of the fittest and rebellion. "Rap Music" connotes a disdain for self-sacrifice for others, it suggests (by omission) an aversion for social commitment and for community service, and it advances (by omission) a despising of individual responsibility and an apparent antipathy for standard accepted interpersonal morality and ethics. Rap is basically un-Christian!

"Rap Music" undermines basic human charity, human decency and human consideration for the rights and properties of others. In the overall "Rap Music" scenario, hate has replaced tolerance, self-gratification has replaced prudence, arrogance has replaced humility and hostility has replaced compassion. To add to the ongoing dilemma other benign abstractions also have been viciously assaulted with this obnoxious "music." Throw the Ten Commandments out the window! In the "Rap World" defiance has replaced respect, sex has replaced courtship, using others for personal gain has replaced basic courtesy, cruelty has replaced modesty and wanton lust has replaced teen romance.

"Rap Music" (in general) is definitely a harmful and dangerous factor contaminating American civilization because the colossal social plague equates (in innocent adolescent minds) pervasive corruptive moral fallacies purporting that: adventure tragically equals thugs and drugs, that freedom is social anarchy, that love is the same thing as sex, that justice is a vigilante-oriented lifestyle, that truth can only be represented as deplorable ghetto misery, that honor is nothing more than revenge and last but not least, that Thomas Jefferson's "Pursuit of Happiness" is really only in practice the pursuit of selfish pleasure. The flimflam known as "Rap Music" is not bona fide music because the blight is without grace, without beauty, without love and without pleasant-to-the-ear harmony and melody, which essentially and truly are the fundamental joyous qualities that are vitally necessary in order to make life both satisfying and worthwhile in any given *civilization*. In short and in conclusion, *we the people* definitely need more harmony and less dissonance in this very complicated world. And the phenomenon known as rap music is basically very annoying dissonance to the human ear.

"Freedom Isn't Free"

I feel inspired and patriotic every time I see a car's back bumper sticker featuring an American flag stating, "Freedom Isn't Free!" The moral clarity of those words rings as true as the *Liberty Bell*. Those Americans that do not fathom the significance of the motto *Freedom Isn't Free* suffer from what I call the very problematic "victim/slave mentality," which ultimately will become a future reality should the majority of U.S. citizens not heed the simple message the sage language conveys.

Yes, it definitely indeed bears repeating, "Freedom Isn't Free!" Its acquisition by our Founding Fathers from King George's England involved struggle; its maintenance throughout the first two and a quarter-centuries of our *Great Republic* required sacrifice, and its continuation into the Twenty-First Century demands perseverance. Wise people fully realize that the principles of struggle, sacrifice and perseverance are the vital characteristics of freedom, democracy and independence and of individual success.

In the late 1930s complaisant European nations were lulled into the jaws of the very dangerous "Victim/Slave Mentality." Weak democracies tried placating and accommodating the tyrannical proponents of the Communist, Socialist and Fascist ideologies and Europe soon found itself in jeopardy with maniacs like Stalin, Hitler and Mussolini threatening the existence of taken-for-granted freedom and human rights. Thanks to the intervention and the military might of the United States, Hitler and Mussolini' were ultimately defeated (despite incredible adversity) and Europe was mercifully salvaged from the scourge of Fascism. But Nazi Fascism did not go away meekly like a lamb into the night. Its defeat required intensive struggle, loss of American treasure, sacrifice and perseverance with over 50 million military and civilian deaths occurring during that *WWII* widespread devastation.

Yes, during *War World II* the social axiom "Freedom Isn't Free!" was definitely validated and verified. Millions of innocent people throughout Europe became "victims and/or slaves." But nearly fifty years removed from the terrible Holocaust, today's gullible anti-war idealists can't logically fathom how and why it is easier to prevent a madman like Hitler (or Saddam Hussein) from threatening our existence than to eliminate his or her power once the madman gets on a conquest roll. "Prevention is always much better than cure!" is a good history maxim to always remember.

Throughout its existence the United States has selflessly liberated more people from tyranny than any other civilization this world has ever known and America truly represents the greatest force for good that this planet has yet yielded. And following *World War II*, U.S. benevolence financed the rebuilding of Europe through the Marshall Plan and during the Reagan Presidency the world witnessed the decline of the Soviet Empire and the relinquishment of Russian Communism dominating Eastern Europe. Thanks to American perseverance, democratic capitalism emerged triumphant over its very formidable totalitarian rival.

And even today America has liberated fifty million people in Afghanistan and in Iraq from the Taliban and from Saddam Hussein's cruel regime but despite the fact that the seeds of democracy have been sown in neighboring Lebanon and in Palestine (not to mention Libya abandoning its nuclear weapons ambitions) many critics abroad and at home cynically insist that the U.S. is to blame for virtually every conflict throughout the world. These "Blame-America-first" skeptics assert that when New York City's Twin Towers were destroyed on September 11th, 2001 "the chickens came home to roost!" These misguided cynical pundits indeed are modern-day possessors of the "Victim/Slave Mentality," for if and when a plurality of Americans think and believe as *they* do, then that certainly will be when this great nation will be vulnerable to takeover from dictators, from repressive foreign ideologies and from more-than-treacherous Fascist Jihadists. These contemporary European and American anti-war Apologists in our midst do not (and will never) understand the maxim, "Freedom Isn't Free!"

The anti-war Apologists in Europe and those in America inadvertently and naively align themselves with the Arab Press and with the Arab Street by proclaiming that al Qaeda and its attendant cells will exclusively attack institutions and people in the United States and in Great Britain because the two long-time allies have a military presence in Iraq. The popular falsehood that the anti-war faction supports is that the Jihadists will only leave the U.S. and England alone when *our* forces jointly pull out of the Middle East.

The best advice to honor is that we shouldn't give the "power of discretion or of choice" to maniacal anarchists. Yet the foolish possessors of the "Victim/Slave Mentality" don't realize that the crazed Muslim Jihadists really want U.S. and British militaries out of the Middle East so that "the enemy" can organize an Islamic Revolution, turn Iraq into a post-war 1990s-type Afghanistan with a Taliban-style regime in command, reinsert a Baathist-oriented government in Iraq (with the nefarious goals of unifying the entire Middle East Arab block against the West) and then systematically extort Europe and America with two hundred-dollar-a-barrel or more oil (to weaken and then paralyze our economies).

The craven Apologists must comprehend once and for all that "Freedom Isn't Free!" and that the several thousand American soldiers that have lost their lives in Iraq have not died in vain. (Please remember that over 405,000 American troops had died in *WWII*). Most of those brave soldiers currently serving in the (all volunteer) U.S. military believe in their mission and fully know that true freedom involves struggle, sacrifice and perseverance.

The easy-way-out Apologist "Victim/Slave Mentality" has no vision of what the world would be like without the United States economy and military giving it stability or what this planet's future would be like if the United States did not take the leadership role in preventing Jihadism and anarchy from spreading their poisonous tentacles around the globe. The last thing that radical Islamic fundamentalists want is the establishment of democracies (like those being instituted in Afghanistan and Iraq) to grant Middle East Muslims (including women) modern-day individual rights.

Let's now analyze in a time-line exactly what the Apologist's philosophy of ignoring the terrorists and hoping that *their* insidious cancer will cure itself has recently accomplished. On February 26, 1993 during the Clinton Administration radical Islamic extremists targeted New York City's Twin Towers with a truck bomb that exploded, killing six innocent "VICTIMS" and injuring a thousand others. Attorney General Janet Reno called the reprehensible blatant execution of terrorism "a criminal act." Without having *their* barbarous evil deed avenged (again during the Clinton Administration) al Qaeda terrorists on August 7, 1998 blew up U.S. embassies in Kenya and in Tanzania killing 224 people (including 12 Americans) and injuring 5,000 others. Then again during the Clinton Administration al Qaeda proponents in Yemen drove a boat into the *U.S.S. Cole* killing 17 American sailors. And who could forget the infamous *Blackhawk Down* debacle in Mogadishu, Somalia? Bill Clinton's Administration did little to counteract the series of unwarranted attacks, merely treating them as "criminal acts" and not as violent terroristic acts of war against the United States of America.

Then of course on September 11, 2001 the Twin Towers in Manhattan came down when a pair of jet airplanes (used as missiles) impacted the structures and over three thousand innocent civilian "VICTIMS" perished. President George W. Bush instantly declared war on terrorism. But U.S. Apologists believe and state that the terroristic acts are isolated incidents of angry Arab reactions to exploitative U.S. foreign policy and that America is to blame for *their* implementation.

Get real now you anti-war dissenters! Nobody in his or her right mind likes war! But sometimes war is necessary to stop tyranny, to thwart terrorism, and to keep Americans "FREE." But liberal elements of the U.S. Press have aligned with the Arab Press and the Arab Street by condemning the "War on Terrorism" as being "Bush inspired." However, this *War on Terror* has gotten Osama bin Laden out of his comfort zone and hiding in caves and safe houses and it has gotten Saddam Hussein out of power and into U.S. custody and eventually executed as a diabolical mass murderer of hundreds of thousands of innocent Kurds. Please remember from the past that because of greedy dictators like Hitler and Mussolini that over 50 million people had needlessly died in *World War II*. And if Americans don't want to see *their* children or grandchildren become "VICTIMS" of terrorists or "SLAVES" to dictators, then they should wholeheartedly support the *War on Terror* and not foolishly give aid and comfort to this country's avowed Islamic Fascist enemies.

The resident U.S. Apologists argue that (if the U.S. does not withdraw its forces from Iraq) terrorists will continue to punish the U.S. and Great Britain by hitting famous landmarks and/or soft targets and that the suicide bombers and assassins will continue to reward France and Germany by favoring those countries and not committing attacks in Berlin, Frankfurt, Paris and Marseilles. And conversely those same anti-war advocates glaringly demonstrate (through their quixotic rhetoric) that they are willfully conceding power to *our* declared enemies by empowering and emboldening terrorists, who do not represent in any way, shape or form any organized legitimate government. The terrorists want the U.S. out of the entire Middle East so that *they* can take over and control the Arab oil. The jealous Arab terrorists are the true "Imperialists."

The terrorists are indeed encouraged and emboldened when they can commit acts of carnage and destruction by destroying trains and killing people in Madrid and then consequently influencing the outcome of Spanish elections. The terrorists are further encouraged and emboldened when they can interrupt the G-8 Conference in Scotland and simultaneously indirectly showing that the 2012 Olympics in London could be in harm's way should the British government not accede to *their* militant demands to vacate Iraq.

And on the home front the resident U.S. Apologists (and anti-war bleeding hearts) are showing the same apathy to danger that the populations of Europe had exercised prior to Hitler's plot to dominate Europe and to threaten freedom all over the world. The Apologists are ignoring the underlying truth in the statement "Freedom Isn't Free!" and history attests (through its habit of repeating itself) that nations that don't oppose tyranny and Fascism soon either become a "victim" of it or a "slave" to it!

And now during a time of worldwide crisis some of America's formerly trusted allies that had been liberated from the *WWII* "Victim/Slave" existence are turning their backs on the United States. But the *USA* is not deterred because there's something marvelously American about mustering up sufficient courage and fortitude for standing up for and doing what is morally right and for doing what is absolutely necessary in order to confront imminent national and international threats. When a tough and dirty assignment needs to be done, thank God that America is still there and willing and able to do it!

While the American and the Arab Press are prattling about inhumane treatment of "prisoners" (a poor euphemism for "war combatants") at Abu Ghraib and at Guantanimo Bay, the prevalent anti-war "Victim/Slave Mentality" wants to protect the civil rights of terrorists that are bent on destroying *our* civilization when the captured terrorists aren't even U.S. citizens protected by the *U.S. Constitution* and its *First Ten Amendments*. And when told this salient fact, the anti-war sophists switch gears and maintain that the "prisoners" deserve *Geneva Convention* rights even though they don't represent any country or army and don't wear any nation's military uniforms but merely desire to eliminate and exterminate all aspects of *Western Civilization.*

But despite the obvious lack of support from France, from Russia and from Germany, the United States wisely refuses to legitimize avowed enemies of this country and contrary to sane reason the naïve Apologists will continue equivocating their talking-points that express that terrorists are entitled to fair trials in courts of law when *their* prime objective is to eradicate all facets of *Western* law and order. The anti-war bleeding hearts throughout the civilized world won't be satisfied until they themselves are either blown up or become "Victims and/or Slaves" to lunatic Islamic anarchists. But then in the final analysis it will be too late for the Apologists to moralize, to politicize, to prevaricate and to give moral equivalency to the enemy because their *freedom to oppose* will have been abruptly extinguished if the Jihadist Fascists ever emerge victorious.

Most European nations have been experiencing zero population growth so to satisfy the demand for low-paying jobs France and Germany have aggressively imported large Arab populations that have not been thoroughly assimilated into their cultures. The French and the German governments don't want to antagonize the already alienated resident Arabs so their option-of-choice has been to tolerate the minority foreigners, many of whom listen weekly in mosques to the inflammatory diatribes of Muslim clerics that espouse the radical decline and fall of *Western* democratic nations.

But most astute practical Americans grimly recognize that tough times and a determined enemy require struggle, sacrifice (in lives and money) along with steadfast perseverance. Terrorists must be ferreted out in the U.S. and abroad and moderate Muslim leaders must show the courage to denounce *their* clandestine activities and demonstrate the desire to help authorities identify Islamic militants and radicals. Hate speech (among Muslims) extolling anarchy and violence does not constitute free speech!

And when the misguided Apologists vociferously cry out that the rights of these "suspected criminals" are being jeopardized, then the sane silent majority should stand together in unity and volley back with conviction, "The rights of the majority must prevail for the safety and welfare of *our* country. These demented extremists being identified are not suspected criminals; they are suspected enemies-at-war with the United States. It's a matter of national security!"

The terrorist bombers of today have much in common with the Japanese kamikaze pilots that committed suicide during the waning days of *World War II. Their'* (the pilots) extreme willingness to die crashing airplanes into battleships (while taking along as many Americans as they could) only confirms the fact that the martyrs had accepted in their minds that the defeat of Imperial Japan had been imminent. The present-day Islamic radicals realize that the Taliban, the Baathists and other repressive Arab regimes will eventually totter and fall once democracy takes hold in Afghanistan, in Iran and in Iraq. That is why the terrorists are committing these desperate heinous acts of violence. The fanatics know that *their* time is just about over and that the sand in their hourglasses is rapidly expiring.

But the vocal Apologists want the USA to fail in Iraq while the Bush Administration is directly staring into victory's face. The Apologists all share the fatal "Victim/Slave Mentality," for that tragedy is what will surely happen to the USA, France, England and

Germany should America falter in its resolve. Then America would sometime in the future fall prey to a newly appeared treacherous dictator who has ambitious designs of conquering the world, or the U.S. will fall prey to a radical predatory ideology determined to snuff out *our* revered human rights. That's precisely why "Freedom Isn't Free" and that's exactly why the preservation of liberty, independence, and civil rights essentially requires struggle, sacrifice and perseverance, three vital characteristics that the Apologists sadly lack and shirk away from. America' will not be destroyed by any external enemy, but we are indeed vulnerable from within as we morally decline and as we lose our sense of purpose and our need for survival.

The next major disaster performed by desperate terrorists might (in comparison) make the Twin Towers destruction seem like a minor event. The fanatics avariciously desire to get their hands-on chemical, on biological and on atomic weapons capable of killing hundreds of thousands of Americans. It really doesn't matter to *them* that these targeted people are ordinary civilians with ordinary families. *Their* wicked goal is to see Manhattan, Washington DC, Chicago, Philadelphia or Los Angeles totally obliterated. We cannot allow this insanity to happen even though our necessary solution might endanger the rights of "suspected war criminals" that think your neighborhood is *their* battlefield. If the anti-war "Victim/Slave Mentality" should ever become the majority opinion in America, then regrettably the lyrics of the rock group Kansas would become prophetic truth, "All we are is dust in wind!"

Let's be wary and vigilant and do our best to not permit horrific catastrophe to happen! Wake up all you' lily-hearted Apologists while you still have precious breath in your lungs to perform your pathetic apologizing! It's now time for all Americans to openly acknowledge that *Freedom Isn't Free* and that these dire times require the tried and true long-honored virtues of struggle, sacrifice, courage and perseverance. Appeasement, negotiations and concessions to terrorists are *not* the answers!

* * * * * * * * * * * * *

The Islamic terrorists' have an evil end game that needs to be disclosed and addressed. Here is the terrorists' end game in a nutshell. The maniacs' headed by Osama bin Laden are modern-day Fascists using Islamic Jihad as their cover and as their modus operandi in an effort to make their evil scheme appear religiously legitimate. Crashing jet airplanes into skyscrapers and detonating explosives in metropolitan subways are merely highly visible means of accomplishing their sinister secret goal.

The determined lunatics want to get their paws on chemical, biological and nuclear weapons of mass destruction in order to kill hundreds of thousands of innocent people and effectively frighten and traumatize millions of others. The principal objective of the terrorists is to instill fear into the hearts of ordinary citizens. But the acquisition and usage of these reprehensible weapons of mass destruction is only another means of achieving *their* evil end game.

The shrewdly concealed wicked end game of the terrorists is to destabilize and inevitably cripple the U.S. economy. This diabolical achievement will cause widespread chaos in the United States, ultimately leading to a Second Great Depression of colossal magnitude. The U.S. will be the first domino to tumble that will soon make England, France, Japan, Russia and Germany totter and then fall into a Worldwide Depression.

A future power vacuum would then be created similar to the one that existed after 1929 right before Hitler, Mussolini and Stalin came to power prior to *World War II*. In a similar future scenario, the United States and the Free World would then be vulnerable to the ascension of Fascist dictators and their radical Islamic ideologies. The Muslim/Islamic suicide/homicide bombers are just naive pawns that Osama bin Laden and his confederates are exploiting as part of *their* sinister plot to take over all Arab oil and to eventually rule the entire world. The Muslim religion is simply Osama bin Laden's cover (and the Jihadists lying justification) for worldwide conquest and for Arab triumph over the Judeo-Christian West.

The Jihadists want to unify the Arab World against the West and then extort Europe, Japan and the U.S. with two hundred-dollar-a-barrel (or more) oil to help bring about the decline and fall of Western and Eastern' civilizations. You don't see O.B.L. blowing himself up now, do you? The maniac has found gullible suckers (young idealistic martyrs) in the Arab World to use and manipulate as tools to accomplish his repugnant purpose, a devastating worldwide depression allowing him and his cohorts to ascend to tyrannical power. Wake up World! The Jihadists are the ones that want to take control of the Arab World and its oil, not the Americans! The terrorists are the damned bad guys, not the United States of America!

"Iraq War Is Necessary and Justified"

This essay is in defense of the current *Iraq War*. President Bush's vocal critics state that over 3,000 American troops have been *sacrificed* in the *Iraq War*. First of all, the word "sacrifice" usually means that a person voluntarily does or gives up something at his or her own free will (like a bunt to advance a runner in baseball or Catholics sacrificing and giving up chocolate for Lent). I don't believe that any of those soldiers that have been killed in the *Iraq War* deliberately intended to die or were "sacrificed" as war critic Michael Moore has erroneously stated. And I'm sure that if President Bush knew beforehand the names of those soldiers that had been killed, I'm certain he would have ordered those individuals to stay on U.S. military bases and not engage in combat in Iraq. The chance of an American soldier getting killed in Iraq is less than a fraction of a percent. I would take those amazing odds at any casino. Our brave soldiers are not being "sacrificed."

Secondly, in *World War II* over 405,000 American military personnel had been killed during that conflict and *that* staggering number happens to constitute over 100 times the *sacrifice* that our nation has made in the combined *Afghan/Iraq Wars*. And besides that horrendous astronomical figure over 671,000 American soldiers were wounded during *WWII*. I agree with the anti-war pundits that American lives should be valued, but when *you* mathematically analyze "sacrifice" in its true context, look to the recent past to equate the true cost of freedom. The 2001 *World Trade Center* twin-towers catastrophe was very comparable to *Pearl Harbor* on December 7, 1941, and in fact more people died on September 11th on U.S. soil than were bombed and killed at *Pearl Harbor*.

Now here's exactly where the liberal mindset suddenly turns philosophical. "The *Iraq War* should not be fought and it cannot be validly compared to *WWII*," they will adamantly argue. I maintain that President Bush does not like or want war, but sometimes war is the only viable measure to take to correct a looming worldwide problem. I strongly suggest that the anti-war doves become students of history instead of naïve idealists of the present situation without any clue of past Holocausts. The rest of the world is not a Utopia and Syria, Palestine and Iran are not heavens or contemporary paradises. Stop this' nonsensical "Blame America first" rhetoric accusing this country of being responsible for all of the world's ills and problems.

I admire President Bush because from the outset he understood one thing very clearly: Problems are easier to solve (despite *sacrifice*) when they are small than when they proliferate and mushroom into something massive. When Adolph Hitler's minions invaded the Sudetanland (Czechoslovakia) in 1939, no one did anything about it. When Saddam Hussein invaded Kuwait, the first President Bush stopped the avaricious tyrant dead in his tracks.

Saddam Hussein's intent was to invade Kuwait and then take over Saudi Arabia, thus controlling most of the Arab oil (and the Arab holy shrines) and holding the U.S. and the free world hostage to both economic and political extortion. Using a valid analogy, later in 1939, Hitler invaded, Poland, Denmark, Holland, Belgium and France. Give the second President Bush much-warranted credit. Saddam Hussein never had a chance to invade Saudi Arabia (and other Arab states) after rebuilding his army after the *Gulf War*. President George W. Bush has very effectively protected and preserved our unparalleled American prosperity and our highly envied American way of life.

Anti-war cynics argue that no WMDs have been discovered in Iraq. But Saddam Hussein showed his true colors when he used WMDs to exterminate 300,000 Kurds, and please remember that over 7 million Jews were systematically eliminated in Nazi gas chambers and death camps during *WWII*. And over 50 MILLION people, civilians (mostly Russians and Poles), prisoners, captives and soldiers "UNNECESSARILY" died in *WWII*. The truth is that the U.S. is currently fighting Arab Fascists that would kill any American anywhere in a New York second (if they could) even though most liberals (innocent random victims) apparently are against the *Iraq War*. According to the terrorists' perverted point of view, any U.S. citizen is just another American warm body that needs to become cold in a hurry regardless of that victim's political "philosophy," either liberal or conservative.

Let's understand one particular thing. The radical Arab extremists have a saying, "An enemy of my enemy is my friend!" This statement means that Saddam Hussein had condoned al Qaeda terrorists living in, training in and migrating through Iraq while traveling from Syria-to-Iran-to-Saudi Arabia-to-Jordan-to Palestine. As long as the radical militants all hated America, it didn't matter one iota to Saddam Hussein. Wasn't our chief terrorist in Iraq a Jordanian and the notorious Osama bin Laden a Saudi? Weren't the 9-11 killers mostly Saudis that hung out and trained throughout the Middle East, including Iraq?

But look at the 1,500 terrorists and Baathist loyalists that were killed by *our* brave soldiers in Fallujah. Fallujah was a giant magnet, a major kill zone where foreign terrorists and Sunni Baathist Fascists were attracted to and then valiantly dealt with, and if any of those fanatics could have the opportunity, they would blow up a New York skyscraper (or New York City if they could) at the drop of a hat. Kill the terrorists and the Arab Fascists in Iraq before they have a chance to enact their hatred here in the USA.

The *Iraq War* under President Bush can only be evaluated in one context: it is actually a legal extension of the *Gulf War* under the first President Bush. Saddam Hussein did not honor the truce terms of the *Gulf War* and ignored over a dozen *UN* resolutions condemning the arrogant dictator, who had been persistently thumbing his nose at the *Security Council*. And there's only one major power (besides England) that correctly interpreted and understood *his* true motivations and held Hussein accountable and liable for his blatant insolence, and George W. Bush courageously leads *that* great country.

To fully understand Saddam Hussein's mindset students of history must first recognize that the dictator modeled his Iraqi regime after the tyrannies of other monsters, *his* boyhood heroes from World History, predators Adolph Hitler and Joseph Stalin.

Saddam Hussein was the Iraqi leader of the Baathist Party. The stated main goal of the Baathist Party is to unify (if necessary by force) the entire Arab World against the West (particularly, the United States). Hussein invaded Kuwait and he was craftily waiting after the *Gulf War* to rebuild his Army and to deploy WMDs when a weaker U.S. President (who would be soft on terrorism and illegal world conquest) would gain office following George W. Bush.

Also, the Baathist Party coincidentally is the dominant political force in Syria and controls the activities of that terrorist-supported government. Right this moment Syria is harboring many of Saddam's former Baathist regime members. And Saddam's WMDs (some of which he used while exterminating 300,000 Kurds) quite possibly have been shifted from Iraq to Syria just before the present *Iraq War* commenced.

When the United States unfortunately allowed the UN to try and persuade Saddam to cooperate with twelve UN resolutions, the stubborn despot used the delay to cleverly spend the UN "oil for food money" to organize the Baathist resistance that our American soldiers are now encountering in Iraq. That earmarked UN oil for food money never went to feeding Saddam's people as *it* had been intended. But at the time left-wingers in the U.S. press and in Congress were accusing

179

the Bush Administration of "starving" the Iraqi people because of the "sanctions" that the U.S. had forced the UN to impose on Saddam Hussein after the *Gulf War* under Bush 41. But the dishonest dictator was secretly using the UN money he was receiving for "food and medicine" for diabolical reasons: to rebuild his Republican Guard Army, to sponsor Palestinian terrorism and to finance the Baathist and Sunni terrorist resistance in order to prevent democracy from taking root in his country.

Saddam also had a secret oil pipeline going from Iraq into Syria that the UN never seemed to know about and Hussein was clandestinely selling that detoured oil to Syria and using that additional "skimmed money" to rebuild his army, to subsidize the Baathist resistance, to promote Middle East terrorism and to generally neglect his people. All the while President George W. Bush was aware that outspoken critics were blaming U.S. sponsored sanctions against Iraq for the deteriorating social conditions prevalent inside that country.

France, Germany and Russia (two of which are UN Security Council nations) had lucrative contracts with Saddam Hussein totaling over 23 billion dollars, in addition to the massive "oil for food" scam that the UN was supposedly overseeing. George Walker Bush got tired of all of the UN lying, cheating, stealing and stalling while Saddam was re-arming and financing terrorism with American taxpayers' hard-earned dollars being squandered by UN Secretary-General Kofi Annon.

George W. Bush was concerned that if Saddam Hussein accomplished *his* invasion objectives and gained control of most of the Arab nations' oil, then *WWIII* would be imminent and hundreds of thousands of American soldiers' lives would be lost in such a cataclysmic global conflict. Our President concluded that a limited *Iraq War* now would be much better than a disastrous war four to six years from now. George W. Bush did not desire to see Saddam Hussein evolve into the next Adolph Hitler. And let's not forget that Saddam's Baathist Party rose to power after *he* personally assassinated the reigning dictator of Iraq and then more recently Hussein had been conspiring to have Bush 41 and Bush 43 assassinated, too.

And finally (for the enlightenment of anti-war liberals), a democracy in Iraq will disrupt terrorism and terrorists throughout the Middle East, particularly in Baathist Syria, in Palestine and in Iran. And please recollect that Saddam Hussein paid each Palestinian suicide/homicide bomber's family $30,000.00 of "UN oil for food money" just to ensure that terrorism in the Middle East would thrive and continue. The same attitude that prevailed among the demented German Fascists exists among the radical Islamic Fascists: "Blame it all on the Jews!"

The United States of America protects all of the free world including anti-war protestors in Canada, Europe and even here in America. The USA is the greatest force for good the world has ever known but our country can only continue being great through strength, economic prosperity, free enterprise and the courage to act, and the nation must persist, must demonstrate leadership and must defend what is right, what is just and what is necessary.

And there's one final essential thing to say to all anti-war liberals. How much money did al Qaeda donate to the tsunami and the hurricane victims? Was it more than the United States of America had contributed? Kindly get on the right side of the fence and stay there.

Below is a "Letter to the Editor" that had been published in the *Press of Atlantic City.*

Iraq War Extension of Gulf War

Editor:

I'm totally tired of reading letters in the *Press* from misinformed liberals that the Iraq War was unjustified because President Bush had lied to the American public about Saddam Hussein's possession of weapons of mass destruction (since none had been found in Iraq).

First of all, Saddam villainous Hussein *did have* weapons of mass destruction because he and his regime had exterminated over 300,000 Kurds with chemical weapons and buried those victims in mass graves. Now the real question is "Whatever became of Saddam's WMDs?" General Georges Sada (Saddam's Air Force Chief) has gone on record stating that Saddam's WMDs had been airlifted into Damascus, Syria just prior to the Iraq War.

According to General Sada, two Boeing commercial jets had had their passenger seats removed and the WMDs had been transported from Baghdad to Syria during fifty-six flights. The secret missions were disguised as "humanitarian aid" for Syrian flood victims because a dam had burst in that country. General

Sada's assertion (about Saddam's possession of WMDs) had been corroborated by similar claims in 2001 by Israel's Prime Minister Ariel Sharon and by General Moshe Yaalon. It doesn't take a rocket scientist or a neurosurgeon to figure out that Saddam Hussein was a Sunni Baathist (a political philosophy that mixes Nazism with Marxism) and that the oppressive regime presently governing Syria consists mostly of Sunni Baathists.

Secondly, it is indeed important to understand that the U.S. did not invade Iraq over the WMD problem/issue. President Bush made the decision because Saddam Hussein had thumbed *his* nose at numerous UN resolutions. His ignoring of UN violations represented Saddam's refusal to honor the terms of truce of the 1991 Gulf War. Hence the Iraq War is really an extension of the Gulf War and not a separate war all to itself as left-wing hacks are claiming.

Thirdly, the USA is the greatest force for good in the world. The Afghanistan War and the Iraq War have liberated over 50 million people from Taliban and Saddam Hussein tyranny. And yes, the Iraq War is also about oil but not in the sense that the liberal left wants us to believe! It's about oil in the context that if Iran and Syria get control of Iraq, and if Iran acquires nuclear weapons, then Saudi Arabia, Kuwait, Jordan and Egypt will be at risk and Israel will be in jeopardy of extinction!

If the U.S. pulls out of Iraq, then be ready to pay ten dollars a gallon for gasoline. Hugo Chavez of Venezuela has just nationalized his country's oil industry and intends to cut off all exports to the U.S., and Venezuelan oil presently constitutes 11% of U.S. consumption. Everyone in America ought to hope and pray that George W. Bush's plan for victory/success in Iraq really works. Let's stop this "Blame America first" nonsense! The radical Jihadists and power-hungry jealous world dictators like Iran's Mahmoud Ahmadinejad and Venezuela's Hugo Chavez are the bad guys and not the U.S. President and Vice-President!

John Wiessner

Here's a "Letter to the Editor" I has submitted that appeared in both the *Hammonton News* and *the Hammonton Gazette*. The missive's theme involves the dangerous motives of radical Islamic terrorists that perceive the West as their avowed enemy in a modern-day crusade/war. Unfortunately, many Americans today believe that the existence of a threat to our civilization is merely a political ruse.

The Terrorists Evil End Game

The destruction of the Twin Towers on 9-11 of 2001 was merely the Islamic Jihadists left jab. To fully understand what the terrorists' right cross knockout punch is, Americans must research the year 1929.

After the U.S. stock market crashed the American Great Depression initiated a "Domino Effect" causing similar depressions throughout Europe. The economic chaos and the corresponding political vacuum that resulted allowed opportunistic Nazi/Fascist/Communist dictators like Hitler, Mussolini and Stalin to rise to power.

Now flash-forward to 2008! Iran's President Mahmoud Ahmadinejad (just like Saddam Hussein had desired to invade Kuwait and then Saudi Arabia) wants to consolidate the entire Middle East's oil under Tehran's dominion. His wicked purpose is to cripple the U.S. economy by raising oil to exorbitant levels and thus causing a Second U.S. Great Depression of such major magnitude that it will make the years 1929-1940 seem like a family picnic.

The militant Jihadists represent approximately two percent of the 1 billion Muslims in the world. Those two million Islamo-Fascists want Americans to tolerate them but they have no tolerance for us or for what they regard as our "sinful" (freedom loving) way of life. The on-a-mission Jihadists are still fighting the medieval Crusades and *their* ugly goal is to see their Muslim religion conquer and dominate Judeo/Christian civilization. The deranged fanatics actually believe that the guaranteed path to "Paradise" is to die for their faith as martyr suicide bombers.

The Twin Towers destruction was just the opening punch of Round 1. The terrorists evil end game (and Iran's President gives his full blessing to them) is to extort the U.S. with two hundred-dollar-a-barrel oil and bring our "neo-colonial imperialist economy" to its knees, which will then create a second monstrous Great Depression that will permit a second wave of tyrannical dictators (preferably radical Shiites) to take control of afflicted nations and their suffering populations. I think it's time for all Americans to remember a valuable lesson from World History. Fascists, regardless if they are past Nazi or present-day Islamic, are detrimental to the peaceful existence of democracies and republics on the Earth. Thanks you so far George Washington, Dwight D. Eisenhower and let's not forget General George Patton.

"Multicultural Education"

I had been named into "Who's Who Among American Teachers!" three times and two of those nominations have been by minority *students* (now Dean's List college achievers), one of whom was black and another Hispanic. Those *minority students* realized that *my* classroom standards were just as tough on *them* as they had been on the majority Caucasian *students* and that I gave them no favoritism, slack or handicap for their minority-status ethnicity. I had always refused to "dumb down" the English curriculum (Grammar, Vocabulary, Literature, Writing Skills) to accommodate Accelerated English *students* that lacked motivation, desire, curiosity, cooperation, respect for teacher authority and a willingness to learn.

A year before I retired in mid-1999 my Middle School's English Department had a special curriculum meeting and the Administration and my Supervisor wanted to change and "modernize" the literature textbook program. The choice eventually narrowed down to two distinct textbook series (grades six-to-eight) and my school's nine English/Reading teachers voted on which company's series to incorporate into the school's English curriculum. Obviously administrative fiat (and pressure and trends from the State Department of Education) was more important than teacher *democratic* input and the English and the Reading Departments' overwhelmingly selected first choice was abruptly discarded because the *other* more "politically correct" literature textbook series from the administratively preferred company happened to have "more cultural diversity" and subsequently was more "multicultural."

For thirty-four years I had loved teaching imaginative literature featuring such accomplished authors including Edgar Allan Poe, Jack London, Alexandre Dumas, Charles Dickens, H.G. Wells, Washington Irving, Jules Verne, Mark Twain, S.E. Hinton, George Eliot, Sir Arthur Conan Doyle, Victor Hugo, William Shakespeare, George Orwell, Kurt Vonnegut, O. Henry and James Thurber. Apparently, the fact that all of the aforementioned famous authors were "white" was a major problem because most of them had been effectively *excluded* in the newly acquired middle school literature texts. The old literature texts and program were too "white-oriented" and were not consistent with New Jersey and USA politically correct trends in "Multicultural Education."

The new eighth grade literature textbook featured on its cover a painting of Sam Adoquei's *Portrait of Rockney C*. A statement inside the text indicated that Sam Adoquei was born in the West African country of Ghana and that Adoquei was a contemporary artist that loved painting landscapes. Older literature textbooks might have featured on their covers works by Michelangelo, Rembrandt, Vincent van Gogh or Leonardo DaVinci but in this day and age those great contributing artists to *Western Civilization* have been demoted (in public schools) in deference to obscure people like Sam Adoquei of Ghana, West Africa.

I must honestly admit that the new eighth grade administratively selected (and faculty overruled) literature textbook did have a token representation of established white authors. However the bulk of the contributors had names like Gloria Gonzalez (Cuban American), Luci Tapahonso (Navajo Indian), Yoshiko Uchida (Oriental American), Gwendolyn Brooks (Black American), Gary Soto (son of California migrant workers), William Saroyan (Armenian American), Maya Angelou (Black American), Diane Mei Lin Mark (Hawaiian American), Julio Noboa Polanco (bilingual poet), Judith Ortiz Cofer (Puerto Rican), Langston Hughes (Black American), Julia Alvarez (Hispanic), Ophelia Rivas (Mexican), Nereida Roman (Hispanic), Rudolfo A. Anaya (Mexican American), Esmerela Santiago (Puerto Rican), Wing Tex Lum (Chinese poet), Naomi Shihab Nye (Palestinian), Ved Mehta (from India), Paul Yee (American Chinese) and Li-Young Lee (Chinese).

There is no doubt in my mind that Multicultural Education is contributing to *socialistically* "dumbing down" American public schools. Many of the obscure "authors" being presented to American *students* in the name of "cultural diversity" have produced works that have weak vocabulary, shallow plots, lackluster characters, non-intellectual subject matter and demonstrably unsophisticated writing skills. Yet these minority *writers* (I wouldn't call all of them "authors") are presented to naïve and impressionable eighth graders as being valuable contributors to literature when *their* works pale in comparison to those of more traditional great *Western Civilization authors* that are presently being systematically removed from literature textbooks and gradually being replaced by (in most cases) obscure or lesser known "minority authors."

The same type of phenomenon is happening in middle and high school "History" classes' as is happening in Literature courses. When *Martin Luther King Day* was established as a National Holiday celebrated in January George Washington and Abraham Lincoln had to be diminished in stature to accommodate *MLK* on the school calendar. The traditional *Washington's Birthday* and *Lincoln's*

Birthday were shrewdly consolidated into *"Presidents Day"* with "Washington and Lincoln's regular February birthdays being abandoned to allow room for *Martin Luther King Day* in January on the school calendar. And February (which used to almost exclusively belong to Washington and Lincoln) is now declared "Black American Month" in schools across the country. It is no wonder that American *children* now know more about Harriet Tubman, Crispus Attucks, Malcolm X, Jesse Jackson and George Washington Carver than they do about George Washington, Abraham Lincoln, Thomas Jefferson, Franklin D. Roosevelt and Dwight David Eisenhower. History (and literature) is being re-written by contemporary *re-visionists* that are attempting to diminish and discredit the accomplishments of white people and simultaneously magnifying the deeds and works of lesser-known minority figures.

One unique irony of all this Multicultural and curricular craziness is that teachers are now being held accountable for higher standardized test scores and "higher academic performance" when *their* curriculums are being systematically watered down and diluted to allow for the priority implementation of "Multicultural Education." Stories (by minority writers) in literature now have simple vocabulary and easy-to-understand (more simplistic) themes, characters and plots. Presently teachers are compelled to "teach down" to the *students'* level of achievement instead of challenging the kids seated in the desks to raise *their* level of performance up to the plateau of superior subject matter content being read and studied in the works of Poe, Twain, Shakespeare and Orwell. And this sort of insane farce is happening in public schools all over America.

Teachers across the nation are being coerced into propagating a system of American public-school education that is both designed and destined to fail. *Catch 22*! Teachers are not only accountable for teaching "weaker subject matter content" with low-academic challenge; they are also now held accountable to the State for *students* acquiring sufficient subject matter skills for the learners to pass state sponsored *"academic* standardized tests." Whatever happened to individual (*student*) responsibility?

"Multicultural Education" should not be eliminated from the curriculum but it should be diminished in influence to allow for a more accurate perspective of Literature and History to be presented to American school *children.* Crispus Attucks and Harriet Tubman should not supplant George Washington and Abraham Lincoln in February as equals sharing common historical prominence. And furthermore M.E. should be a part of regular traditional public school

187

history, literature, math' and science courses, but it should not constitute the entire curriculum in core subject areas.

And there's no way that Sam Adoquei is in the same league as Picasso or that Gloria Gonzalez and Yoshiko Uchida are the literary equivalents of Mark Twain and O. Henry. Our great American culture is being distorted and perverted enough by *MTV*, *VH-1* and by the *Comedy Channel* without ineffective social engineering and an excess of Multicultural Education polluting our American public-school *students* and also our public schools' already ambivalent academic standards.

I have been scrutinizing and studying Multicultural Education for four decades now and have heard too-many-times the lackluster educational jargon originating from college professors and from misguided advocates of M.E., and quite frankly those "elitist arguments" have become rather redundant, hackneyed and monotonous, and to think that I once wholeheartedly espoused those ethereal Multicultural Education principles as an idealistic teacher beginning my classroom career back in September of 1965.

Despite the "Happy Face" that supporters of Multicultural Education are attempting to promote and propagandize, one distinct adjective comes to mind whenever I think about Multicultural Education and that particular word is "insidious." To the unsuspecting layman or college student "Diversity through M.E." is a nifty catch phrase that sounds awfully noble and pleasant to the ears upon hearing its utterance, but the process is actually quite detrimental to the implementation of effective American education. I deliberately describe the scourge as *insidious* because over the past forty years M.E. has imperceptibly and very cunningly been introduced, advanced and perpetuated by its militant proponents without the American public realizing exactly how harmful, how treacherous and how detrimental the seemingly benign terminology appears to be.

Multicultural Education never clearly defines and identifies itself to the American public for what it really is. U.S. citizens automatically equate and associate M.E. with Bilingual Education and *ESL* (English as a Second Language), which the clever campaigners for M.E. never lucidly delineate and differentiate. Bilingual Education and *ESL* are indeed definite, positive, beneficial and necessary programs in our American public schools. Those two activities encourage and facilitate the cultural "Melting Pot" ideal whereby immigrant and certain minority *students* learn English along with *ESL* and are hopefully successfully assimilated into regular grade-level classrooms after two-to-four years of exposure to a new language and a new culture.

188

But Multicultural Education is the complete opposite and inverse of Bilingual Education and *ESL*. Here's what Multicultural education really is: It is an attempt to manipulate history, English, literature, math' and science to make those subjects appear to *all students* in *all classrooms* that blacks, Hispanics and other minorities have contributed as much (if not more) to *Western Civilization* than Einstein, Jefferson, Washington, Thoreau, Shakespeare, Cervantes, Hugo, Twain, Newton, Steinbeck, Hemingway, Poe, Socrates, Plato, Aristotle, H.G. Wells, Arthur Conan Doyle, Abraham Lincoln and other noteworthy Caucasians have. Multicultural Education attempts to diminish the great "White" benefactors of the *Western World* while simultaneously elevating the works of obscure minorities to *their* plane. And the entire *student* body is exposed to and forced to suffer through this ruse in *their* various core curriculum textbooks and it's not just *ESL students* and Bilingual Education *children* being exposed to the ongoing brainwashing. And once the American public fully recognizes *that* important concept' separating M.E. from Bilingual Education and *ESL*, then Multicultural Education will finally be satisfactorily challenged and ultimately rejected.

Although the Multicultural Education academic elitists claim to be "visionaries" they are in effect *revisionists*. Their impractical goal is to create a Utopian *future* by first rewriting the *past* and next changing the *present*. First relegate icons like Shakespeare, Cervantes, Jefferson and Newton and then give equal or greater stature to James Baldwin, Langston Hughes, Jesse Jackson and George Washington Carver. It is true that George Washington Carver remarkably found over three hundred applied uses for the peanut but the Multicultural Education activists want us to believe that the black scientist is just as important to American culture, science, technology and history as is Bill Gates and Thomas Edison. I don't think so!

This is not to say that minority inventors and authors are not to be studied in public schools. As a teacher I remember enjoying reading terrific biographies of Louis Armstrong, Harriet Tubman and Ralph Bunche with my literature classes but if Multicultural Education advocates had their way, *that type* of minority-oriented reading would constitute the bulk of the literature, history, math' and science curriculums taught in our schools. And I truly admire the accomplishments of Colin Powell, "Condie" Rice and Clarence Thomas because they didn't need any cause, movement or national organization to inspire them to excellence. They (according to the American free enterprise tradition) reached deep-down inside and motivated themselves "as individuals" to strive for greatness but many

189

liberal socialistic Multiculturalists will call the three cited black achievers "Uncle Toms" since they have succeeded in the highly competitive American capitalistic culture on their own without a massive crusade or national "special interest agenda" advancing their *individual* attainments.

To get their way the M.E. elitists must shrewdly label and demonize traditional curriculum by calling it "Eurocentric," which automatically connotes a bad moniker. The long-range objective of the M.E. masterminds is to first condemn "Eurocentric" history, literature and science and then to systematically dismantle *"Western Civilization,"* which in reality is what the stereotype "Eurocentic" means.

I have eight elementary questions that pertain to significant developments in the history of mankind to ask the Multicultural elitists:

1) Where did the concept of *Democracy* begin? (Clue: the city is the capital of Greece)
2) Where did the *Renaissance* happen? (Clue: a country that has cities Florence, Rome and Venice)
3) Where did the *Age of Exploration and Discovery* begin? (Clue: cities like Genoa, Lisbon and London)
4) Where did the *Age of Enlightenment* have its roots? (Clue: Cities are found on rivers *Seine* and *Thames*)
5) Where did the *Protestant Reformation* take place? (Clue: Main players were Martin Luther of Germany and Henry the VIII of England)
6) Where did the *Industrial Revolution* get started? (Clue: a country that has cities named Manchester, Coventry, Sheffield, Leeds and New Castle)
7) Where did the *Atomic Age* happen? (Clue: the country has an eagle and an old chap named *Uncle Sam* as its symbols)
8) Where did the *Computer Age* have its origins? (Clue: corporations named *IBM, Microsoft, Intel* and *Apple* inspired it to happen).

The phenomenal freedoms that Americans enjoy today are outgrowths from the eight Eurocentric eras enumerated above. The concept of *Democracy* originated in ancient Greece. The *Renaissance* liberated the human spirit and gave birth to cultural creativity. The *Age of Discovery* and *Exploration* sent men on great adventures to distant continents. The *Age of Enlightenment* swiftly led to the development

190

of modern-day political philosophy. The *Protestant Reformation* loosened church authority and created an atmosphere where thinkers could contemplate and publish their works, where scientists could freely experiment and where inventors could create.

This newfound freedom of thought and expression eventually led to the development of Constitutional governments where for the first time in history the rights of citizens were protected under law. This fantastic revolutionary *"Western Civilization"* newfound liberty led to freedom of thought, which led to discovery, which led to technology, which led to progress and to our contemporary American (and European) way of life and high standard of living. But if the determined Multicultural Education zealots had their druthers the eight important eras of *Western Civilization* would be diminished and relegated because they are "Eurocentric" while the accomplishments of minorities will be elevated, given accolades and praised in our public schools, thus dooming our *students* to perpetual mediocrity.

Now knowing the above-mentioned salient facts, the majority of adult Americans would prefer having their *children* exposed to the same kind of "Eurocentric" education that *they* had received and understood as *"Western Civilization."* Every mature U.S. citizen with any scruples wishes to have the culture and history of America expertly transmitted to the younger generation, for that particular function is the central purpose of schools besides teaching *students* vital skills in reading, writing, speaking, mathematics, science and thinking. But if the adamant M.E. crusaders had their way teachers would have to pretend that *Western Civilization* never happened and that minorities were equally (if not more) responsible for the prosperity, economy and government that America presently maintains and enjoys.

The goal of Multiculturalists is to make every public-school *student* into a tribal member of a *UN* model "global village." This is why Multicultural Education is both un-American and unpatriotic. And those stubborn Multicultural Education advocates are very inflexible and quite obstinate too. They want you to believe that M.E. is a powerful new "science" and not a topic that should be comprehended as a "debatable controversial issue" having an opposing point of view.

Several years ago I had submitted a critique of M.E. to a college professor that maintains an "Essays on Multicultural Education" *Internet* website. The academic elitist refused to post my article on the basis that it was a prejudiced and biased view of Multicultural Education based on "stereotypes." Well now, isn't that a wicked contradiction! The M.E. proponents suddenly take on a "ban-the-essay censorship Fascist mentality" when someone who values *Western Civilization* dares to present an alternative position on *their* pet subject. And this is perhaps the greatest danger that will materialize should intellectual democratic elitist educators get their way: intolerance to other people's points of view and a blatant violation of *First Amendment* freedom of speech rights. And the irony of it all is that Multicultural Education is masked, marketed and sold as "democratic education." Such a canard is advertised as making American public-school *children* more aware of "diversity." I suppose *that* specific definition does not include *diverse* opinions or contrary philosophical positions about Multicultural Education.

Once the general public eventually fathoms the true nature of the Multicultural Education fanatics' motives, I am convinced that the adherents and their movement will subsequently be soundly defeated. Their agenda (and they do have an agenda) is disguised as and masquerades as a necessary feature of "Educational Socialism," which conceals itself under the mantle of "Educational Democratic Equality for All." But if all *students* are *equal*, therefore no *student* could ever become more *academically* superior, more-wealthy', more outstanding, more achievement-oriented or more creative as long as he or she remains in a public school under the dominion of "Educational Socialism." In the Multicultural Education Universe there can be no Valedictorians or Salutatorians because that type of *academic* honor *discriminates* against the masses and makes the average *student* (minority or otherwise) feel inferior. "Just try and blend in with everyone else! Let's have a Melting Pot or giant cultural salad!" is the watchword of the M.E. enthusiasts.

Educational Socialism and Multicultural Education are conveniently bolstered in classroom subjects with the implementation of a Neo-Industrial Education Factory-Oriented Classroom Model. Our American public schools are run like factories. Administrators and supervisors are the bosses, boards of education are the boards of directors, taxpayers are the stockholders, teachers are regarded as the employees in the system and the *students* are the products of a twelve-year-long manufacturing process. This obsolete educational factory model has been in existence for over a hundred years now and as long as it persists and as long as administrators are influenced by state-supported mandates like Multicultural Education, then mass mediocrity will in the final-analysis be the result. Schools are operated like factories and Multicultural Education will still guarantee a very nondescript product (the homogenized "salad-Melting Pot *students*" constituting the entire *student* body).

Now here's where and why I believe that Multicultural Education will ultimately be vanquished. Multicultural Education proponents are generally also Educational Socialists. In addition to desiring to dismantle *Western Civilization* (calling it "Eurocentric") they absolutely loathe capitalism, the indispensable economic engine of America. If it weren't for "free enterprise" (capitalism) and the economic security that the accumulation of personal wealth affords and provides, then our great American democracy would be vulnerable to eroding, eventually decaying into civil unrest and gradually heading in the direction of anarchy. Think about it! Our *free* enterprise economy is what makes Americans truly *free* and the essential economic idea of "risk-reward" is hardly ever taught in our public schools because it involves free enterprise and individual achievement. School philosophy is indeed anti-free enterprise.

But Ivory Tower Educational Socialists think that "capitalism" and "competition" cause *students* to become selfish and greedy without *sharing* with others. They frown upon capitalism as being a negative influence because it engenders *students* becoming too egocentric and arrogant and therefore capable of being distinguished as achievement-oriented individuals from the rest of the group (their *student comrades*). In M.E. classrooms, *students* are discouraged from thinking outside the box because then they would be an obvious danger to the system and a threat to the dominance of Educational Socialism. Blend in and be exactly like everyone else in the great *Melting Pot*. Be an average pepper, carrot or onion in the Giant American Salad. Don't aspire to accomplish more than your fellow *students* and never be exposed to the evils of capitalism and free enterprise. "Now let's eliminate grades so that everyone can think and be on the same level at all times because we're all *equal.*" *That* is another immediate goal of these educational socialistic maniacs.

Capitalism (a wonderful concept of Eurocentric *Western Civilization*) is the great hope and foundation of any free and democratic society. Capitalism (Wall Street and Main Street) is what gives the *United States of America* its stability and security. Heaven forbid if our entrepreneurs and risk takers are ever silenced! They employ people', and these ambitious pioneers open new frontiers and establish new dynamic businesses and corporations. It's all quite simple and "Elementary, dear Watson!" as Sherlock Holmes often stated. Without capitalism in America there would be no profits, no employees, no taxes being paid, no companies, no businesses, no government programs, no public schools, no colleges being financed and contributed to, and no wealth being created. Without capitalism the *United States'* flourishing economy would soon deteriorate and go the way of the *Soviet Union.*

Thank Heaven that free enterprise is still the most vibrant and productive force in America! But please remember: college professors in general are liberal-minded and many of them are elitists that despise free enterprise and competition while *they* advance the "cooperation causes" of Educational Socialism and Multicultural Education.

Instead of endorsing a hypothesis that postulates that America is a great Melting Pot where all public school students are *equal* (the same), American Education needs to get on the right track and instruct its students, "If you want to achieve individual prosperity become a capitalist and not a factory or office worker. You have the potential to become an employer and not settle for just being an employee. Pursue excellence and work hard towards everything that you attempt or do, and by all means never simply settle for being just like everyone else in a cultural salad! Dig deep down inside yourself and produce more than your peers! Strive to become an individual and don't be satisfied just being referred to as one!" But that inspiration will never happen on a broad scale as long as Educational Socialists (that hate American capitalism) and Multicultural Educationists (that resent "Eurocentric" history and literature) are at the academic helm and wielding tremendous influence over the fate of millions of American public-school *students.* "Ambition" is now an absolute dirty word in American education! It suggests that an aggressive self-motivated *child* will distinguish himself or herself from his or her fellow *students* and learn to grow and excel as an individual.

The elitist critics of free enterprise again use labeling to endeavor smearing and debunking capitalism, accusing the greedy method as being "trickle-down economics!" But will someone please explain to me how gravity could be successfully defied by having "trickle-up economics?" And I boldly venture to state that most Multicultural Education elitists are also Educational Socialists. Public school students must learn to first help themselves and *then* help society!

In conclusion only free enterprise (and our *students'* awareness of and their belief in its greatness), a continuation of the teachings of *Western Civilization* along with some sober realistic thinking will ensure the future of the *United States of America.* The public must first become aware that Multicultural Education is the problematic antithesis of this country's past glory. But as long as Multiculturalists are powerful elements performing their egregious harm inside

American Educational Philosophy and Psychology, our public schools are destined and doomed to mediocrity.

There' will be no future Multicultural Utopia produced by the Educational Aristocracy (college professors, school administrators, school supervisors, curriculum coordinators, and State-Mandated Programs) as the academic boyars would like us to believe. Multicultural Education isn't even a placebo let alone a civilization-saving elixir. Our only hopes for a prosperous future are Free Enterprise (capitalism) and the preservation of *Western Civilization*, two extraordinary disciplines that the educational elite (in general) ignore, abhor and reject. Please remember that the opposite of "Cultural Unity" is "Multicultural Diversity." This is the principal reason why M.E. is so dangerous and so detrimental to American education.

And it was essentially because of that "politically correct and multicultural" new literature textbook series that had been administratively imposed on my middle school's English Department that convinced me that it would be expedient for John Wiessner to retire from the teaching profession after thirty-four years of dedicated classroom instruction.

"School Holidays"

Below is a "Letter to the Editor" that had been published on Wednesday, November 2, 2005 in both the *Hammonton News* and the *Hammonton Gazette*. The writing pertains to the changing of "Halloween Day" in Hammonton, New Jersey's Sooy Elementary School to "Orange and Black Day."

Editor:

Now that Halloween has come and gone, I wish to describe what I believe is actually happening concerning Halloween on a national level that has had its repercussions right here in the Hammonton School System. Halloween has recently been changed from an annual school tradition to "Black and Orange Day." Local school administrators have publicly stated that the conversion is due to "safety reasons." How many incidents involving violence or student injury during past Halloween celebrations have happened in our public elementary schools? I'll bet few if none! Certainly, if safety is a major concern the elementary school kids could continue to enjoy their parade and celebration without wearing masks while parents could stay out of the school building and hear about the festivities over nightly supper. I suspect that other more sinister factors are at work here besides a "concern for safety."

First of all Halloween has much of its origin attributed to the medieval idea of ghosts of saints (spirits) populating the earth just prior to All Saints Day and All Souls Day in early November. To be a saint one has to obviously be *dead* so naturally Halloween (as we know it with ghouls and goblins) is an extension of that ancient belief in ghosts. Please remember that "Halloween" means "Holy Eve."

The essential problem of contemporary social revisionists (those in powerful positions attempting to rewrite American history and culture) is that (in *their* demented point of view) all references to Christian holidays in public schools must be eliminated to allow for "the Separation of Church and State." Our Founding Fathers thought that the "Separation of Church and State" meant to *not* have a State Religion in America dominating political thought such as the Anglican Church was doing in England. The Pilgrims and the Puritans had migrated to America because they were being persecuted by the more elite and influential religious denominations in England. So to our Founding Fathers, the "Separation of Church and State" simply meant to not have a predominant religion influencing secular government decision-making. However modern revisionists have insidiously re-defined this revered historical notion of "Separation of Church and State" to meet their own fancy, specifically to mean no religion in public schools.

Let's examine what has happened on the national scene that has been initiated and will be gradually completed by social revisionists. Christmas has been diminished to "the Holiday Season" in our public schools, Easter has become "Spring Break" and now Halloween has become "Black and Orange Day." When Martin Luther King Day was established as a national holiday on the January school calendar Washington and Lincoln had to be diminished in stature to accommodate MLK. February used to exclusively belong to George and to Abe but now we celebrate "Presidents Day" (seemingly to honor all Presidents) and February has suddenly magically appeared as "Black History Month" in our public schools. The next holidays to be hit in this diabolical domino effect will be St. Patrick's Day becoming "Green and White Day," St. Valentine's Day becoming "Red Day" and Thanksgiving becoming "Grateful Day" simply because all three of those remaining holidays have all-too-glaring Christian references and origins. Do you see a pattern here?

In addition to "history and cultural revision" the phenomenon known as political correctness also is responsible for this sudden change in the traditional Halloween venue to the "Fall Festival." When I was teaching eighth grade English in the late 1990s, I had been developing a creative writing activity while using excerpts from the movie "Beetlejuice" to show to several of my classes. A small faction of vociferous parents (for religious reasons) didn't want their children exposed to "Ghosts" in a public-school setting and vehemently protested my creative writing lesson to school administrators. Their children had to go to the library to work on an alternative writing assignment while the movie was being shown in my classroom and school administrators advised me to not in the future show a film that "certain elements of society find offensive."

And so if you honestly believe this "standard company line" business of Halloween being altered to "Black and Orange Day" because of safety concerns then you don't fully understand that the "standard corporate line" (Federal Department of Education and the State Department of Education) dictates "guidelines" to school administrators and that *their* decisions are also being influenced by powerful educational bureaucratic professors who are calling the shots in teachers' colleges and universities. These radical educational and societal "revisionists" (who incidentally author and/or approve your child's textbooks) are endeavoring to re-design U.S. history and re-define time-honored American traditions in order to reconstruct the past and the present for future generations to study. Their policies and agendas are advanced by their need for "political correctness" (don't offend anyone in the minority community by your time-honored national cultural traditions) and by *their* need to abolish Christianity and all of its vestiges from American society starting with the public schools, where vital socialization of the next generation is being practiced.

If you believe that the elimination of the Halloween heritage in the local public school has to do with safety, then you must be living in *Oz* instead of in Hammonton. Safety has little to do with the transition the town of Hammonton is witnessing in regard to Halloween. The entire issue is politically motivated on both the national and the local levels. The transition from Halloween to "Black and Orange Day" is really all about political correctness and about the ongoing secular war on Christianity, its teachings and its symbols.

John Wiessner

Here is another "Letter to the Editor" that was published in both the *Hammonton News* and the *Hammonton Gazette* on December 8, 2005. The theme of the letter is the transformation of the saying "Merry Christmas" in local public schools to the more politically correct "Happy Holidays."

How Does the Hammonton School System Stand on "Merry Christmas"?

Editor:

Now that the Hammonton Sooy Elementary School's primary grades have made a travesty out of changing the traditional *Halloween* parade and corresponding classroom decorations into Black and Orange Day and the celebration of *Thanksgiving* into "Turkey Day," the next cultural barrier the school administration must face is the elimination of "Merry Christmas" anywhere in the school buildings. Instead "Happy Holidays," "Winter Break" and "Holiday Trees" must replace the mentioning of the taboo word "Christmas." And you probably thought that the nefarious old Grinch was only a fabrication of Dr. Suess's fertile imagination.

Powerful secularists and history revisionists are again rewriting the past, trying to make us all pretend that the *Christmas* tradition was never honored or celebrated in our public schools. And your public-school administrators are so influenced by these educational and cultural revisionists that the bureaucrats will wholeheartedly ignore the past and conveniently change the present (at your child's expense) in order to accommodate *their* politically correct superiors in the State and Federal Departments of Education.

The United States of America, our *Constitution* and our *Declaration of Independence* were all founded on Christian values based on the principles that man is basically good and that man's nature can be trusted with "unalienable rights." A rather grotesque convolution has been occurring in America the last sixty years where secularists and revisionists are using the First Ten Amendments of the U.S. Constitution to undermine the teachings of the Old Testament *Ten Commandments.* Legality is currently at war with conventional morality and now *Halloween* and *Christmas* are at the core of the religion/law controversy.

And when the secularists and the revisionists are clever enough to figure out that the appellation Santa Claus is simply an Americanization of the European Saint Nicholas (Father Christmas), then old St. Nick will most definitely be under attack too during this time of year because of obvious political/religious implications. This rising anti-Christian sentiment in this great nation really "sleighs" me.

The biggest problem that the agenda-oriented secularists and revisionists face in regard to December 25th is that not only is *Christmas* a religious holiday but it is also a declared national *legal holiday* established by President Ulysses S. Grant in 1870. Hebrews and Jehovah Witnesses should not be offended with the nomenclature "Merry Christmas" because they share this nation's rich Judeo-Christian *Ten Commandments'* heritage. In fact, eighty-five percent of Americans call themselves Christians and if the majority opinion rules in this "democratic" country, then the popular December holiday should be recognized in public schools despite the objections of Muslims, Buddhists, atheists and other "offended" vocal minorities.

The secularists and revisionists argue that "Happy Holidays" is a more inclusive term than "Merry Christmas" is. Stores like Target, Wal*Mart, K-Mart and Toys "R" Us don't want to discriminate against certain minority interest groups so they prefer to call the reason for the annual December shopping bonanza "Happy Holidays" while simultaneously banking on the theory that Christians will not be offended (by being snubbed) and will not boycott *their* stores. We live in an age where militant minorities get their gears greased while the silent majority often suffers the consequences. Hopefully all of this detrimental cultural dismantling insanity is about to change. But in the past great civilizations have collapsed and crumbled from internal moral decay (and not from external conquest) because over time those entities had lost their sense of purpose and original identity. This butchering of "Merry Christmas" is stark evidence of the same type of destructive phenomenon occurring in America right before our very eyes.

Secularism has now taken over as the dominant social/ethical philosophy in most of Europe and in Canada. Guess what country has been protecting and defending Europe and Canada for the last sixty years? If the secularists and revisionists have their way then the United States will eventually become militarily weak and morally bankrupt and will be compelled to join the ranks of France, Germany and Canada in "an equal new world UN order." Just think about it. Where would the world be and what would this planet be like without the moral clarity of the United States of America leading the way?

Citizens, school administrators and boards of education should not be intimidated by these zealous secularists out to create "a global community" and Americans should not allow our revered traditions such as *Christmas, Thanksgiving* and *Halloween* to be gradually and systematically disposed of because of opposition from highly audible and supposedly grievously offended minority factions, the on-a-mission *ACLU* and fanatically determined secularists and revisionists.

I urge all parents of students in the Hammonton School System to contact your school administrators and school board members to find out the local school system's philosophy in regard to the expressions "Merry Christmas" and "A Christmas Tree" on classroom and hall bulletin boards. Don't let them tap-dance and waltz around the issue! Phony euphemisms (attempting to rewrite history and culture) like "Happy Holidays," "Holiday Tree," "Winter Break," "Turkey Day" and "Black and Orange Day" do not reflect the true values formerly deeply embedded in our still-enviable American culture.

Forget about politically correct expediency! It's time for the silent majority to step up to the plate and go to bat for what's morally right. *Christmas* should remain an essential part of our American civilization to be recognized in local public schools, and this cherished practice should be emphatically and redundantly reinforced to "don't rock the boat" school authorities.

And finally, here's a third "Letter to the Editor" on the subject of "Holiday doubletalk" that appeared in the February 1, 2006 editions of the *Hammonton News* and the *Hammonton Gazette*.

Administrative Doubletalk is Really Bureaucratic Trouble-talk

School administrative doubletalk concerning the renaming of Christian holidays is really trouble-talk that the public should not dismiss as typical mere adminis*trivia*. A bad habit of casually renaming a Christmas Tree a "Holiday Tree" might seem like a picayune matter but when the discerning observer connects all the dots of many other similar phenomena going on in our public schools in particular and in American society in general, a distinct pattern of insidious secular malfeasance is being conducted and perpetuated to callously expunge all semblances of Christian holidays from public school children's academic experiences.

The public schools, which should be transmitting our great American culture to the younger generation, are actually renaming, erasing and (in many cases) eliminating vital aspects of our heritage (and our traditions) simply to comply with the demands of radical squeaky-gears secularists. Let's examine the school calendar to get a better perspective of what's really going on.

In the month of October, Columbus Day has traditionally been celebrated but don't be surprised if in the future some secular factions are going to figure out that the Italian explorer came to America in 1492 with the Nina, the Pinta and the Santa Maria to enforce the three G's: gold glory and gospel. The religious words "Santa Maria" and "gospel" might just get the secularists going and have school administrators inventing things like "Three Ships Day" and "Columbus, Ohio Day." And oh yes, let's not forget that also in October Halloween has now been re-invented and renamed as "Black and Orange Day."

And please remember that Veterans Day in November and Memorial Day in May have been set aside to honor America's war soldiers, both living and dead. Secularists are basically elitists who despise the notion of war. They' naively think that war is childish and akin to schoolyard bullying (when crazy dictators and fascist maniacs like Hitler, Stalin, Saddam Hussein and al Qaeda are around jeopardizing the world), and these on-a-mission secularists don't like the idea that crosses are in military cemeteries, either on tombstones or serving as grave markers. If the secularists and the ACLU have their way these revered military holidays might in the future be imaginatively renamed Veterinarian's Day and Cemetery Flower Day.

To those all-too-numerous misguided secularist peaceniks I have two basic questions to ask: What would the world be like without the United States of America? What would the USA be like if it were a pacifist nation without any military to protect it?

And oh yes dear secularists, the Pilgrims came to America to gain religious freedom and upon arriving they thanked God for their new land. The ideas of religious freedom and Thanksgiving to God are offensive and repugnant to secularists, to the ACLU and to atheists, so that's why in late November we now have "Turkey Day."

And please don't forget what's happened to Christmas. We presently have the un-traditional Holiday Tree and also in elementary schools Santa Claus is becoming taboo too because the name means "St. Nicholas." And the phrases "Happy Holidays" and "Season's Greetings" are quickly replacing the standard "Merry Christmas." Well, this is a hard one for the secularists and for their all-too-accommodating puppet school administrators because the word "holidays" is derived from "holy days," since most holidays originally were holy days, and quite confidentially the new terminology is also tough on the new iconoclasts because there's a reason for the "Season's Greetings," and guess what folks, it's not Kwanzaa.

Martin Luther King Day in January might seem pretty safe from school administrative tampering but wait a minute! MLK was a black Christian minister, the Reverend Martin Luther King. Heaven forbid! This no-no Christian title represents a big potential hitherto unforeseen problem for school bureaucrats because administrators encourage their teachers to discuss Dr. Martin Luther's King's biography each and every year just exclusively thinking that "The Reverend" was a black civil rights activist and not a man of God.

February is another headache for wishy-washy school administrators because even though Washington and Lincoln have been recently relegated in importance by having to share Presidents' Day, Washington was a Mason who strongly believed in the motto "In God We Trust" that the secularists absolutely abhor appearing on our U.S. money and coins, and Lincoln was a religious man who loved the opening lines to the "Battle Hymn of the Republic," "Mine eyes have seen the coming of the glory of the Lord." Lincoln wasn't referring there to Alfred Lord Tennyson or to Lord Byron, you know!

And don't forget that Valentine's Day in February has its origin with St. Valentine (scholars believe there were two St. Valentines), a martyr who gave his *heart* and his life for third century Christianity. Big trouble here school administrators with the appellation St. preceding the name Valentine! And naturally St. Patrick's Day in March has to be renamed "Leprechauns Day," "Irish Day" and "Clover Day," even though Strawbridge and Clothier ("Clover Day Sales") department stores are no longer viable and dominant business enterprises.

As we all now know, the Easter Holidays are now euphemistically referred to as "Spring Break" because of obvious religious overtones and don't be surprised that in the future such seemingly innocent allusions as the New Orleans Saints, the California Angels, the Jersey Devils (ice hockey team) and the Hammonton Blue Devils' names and mascots might be in jeopardy because of certain religious and quasi-religious associations made by politically correct numbskull radical secularists.

I've saved Labor Day for my last school holiday. It doesn't have any outstanding Christian or religious association and it seems rather harmless, but it's all remotely-but-essentially connected to the theme of this writing. Labor Day is an American capitalistic tradition but most secularists are also socialists that despise competition, that hate free enterprise and that detest capitalism, and when these militant-and-determined "socialistic-minded" college professors and powerful upper-echelon educational bureaucrats influence the judgment of local school administrators, a great disservice has been rendered to the citizens of Hammonton and to their school age children.

We all hear every day on television news about the "Establishment Clause" in the United States Constitution but nowhere in that document are the words "Separation of Church and State" ever written. The First Amendment of the Bill of Rights states, "Congress shall make no law respecting the establishment of religion, or prohibiting the free exercise thereof." The clause simply and explicitly means that there is to be no specific United States national religion but everyone can practice the religion of his or her choice.

The so-called "Establishment Clause" actually guarantees Americans freedom of religion (as opposed to the elimination of it) along with its references and symbols. But the ACLU and powerful secularist hypocrites and educational pseudo-intellectual elitists, (as erroneous as their thinking is), happen to believe otherwise. And out of fear of expensive ACLU lawsuits wimpy school administrators take the easy way out banking on the hope that the public will be apathetic to *their* cultural tinkering shenanigans and in the final analysis will not care about what harm to which *they* have been accomplices.

I hope that the public now understands the real dangers of administrative doubletalk being culturally destructive bureaucratic trouble-talk. Perhaps the apprehensive school executives should consult with the Hammonton High School wrestling coaches on how to grapple with their' ongoing "holidays crisis."

When the meanings of words are changed and redefined to conform' with a radical political agenda, then the jargon originating out of school administrators' mouths begins to sound like the doubletalk babbling originating out of the Biblical Tower of Babel. Now that we have connected some of the dots, everyone can plainly see where school administrators are (either deliberately or inadvertently) doing the opposite of what they were entrusted to do, transmitting the nation's values and culture to the next generation. Administrative doubletalk in regard to Christian holidays is indeed trouble-talk that without a doubt is detrimental to both the present and the future stability of the United States of America.

"Gerunds, Verbals & Participial Adjectives"

I've always found the *I-N-G* words in English grammar rather annoying and bothersome. Of course, Gerunds are I-N-G words that look like verbs but act like nouns in sentences. For example the sentences "Skat*ing* is fun," "My favorite sport is skat*ing*," "I like skat*ing*" and "There are many moves in ice skat*ing*" show the Gerund skat*ing* acting as a subject, as a predicate nominative following a linking verb, as a direct object following an action verb and as an object of the preposition "in." Gerunds only occasionally give me a hard time as in the cases of me not wanting to own a lightn*ing* rod out of fear of being electrocuted or me wondering in which direction a newspaper head*ing* is actually head*ing*.

The I-N-G ending (or Present Participle) words that behave like verbs occasionally give me a hassle. I sometimes speculate that "mow*ing* lawns" could cut me up pretty good and that "pet groom*ing*" advertised on a sign makes me think, "I don't want any pet groom*ing* me!" I mean "paint*ing* houses" could change your skin color in a hurry' and "hear*ing* aids" sounds plenty more dangerous than H-I-V. Revolv*ing* charge accounts can make you dizzy if you watch one long enough, and I often wonder if fenc*ing* companies sometimes abandon using sabers and instead fight with swords? If an idea' is swimm*ing* around in my head, would I then be a candidate for contracting water on the brain? Incidentally, I believe that eat*ing* crow is for the birds, particularly the buzzards, but I prefer tell*ing* the truth while stand*ing* up rather than ly*ing* on the ground. And how could a person ever be caught throw*ing* a tantrum unless the spectator knows exactly what a tantrum looks like and how much it weighs. And once at a circus sideshow I was gullible and paid a dollar to see "the man-eat*ing* crabs" only to walk into a back room and see a man sitting at a table eat*ing* crabs.

Sure stupid jokes can be made by inter-playing *ing* verbs but it's when the Present Participle is used as a Participial Adjective that my patience and tolerance are absolutely tested to their limits. I mean how would you like to go into a large contingent of stores and have to compete with a shopp*ing* mall. And why don't hunt*ing* lodges walk around in the middle of the forest with loaded shotguns? Astronauts have to worry about being wounded by shoot*ing* stars and museum visitors often must duck down when entering a shoot*ing* gallery. And baseball umpires occasionally have to call a slid*ing* board or a slid*ing* door "Out" at second base and heaven forbid if you intrude on and embarrass a dress*ing* room. And in my home's kitchen I always keep my head away from the chopp*ing* block and I often question why smok*ing* chimneys never get cancer or emphysema.

And to really aggravate me about Participial Adjectives, park*ing* lots make it difficult for me to find a place to put my automobile and I don't desire to be maimed, mutilated or injured during TV break*ing* news. And I feel extra tall when in the presence of a shrink*ing* violet and I wish I had a local plann*ing* board on my wall so that I wouldn't have to think about what I had to do next. And quite confidentially one of my biggest apprehensions is to be consumed and incinerated by a burn*ing* desire.

These very troublesome commonplace Participial Adjectives are both abominable and horrendous! How come swimm*ing* pools are never seen doing the breaststroke out in the Atlantic? And if a person is in a swimm*ing* pool then that individual must be careful not being injured by a div*ing* board. Naturally I fear being gulped down by drink*ing* water and I don't want to be threatened or molested by drink*ing* cups. And besides that remote possibility, driv*ing* rain doesn't even have any steering wheels and speaking of driv*ing* (a Gerund here), I make it a habit to stay out of the pass*ing* lane (Participial Adjective) because I don't want to get run-over by part of the highway. And despite how intelligent they may sound, writ*ing* tablets still require the use of pens and pencils and in addition they should never be swallowed.

And how come runn*ing* water has no feet let alone no legs? And how come the school cafeteria ladies are never serv*ing* tennis balls? And why does my liv*ing* room make the other parts of my house seem dead? And how come I've never been cleaned by a wash*ing* machine or physically defeated by a winn*ing* lottery ticket? And how does a student start finish*ing* school? My mother once authoritatively told me, "You have to look quickly or else you'll miss seeing the vanish*ing* cream!" and I remember my sister once saying, "This gust*ing* (Participial Adjective) wind is totally disgust*ing*!" (Participial Predicate Adjective).

Other relevant questions often confound my cerebral function*ing* (Gerund). Do print*ing* specialists also know how to write in cursive? Why do citizens participate in elections if we already have vot*ing* booths to do the job for them? And why do hospitals need surgeons when they already have operat*ing* rooms and operat*ing* tables? And did you ever cower away from the idea that a hang*ing* basket might actually strangle you? And just think about the poor innocent Mesopotamians that were lynched in the Hang*ing* Gardens of Babylon

208

even without the essential services of hang*ing* judges, who might have also been suspended from ropes in the Hang*ing* Gardens! And why don't fly*ing* insects require pilot licenses when fly*ing* humans do? Can fish*ing* boats really catch tuna all by themselves and can Mexican jump*ing* beans pole vault too? I wonder!

These very frustrating I-N-G Participial Adjectives can easily drive an emotionally disturbed person (like myself) to the brink of insanity. A paranoid college student might never take a test next to a copy*ing* machine out of fear of getting caught in a scandalous cheating incident and I never show my novels to employees at bookkeep*ing* companies because I'll never get my hard covers or paperbacks back. And I can tolerate my telephone answer*ing* machine until it begins to challenge my statements and then defiantly answers me back. And I definitely avoid tann*ing* salons because when I was young I once threw a football and broke a window, and my father tanned my hide pretty good. Once I had eavesdropped on a private conversation between two meet*ing* rooms and when I go to Atlantic City casinos I pick up bad habits from gambl*ing* devices that coincidentally have had one of their arms amputated. And mov*ing* vans are still called mov*ing* vans even when they are parked or when they are stationary at a red traffic light!

Over the years I have learned to stay away from practic*ing* physicians and dentists because I don't like any rank amateurs experimenting on me and recently, I have mastered the art of runn*ing* (verb) away from walk*ing* (Participial Adjective) pneumonia. And I was recently shocked when I drove by a local manufactur*ing* company because I had formerly believed that only people made and assembled things. But my biggest concern is not gett*ing* (Verb) my legs mangled when ambl*ing* (Verb) by the area bowl*ing* (Participial Adjective) lanes. Quite frankly, that kind of bowl*ing* (Gerund-Object of Preposition) is not up my alley!

"A Nightmare Vacation Trip"

During my fifth year of teaching my wife and I had taken a three-day mini-vacation to West Virginia. We stopped at Harpers Ferry, the sight of John Brown's raid, and also the scene was a historic landmark rich in *Civil War* era heritage. Then my faithful spouse and I proceeded south on scenic Skyline Drive through the Blue Ridge Mountains to Luray where we had planned to tour the famous underground caverns. It was getting dark and a heavy mountain fog began settling along the elevated highway.

I instinctively turned on the headlights to forewarn oncoming traffic of our presence while nervously holding and blasting my horn around each successive curve and bend.

"Your headlights are becoming dimmer!" my observant wife related.

"You're right!" I concurred. "And now my horn has the blast of a dying mouse caught in a trap!"

Luckily my expert driving had safely gotten us through the dense fog to Luray where we tarried for the night inside a well' appointed motel room right near the acclaimed caverns. The following morning we toured the beautiful subterranean hollows and later consumed a casual lunch. Then Joanne and I returned to our motel, packed our bags, paid our debts and put all of our belongings in the car trunk.

"Oh no!" I moaned to my wife. "The engine won't start!" The ignition kept making a pathetic groaning noise that sounded as if it was suffering from a severe case of laryngitis.

I paced to a nearby phone booth, leafed through the yellow pages, located a number and spoke with a service station mechanic. After an hour of patient waiting the repairman finally arrived at the scene of distress in his tow truck. After examining my wife's car's engine the expert's diagnosis was that the auto' needed a new battery cable.

"Do you have one on your truck?" I inquired. "If not can you get one?"

"Sure do have one sir," the jolly fellow with a strong southern accent replied. "I'll need to charge up the battery after I change cables. The whole deal will only cost you thirty-five bucks for parts, labor and installation!"

After the defective battery cable had been removed and the new one installed, I gladly paid the good-natured mechanic for his polite service and generously gave him a five-dollar tip.

I proceeded out of Luray and drove through a piedmont section gradually heading down from the mountains toward the valley. We stopped at several places of interest along the route including a gift shop and a farm market. It was autumn and the tree' leaves in and around the beautiful *Shenandoah Valley* were turning to spectacular brown, red and yellowish hues.

"Isn't the scenery magnificent?" I asked Joanne. "This is one of the prettiest sights in America!"

"Yes, and this is the vicinity where Johnny Appleseed is said to have planted all those apple trees! We read a story about John Chapman in school!" my wife (a third-grade teacher) added. "You're right John! It's quite a fantastic panorama!"

It was late afternoon and twilight was slowly descending on the region. I flicked on my headlights to prepare for nocturnal driving. The radio announcer's voice sounded as if he was going unconscious while suffering from yellow fever. My wife turned the station selector dial and the next speaker sounded like a hospital patient in traction broadcasting from a very distant intensive care ward.

"There's a gasoline station just up ahead!" my alert spouse noticed. "Let's stop and see if the new battery cable is loose!"

My automobile sputtered to a halt just beyond the entrance to the garage. Several flabby grease monkeys came ambling over and then helped me push the green *Pontiac* into the service station bay.

After raising the hood and generally inspecting the motor, the chief neurosurgeon said, "Your car needs a new battery!"

"Install it!" I commanded. "My wife and I are on the brink of mental and physical exhaustion. Just install it!"

The battery transplant was successfully completed without the use of any anesthesia. I forked over the forty-seven dollars for the new battery, a reasonable sum even by 1970 standards.

"Thank goodness that the car didn't stall-out in the middle of nowhere!" my wife attested.

"I hope this new car isn't a lemon, even if it is a belated wedding gift from *your* father!" I answered.

"Just drive and keep your negative comments to yourself!" Joanne sarcastically chastised. "Your motor mouth isn't too appreciated!"

My wife and I waved to the accommodating service-station technicians and then re-embarked on our northern itinerary fully believing that the electrical difficulty had been effectively corrected. Several hours of carefree driving elapsed and we were heading northeast toward Harrisburg, Pennsylvania. A road construction project got us detoured onto a less traveled thoroughfare that had scarcely any traffic.

"You must've made a wrong turn somewhere!" my upset wife theorized and declared. "I wish you'd pay more attention to what you're doing!" she criticized.

"I don't remember ever seeing any additional detour signs!" I responded. "There's hardly any other cars on the road we're on and it's now pitch black out. It's almost as if we've drifted into some mysterious *Twilight Zone!*"

"Just stop talking and drive!" my wife exclaimed. "Your annoying drivel is of no help whatsoever!"

I nearly swallowed my tongue when I perceived my headlights again dimming and then flickering on and off doing an animated dance across the deserted two-lane highway. My wife was indeed a nervous wreck. Apparitions of looming disaster haunted my cerebral processes. We intensely discussed being marooned on a forsaken country road infested with hungry bears, aggressive skunks, rabid raccoons and ferocious bobcats.

By a miraculous stroke of good fortune the green *Pontiac* coupe coasted down a hill and into a quaint village that featured a small service station. The gas station attendant was very cordial and cooperative. He opened the hood, browsed the engine with the aid of a trouble light and then intelligently traced the origin of the problem down to the distributor. My wife was almost in shock from the series of car-trouble' crises we had been experiencing and our only desire was to get back on the road as quickly as possible and make it safely to New Jersey at any expense.

"I just happen to have the necessary part in stock!" the gas station guru stated in a cute Pennsylvania Dutch accent. "It's used but it'll work perfectly!"

The quite benign fellow performed the needed *GM* distributor exchange, charged up the recently acquired battery, checked the replacement battery cable at my request and merrily charged me ninety dollars for his labor, expertise and parts.

"How can we get onto the *Pennsylvania Turnpike*?" I asked. "Once we're on that highway I know exactly how to get home!"

"Go down three miles and make a right at the fork in the road," the obliging fellow instructed. "Then go three more miles and ya' can't miss the big sign."

"Thanks for fixing our car!" my wife exclaimed with a sigh of relief. "I've spent worse three-hours just sitting in the hairdresser's getting a permanent!"

213

After a half-hour traveling east toward Philadelphia on the *Pennsylvania Turnpike* my headlights again began to dim and then flicker. Almost having conniptions (and almost becoming a total basket case) I pulled into the next service plaza. The night mechanics on duty were cheerful blokes and they ingeniously hypothesized that my car's ailment was electrical in nature.

"Do what you need to!" I insisted. "All I want to do is drive back to Jersey alive! We should have taken the trip in my *Triumph Spitfire* sports car!" I told my already traumatized wife.

I just had to marvel at the mechanics' mental alacrity. Two servicemen put new spark plugs in, changed several crucial wires, adjusted the points and retested the battery after charging it. I realized that the car probably didn't need a few of those items but I was so stressed out that I didn't care how much the parts and labor would cost. I just wanted to get home and escape the living nightmare my wife and I were trapped in.

"Your oil is dirty!" one mechanic brought to my attention. "I think you ought to change it just to be safe!"

"Go right ahead!" I agreed. I was on the verge of a mild coronary but now the engine wizards had to verbally degrade the quality of my engine oil and virtually accuse me of being derelict in maintaining my wife's undependable car. But I did not dispute their claim or challenge their apparently superior mechanical knowledge.

"Anything you have to do to make this tin pig run better!" I answered as my wife gave me a terrible frown as I critiqued the automobile her benevolent-but-parsimonious father had given us. I even consented to the men adding two quarts of anti-freeze and a pint of transmission fluid just to make the car run more efficiently.

"They could tell me I need a new cigarette lighter and I would insist that they put one in," I revealed to my perturbed and impatient wife. "Neither of us smoke but I would still have *it* done just to achieve peace of mind!"

"It was your idea to go on this relaxing trip!" my spouse reminded and scolded me. "Have you got any other great ideas?"

We remarkably made it to Philadelphia and passed over the *Walt Whitman Bridge* into New Jersey. About three miles from our home the lights again began losing their illumination. I turned into our driveway, shut off the ignition, took a deep breath and then began unloading our suitcases and souvenirs from the jinxed car.

The following morning I just managed to get the engine started. Then I drove the accursed auto' to the local garage mechanic. He inspected the engine without the aid of a sage *Ouija Board* and immediately determined that the fan belt that cranks up the alternator had snapped off and its absence was paralyzing the car's entire electrical system, especially at night when additional power was required to operate the headlights. The fan belt cost me $3.98 plus labor, but the point is that I had recently spent almost three hundred hard-earned dollars in parts and labor for a vital $3.98 part.

A dozen pleasant mechanics had seen the same thing and had come up with the wrong theories as to why the lights had been incessantly flickering. But only the last automobile guru in my hometown had the ability to pinpoint and finally alter the deficiency. All of the "mechanics" I had encountered were courteous and amiable but only one of them knew exactly what he was doing.

"I now know that education isn't the only field where incompetent performance flourishes," I told my wife at the supper table. "Without a doubt this country needs more knowledgeable automobile mechanics."

"Be quiet and just eat your lima beans!" Joanne succinctly answered back.

But then a revolutionary thought occurred to me. In speaking with each of the "mechanics" I had learned that they all had graduated from high school, even though they were inept at diagnosing engine problems. And they all also had congenial dispositions and temperaments. But *their* bungling had cost me in excess of three hundred dollars in unnecessary expenses. Then it all came to me like some supernatural revelation.

"Incompetent performance in high school education is the genesis of the irresponsibility *we* had experienced with the untrained garage mechanics," I informed my wife. "They learn how to socialize and get along with each other in high school classrooms but their educations grossly unprepared them for their future occupations. We have to begin accurately assessing the true damage schools are doing to young people!" I argued.

"Now that you've eaten your lima beans," my spouse uttered, "you can now start on your delicious broccoli!"

"Joanne, of what value is a society of friendly workers that can't produce results, that cost others valuable time and money, and that lack adequate skill in their jobs?" I asked. "Of what benefit are nice guys that make a motorist pay over three hundred bucks for a four-dollar fan belt?"

"Don't forget your mashed potatoes," my wife reminded me. "I had to mash them all by myself because *you* were at the auto' mechanic's garage!"

The real education in America is not done by public schools. It' is done by large corporations like *IBM, AT&T, Microsoft, General Motors and GE.* Those companies *train* (there's that evil word) prospective employees to perform highly *specialized* tasks. The thrust of corporate America is to turn a profit and company executives realize that highly *trained* workers contribute to the prosperity of the firm and to the stability of the country when they *train* (teach) people to do specific jobs.

High schools could best serve non-college-bound *students* by setting up curricula with large and medium-sized corporations to begin *training* the future blue-collar workers and technicians that are presently vegetating in academic English and history classes and terrorizing teachers in home economics, the school cafeteria, mass study halls and in family living classes.

An incredible Great Barrier Reef separates the concept of "child-centered curriculum" with its liberal expectations from the tough standards that are demanded of employees by corporate America. While pursuing the *Holy Grail* of *democratic* education public schools are performing a terrible disservice to this great nation. The *child-centered curriculum, democratic* sociological education, the lack of tough academic standards and the promotion of "cooperative learning" are really the antitheses of orderly self-responsibility and self-accountability in adult life. Just imagine the fate of American corporations if the companies practiced "worker centered production," "psychological cooperative production among employees," "democratic rights on the assembly line" and "sociological bottom lines."

In the final analysis, the U.S. "*democratic* comprehensive high schools" are producing non-college-bound graduates that are grossly unprepared to be absorbed into the mainstream of the American free enterprise system. A future citizen needs food in his stomach before needing to "socialize." He or she needs clothes on his or her back before he or she needs to get along with others in cooperative groups, and *students* need secure jobs based on sufficient *training* before they need a devalued piece of parchment inscribed with the official school emblem.

216

"Why Jimmy Brown Doesn't Write"

In 1972 I had read in local New Jersey newspapers where the Federal Department of Education had blasted American education for being responsible for declining standardized test scores. I had to chuckle when I read that one of the suggestions for improving the quality of education was to have the school year extended from a hundred and eighty to a whopping two hundred and ten days. As usual quantity was the oversimplified solution where quality should have been the prime consideration.

Teachers know the real reasons for declining test scores from the inside of the warped academic fishbowl looking out. The present *democratic* comprehensive American educational system (over the past fifty years) has generated massive waste and is grotesquely inefficient. For education to improve certain simple basic common sense steps need to be taken.

Students have to be sorted out and then tracked into academic and into vocational curriculums after eighth grade. Rigid academic standards must be maintained for the college preparation tracked *students.* Teacher duties must be eliminated so that the professional staff can do more direct teaching and individual tutoring of *students.* The fifty-to-seventy-five perpetual troublemakers that cause turmoil in the average high school must be extracted out of the academic educational setting and placed either in the vocational curriculum or in alternative schools. Teacher duties should be handled by aides and tough stints like the cafeteria that require crowd control and the stoppage of fights should be the responsibility of the local police department. And finally, teachers must become first and foremost respected *specialists.*

In 1972 I had driven to the town Pony League field to watch some of my fourteen-year-old *students* play baseball. I never really liked going to local public sporting events like organized baseball games because invariably there would always be some parent that recognized my identity and then would give me a tin ear about how much expertise he or she had about schools and about public education. Parents have always had the bad habit of trying to impress teachers when *they* automatically christen themselves official authorities on American public-school education.

I glanced up at the home team bleachers and noticed four parents of *students* I had been teaching that year sitting up there masquerading as baseball' fans. I discreetly decided to amble over to the visiting team's bleachers to quietly enjoy and view the game. No sooner had I parked my hindquarters on a wooden plank when' Mrs. Brown, a very attractive and affable mom, climbed up the bleacher steps and then occupied the space right next to me.

"Mr. Wiessner," Mrs. Brown began, "my son Jimmy has really learned a lot of literature, grammar and vocabulary in your English class!" she voluntarily complimented.

"Thank you very much!" I tersely answered while trying to suggest that I preferred to be an anonymous Pony League baseball fan rather than an itinerant English teacher at that particular time.

"But honestly Mr. Wiessner," Mrs. Brown continued her impromptu oration with a forced smile, "I do feel that you should've taught more writing lessons this year. As you know Jimmy is really weak in composition writing."

"He's not in an Accelerated English class," I reminded Mrs. Brown. "Those *students* in my two Accelerated English sections write two dozen compositions every year. Jimmy's section writes two final drafts a marking period and that comes to eight every school year."

"Maybe Jimmy will have more writing in his ninth grade English class next year!" Mrs. Brown speculated while indirectly criticizing my writing teaching methods in my *general* English classes.

"You're right Mrs. Brown!" I agreed. "Jimmy should have had more composition work this year." Then I thought, 'If Jimmy worked a degree harder and was in an accelerated class, he *would have had* sixteen more compositions to author,' but I refrained from antagonizing the overly concerned parent.

"Mrs. Brown, this school year I had almost burned myself' out reading and correcting nearly three thousand compositions," I commented before clearing my throat, "and I already need reading glasses and have arthritis in both my hands!" That remark seemed to silence Mrs. Brown's attitude about my implied lazy work habits.

Mrs. Brown saw one of her lady friends ascending the visiting team's bleachers so she excused herself to join her acquaintance, leaving me alone to ponder my most recent undesired spur-of-the-moment parent conference with a *grandstanding* mother.

'If only Mrs. Brown knew the entire truth rather than bits and pieces here and there!' I chuckled to myself. 'Then her opinion of the big picture might be a little more accurate than it is right now!'

Jimmy Brown's language problems begin, end and revolve around two central facts. Jimmy was a well' behaved above-average *student* who was well' liked and socially adjusted. Because of those initial sterling qualities, secondly Jimmy was an aspiring virtuoso who

218

played saxophone in the school band. In my junior-senior high school, band was the ultimate activity besides football. Influential people in the community valued band and football over *academics*. And so the entire value system was inverted where academics were treated as extra-curricular activities and band and football were handled as if they were core curricular school subjects. English, science, mathematics and social studies had been demoted in rank while over the years band, football and other vital cherished extra-curricular activities had been elevated and glorified.

Here are the central issues. Jimmy left my English class once a week to take saxophone lessons with the music instructor. The message Jimmy received from the sax' practice was that music was primary and English was secondary because he never had to leave his music lesson to go to English class.

The band *student* missed thirty or so English classes that school year, the lad taking once a week saxophone' lessons. It then was *my* responsibility to make sure that Jimmy Brown completed all of the work that he had missed while strenuously blowing into his saxophone. Consequently, I had to provide Jimmy with worksheets and homework assignments and then make sure that he completed what he had missed when he should have been ambitiously working in my third period class. And please remember that little Jimmy was but one of a hundred and thirty *students* I had been assigned to teach every single day.

I couldn't help but believing that Jimmy Brown was really missing out on some serious insights when the class had to read stories by: Arthur Conan Doyle, O. Henry, Mark Twain, Washington Irving, Jack London, H.G. Wells, James Thurber, Herman Melville, Hans Christian Andersen, Jonathan Swift and Edgar Allan Poe. Because of his saxophone playing Jimmy Brown had to read and study all of that literature work that he had missed in class *on his own* for homework. The message Jimmy Brown received from that time-substitution was that saxophone lessons were more vital than the masterpiece works of all of the above distinguished authors.

And then Jimmy Brown missed out on interesting vocabulary words like "prodigious, loquacious, surreptitious, assiduous, egregious" and "avaricious." He also could have better mastered complex sentences with relative pronouns and adjective subordinate clauses and those other complex sentences containing subordinating conjunctions and adverb subordinate clauses not to mention noun clauses. So, because Jimmy's wonderful mother wanted him to play saxophone in the band and have individual lessons to perfect his tooting and blowing, English class had now been mathematically reduced to a hundred and fifty-day activity for little Jimmy Brown.

Jimmy Brown, just like all the other eighth grade *students* had to take the school-mandated standardized tests to determine how his individual skill levels compared to national norms. Jimmy spent three English sessions taking the *California Achievement Test* and two English classes were devoted to the *Differential Aptitude Test* for the Guidance Department. One additional English class period was used for the *Otis IQ Test*, the results of which were placed and kept in the *child's* "Confidential Guidance Folder." Now Jimmy's English class time was down to a hundred and forty-five sessions out of a possible hundred and eighty forty-five-minute periods.

Jimmy was absent from school the day the *Differential Aptitude Test* had been administered so he had to leave English class to take the Guidance Test he had missed. That same day I had given an English test, which Jimmy had missed because he was making-up the heralded *DAT* he had missed because he was absent from school the day the Guidance Department had scheduled it. The message Jimmy Brown received from all of that *democratic* educational bureaucracy was that Guidance Office tests were more important than English class, English tests and English teachers.

The classroom teacher was the one that really had suffered from all of Jimmy's absentee problems and school unfinished business outside of English class. I had to schedule a time slot after school later in the week so that Jimmy could make up the English test that the boy had missed because *he* had to take the Guidance Department's *DAT*. The *child* had missed the *DAT* because he had been absent from school the day Jimmy's entire class had also missed English class.

Standardized tests the year before had identified Jimmy as a "gifted *child*" that had only average *academic* skills in reading and writing. So now the eighth-grade *student* was also in the "Gifted and Talented" program and consequently missed several English classes each month to participate in that special placement. Then Jimmy Brown had been selected to partake in the countywide "Olympics of the Mind" competition that required three more lost English periods in which to adequately prepare for the important interschool event. Jimmy's total English class days were now down to around a hundred and twenty-two.

Jimmy Brown and his eighth-grade peers were to be making a tremendous transition to their freshman high school year and to accommodate that serious *social* adjustment, the guidance counselors met with each class section ten times. The purpose of the Guidance

Department sessions was to ensure that the switch from eighth grade to high school was not too traumatic for Jimmy Brown and his fellow eighth graders. Of course, important matters like course descriptions and subject selections, electives, regular subject requirements for high school graduation (still over four years away for Jimmy) and college choices were all thoroughly discussed.

Even though the ten scheduled guidance meetings were distributed between regular English, science, social studies and math' core curriculum classes, Jimmy still wound-up missing four additional English sessions. Now it was important that Jimmy and his classmates knew where the cooking rooms, woodshops, family living rooms and auto mechanics shops were located so another English period was wasted so that Jimmy could tour the same junior/senior high school building he had been attending school in since September. Jimmy's grand total was now down to a hundred and seventeen English sessions.

Please notice how educational *academic* inefficiency was being generated because the school officials were so concerned about Jimmy Brown's sociological and psychological needs that academics had been coincidentally neglected. But already sixty-three days of English class periods had been squandered for Jimmy Brown's delicate mental and emotional needs.

Jimmy Brown was smart, gifted and talented, articulate and sociable (but average in *academic* skill proficiency) so the administration along with the class advisor nominated the *student* to be a *School Guide* for the sixth graders coming over from the elementary school to become familiarized with the junior-senior high school. So Jimmy Brown (who was developing *socially* but not *academically*) lost two additional English sessions guiding sixth graders around the same building he had lost five days being guided in and around by the Guidance Counselors, who were definitely experts on all kinds of guiding. His English class total was now down to a hundred and twenty sessions.

I am not being facetious, trite, cynical, exaggerating or picayune here. I am stating exactly what had happened to little Jimmy Brown that school year and am demonstrating that it was quite remarkable that the *child* got to write and submit two compositions each of the four marking periods.

Now I can do some more statistical tinkering. Jimmy Brown also missed three English classes because of scheduled school assemblies when the teacher had to bring the entire class to the auditorium. And then Jimmy missed out on three other English sessions where the class was reading the wonderful literature to Charles Dickens' "A Christmas Carol" because the band had to rehearse for the annual *Christmas* assembly show that had to be given twice to accommodate the entire *student* body.

Then also English class had to be postponed twice that school year so that the *students* could view the *Christmas* movie and the spring *Easter* movie at other school assemblies. And Jimmy missed one other class because of a football pep' assembly that had been held in the gymnasium. Jimmy's English class total has now been diminished to a hundred and eleven sessions.

And to top everything else Jimmy Brown had missed eleven additional school days because of bouts with bronchitis, the common cold, high fevers and the flu. So now we're down to a hundred school days where Jimmy Brown must master the intricacies of English grammar, composition, vocabulary and literature.

And don't forget that the teacher was also absent ten days that school year because of sickness, funerals and personal business. So actually, the total classroom teacher/*student* learning time Jimmy had *me* as his instructor was around a half a school year. Compound Jimmy Brown by a hundred and twenty-nine other *students*, and you can appreciate why teachers often become frustrated, cynical and depressed.

Now here is the reason I had gone to the baseball park on that 1972 Saturday morning. I was still recuperating from a terrible Friday at school the day before. I figured I would watch a relaxing baseball game and then return home and mow my lawn.

That Friday morning, I was scheduled to have bus duty outside my school wing. It was a bleak, damp morning, but since it wasn't raining I had to wait outside and supervise the *children* until it was time for them to enter the building. That fifteen-minute interval before school was normally spent getting my homeroom attendance cards ready in alphabetical order, filling out lunch slips and recording late homework assignments in my grade book from twenty-two *students* that had been absent on *Wednesday*.

That morning a pretty bad fight erupted on the backside of the asphalt and I had to run over and break-up the melee as three hundred *children* were screaming and shouting. Then I had to admonish and warn other *students* that were throwing stones at each other to avoid a racial incident if the violators should get involved in a second altercation.

When the entrance bell finally rang I had to escort the first two combatants down to the main office for fighting. At the office I had to pick up Discipline Referral Cards to fill out on both combatants during homeroom period while I also had to take attendance and cafeteria lunch counts.

The second period 8-6 class was nerve-racking but I valiantly managed to make it to fifth period cafeteria duty. I had to admonish *children* and *students* that were bending spoons and flinging *Jell-o* at each other with their newly invented catapults. Toward the end of the forty-five-minute cafeteria period the din sounded like an ancient chariot race crowd that had gone berserk inside the *Roman Colosseum.*

"Wouldn't it be wonderful if teacher aides could do this job along with a few policemen!" I shouted to Tim Amoro (who later in life became a guidance counselor and then an elementary school principal).

"Yeah!" Tim agreed. "I already had my nose broken trying to break up that big January fight we had in here. I want to retire from this job with two nostrils!"

"If we didn't have to be in here," I yelled to Tim, "then we could be assigned to either teach a class or tutor *students* in writing skills!"

"That will never happen!" Tim shouted above the exodus din. "That's why I'm taking graduate courses to become a guidance counselor and evolve out of this crazy daily existence!"

At last I made it to seventh period, my *PPSA* (teacher Preparation, Planning and Special Assignment). My eighth period general English class was almost as challenging as my second period 8-6ers so I needed the free time to rejuvenate and catch my breath. 'I'll run-off some worksheets for Monday in the office and then take it easy the rest of seventh period!' I thought. 'Teaching is about the only job where you have to have the next school day's work done today!'

Six teachers were absent that day. The junior/senior high school no longer had permanent substitutes so I was notified over the intercom by one of the main office secretaries that I had to surrender my prep' period to teach "American Government" for the absent seventh grade social studies teacher.

At the time the daily substitute pay was only $35.00, so you could imagine how many times teachers were asked to sacrifice their *planning* time to have a *special assignment* (remember, *PPSA*) in another teacher's specialized subject area. And so the school system had saved itself a remarkable $35.00 and had successfully inconvenienced six teachers that showed up that Friday to cover the absent instructor's classes.

During my eighth period class the principal had me yanked out because an irate parent had stormed into the office and wanted to see me right away. A science teacher had to give up his *PPSA* to cover my last period class while I was confronting the livid parent about something of which I hadn't the slightest idea. The parent had misconstrued a comment I had made on Monday (remember it's now Friday) and then left the school more peacefully than when he had arrived in an angry state of mind.

I returned to my English class only to discover that the science teacher covering for me had abandoned Edgar Allan Poe's "A Tell-tale Heart" and was lecturing the *students* all about entomology and insects after a certain passage in the famous Poe story described "night watches" in the wall. After the science teacher excused himself for the last fifteen minutes of eighth period, I noticed some drawings and scribbling that had not been on five student desks before I had been summoned by the principal out of my classroom to appease an irate parent.

Then that entire week after school I had Office Detention, the "Devil's Island Howdy Duty Show" (being assigned to teachers at no extra pay by the administration). I didn't know six of the twelve *students* in the detention and had trouble with three of the high school *children* that didn't like taking orders from an eighth grade English teacher.

The shades to the side windows were closed and several of the *student* friends of the *detained* high school *children* were outside banging their fists against the windows for the amusement of their *punished* pals.

When I finally made it home alive and still breathing, I had to work on the new computerized report cards. The new system required teachers to use a number two pencil to methodically circle in grades instead of writing A, B, C, D or F on sheets of paper. Also, four comments for each *student* had to be shaded in requiring two circles for each comment. For example, 47 (two numbers) shaded in means "talks too much in class" and 59 (two numbers) shaded in means "more study needed at home."

It required three and a half-hours' to do the new report cards instead of the customary hour, but on the plus side of the coin the new system saved the office secretaries time they used to spend transcribing the written grades from the "Teacher Grade Sheets" onto the actual "Report Cards."

Because of all the stress I sometimes took "mental health days" when I wasn't actually physically sick. But the administration would call teachers on the carpet if they missed more than eight sick days of the twelve allotted by school/teacher contracts each year. A recent government report indicated that teaching is the third most pressurized job there is. An administrator once told me, "Teachers that miss more than eight days a school year are *unprofessional* because they are disrupting the educational continuity and hurting *student* learning." Right!

If the public wants to improve standardized test scores, then the answer is quite simple. Keep kids inside their assigned classrooms where they're supposed to be learning core curriculum *academics*.

I hope that two things are now quite evident: why good teachers leave the profession or evolve into guidance, college-professoring or administration *and* why little Jimmy Brown only wrote eight compositions in his *general* eighth grade English class. And incidentally Jimmy Brown's team lost the *Pony League* baseball game.

"Agents, Editors and Writing"

So, you just wrote your first science fiction novel. Your friend read it and told you that you were the next Ray Bradbury or Gene Roddenberry. Your fertile mind fantasizes your name up there on a Borders' wall poster right next to images of Isaac Asimov and Jules Verne. Before going off the deep end and equating your excellent achievement with Hemingway and Steinbeck, give your ego a vital stiff reality check.

Few of us mere mortals are literary Mozarts that can plop down in front of a computer screen and author a perfect manuscript the first time around. Let's get one thing straight right now. You wrote a *manuscript* and not a book. After an author takes the time and care to read, analyze, evaluate, edit and rewrite the manuscript at least five times, the work has finally evolved into a publishable *book manuscript*.

Literary agents have represented several of my books. Truthfully, I never learned too much from literary agents except that they will show a strong interest in you and your work only if publishers and film producers do. If the power brokers in the literary world think your work is marketable, then you are a viable commodity. If you have no track record in the publishing industry, then forget all about your friend's praise and about your artificially inflated ego. You're going to have to accept criticism from your agency's all-too-busy editors, compromise ideas and plots in your artistic masterpiece, rewrite paragraphs, sentences and pages to conform to editorial evaluations and suggestions, admit making errors, learn from these grave "mistakes" and conscientiously avoid them when constructing future "manuscripts."

Although I never had learned too much of importance from my literary agents, I absorbed plenty from editors I had worked with. It took me three years to finally master what the editors considered the "mechanics of the writing craft." I reluctantly learned that good writing involves much more than the knowledge and demonstration of grammar, spelling and punctuation skills I had mastered as an English teacher. I picked up a hundred or so "recommendations" from my "literary editors" and I will now share some of them.

To facilitate good transitions and chapter integrity, don't begin sentences and/or paragraphs with pronouns (when writing in the third person). Stay away from "lazy sentence patterns" such as starting out with constructions such as "There are" or "There is." And above all else, if you plan to be refreshingly original and creative, stay away from using stereotypical cliches and hackneyed idioms, which tend to irritate book editors.

A good sci-fi' novel or any other genre novel should first be a "love story" at its core construction with the attendant genre decoration adroitly wrapped around that core. For example, H.G. Wells' classic breakthrough novel *The Time Machine* is at its core a love story between the Time Traveler and Weena and secondly, the work is a wonderful adventure story about the ongoing conflicts between the Eloi and the Morlocks. In Ray Bradbury's masterpiece *Fahrenheit 451,* the success of the novel has as much to do with the struggle in the main character Guy Montag's personal love relationship with his dysfunctional drugo' wife as it does with the tyrannical government controlled by the powerful fire department that Montag works for. Guy Montag is searching for love as much as he is in quest of truth and justice. So, if you think that genuine sci-fi' is simply about alien invasions, green-headed one-eyed monsters, laser attacks and wars between planets with lots of terrific action scenes with Apache helicopters and UFOs exploding, you are dooming your *manuscript* to both mediocrity and to commercial failure. Your main character must have love or/and must be searching for it while he's saving the world.

The main character cannot be a villain or an evil person. Perhaps he could start out that way but he must change for the better as the story progresses, and the quicker, the better. He or she must be a compassionate protagonist that the reader can sympathize with and care about. The reader has to identify with the main character's noble conscience and his (or her) extraordinary empathy for others. Reader' allegiance is the author's greatest weapon. Yes, you can have bad guys in your novel but they have to be the definite antagonists and not the heroes. And the bad guys should hang around until almost the end and if they do hang around until then, they ought to relinquish some of their devious traits and be positively influenced by the good guy's superior demonstrable personality strengths. The main *character* must have "character."

The protagonist (good guy main character) ought to be present engaging in dialogue and showing activity in every chapter, and the nefarious antagonist must appear or at least be mentioned in each and every chapter.

Each character in your novel should have a separate and unique personality. No two characters should seem alike to your readers. In my satirical novel *Ron Coyote, Man of La Mangia*, Ron Coyote is the idealist, the dreamer out to change the immoral world and his companion Pancho Sanza is practical, naughty and hedonistic. The two engage in many amusing conversations, and their polarities in interests and values facilitate and support the humorous theme of the adult-oriented novel. Ron Coyote is out to change the world and convert it to Christian morality while Pancho Sanza is quite happy with the way that the planet's population is dysfunctioning.

No easy formulas exist that can guarantee success to an author. One must find his (or her) writing style and writing voice through years of experimenting, rejection, frustration and failure before fame and fortune become realistic products of your labor. But most importantly, accept criticism from knowledgeable editors, admit you've made mistakes and then the author must learn something from them. You've finally made it when a reader could be shown a paragraph from an unidentified work and immediately recognize the words as special language originating from *you*. Then it is quite apparent *you'* have developed a unique "writing voice."

Writing a novel is not a task; it is a labor of love that represents an ongoing project. If writing seems tedious and too much like work, you'd be better off organizing letters or newspaper ads than attempting to professionally author a noteworthy book. Novel writing is like a sickness that you are addicted to love to do. It is mental madness that must be completed, and while your masterpiece is in progress, your book is the most important thing in your life that exists on a higher plane than even food and oxygen.

Characters alone do not make a good story. Plots and subplots by themselves do not make a good novel. Novel writing is akin to the famous double helix DNA model. Your tale's characters are on one strand and your plots and subplots on a second strand wrap around each other in an upward spiral, forming a dynamic symbiotic relationship. Together their chemistry should unite in a synergy that builds and expands and reinforces itself from chapter one until the final chapter's last sentence. Good characters need good plots and subplots, and good plots and subplots need good characters. One factor cannot sustain a strong novel without the aid of the other. It all sounds quite simple and rather elementary, doesn't it?

Okay, your sci-fi' novel now has terrific characters, both protagonists and antagonists, and an extraordinary plot and well-synchronized subplots moving upward in a well' organized inverted pyramid structure. Congratulations! You now have seventy percent of the elusive good novel writing mystery competently solved. But please remember that the fiction book industry itself is also a giant pyramid, and only the top three percent of the "damned' hard-working" authors at the apex of the writing matrix make the big bucks. To enter into *their* eminent and lofty 3% domain you have to be better than the 97% of "wannabe' writers" in the base of the overcrowded literary pyramid. This is where diligence in pursuing excellence must be both honored and implemented.

Setting is another crucial element of novel writing that novice authors take for granted. My editors at the literary agency kept reminding me, "Everything that is said, all dialogue, must have a definite time and place where the characters are exchanging conversation. You can't state something like 'Tom Smith once told Bob Jones that Jones was incompetent'." When did Tom say that? What year, and what date was it? Where were Tom and Bob when the comment was made? It is the author's responsibility to extend the courtesy of time and place setting to the reader in everything that is alluded to in both real time and in "flashbacks," and by all means do yourself a mighty big favor by leaving "foreshadowing" to the motion picture industry.

Another must in good novel development is balance between dialogue and narrative. If you insert too much dialogue, you've written a script for a movie or for a screenplay; but if your story has too much description, your sci-fi' narrative then reads like a non-fiction book. In this regard an author must practice discretion and always be judicious while weighing "narrative versus dialogue."

Mingled into the delicate mix of dialogue and narrative usage are such significant elements as theme, suspense, drama, author's writing style, writing voice, tone, conflict, setting, action, adventure, plots, subplots, grammar skills, creativity and acceptable character definition. If the *author* can weave all of these intangibles into a viable series of chapters of seventy-five to one hundred fifty thousand text words, then he (or she) has advanced from being a *writer of manuscripts and stories* to an authentic *novel author*.

Above all else, the concept of "show and tell" is not limited to elementary school classrooms. It is also indispensable to authors of successful novels. The author *objectively* "tells" the story but the characters' conversations and actions "show" the story. *Show* is better than *tell*. Good dialogue (and action) is better than good narrative. And a good novelist knows the difference between *active* and *passive voice* and habitually prefers the former to the latter.

Generally, stories come across as more believable when written in the first person. The author's big problem with utilizing the first-person technique translates into how not to overtax the reader with the

230

repetition of the pronoun, *I*. Most novels are written in the third person but I have written two in the first with the main character recalling the story as "a testament" of what had truly occurred. Good fiction must always read as if it was good non-fiction and conversely and ironically, good non-fiction must read as if it was fiction.

Presenting a novel in the third person (speaking about the characters) gives the author a distinct choice. The narrator (author) telling the story can *objectively* advance the tale as the "detached presenter" revealing events either in chronological order or arranging episodes accompanied by flashbacks and/or foreshadowing. Flashbacks are more desirable (remember to include setting) because they promote "show," where "foreshadowing tends to orchestrate "tell" and leans one in the direction of "author interference," a major mortal sin of novel writing. Stay out of your story and keep your opinions to yourself! Allow a character to express what *you* (the author) might think and feel!

This next part is rather tricky. The third person method of writing could also implement the "omniscient narrator" technique. The storyteller knows all about the characters, even some things the characters don't know about themselves. You can't be both the "objective narrator" and the "omniscient narrator." You have to choose one or the other approach and stick with that pursuit throughout the novel. The "omniscient narrator" method dangerously points the author in the direction of "author interference," which is recognized in the publishing industry as literary quicksand that must be avoided at all costs.

"Author interference" is something that all good writers can recognize and sidestep. Stay the hell out of the story you are telling. Again, permit one of the characters to possess your attitudes and opinions if you feel they must be expressed but by all means, don't editorialize or opine. You are writing a novel and not an essay or an opinion column for the local newspaper. And by all means, don't be preachy in *your* carefully arranged narrative that appears in between characters' dialogue, and if one of your fictional human creations coincidentally has your attitudes and opinions, make sure that he or she is not too preachy or boorish, too!

Give some credit to your readers' intelligence. They have minds of their own, and they are continuously perceptively hypothesizing, evaluating and deducting conclusions as your story progresses and evolves. You don't have to tell them everything and explain every little detail. Leave some things open for their hungry imaginations to ponder. Don't over-describe and "overwrite," although this suggestion

231

is easy to give but hard to employ. Your reader will genuinely respect you and your story if you reasonably stay within those particular guidelines.

Finally, this last advice is the hardest part of all. Once you have finished writing your fantastic masterpiece, do not run to the post office and send it off to a publisher. Remove yourself (your emotions and your heart) from your work for at least one month. Distance yourself from your marvelous product. Harness your wonderful enthusiasm pertaining to your great contribution to American and World literature. Writing is an art, and that's where the "talent" part is exhibited. But an axiom to remember is that patience and prudence are paramount parts of being "talented."

At last, you are en-route. You're now seriously involved in making the art of writing into a "science." And only when there is a true marriage between *art* and *science* that then your work is ready for public presentation and consumption (if you want to distinguish yourself from the 97% of the writers that are comparable to crabs in a bushel, crawling over each other desperately and frantically trying to get out of their mediocre enclosure).

Confidently show self-control and put your *manuscript* on your closet shelf. After a full month, take it down and read it again from stem to stern. Now you are better able to evaluate your work, your errors, and your inadvertent departures from good novel writing methods (that should now stick out like ugly poisonous thorns throughout your comprehensively prepared work). You can now be more *objective* in doing your final *revision,* which should be a "new vision" of your work as you proudly steer your stellar literary contribution onward toward perfection and deftly bring your writing ship into port. After *that* very necessary procedure is enacted and accomplished, it is finally time to launch your splendid masterpiece into the literary universe.

"Journalism Versus Creativity"

On January 1, 2002 I had finally finished authoring my fiction book, which is titled *The Great Teen* Fruit *War, A 1960' Novel*. The work was quite a Promethean task to complete, having 162,000 words organized on 468 pages presented in 46 Chapters. When I read my final draft, I think I felt a little like Victor Frankenstein must have when he first fully viewed the monster that *he* had *created*.

The Great Teen Fruit War is set in 1960 Hammonton, New Jersey and involves conflict between the Blues, the sons of wealthy blueberry farmers and the Reds, the sons of peach farmers (please remember, a novel is *fiction*). The Blues are the antagonists and the gang members wear button-down blue denim jackets and the Reds are the naughty protagonists and wear zip-up red James Dean jackets like those worn by the famous actor in the 1955 classic film, *Rebel without a Cause*. The *Great Teen Fruit War* is the sequel to *Black Leather and Blue Denim, A '50s Novel*. A third book *Frat' Brats, A '60s Novel* completes the coming-of-age trilogy.

In *The Great Teen Fruit War*, Bellevue Avenue in the center of Hammonton is the dividing line between blueberry country to the east and peach territory to the west. To spice up the story, the Reds have one "antagonist" in their gang named Ronald "Goose" Restuccio, the son of a Mafia kingpin. Complicating matters even further is a third gang, The Ramrodders, a group of greasers that occasionally violently interact with the Reds and the Blues.

Now here's the essential difference between fiction and non-fiction. *The Fruit War's* setting is real but the story and the characters are not. Most of the "characters" are composite, a combination of two or more people I have known from my teenage past. I have taken personality elements from these past acquaintances and *synthesized* each of them into a new person just like Victor Frankenstein had done with *his* formidable monster.

In all due respect to Gabe Donio and Gina Rullo of the *Hammonton Gazette* and to Ben Meritt and Susan Leiser of the *Hammonton News,* front-page journalism or standard news reporting is relatively easy. Journalism is basically accurate descriptive narrative writing that involves responding to the rudimentary questions: *Who? What? When? Where? Why? How*? And then the typical newspaper article provides a few direct quotes and a first paragraph *hook* that seamlessly captures the reader's attention.

Now Gabe Donio, Gina Rullo Ben Meritt and Susan Leiser take *the Hammonton Gazette* and the *Hammonton News* to higher levels of thinking when they *write* the Editorial Pages, because now we have opinion based on fact, which involves (mentally relating) the thought processes of interpretation, analysis, problem solving and controversy. Those elements are "higher level thinking skills" existing above front-page reporting and description of events. On the "Editorial Pages" some local citizens might become incensed because they didn't exactly savor the way certain facts have been interpreted, analyzed or problem solved so they contribute their own letters-to-the-editor to explain *their* positions on certain disputed issues of town interest.

However, on the "Editorial Pages" Gabe and Gina and Ben and Susan are still honoring their oath to good journalism by basing their judgments, deductions and conclusions on *fact,* even if in the meantime they adroitly employ persuasive writing techniques.

Both short story and novel writing use facts as their basis also, but then the author deviates from factual writing (journalism, biography, etc.) when the *writer creates* imaginary characters, plots, situations, subplots, themes and conflicts. Novel writing requires the highest forms of thinking skills, a continuous combination of *creativity* and *synthesis.*

It is always easier to borrow than to invent. Most authors know this essential truth very well. It is hard to be absolutely creative where everything in *your* book is original and invented. And so, most *authors* depend heavily upon "reactionary creativity," combining personalities we have known into a new protagonist or new antagonist or taking ordinary objects and attributing to them extraordinary functions.

For example, in *The Great Teen Fruit War* the Reds had a mammoth problem. They had stolen seven hundred fifty thousand dollars from a Blues' father and had to dispose of the cash in a hurry. Waaa-la! They break into Bruni's Pizzeria, put the cash inside one of the ovens, set the temperature to five hundred degrees and then hastily evacuated the premises. The author had once read Ray Bradbury's *Fahrenheit 451* and knew that books (paper) burn at 451 degrees, and naturally, the paper money would disintegrate overnight at a 500 degrees temperature. "Reactionary creativity" had been effectively and logically scientifically employed.

In another scenario, the diabolical Blues capture two Reds and vertically attach the dual victims' crucifixion-style to the Fairview Avenue railroad crossing gates. When a train zips by, the gates are lowered with the two peach-gang kids still attached. Whether or not this is possible in terms of physics or mathematics is unknown by the

234

author (or most of his readers). However, it is another example of taking familiar ordinary objects (railroad crossing gates) and ascribing a different function to them, or what I call "reactionary creativity."

In another *Fruit War* chapter called "The Scavenger Hunt," two teams of Reds and Blues must visit fifteen places in 1960 Hammonton and vicinity. Greenmount and Oak Grove Cemeteries, the giant Renault Champagne bottle on *Route 30* in Elm, the Sons of Italy on 3rd Street and Angelo's Store in Rosedale (among other local places) must be visited in a competition to obtain certain information from inscriptions and signs. The data retrieved must then be deciphered to solve a riddle encrypted inside the correct information that had been gleaned during the scavenger hunt contest.

In conclusion to this brief writing seminar, I believe that *writers* pursue non-fiction and that *authors* write fiction, but in the final analysis that is worth repeating, good fiction must read like it's non-fiction and good non-fiction must read like it's fiction. And oh yes, life often does seem quite ambivalent!

"Dickens, Thurber, Andersen and London"

As far back as I can remember my mind has always thought and learned by association. My brain fancifully connects things like computer terminals and bus terminals, Indian reservations with plane ticket confirmations, and carpetbaggers with ruthless rug stealers. Don't ask me why, but I think I get bored with ordinary human communications and then out of sheer depression lapse into my imaginary fantasy association world, finding *that* mental paradise much more fascinating than the nightly news, soap operas and talking head yakety-yak cable tabloid shows.

Because my cerebrum delights in working by making bizarre associations, whenever my mind thinks of Charles Dickens, the great English author is filed and classified in a "mental cabinet" along with James Thurber, Hans Christian Andersen, Jack London and surprisingly, the mythical ancient Greek hero, Perseus, all of whom had to give somebody "the dickens" at one point in their lives. All of those marvelous personages had to also overcome obstacles, challenges, trials, tribulations and adversity. They elevated themselves above grief and ridicule, stayed focused on their goals and in their individual lives and exploits were not defeated by an abundance of public criticism and rejection. I admire each of them because all five were *motivated by failure.*

Charles Dickens' (1812-1870) father had great financial difficulties. The boy had a rather miserable childhood and the lad spent much of his time in cheerless poorhouses and workhouses. Did poverty overwhelm Charles Dickens? Was his cruel negative environment to blame for an unproductive and fruitless life? No it wasn't. Dickens retreated into his secret imaginary world and incisively wrote about the need for social reform in what later became such immortal literary classics as *Oliver Twist* and *David Copperfield.*

James Thurber (1894-1961) ranks as one of America's most popular humorists. The author is most renowned for his classic short story "The Secret Life of Walter Mitty," who was a meek absent-minded hen-pecked character who daily suffered the sharp-tongued ire of a dominant bossy wife. Thurber's hilarious stories and self-drawn cartoons appeared for over thirty years in the reputable classy *New Yorker* magazine. James Thurber had been blinded in one eye in a childhood accident and then he unfortunately lost vision in his other eye in later life. Despite those difficult and encumbering hardships, the determined author still continued his unique storytelling pursuits and he even appeared late in life as himself in a popular Broadway play *The Thurber Carnival.*

Hans Christian Andersen (1805-1875) was born in a small fishing village in Denmark. (If a last name ends in *sen*, the person is probably from Denmark; in *son*, probably from Sweden). At age fourteen Andersen journeyed to Copenhagen to diligently pursue either an acting' or writing career. Hans auditioned as an opera singer, was a humiliating failure and spent the next three years anguishing in abject poverty. Much to his utter disenchantment his first plays and novels received little acclaim. Was Hans Christian Andersen soundly defeated by rejection? If he had been, *poor* Hans Christian and his delightful fairy tales would have remained wallowing in obscurity, his literary work undiscovered, his reputation hiding in the giant anonymous void that history so aptly calls "the masses."

Jack London (1876-1916) has to be one of my favorite authors in American literature. He certainly is a source of inspiration whenever I feel depressed. London was born into grim poverty, had little formal education, and was definitely heading toward a criminal life. As a teenager he was an oyster pirate on San Francisco Bay and spent several years roaming the city as a hobo. But Jack London loved going to the library and reading books, so much so that he decided to endure what he had possibly hated most, formal education. Consequently, Jack became a "student of life." London managed to finish high school and then eventually enrolled into the *University of California.*

I admire men such as Charles Dickens, James Thurber, Hans Christian Andersen and Jack London. I find inspiration in considering the fact that formidable negative social and economic environments had not overcome the spirit of any of the four great authors. Each man elevated himself above mediocrity through sheer determination and tenacity. Failures and handicaps made them tougher, more resilient and more adamant about achieving success. They didn't blame society for the bad cards they had been dealt. These great authors were motivated at being shunned by the literary establishment. The stellar writers refused to be mere products of their environments. Instead the admirable men' transcended adversity by having faith in their dreams and then being able to subsequently define themselves, find a reading audience and ultimately shape *their* environments.

Now, how do I *associate* the mythical Greek hero Perseus with Charles Dickens, James Thurber, Hans Christian Andersen and Jack London? Perseus had to overcome many obstacles in his pursuit of honor and glory. Kings and noblemen rejected his ambition. The hero was about to surrender to failure when the goddess Pallas Athene appeared to him and asked, "Perseus, which would you prefer to have, a soul of clay or a soul of fire?" Obviously, Perseus answered a "soul of fire." Translated, this awesome statement means that the hero intensely wanted to distinguish himself from the faceless masses, all of whom possessed souls of clay.

This exceptional quality is what Perseus has in common with Charles Dickens, James Thurber, Hans Christian Andersen and Jack London. Success wasn't given to them; they earned it by defeating challenges that only temporarily obstructed their achievements. They all realized how ephemeral human existence is and that every second counts. They made the most of their lives by seizing opportunity the moment it came their way, and when it didn't come their way, their industry, their' perseverance and their inner strength compelled them to create opportunity. The five would not accept *"no"* for an answer from anyone. Each man opened his own window of opportunity. Those great "heroes" of mine transcended the bitter sarcasm, the banality and the castigation that surrounded them. They refused to go through life satisfied being sheepish men having *souls of clay*. The four champions of literature (like Perseus) aptly demonstrated to the cynical world that they possessed "souls of fire."

"Riding the Cape May-Lewes Ferry"

I remember taking ferries across bodies of water when I was a mere toddler. Before the *Delaware Memorial Bridge* (originally one span) opened for business in 1951, a small fleet of ferryboats shuttled cars, buses, tractor-trailers and foot passengers back and forth between Pennsville, New Jersey and New Castle, Delaware. As a young teen newspaper boy delivering the *Philadelphia Bulletin* in Levittown, Pa., I had won a subscription contest that entitled me to a free trip on a passenger ferry down the *Delaware* from Philly' to Riverview Amusement Park, Pennsville. So ferry transportation was a quite common experience for kids growing up along the eastern seaboard in the 1950s.

Between the exciting years 1967-'81 I had co-owned boardwalk businesses in Ocean City, Maryland, Rehoboth Beach, Delaware and Atlantic City, New Jersey. I was like a veritable jackrabbit each year from weekends in May right through October jumping up and down the east coast between the three popular resort cities. The highlight of each trip was the seventeen-mile ferryboat-cruise across *Delaware Bay* from Cape May (New Jersey) to Lewes, Delaware. I estimate that I had taken the excursion at least six hundred times between '67 and '81, transporting merchandise, tee shirts, arcade prizes and finally loose (non-carton) stuffed animals between my home's garage and cellar in Hammonton, New Jersey and the three summer resort destinations.

The price of the crossing was quite cheap back then. I recollect spending a mere five dollars to cross the bay with a car-full of merchandise (today the expense is twenty dollars from April-October for just the driver and car). I recall that fellow ferry passengers would request buying stuffed animals from me and I would politely refuse, telling them that "the plush" (boardwalk/carnival slang) happened to be arcade prizes that had to be won and not purchased. I would jam as many ferry furry creatures inside my Pontiac station wagon as I could. And when curious ferry riders would gawk at all of the bears, giraffes, cats, dogs and elephants crammed inside my vehicle, I would yell up to them on the main deck, "Now you know why they call these things stuffed animals!" That silly comment would always elicit a chuckle or two.

I would always leave Hammonton at six a.m. and have sufficient time to board the Cape May-Lewes Ferry for a seven-thirty departure. I enjoyed many bacon and eggs' breakfasts on the boat during the hour and fifteen-minute leisure bay crossing. My memory recalls that one foggy morning in late September the captain made an error in judgment and the almost empty ferryboat wound-up on the wrong side of the jetty on the Delaware side. We were nearer to Cape Henlopen than to Lewes, and the general contemplation my fertile mind imagined was me' being a hostage on a mysterious lost ghost ship adrift at sea.

Occasionally I would encounter certain Hammonton area people on their' way south for business or for vacation. One time I struck up a conversation with Egg Harbor City undertaker Larry Winberg (who had attended St. Joseph High with my wife). The mortician was on his way to Delaware to pick up the corpse of a new client, and another time in June I met and conversed with Mike Palmieri, owner of the Farmers Daughter Market. The farm market proprietor was going south to the Delmarva Peninsula to procure a load of early season cantaloupes.

Sometimes my being a conscientious person wickedly backfires. One busy Friday just before *Memorial Day* I stopped at a Hammonton (New Jersey) bank to deposit my wife's and my teaching checks. I had my green station wagon loaded to the gills with prizes and my wife was reluctantly accompanying me down to Ocean City, Maryland. I thought that one of my back tires was low so en route toward the shore I pulled over on the *Garden State Parkway* just before Cape May. Hammonton's Richard and Teresa Lanza (blueberry farmers) pulled over and asked if my wife and I needed help. I thanked them for their good intentions, saying that the slightly deflated tire would be "all right."

When Joanne and I arrived at the Cape May Ferry Terminal the Lanzas were the last car able to squeeze aboard the final boat to Delaware. As a result, I had to drive the entire distance across New Jersey to the *Delaware Memorial Bridge* and then down the Delmarva Peninsula to Ocean City, Maryland. An ordinarily three and a half-hour trip had suddenly transformed into an extended nine-hour nightmare.

I was in Hammonton one 16th of July. I needed to buy a new portable TV for my apartment in Ocean City, Maryland. I remember being under duress trying to get around the crowded Hammonton streets during a local town religious festival/procession and to make it to Colonial Electric. Louis Valenti sold me a set, which could just squeeze onto the already packed front seat. Driving down Twelfth Street, I ran over a board that had protruding nails. Ten minutes later I felt my steering wheel wobbling so I drove into the Frank Farley Rest

Area on the *Atlantic City Expressway* and filled-up the left front tire. The same thing happened near Pleasantville, where I exited the crowded *Expressway* and repeated the inflation procedure at a local gas station. I filled the tire twice more, once on the *Garden State Parkway* and finally again on the outskirts of Cape May.

When I finally arrived at the Cape May Ferry toll-booth I turned up the volume on the car radio and paid the collector the exact amount so that she could not hear the air sizzling out of my left front tire. Then my green station wagon boarded the boat. I sat in my vehicle until the tire went flat, stepped upstairs and had lunch, and when the ferry was in the middle of the seventeen-mile-long bay crossing, I confidently reported my "newly discovered dilemma" to the captain.

After the boat docked in Lewes two burly ferry employees came to my assistance by inflating my maligned front tire, injecting it with tire-sealant. I departed the vessel much relieved and safely made it to Ocean City, Maryland without incident, and to this day, I still occasionally laugh to myself every time I think about how I had made my very aggravating flat-tire nightmare the instantaneous problem of the Cape May-Lewes Ferry personnel.

"The Columbine-Type Student"

Don't "kid" yourself. There's trouble in paradise that escapes the vision of folks wearing rose-colored glasses. I'm not a contemporary Chicken Little recklessly running around screaming, "The sky is falling! The sky is falling!" And I'm not a facetious little boy crying out "Wolf!"

I am a former English teacher with thirty-four years classroom experience. I've taught through wars, recessions, political assassinations, disco music and public anti-war protests. I've seen and broken-up hundreds of bloody "student" fights. I've been threatened by enraged "students" and by their irate "parents." Been there; done that!

Columbine-type "students" attend most high and middle schools across the country. They attend Hammonton High, Hammonton Middle, Winslow Township High, Oakcrest, Palm Springs and even Beverly Hills High. They might not always wear trench coats and carry concealed guns and grenades. But the Columbine "student" mindset is definitely present and ubiquitous across America.

These troubled Columbine-type youths (many of them Goths and Satanic disciples) are scarier than the obnoxious wise guys that daily defy teacher authority and these often reticent loners are more frightening than the "student" bullies that terrorize weaker peers and start brawls in the school cafeteria or in the crowded hallways. The tacit behavior of Columbine-like *students* makes *them* a formidable challenge to school authority.

Sure, high schools have "peer mediation." The basic problem is that these "Columbine-like" *students* don't want to communicate with representatives of standard academic school society. The sinister-minded teens often don't even communicate with each other. That's what makes these stealthy mavericks walking and sitting time bombs ready to detonate. They prefer having an insular existence that does not want to be disturbed. They don't express themselves or their emotions until it's too late.

The "Columbine student mentality" has a certain behavioral "profile." That's right all you politically correct critics out there, I emphatically stated the improper word "profile." The kids say little or utter nothing at all. They keep their feelings and thoughts mainly to themselves while sitting in their desks, often seething beneath cool external façades.

Columbine-type kids seldom participate in classroom discussions or volunteer to do constructive things in school. To them, activities like athletics, school clubs and achievement awards are not worth pursuing. Their rebellion is silent, furtive, cold, cunning and calculated. Their ongoing rage is adroitly camouflaged; they could erupt and explode without warning at any minute. These kids, probably around five percent of any middle or high school's student body, are individual sticks of dynamite ready to be lit. Not even the *students'* guidance counselors have any psychological handle on what these wily emotionally disturbed youths are thinking, feeling, believing or plotting.

The Columbine-type kid often feels picked-on, hostile, frustrated, alienated and persecuted. Bigger, tougher teens, maybe football jocks, track stars or biker-type kids take pleasure in badgering physically weaker "students." Sooner or later there comes the straw that ruptures the camel's spinal cord. That's the dreadful kindling point where resentment and despair instantly transform into horrifying tragedy. Columbine-type kids don't relish their lowly perch in the school pecking order and suddenly reach the Popeye syndrome, "That's all I can stands, I can't stands no more!"

Columbine-type kids *covertly* perceive weapons as equalizers that could quickly neutralize and extinguish the *overt* power exhibited by peer bullies. In *his* and *her* cerebral dynamics, the Columbine-like "student" *needs* to empower himself or herself to stand-up to insensitive, arrogant peer adversaries. A gun or a knife could easily accomplish that objective and instantaneously narrow the power gap.

Parents should discourage bullying, especially in this treacherous and unpredictable day and age. The perpetual school hazing all-too-frequently results in lethal situations. Bullies have got to learn that a weakling's concealed gun could discharge bullets that travel a lot faster than fists do. This is the risk that a bully now faces when he or she antagonizes a Columbine-type kid; dishing out humiliation might literally trigger *your* own elimination.

Columbine-type "students" are often *lone wolves*. The disturbed kids don't like themselves, don't like school, don't like *normal* kids, don't like normal activities and certainly don't like authority figures like teachers and policemen giving them directions or making demands that seem contrary to their wills. When their fuses reach their ignition point, the disenfranchised youth's radical solution to his/her torment is to blow up the school and send everybody (or as many as possible) to the Eternity Hotel. That *statement* is their quick and violent answer to the emotional anguish that they perpetually silently feel.

I recall a particular eighth grade *student* I had taught in the early 1980s. I remember walking up and down the aisles of Room 103 of the Hammonton Middle School while closely monitoring an English literature silent reading activity. I looked down and detected a bulge underneath the *student's* lightweight jacket. Beneath the jacket was a vest, and under the vest my eyes glimpsed a holster with a gun nestled inside. 'I have to do something in a hurry!' I nervously thought. 'This is serious business!'

I bent over and quietly told the "student" that one of the office secretaries wanted to give him a message. I didn't say "principal" or "assistant principal" because those designations might have transformed the "student's" mental condition into a panic-state.

While the class was still working on the silent reading task, I gingerly escorted the "student" out the back-classroom door and then across the hall to the Main Office. Hastily I reached inside his jacket and grabbed under his vest, roughly removing the gun in a short scuffle. Then I wildly tossed the object onto the office counter (not thinking that it might discharge). The very surprised office secretaries gasped in shock and horror.

"Don't worry, it's only a toy," the embarrassed and surprised "student" apologetically remarked.

Upon closer inspection the gun was indeed a toy but its barrel was made out of metal and the thing had an authentic-looking wooden handle. The false pistol looked and felt like the real McCoy.

The "student" was suspended for his bad decision of bringing the object to school. I believe that this is where our schools and our "educational psychology" fail us. Punishments for flagrant violations are too lenient and too moderate. Events like fighting and taking weapons to school should be handled as if they were "felonies." Police should be called in, charges presented, and the "student" or "students" ought to be removed permanently from the normal middle and high school and sent to alternative schools. Students' criminal activity within the school should not be diminished as if they had been mere minor misbehaviors.

When boards of education have the courage to stand up for what's right and when administrators finally have the guts to state to "students" that schools are sanctuaries of learning where policy does not tolerate fighting or weapons under penalty of expulsion (and not suspension), and until those things happen, the status quo will remain the rule. Fights and weapons will continue to flourish in public schools as long as administrators treat the events as "business as usual discipline problems." Fighting and weapons should not be dispensed with as if they are normal everyday occurrences, but that's exactly how they are addressed and treated.

The eighth grade "student" vehemently protested to the principal about the rough treatment he had received because I had assertively disarmed the toy gun from his possession in the main office. The "in-denial transfer of blame" lad complained to the school administrator that I had "manhandled" him. Fortunately, the school authorities placed no credence in *his* contrived grievances. But nevertheless, I had nearly suffered a coronary over the very tense "false alarm."

The eighth grader had brought the toy gun to school for the expressed purpose of impressing other students that he could be a threat to bigger kids that would daily harass him. His scheme was that he would scare them off in front of witnesses (and gain prestige among his peers) with his fake pistol, empowering himself before his classmates. That nerve-racking event I have just described transpired over twenty years ago.

The principal difference between now and two decades ago is that "the gun" would probably be real and loaded in 2008. So you see, the Columbine-student mentality really existed in my school over twenty years ago.

Whoever says that middle and high schools don't need policemen patrolling the corridors, the bathrooms and the cafeteria has never had to disarm a "student," break-up a difficult combat between several two-hundred-pound *children* or take control of a dangerous school hostage situation in a hurry (without any police training). In my teaching career (34 years) I had broken-up over two hundred and fifty student altercations.

The school population has to be protected from these Columbine-type kids and these Columbine-type kids have to be protected from themselves and from each other. Teachers and students must be safeguarded from whatever covert turmoil is swirling around within *their* confused adolescent fantasy-oriented minds. The general safety and welfare of the school population should always be our top priority.

The Columbine-type student is "out there" right now in every American community but when he or she attends school with your son, daughter, nephew or niece, the "student" is "in there."

Disclaimer: The author realizes that the majority of the students who attend (or attended) Columbine High School are good kids. Unfortunately, the terrible incident that had occurred at that institution has led to the media's usage of the stereotypical term "Columbine-type student." The author does not intend to disparage the school's fine faculty and student body in this article. The author recognizes that Columbine High School has always been an excellent educational place of learning. I believe that everyone reading this article should feel the same way. As usual the reputations of the majority suffer because of the random irresponsible actions of a minority.

"Fighting in School Should Not Be Tolerated"

The sacred Teachers Handbook states in regard to *student* discipline: "Since the success of a *democratic* nation relies on the ability of its citizens to exercise self-discipline, it is the purpose of the school to teach *boys and girls* our main objective, which is the philosophy of self-control." Everything looks good on paper where *democratic* education in the comprehensive school is concerned, but a tremendous *Grand Canyon* exists between educational theory and everyday public-school reality.

A core of seventy-five to a hundred nasty *students* are continuously disrupting the smooth operation of the average sized middle or high school and also suckering good kids into altercations and committing uncivilized behavior through peer pressure, intimidation, extortion and other sinister tactics. Those hundred young barbarians are as *self-disciplined* as a colony of wild baboons. Educational psychology, the law and ultra-liberal *democracy* in a comprehensive school protect those seventy-five to a hundred terrorists from much needed reprimand and police intervention.

The public schools are often dumping grounds for recalcitrant *students* that have been *expelled* from parochial schools and from private schools. The hands of school officials and teachers are tied when dealing with the "comes with the territory" riffraff so the standard approach is to tolerate their antics and attempt to rehabilitate them by being especially nice to the young thugs.

And then inequality in punishment when it is meted out in small community schools is a daily practice. Given the same offense the son of the village drunk is more likely to be suspended than the son of a prominent citizen is. The internal problems inside schools are often concealed, whitewashed and squashed while only the good tidings filter out into the newspapers. The only time bad news is published is when police reports are organized and available to journalists, so *that* is precisely why school public-relations-minded administrators are reluctant to call in the local cops.

I remember one year when I was teaching at the high school that one of the boys' lavatories was virtually demolished. The crime scene looked almost as bad as San Francisco after the great earthquake of 1906. Ceiling panels were reduced to what looked like shredded wheat, sinks had been yanked out of the wall and cherry bombs had rocked the commodes from their anchoring. The story of the vandalism had circulated around the community but since the police were not called in the destruction was only a rumor to the common taxpayer. Administrators want only the superlatives leaking out to the public and the chance of the total school picture being accurately portrayed in the mass media is very slim indeed.

I want to emphasize that I had taught in what is regarded as a model school district so I can't imagine what's going on in urban schools or in schools with bad reputations for violence and vandalism. One thing is for sure and that is fighting in any public high school with a *student* population of a thousand or more teenagers is as certain as death and taxes. But administrators regard student fighting as "business as usual" when the local police ought to be notified and come into the building and arrest the brawlers with assault charges being issued against the main perpetrator.

I once had the displeasure of intervening in a juicy brawl in the C-Wing corridor while I was on my way to cafeteria duty. One fairly large *student* had another in a headlock with his left arm while the lad's right fist was riveting off the other *child's* head and face like a jackhammer destroying an ancient sidewalk. The recipient of the brutal blows' cheeks looked like crushed hamburger meat with a thick layer of ketchup squirted on.

I used the ice hockey official's approach and waited thirty more seconds until the *student* that was hammering away finally became a degree fatigued. After I separated the combatants I sent the bloodstained victim to the nurse's office for medical attention and then escorted the aggressor down to the main office where I had to write out Discipline Referral Cards on two antagonistic *students* I didn't even know.

That afternoon I encountered the principal in the main corridor. "Just look at these bloodstains splattered all over my sport coat from breaking up that vicious brawl this morning!" I complained. "Do you think that the board of education would defray the cleaner's expenses if I submit a voucher?"

"That's okay Mr. Wiessner," the principal jokingly responded. "The red stains almost blend right-in with the cranberry colored jacket you're wearing."

At that particular moment I vowed to my conscience that I would disappear into the woodwork the next time I would observe a *student* fracas erupting. "That's just great!" I answered the high school administrator. "Tomorrow I definitely will be wearing my green leisure suit with no tie!"

A teacher might suspect that a *student* involved in a bloody altercation might be on drugs or maybe on alcohol. One time back in the mid-'70s three eighth graders arrived at my homeroom hung-over from a wedding reception they had attended the night before. I dispatched the trio down to the nurse's office for medical exams' and verification of my theory. The nurse (under administrative suggestion) diplomatically had the boys sent home for "headaches" and for "feeling ill," thus averting adverse publicity in the newspapers.

If certain *students* are on drugs (illegal or prescription), it is more difficult to prove than when they have imbibed alcohol. Hazy eyes might suggest narcotics usage and the teacher is reluctant to report evidence of drowsiness, hyperactivity, depression or nervous twitching to the nurse because many *students* show those same symptoms normally every day.

If a teacher is daring enough to send a *student* to the nurse on suspicion of drug usage, and if the instructor's observations prove to be false then the possibility remains that a lethal libel suit might result claiming that the *child's* integrity had been maligned by a false allegation. The lawsuit might be filed against the teacher by the parents if the instructor had written a descriptive note to the nurse. That innocent teacher memo' could be used by the plaintiff's attorney as evidence against the instructor'.

Once in the early '80s (after an intense home high school football game with a cross-town rival) one of the more eminent *students* was screaming a collection of assorted profanities at the opposing team's players. An assistant coach on the home team yelled over to the *child* making the grotesque linguistics to stop in the interest of good sportsmanship.

The dastardly *student* resented being rebuked by the assistant coach in front of his equally obnoxious cohorts. The belligerent *student* then defied the coach by verbally bombarding *him* with a flurry of obscene idioms that are seldom heard in monasteries and convents. In seconds the assistant coach and the vile instigator wound-up on the ground hostilely flailing away at each other and thrashing around.

Coaches and players finally separated the two combatants. The *student's* eyes were rolling around like cherries and lemons in a slot machine's windows. The teachers on the faculty had long suspected for quite some time that the abusive *student* had been experimenting with drugs, but since his father was always quick to defend his son's bad deportment, no one was going to ever accuse the teenager of narcotics usage and then have to defend that daring position in court.

Daily cafeteria duty was without a doubt my greatest headache. Most high school teachers would prefer being trapped in an endless maze having a multitude of cul-de-sacs rather than being exposed to the cruel and unusual punishment known as the cafeteria. Just imagine two hundred and fifty howling adolescents bending spoons into goose eggs, tossing macaroni and *Jell-o* at each other and deliberately making messes to upset the teachers on duty. The poor head teacher's incantations over the microphone are ignored because the PA system is weak', the acoustics are bad and the microphone works every other time. Yet the teachers are responsible for an orderly dismissal.

I found that the best way to patrol the cafeteria was to revolve around the perimeter with my back to the walls facing the *students* at all times. When I was courageous enough to patrol the aisles between cloistered tables, then I constituted a convenient moving target for flying debris and miscellaneous (*missile*aneous) food chunks hurtling from behind toward my head and my back.

Sometimes my wife claimed she could tell the school menu that day by inspecting my sport jacket's fabric. She saw and identified pea smears, string bean stains and carrot splotches on different occasions that had added a new exquisite design to my school attire.

The cafeteria is a mass situation where fights are most likely to flare-up in a hurry. In 1971 before John Rizzotte and I could stave off a *student* altercation, one teenaged anarchist had hit the *student* sitting across the table with a sticky meat particle. The victim then escalated the stakes by picking-up a pickle slice and a handful of lemon meringue pie and hurled the food into the first *student's* face. The crusaders that were supposed to be good friends then leaped-up onto the cafeteria table and started flailing away. That was a hard fight for John Rizzotte, Tim Amoro and myself to break up because the brawlers were standing above us on the table. Tim Amoro wound-up with his glasses being crushed and a broken nose to boot.

Whenever a cafeteria fight is triggered a sudden dichotomy of *student* loyalties develops, and if the teachers aren't quick to intervene other *students* may enter the battle. A distinct occupational hazard indeed exists. The teachers have to focus their energies on immediately separating the first two junior (or maybe even senior) gladiators, yanking them down to the vice-principal's office and then dutifully returning right away to the "rectum of the school," its cafeteria.

In my younger days I used to be more aggressive in stopping lunchroom altercations but after being involved in over two hundred and fifty different *student* fisticuffs over a span of thirty-four years I gradually became less assertive. And if the *student* that I despised more was getting the worse of it on the bottom while being pummeled, then I would make sure I got to the fight scene a little slower than I ordinarily would have.

In my school district an effective cafeteria disciplinarian was usually awarded an asterisk next to his or her name on the cafeteria duty roster. The un-coveted star signified that the teacher with the asterisk was in charge of the cafeteria and responsible for keeping order during the raucous forty-five-minute lunch period.

The asterisk did not bring any additional monetary reward for being the official charge d' affaires. The only honor of being the possessor of the un-envied asterisk was having a defective microphone, of having a *student* audio-visual club (with the mechanical skills of the Marx Brothers) to repair the sound magnifier and the distinction of being abused daily by the merciless juvenile mob. The asterisk certainly didn't qualify me to be a certified boxing referee.

Usually the same teachers pulled cafeteria duty each year while the balance of the faculty members were assigned to easier study hall' situations. Several cafeteria-assigned teachers learned that when they had performed a mediocre job in the lunchroom they had been re-assigned to "easier to cope with" study hall duties the following school year.

Administrators and school board' members often contended that teachers can command respect from *students* in the cafeteria, whereas, cafeteria aides cannot. Teachers are saddled with the ugly duty because the public believes that certified instructors know how to manage *students* in mass situations.

The truth of the matter is that there is little transfer of *student* respect from the classroom to the school cafeteria. The same *students* that love a teacher in English might emulsify the instructor in the cafeteria. Teachers seldom have serious trouble with *children* in their classrooms but in the cafeteria sometimes even the good kids go sour or bonkers. Instructors are continually getting into hassles with *students* over who threw the napkin on the floor, who left the tray on the table or who' threw his or her silverware into the food garbage can. Teachers suddenly have to become police investigators.

Daily cafeteria duty is one of the best ways to ensure acid indigestion. And then when the *students* finally return to their classrooms after lunch, oftentimes they must face a strung-out exasperated teacher that had spent a very hectic forty-five-minute interval in the cafeteria dungeon. The emotions known as anger and frustration are not faucets that are easily turned off. A teacher must be careful to not carry his or her petulance from the lunchroom into the classroom. Several times I had overly admonished *students* in the classroom immediately after cafeteria duty and then had to contend with parent-initiated hostile conferences.

In the early '70s two brawny high school *students* were really hammering away at each other in the cafeteria. By the time John Rizzotte and I hustled to the battle scene boisterous *students* were shrieking and also scurrying to the battle to add an additional dash of pandemonium to the mounting crisis. John and I tried tugging the brawlers apart but they were interlocked in a clinch like two magnetized mastodons. By that time the cafeteria marathon fight scene sounded like a blend of the *Kentucky Derby's* homestretch and the climax to the Roman *Circus Maximus*. The teachers' inability to separate the grapplers added a dimension of slapstick comedy to the already exciting event.

The bigger *student* had the smaller one in a bear hug while the more diminutive *child* had his arms locked around the huskier kid's head and neck. I leaped upon the bigger kid and eventually managed to separate him from his opponent. The bigger *student* whirled around with the two-hundred-pound teacher attached to his back. I felt like I was a rodeo cowpuncher atop a berserk Brahma bull.

The larger *student* (with me on his back) re-entered the fight with the smaller *child,* who had broken away from John Rizzotte's grasp. Siamese twins would have been easier to separate than those two battlers were. The other two hundred and fifty maniac spectators were clamorously cheering the zany scene that was crazily transpiring before their eyes. Thank goodness a rescue squad of five male teachers zoomed into the cafeteria from the nearby teacher's lounge or John and I would have lost what represented the *main event* of the day for the thoroughly delighted *students.*

In another cafeteria period several enterprising *students* thought that they would evoke certain behavioral responses from the female teachers on duty. Two boys stripped the husk from a healthy-looking banana and in a gesture of inspiration they ingeniously stretched a prophylactic over the fruit, which was then placed perpen*dic*ularly on the lunch table for other *students* to *rubber*neck and admire. Perversions of that nature are designed to rattle or unnerve teachers, so the worst thing an instructor should do is act appalled. But if the bad cafeteria behavior is not handled properly, a heated argument between the teacher and the mischievous *students* might ensue and that's precisely what the *students* were attempting to instigate, an argument with a teacher over a stupid inappropriate behavior.

I took the wind out of the violators' sails by stating, "I didn't know that bananas were capable of contracting venereal diseases!" I had successfully stolen the boys' thunder and had reduced their queer impropriety to the level of "So what!" If one plans to last for thirty-four years in the educational field, minor occurrences like the banana/prophylactic incident should not ruffle a teacher's feathers.

Students' cutting into the cafeteria line could constitute a major daily challenge for lunchroom duty teachers. Many of today's *students* belong to a peculiar breed. Besides thinking that *Hamlet* is some sort of new breakfast sensation (like an omelette), many *children* adhere to advocating a unique relative morality where lying, cheating and stealing are acceptable modes of behavior. It might be easier to lasso a bucking bronco with a rubber band attached to a shoelace than to get the truth from an uncooperative *student*. Perhaps schools should teach more wisdom and less knowledge and more ethics and less irrelevant facts.

I remember noticing a husky lass slipping into an already formed cafeteria line. I thought that her action had been unfair to the other *students* so I told the young lady to have a seat and then get up to be served last. Although the girl heard my directive she acted as if I had been addressing her from a soundproof booth. I repeated my command more vigorously.

"Man, stop spittin' in my face!" she indignantly sneered at me.

"Sit down and then get in the back of the line!" I repeated.

"Fuck off bro'!" she snarled back, much to the amusement of her appreciative peers.

In the midst of a temper tantrum I told the cafeteria brunhildas not to serve the girl when she came through the line. The *student* defied my authority by grabbing a platter of food and putting it on her serving tray and then she promptly proceeded to the cashier. I notified the office. The vice-principal was tied up with another discipline problem so the principal cruised into the cafeteria.

I explained the situation and the chief school executive told the bellicose girl, "Bring the tray back to the cashier because you didn't pay her!" the principal diplomatically commanded.

The hysterical girl arose from her cafeteria seat and sauntered back to the serving line carrying her red tray. The perturbed principal followed the *student* into the serving area to ascertain that the girl would return her tray and then take a seat before moving to the back of the food line as I had directed.

A verbal exchange then ensued between the defiant *student* and the principal. The angry girl threw food particles from her tray that instantly ornamented the school official's haberdashery. The administrator reached to apprehend the disrespectful girl and she took a wild swipe at his face. The female violator zipped out of the cafeteria and fled to a place of hiding.

The principal notified the police and the girl was found seated in a telephone booth in the main corridor, holding the door shut while calling home for advice and counsel. The principal and two policemen attempted wedging the door open as the young lady kept it shut with one hand while talking on the phone with the other. I casually dismissed the craziness by thinking, 'Our' great American *democratic* educational system is for all the *children* and it is not just for the elite college-bound *students!*'

In the mid-80s a juicy fight had broken-out in the middle school cafetorium. Two boys were really doing damage to each other's faces. I separated the brawlers three times but then they continued their donnybrook. I became angry from the continuous fighting so I got the more aggressive *student,* flung him into the ice cream freezer, quickly put the lid on the refrigeration unit and then sat on top. The *student* inside was smashing the top from the frigid dark interior but could not move the covering with my body weight holding it down.

"Chill out!" I yelled to the trapped instigator inside the ice cream box.

A minute later I opened the freezer. Several dozen ice cream sandwiches and chocolate pops had been destroyed during the bizarre fiasco. Another teacher on cafeteria duty then escorted the cooled-off violator to the main office while I enjoyed eating one of the lesser crushed' chocolate covered ice cream pops.

Another time I was in after-school Office Detention with a seventh-grade *student* that had told one of his teachers to "Fuck off!" The *student* had to write a sincere letter to the teacher apologizing for his misdemeanor so I was kind enough to depart from Office Detention policy (as prescribed by the administration) and allow the *child* to write the theme under my jurisdiction.

At the end of the Office Detention session I commented to the *student,* "I'm glad you used your time constructively!"

"Blow me asshole!" he nastily responded.

Sometimes it just doesn't pay to say anything at all (polite or otherwise) to a nasty *student.* "What did you say?" I politely requested to know.

"I said 'Eat me raw asshole'!" the manner-less individual replied.

The *student* was given three additional days of Office Detention for using profanity directed toward a teacher. A week later the *student* got into a nice bloody fight in the cafeteria while I was on duty. I broke the boxers up twice but they still were going at it. The *student* that had used the obscene references in Office Detention again began swinging at his adversary.

In a fit of anger, I un-gently grabbed the aggressor and pushed him through the cafeteria doors. The *student* had been broken open with blood cascading down his face and cheeks from his forehead.

"Go to the nurse's office right now!" I bellowed to the *student* bleeding profusely on the corridor floor.

"Fuck you!" The upset *child* yelled back as he got up onto his feet. Before I could utter another word, the *child* darted out of the building, scurried across the avenue and entered the police department to cite me for corporal assault. Luckily the police chief returned the brawler to school jurisdiction, but I recently read in the newspapers of a similar episode in a Pennsylvania school where the police came to the school and then arrested the teacher for assaulting a *student*.

In another cafeteria fistfight involving two huge eight graders, I forcefully pushed the main aggressor against the closed entrance doors in an effort to separate the fierce combatants. The kid hit his head against the wooden frame and some blood was trickling-down from a cut on his forehead. I quickly instructed the pugnacious student (who incidentally loathed me because he was failing my English class) to immediately go to the nurse's office, after which I soon wrote-out a pass and then directed a better-behaved student to deliver the message to the nurse. The belligerent instigator, instead of going to the nurse, intentionally entered the downstairs bathroom and proceeded to repeatedly slam his head against a toilet stall, thus making his head bleed excessively. The insolent kid then stepped across the hall and told the nurse that I had caused the head wound during the brawl. However, the time of the pass I had written compared to the lad's appearance in the nurse's office was a five-minute lapse. A half-hour later the janitor discovered fresh blood stained upon the bathroom stall wall, and thus I was exonerated by the school administration from the frivolous accusation of beating-up the defiant student in the school cafeteria.

Fighting is not only limited to the cafeteria. Brawls erupt in the halls and in study halls too. A large study hall in the lunchroom can rival the treachery of cafeteria duty. On several occasions fistfights had broken out in the cafeteria study hall before I could arrive there' from my classroom on the other side of the building over three hundred feet away through crowded corridors.

I have had as many as a hundred and fifty *students* crammed into a cafeteria mass study hall and out of that number only about fifty of them were genuinely studying. Study halls in public schools are generally vast educational wastelands that operate on maybe a forty-percent efficiency level. Teachers are constantly taking attendance, moving talkative *students* to specially isolated seats and correcting those infidels that are determined to violate the sanctity of the forced silence the teachers are trying to maintain. And one time during a study hall fight I was punched twice in the back by a craven spectator while I was breaking-up the fracas.

A fight may erupt in the halls while a teacher is casually en route to his or her next class. In 1999 two eighth grade girls liking the same boy got into a real fingernail hair-pulling cat-fight. I was exiting the main office with a hundred and forty worksheets in my hand that I had just *Xeroxed*. A short substitute teacher was already on the scene trying to intervene in the fracas but he was taking as much of a beating as the two combatants were.

I dropped my papers on the corridor floor and assisted the substitute teacher in his grave enterprise. I yanked one of the girls off but she raised her feet and was savagely kicking away at the other cat-fighter. The *student* in my clutches then kicked the fire extinguisher attached to the wall and it tilted sideways, mixing its chemicals and then giving off a noxious spray. The corridor was immediately filled with choking *students* and the chemical vapors swirling in the air looked like a miniature atomic mushroom cloud. The vice-principal exited the office, lifted one of the combatants onto his right shoulder and carried her into the main office like Little Abner eloping with Daisy May on Sadie Hawkins Day.

I remember one instance where a school janitor attempted to break up a brawl between two pretty big *students* and the custodian wound-up in the hospital getting stitches and treatment for multiple lacerations for his benign intervention.

Finally, I recollect a really terrible girls' fight that had erupted outside on the asphalt playground between an eighth-grade *child* bully and a new seventh grade transfer *student*. When I arrived to the combat zone the two girls were really pummeling and mauling one another in what amounted to a vicious battle featuring wicked hair pulling and the violent scratching of faces and arms.

Charlie Southard (an affable math' teacher) and I separated the felines three times but the marathon battle ensued. It was one of the most difficult struggles I had ever dealt with and it took Charlie and me five full minutes to restore order among the shrieking *student* eyewitnesses.

Three weeks after that horrible ordeal Charlie Southard died from a massive heart attack. I have often wondered if there had been any

260

connection between the stress and strain of separating the two girls in that terrible fight and the passing away of my good friend and colleague.

I really still consider it a minor miracle that I had managed to survive in public school teaching for thirty-four years. *Student* fighting comes with the total teaching package and it has nothing at all to do with either teaching or with learning.

But today's school fights are not always one-on-one with fist against jaw combat. Honor (one-on-one fighting) is now often abandoned. The "wolf pack mentality" is presently pervading many urban schools and *students* are now employing the herd attack practice in rural high schools as well. Four *children* will now fight maybe six *students*. Sometimes a *student* will be knocked to the ground outside the building or to the floor inside the edifice and five or six members of the assaulting wolf pack will stomp and trounce the ribs and face of the unfortunate recipient of *their* collective hostility.

If a *student* fight happens first thing in the morning, it could set the tone for and ruin a teacher's entire day. Fortunately for the already encumbered instructors most days are more tranquil than those dates that are tainted with wall-to-wall *student* conflicts. On those chaotic mind-boggling days (usually before extended holidays like *Thanksgiving, Christmas* and *Easter*) public school teaching could seem like the *Wild, Wild West*.

* * * * * * * * * * * *

I firmly believe that all *students* between the ages of thirteen and eighteen should be required to spend six weeks of each summer vacation involved in community service in order to develop a spirit of commitment and responsibility so that adolescents could realize from experience that there's more to life than the all-too-prevalent "me-first" attitude that most egocentric teenagers of today assume and practice. A strong sense of purpose among juveniles could drastically reduce the number of *student* fights that currently take place. And administrators and boards of education should treat school fighting as serious assaults and batteries worthy of police investigation and not as business-as-usual events resulting in mere *student* detentions and suspensions.

Also, I think it would be beneficial to our great American society if each high school graduate be put on hold and have college (or work) delayed for two years so that every eighteen and nineteen-year-old could fulfill a societal contribution by either serving in the military or by assisting in their communities as voluntary helpers given assigned responsibilities and duties. Then perhaps our college dropout rates would be diminished when more mature, more disciplined and more ethically minded twenty-year-old freshman *students* enter those hallowed university halls to finally engage in serious academic pursuits.

"Starting an Internet Publishing Business"

On July 1st, 1999 I had retired from the Hammonton, New Jersey Public School District as a middle school English teacher after thirty-four years of dedicated service. I knew there would be an eight-hour Monday-through-Friday daily time-void in my life (until my wife would retire from public school education in 2005), so I decided to fill the vacuum by making my avocation (writing) my vocation. The task of becoming a successful *Internet* author was much more formidable than I had originally anticipated.

I had written and re-written two-dozen book-length manuscripts over the past three decades and knew I could get over two million words in print within several months. My naïve strategy was to blitz the *Internet* marketplace with my two-dozen e-books and cause a robust chemical reaction. 'People tend to be binge readers,' I thought, 'and if someone were to read one of my books, I figure *that* person would immediately desire to read another of my works.' Right? Wrong!

My first assumed task was to find a workable pen name. Samuel Langhorne Clemens used the pseudonym Mark Twain, William Sydney Porter was O. Henry, H.H. Monroe became Saki and Mary Ann Evans did pretty well using the name George Eliot because she was trying to be an author during a very chauvinistic male-dominated era. After several weeks of serious deliberation John Wiessner reckoned his pen name would be a corruption of his initials J.W., Jay Dubya.

You could imagine the elation I felt on Monday morning September 16, 2002 when I turned on my computer and first visited Amazon.com to see how my e-books were doing. My *Black Leather and Blue Denim, A '50s Novel* was Sales Ranked at #108 on Amazon.com out of over three million products in books, videos, toys, games, DVD's, CDs, software, music, electronics and kitchenware.

Then I excitedly visited Amazon.co.uk and found that *BL&BD* was Sales Ranked #438 in the United Kingdom and after visiting Amazon.co.de (Germany), my e-books *Pieces of Eight* and *Pieces of Eight, Part II* were Sales Ranked #67 and #68 respectively in Germany. My young adult fantasy trilogy of *Enchanta, Pot of Gold* and *Space Bugs, Earth Invasion* was beginning to move in Japan. On September 16, 2002 some of my e-books were competing very well with Harry Potter novels and most Britney Spears CDs and DVDs around the world. How had all of that come about? Believe me, it wasn't easy.

I had known from preliminary research that e-books were at the time selling fairly well on Amazon.com. The *Art of War* by Sun Tzu was for months one of the best-selling products on Amazon.com and it *was* an e-book. E-books by established writers associated with big New York City publishers were also highly ranked, and *Amazon Press* had re-published novels and novellas by famous authors in e-format and those works were also selling big. What I did not understand at the time was that e-books by *non-established* self-published writers like Jay Dubya were selling zip.

I enthusiastically signed on with three Australian, five American and two Canadian e-publishers. I had my e-books produced in Adobe Reader and Microsoft Reader downloading formats for desktop computers and in Mobipocket Universal Download for all hand-held computers. Expensive artwork for all twelve titles had to be done for *Internet* display, so already I'm out about a thousand dollars an e-book, or twenty-four thousand bucks without recouping a single penny.

I had eagerly e-published my books with cyberread.com, ebookmall.com, ebooksonthe.net, electricebookpublishing.com, ebooks-for-sale.com, ebookland.net, ozonebooks.com and ebookstand.com in Adobe Reader downloading format. Ebookstand.com also would produce Print-on-Demand paperback versions of my books. Pretty neat strategy? Well, not really! Sales were still zilch!

I then spent countless hours listing and describing my books in *Internet* directories such as ebooksnbytes, ebookpalace.com, authorsden.com, Hammonton High School Directory, Bookzone, Bravenet.com, ebookheaven.com, e-book directory and knowbetter.com. Most of these listings were free so I thought I was developing a good base. Jay Dubya and my book titles soon appeared on Yahoo, Google, AOL Search, MSN Search, Lycos and FAST, Netscape, Hot Bottom, Alta Vista, Ask Jeeves and All-the-Net search engines. I was happy but then I reluctantly realized that I still wasn't selling any books.

I published articles on writing at SFF.com, ebookpalace.com, Essay Depot and authorsden.com. This brought me certain recognition but I still was not selling any books. I was becoming mighty frustrated but I persisted and persevered. Google and Yahoo featured over 5,000 web pages for "Jay Dubya," but I still wasn't selling any books. It was as if I was functioning in a foreign reality, in another universe! I concluded it was futile being a free-lance author and going up against the omnipotent New York book publishing industry.

I sent out paperback review copies and obtained satisfactory book reviews from dreamwater.com, allreaders.com, storyweaver.com, Northwest Book Review and my hometown newspapers, but still I wasn't selling any e-books or paperbacks. All in all, I sent out over a hundred paperback review copies at an expense of over two thousand dollars (for I had to pay for each paperback copy), and I was on the edge of insanity when I noticed that no tangible results were occurring from all of my vigorous enthusiastic promotions. 'Perhaps I'm being a complete fool thinking that I can compete with the powerful traditional New York City book industry?' I again suspected and theorized. A hundred powerful publishers and five hundred influential book agents control the entire industry.

I quickly realized that I needed allies to help me sell my e-books on the *Internet*. I teamed up with ebookpalace.com, authorsden.com and ebookstand.com to promote my books. In the first six months, those three sites generated over fifty thousand hits for Jay Dubya, but out of fifty thousand *Internet* hits, I had sold less than a dozen books. 'What is wrong here?' I wondered.

The answer to my quandary was CREDIBILITY. Jay Dubya had *none* as an author. My big break came in February of 2003 when cyberread.com of Seattle, Washington bought ebookstand.com and then signed contracts for e-book distribution with Amazon.com, Borders, Barnes and Noble, Buy.com, Bookbooters (which has since gone out of business), Powell's Books, e-Novel (now out of business) and finally Books-A-Million. My e-books, (hardcovers produced by Lightning Source) and paperbacks (produced by bookstand.com) were now being displayed online in lists alongside famous authors whose books were in hardback, paperback, audiocassette and also e-book formats.

I believe I caught a real break when I self-reviewed my *Great Teen Fruit War, A 1960 Novel* at AllReaders.com. The web site will have the author fill out a long form describing characters, plots, subplots and settings, and it turned out that my novel was very similar in construction to a famous work of fiction, S.E. Hinton's *The Outsiders.* That development brought many more visitors to my various *Internet* sites, but I still wasn't selling any books.

A month later in March of '03 *Black Leather and Blue Denim* soared to 2,300 on Amazon.com after it was placed ALONGSIDE (for the keyword searches Black, Blue) the works of James Patterson (*Violets are Blue*) and Ian Rankin (*Black and Blue*). Amazon.com gave my two-dozen books parity and *instant credibility* on various web pages and after that happened, my chemical reaction strategy then started working. The public finally began perceiving me as being legitimate. I still can't believe that by typing in "Eight" at Amazon Germany will yield my *Pieces of Eight* and *Pieces of Eight, Part II* (at this moment) Sales Ranked ahead of *Hard Eight* by Janet Evanovich, which has been heavily promoted by a huge New York publisher.

E-books are quite alive and selling, and in some cases, they are outselling printed books. They are about one-fourth as expensive as hardbound copies, with my e-books selling from $4.95-$6.95. E-books save trees and are environmentally friendly. An electronic book is conveniently obtained because the product can be downloaded from the *Internet* in less than fifteen minutes. Also, the e-book print is large and can be adjusted in both Abobe Reader and Microsoft Reader digital encryption versions. But hardcover Print-on-Demand books are what really gave me credibility on various retail Internet sites.

In 2004 Cyberread.com (my principal publisher) signed a contract with Lightning Source to have authors' works produced in hard cover format on a Print-on-Demand basis. Of course, the author must finance each book for Print-on-Demand file setup, and now my books exist in five formats: hard cover (Lightning Source), paperback (ebookstand.com), and three e-book formats, Adobe Reader, Microsoft Reader and Mobipocket. The total cost for each book in five formats (along with ISBN numbers and *Internet* cover art display) averages around two thousand dollars for a hundred and fifty-page book' like *Enchanta* to twenty-eight hundred for a five-hundred page manuscript like my *So Ya' Wanna' Be A Teacher*.

The upside to book publishing is that I have a "Non-Exclusive" contract with cyberread, which means that I retain all of the subsidiary rights to my books and I have control over their intellectual content. The downside to e-book and Print-on-Demand publishing is that standard literary reviewers like the *New York Times* and *Publishers Weekly* will not review your book (or books) because those influential publications regard e-publishing as a form of "vanity publishing." And unfortunately, at the present time (2008), my books are exclusively sold over the *Internet* and are not sold in bookstores or distributed to libraries, even though Barnes and Noble and Books-A-Million sell my books on their *Internet* web sites they still don't carry my works in their brick and mortar retail stores.

In conclusion e-books and Print-on-Demand paperbacks and hard covers are a definite threat to the standard publishing industry. Up until recently a hundred big New York City publishers and about five hundred agents acted as a giant filter deciding what the general public should or should not read. E-books will eventually change all that "Big Apple Gatekeeper stuff' and swing power to the reading public, giving *the people* the right to decide what they want to read and what they don't want to read.

I desire to be a part of this e-book revolution. I want to be a pioneer helping to lead the e-book and Print-on-Demand industries into the twenty-first century publishing frontier. I don't think it's right that an author should receive only 7-10% of a retail book price and surrender his subsidiary rights to a print-publisher. I'm now partners with Amazon.com (and many other online retail outlets) and make 40-50% of retail e-book sales and approximately 20-25% of the hard cover sales price. And I still retain all rights to my books. But again on the ugly downside, my books are *not* presently sold in bookstores or distributed to standard libraries as "conventional" printed books are and also, I must do all of the promotion and most of the marketing myself.

Nothing gives me more satisfaction than to type in "Black and Blue" at Amazon.co.uk and seeing my *Black Leather and Blue Denim* novel often Sales Ranked above *Black and Blue* by Anna Quindlen, a book and author aggressively promoted by Oprah's Book Club. I did it on my own without any super-publishers or promoters helping me and if it weren't for the *Internet*, cyberread.com, Amazon.com and a bit of serendipity, my career as an author would have never blossomed. For example, all three of my Australian e-book publishers have gone out of business.

So contrary to popular opinion e-commerce is not dead. I think that within the next several years there will be a definite resurgence of .com mania and more and more people will be purchasing e-books and Print-on-Demand titles.

"American Education Is Wasteful"

I am not anti-patriotic. I am an educational realist who has taught English for thirty-four years in public schools. I know from personal experience that American "democratic" education is a costly wasteful inefficient enterprise.

Educational philosophers, bureaucratic administrators and school board members will proudly tell the public that our American educational system is "democratic," based on our noble form of citizen-oriented government prescribed by Thomas Jefferson. The inspiring rhetoric sounds mighty good, doesn't it? So good that it wastes billions of tax dollars each year in thousands of communities across the United States.

In most American middle and high schools, eighty percent of the "students" are good kids. It's that remaining twenty percent of the student body that causes massive community waste and excessive academic inefficiency. "Democratic" education ensures that "student rights" are protected by the Constitution. The twenty percent of the *student* population that instigates disruption inside most American middle and high schools knows all about their "rights" guaranteed by the First *Ten Amendments* to United States Constitution, but the bad feature is that *they* care little about the moral responsibilities associated with the *Ten Commandments*. U.S. law often undermines the enforcement of *student* moral behavior.

Take the Hammonton Middle School for example. There are now four hundred "students" attending the facility. A hundred of them are classified as "special needs students." Around seventy of the four hundred *students* aren't *students* at all! The designation' *students* is one that represents a false and misleading reference to describe these certain juvenile anarchists. They are disrupters, saboteurs and educational punks who daily use peer pressure to influence good kids to join their rebellion against teacher authority. Unfortunately, the good apples seldom cure the rotten ones inside the barrel, especially when the bad apples habitually intimidate the benign ones.

The middle school's disruptive twenty percent (some of whom *are* special needs "students") are placed (mainstreamed) in regular classrooms where their havoc is defended and guaranteed by the U.S. Constitution and by "American democratic public-school education." Victimized teachers must contend with these junior terrorists every day *they* attend school when *they* aren't playing hooky, suspended or sitting in the vice principal's waiting area not caring one iota about being "disciplined" for the twentieth time since school started in September.

Similar bands of seventy *students* exist in most large middle and high schools across suburban America and those disruptive teens are also perpetually instigating trouble, making a mockery out of school rules and teacher authority, terrorizing weaker good kids and causing general chaos throughout their buildings. These junior nihilists seldom or never do homework or participate in class discussions. Most of these *students* come to school to fool around, to harass other kids, to eat lunch, to aggravate teachers, to sucker good kids into fights, to steal personal property from others' lockers, to see what they could get away with, to deface property and to sell or buy drugs. And their rights are protected by "democratic public-school education." These difficult to deal with *students* need to know as much about their *wrongs* as they do about their *rights*.

Juvenile hooligans cost towns and boroughs across America billions of dollars annually in unnecessary expensive waste. Each undisciplined *student* (in New Jersey) costs around ten thousand dollars a year to *educate*. Multiply that number by seventy in the middle school and another seventy in the high school and the town of Hammonton squanders over a million dollars each year on *educating* apathetic disruptive *students*. Multiply that unsettling sum by the number of high schools and middle schools across America and you will be able to fully assess the problem's magnitude.

And so, each year it costs the town of Hammonton over a million dollars annually to have teachers baby sit, tolerate and discipline insolent and defiant *students* in regular classrooms. It would be wiser and easier for the local board of education to stuff a million dollars into a suitcase, label the luggage *Hammonton Public Schools* and then burn the loaded baggage.

And that's only the tip of the educational iceberg. When these arrogant *students* act up in class and defy teacher authority they must be corrected. If it requires five minutes of class time to discipline one unruly *student* and settle a class down, then multiply five minutes by the number of kids in the class. Probably over 140 minutes of academic time had been wasted on one incident. Over two hours of total student learning time has been lost and cannot ever be retrieved. Multiple that one classroom event' by the thousands of minor and hundreds of major discipline incidents that annually occur in the average public school and you will understand the enormity of the massive educational behavioral crisis.

The worst part of the public-school discipline scenario is that administrators expect teachers to accept disturbing erratic *student* misbehavior as part of *their* daily routine. Ironically *student* misbehavior is the major justification for school administration. If all students were respectful, serious about work, honest, courteous and sincere to their teachers, then school systems would not need administrators to "interview," to "interrogate" to "investigate," to "discipline" and to "suspend" unruly rule-breakers. Principals and vice-principals would not be needed. American schools could run perfectly well with just department chairmen and faculty members. Each district could simply have a superintendent to hire and manage faculty and a business administrator to requisition supplies and to make payroll. Plenty of bureaucratic waste would be eliminated.

A very weird symbiosis exists in American schools, a dependent relationship where plenty of discipline problems support the need to have principals and vice-principals. They need each other to exist and flourish.

After a graduation that is not really earned, most of the unskilled defiant "students" venture out into society and interrupt the normal flow of activities in their communities. And it is that same twenty-percent (whether in school as dysfunctional *students* or at large as dysfunctional adults) that costs towns across the country millions more in police protection.

If all citizens were honorable, decent, law-abiding, respectful adults, how big would the local police departments really have to be? The police, lawyers and prosecutors need criminals just like school administrators need recalcitrant *students* to stay in business. Why would a large number of policemen, criminal lawyers and court prosecutors be needed to protect good, moral and ethical citizens from one another?

Here's what is needed to reverse the great wasteful dilemma caused by American "democratic education." Those hundred and forty middle and high school kids that daily sabotage the smooth operations of local school systems must be channeled into vocational educational schools (or alternative schools) where *they* can work with their hands and learn a trade. The *students* could then learn hands-on skills that *they* could use later in life when they will eventually mature and become productive taxpaying members of local society.

If those identified and detoured *students* find that they don't like vocational school (or alternative school), *they* should be given the option of returning a year later to the regular school system. However, *they* and their parents would have to sign contracts stating that the *students* promise to be respectful of school rules and teacher authority or else have to return to vocational school or to alternative school until graduation. The vocational school diploma would be given equal status to the regular high school diploma to erase any stigma being associated with attending a "Vo-Tech or an Alternative School."

If the hundred and forty former school system troublemakers learn practical trades and skills (computer skills included) at the Vo-Tech institutions, then the taxpayers' investment in their education would be wisely utilized. As long as American public schools tolerate the antics of arrogant and belligerent *students*, our school systems are doomed to mediocrity at best. Schools need to become "academic institutions" and not "sociological experimental places" where *student* insubordination and rebellion are condoned by administrators and defended by the *First Ten Amendments*.

Mandatory vocational school is one very practical solution to "democratic education's" squandering of hard-earned taxpayers' money. If lawyers and judges insist that mandatory vocational education violates a *student's* Constitutional Rights, then school systems should have the courage to implement other practical solutions. A definite police-beat presence should be evident in middle and high schools with a community or borough cop substation in each school. The safety of good students and their teachers should be insured against the growing horde of bellicose and obnoxious uncooperative troublemakers. Schools must be viewed as microcosms of our communities. We all accept the presence of patrolmen on our streets and in our stores. Let's finally have the guts to admit that their presence is also welcomed and needed inside our school buildings.

Also, every middle and high school should have two disciplinarians: a vice-principal in charge of *student* behavioral discipline and a vice-principal responsible for enforcing academic discipline. When *students* don't do homework or when they refuse to do class-work they need discipline and not *guidance*. When *students* tacitly exhibit negative attitudes about learning and when they chronically complain to the teacher that a subject is boring, they require discipline and not *guidance*. When *students* fail to perform teacher expected classroom activities, then they should be referred to the "academic disciplinarian" for discipline and not to the guidance department; and if the problems persist, detentions, suspensions and transfers to Vo-Tech and alternative schools should be assertively prescribed and *administered*.

Two Septembers ago the new middle school principal asked if I wanted to come out of retirement and have my "old *job*" back while my successor was out on maternity leave. The Hammonton Public

School District requires that each *student* from grades six to twelve read a listed book compatible to their grade level over the summer and then submit a "critique reaction" to each chapter and hand the work in to the English teacher the first week of September. The assignment is called a "summer reading *requirement.*"

When I had retired from the Hammonton School System in June of 1999, I had 105 *students* spread out over six teaching classes. When I returned to my "old job" I suddenly had 142 *students* in six teaching classes. No public-school teacher should ever have a daily workload of more than 100 *students* (not counting homeroom) and be expected to create a satisfactory academic environment in each assigned class.

Thirty of the hundred and forty-two *students* did not have their summer reading reports done on time. At the end of the first marking period twenty of the thirty *students* also owed compositions (course proficiencies). Verbal conflict often arises when teachers must put pressure on derelict *students* to turn-in overdue work. I approached the vice-principal about the troubling problem.

"Oh, just give them a zero for not doing the summer reading critiques," the administrator said.

"But they failed to submit a course *requirement,* which is the same thing as refusing to turn-in a course proficiency," I replied in astonishment. "It isn't much of a *requirement* if thirty kids don't do the important assignment and then still wind-up passing the course."

"Just count it as a failing test grade," the vice-principal insisted, obviously thinking that when *students* neglect or refuse to do required assignments it is NOT a school discipline problem.

If the school had an "Academic Disciplinarian" to refer the delinquent slackers to, then I believe that a good deal of the "attitude adjustment" and lack of cooperation problems could have been addressed. Then I would not have had to come into verbal conflict with *lazy students* (I'm not afraid to use those taboo and politically incorrect words). I wanted to give each of the uncooperative thirty *students* a U (Unsatisfactory) for conduct, but the school brass maintained that U's should only be given for flagrant *student* misbehaviors like fighting, stealing, school vandalism and cursing and not for simply neglecting to do *required* work.

It's about time that school boards and administrators demand *student* accountability and *student* responsibility. Let's get disruptive *students* out of classrooms, and please, stop calling them *students* until they learn self-discipline and demonstrate self-control and respect for others. Make teachers responsible for just "teaching" and not also liable for "*student* learning" and for "*student* behavior."

It's about time that *students*, their parents and society begin viewing and understanding public school education as a *privilege* and not as a *democratic right*. Privileges can be revoked if not honored; rights can't be taken away.

I firmly believe that six-weeks of compulsory summer community service should be required of all *students* ages thirteen to eighteen. Maybe then *that* twenty percent of disruptive *students* in almost every public middle and high school will begin to appreciate the value of American education and will start to comprehend that schools are places where dedicated teachers impart subject *disciplines* to genuine *students* that have the *self-discipline* to learn.

In a Letter-to-the-Editor to the *Hammonton News* and the *Hammonton* (New Jersey) *Gazette* the author provides some constructive suggestions on how to alleviate the high cost of American school education:

Refrigerators and Vats Could Save Taxpayers Billions

Imagine your refrigerator without a separate freezer compartment. Just think of all the expensive food that would be wasted and how foolishly inefficient and cost ineffective such one-storage-area refrigerators would be. Well, that's exactly how our American public schools operate. Instead of having two curriculums (*academic* and vocational), high schools utilize the "one-size-fits-all" approach by forcing teachers to teach *academics* to all *students*. The Commissioner of Education (and local school bureaucrats) then give upper grade teachers "The Rumpelstiltskin Mandate: "Okay, now here's 120 *students*. We want you to spin straw into gold and then the State of New Jersey is going to give your students an *academic* High School Proficiency Test to ascertain that you've performed that simple task and then hold *you* the teacher accountable for *academic* excellence.

The "one-size-fits-all" high school practice is why local taxpayers do not get the educational "bang for the buck" that they deserve. As soon as government bureaucrats touch hard-earned tax dollars, good money suddenly becomes wasteful money. For example, thirty to forty percent of the students at Hammonton High School are not *academic* students and they should be attending a County Vocational School. Yet the State compels high school instructors to teach *academics* to *all* students and then tests those 30-40% reluctant learners on their knowledge.

To be fair to everyone involved, if the State insists on an *academic* test then all public high schools should be converted into high standards' *academies* with the thirty-to-forty percent of vocational-oriented *students* removed and sent to technical prep high schools better tailored to their future careers. If the present "one-size-fits-all" democratic comprehensive high school scenario must exist (without *student* redistribution into separate academic and vocational high schools), then the most ethical State solution should be to have two *student* performance tests administered: an *Academic Test* for college-bound scholars and a *Basic Skills Test* for the remaining 30-to-40% of the *student body*.

The United States is the greatest nation in the world in spite of its lackluster public-school education system. Up until most recently property owners could afford financing an inefficient system of education. We all must recognize that those thirty-to-forty percent vocational-oriented *students* must (after high school graduation) be re-educated and re-trained by technical schools, by the U.S. military and by profit-oriented corporations because their "comprehensive democratic high schools" didn't adequately prepare them for their future careers. Our "democratic comprehensive high schools" are so pretentiously concerned about the vocational-oriented *students* while force-feeding them four years of *academic* education but when those many unprepared seniors graduate we dispassionately say to them, "Now you're on your own! Good luck!"

Local taxpayers shouldn't fault their Hammonton Board of Education for representing a highly wasteful "democratic comprehensive high school" philosophy. The high per-pupil-cost of public school education cannot be fixed or repaired on the local level, even if the Board wanted it corrected. The Board is only following policy dictated by the State of New Jersey, which is mimicking the Federal Department of

Education's quixotic instructions. The difficulties of the "teach *academics* to everyone and tolerate everything" democratic comprehensive high school can only be addressed and solved on the national level, and then the all-too-familiar "trickle-down Chameleon Effect" could change things for the better on the local educational front.

Most of those who object to the content of this letter are probably apologists for the present status-quo form of education that's currently in place and who also have vested interests in maintaining the in-progress mediocre public-school system now functioning. Most school board candidates advocate "quality education at the lowest tax cost" without realizing that our public high schools squander millions of dollars annually by perpetuating weaknesses in the areas of tolerating chronic discipline problems and improper student distribution into the most desirable curriculum divisions, local high school *academic* and county high school vocational programs.

The public must understand that the terms *academics* and education are not synonymous or interchangeable. In 2008 *academic* instruction is what happens in private *academies* and education is what happens in public schools. Yet in today's reality public schools are sociological institutions merely reflecting the appearance of being *academic* places. If the State of New Jersey wishes to give public school *students* an *academic* test to qualify for graduation then it should take the sociological aspects out of the curriculum and convert its democratic comprehensive high schools into high standards *academies* and build county vocational schools to accommodate the remaining vocational-type *students*.

In addition to studying how refrigerators operate, federal, state and local public-school officials ought to understand how vats can be another partial-but-creative solution to our national educational dilemma. In Europe (VATS) Value-Added-Taxes help alleviate property assessments. Whenever an item is purchased, a VAT is added onto the total cost of the commodity to provide additional government operating revenue. Besides revamping our cost-inefficient public-school systems by eliminating the central problem that *academics* must be taught to all *students*, it's time for Americans to understand how both refrigerators and vats can make public school education more practical and affordable and thus annually save American property taxpayers billions of dollars.

"The Need for Competition in Schools"

Cooperation is emphasized in American public schools while competition is generally discouraged. Competition is even being downplayed among the most gifted students because educational psychology maintains that competition breeds selfish arrogant adults that only care about themselves and not about the needs of the less fortunate. Everyone involved in education has to get back to the idea that competition is a worthwhile pursuit that is consistent with our great free enterprise system of economics. That is why it is so important that public school philosophy pragmatically follows the free enterprise economic model rather than the current ineffective political democracy model of education that squanders billions of dollars annually.

Industry is keenly aware of the need for competition as the true instrument of societal prosperity and personal improvement. Surely *Nissan* and *Toyota* have forced *General Motors* and *Ford* to manufacture better cars or else go the way of the dinosaur. But our schools just don't get it! Rivalry is the key to individual self-sufficiency and to corporate progress everywhere in America except in our public schools.

As it is, our schools are eroding away the essential tradition that has made America great. Why should *students* attempt to excel if they are working in a *democratic* sociological system that accentuates grade inflation and the status quo? The entire average high school's curriculum is gradually drifting away from academic competition toward a median that promotes sociological growth under the guises of *democratic* education and cooperative learning. Instead of *group adjustment* schools should be emphasizing *student* exploration of individual potential, tough grading standards and rugged individualism.

Educational philosophy must reflect the true values of American tradition. Americans are more materialistic than they are aesthetic. Our traditions have supported the premise that success has more to do with individual pursuit of happiness than with group adjustment to happiness. Success in the real world has more to do with individual competition than it does with group cooperation.

Philanthropists had to be selfish to accumulate fortunes so that they could then become benefactors of society and effectively contribute to the stability of our "economic civilization." The wealthy are the biggest contributors to American government paying over seventy-five percent of taxes. When schools begin teaching *students* how to better their own lives economically then this country will again be steadied on the right track. But high schools persist in putting the cart in front of the horse!

The United States defeated the Soviet Union in the *Cold War* because of our free enterprise economic system and not because of our educational system that promoted *group assimilation*. The Russians shot a cannonball across America's bow when the communists sent up the first *Sputnik* in 1957. The U.S. knew it was in a do-or-die competition for survival so we got tough, developed a space program and put the first man on the moon. But it was the threat of *competition* from Russia that brought out the best in America! Competition is good, and as long as educational psychology sees *student* academic rivalry as being the opposite of societal needs our educational system is doomed to mediocrity.

For over half a century our American schools have been implementing *democracy* but despite all of this energy and expense crime and delinquency run rampant, drugs, AIDS and alcohol are destroying city and suburban teens and American society as a whole is degenerating towards disintegration.

Why do kids join gangs and experiment with dope? It is because the *group pressure* exceeds the will of the individual's conscience. And what do schools teach *students* to do? They teach kids how to sacrifice individual will for the sake of *the group*. Peer pressure can make almost any *student* yield to temptation and bad habits. A teenager's friends at age fourteen are more influential on his or her development and choices than his or her parents are. Have the wrong friends and then a *student* is easily led down the wrong path and *cooperative learning* in a group is partly responsible for that peer pressure social phenomenon.

In the classic science fiction novel *The Time Machine,* H.G. Wells suggests that it is man's aggressiveness, his sense of competition geared to his need for self-survival that drive individuals to invent, create, explore and discover. The novel teaches that it was because mankind became *too secure* and too happy and contented that caused the inferior Eloi race to evolve and be exploited and massacred by the heartless Morlocks.

As long as schools pursue making *students* socially secure and happy our civilization will be drifting towards complacency and starting to author its self-destruction. It is a testament of history that empires and civilizations usually decay and decline from within and not from external attack. That's what happened to Russia, Rome and ancient Persia, Egypt and Mesopotamia. If we as a nation lose our original sense of purpose as outlined in the *Declaration of Independence*, which is currently being undermined by radical interpretations of the *United States Constitution*, then we are surrendering the essential principles that made this country the envy of the world. As long as psychology and sociology govern law, culture and education, the decline of this nation will continue to accelerate.

Education in America should reflect the values of the adult world. If high school *students* earn good *academic* grades, the school systems should reward their achievements with pay, and the money earned from good high school grades could be set aside for future college tuition. All kids understand money but many teenagers find high school irrelevant and the philosophy of learning for the sake of learning alien to their natural survival instincts. Teenagers as a whole don't buy the false teachings that maintain, "You are here for a non-future because we are not training you to do anything but sit there." Those *students* that can't cut stiff competition in academic courses should not be allowed to take them.

Only the best *students* should be paid for attaining honor roll averages in valid *academic* courses that have not been diluted to accommodate mediocre and unmotivated *students*. In other words, academics should be the *privilege* of the minority and not a *right* of everybody. When that important transformation happens there will automatically be more *privileged students* because teenagers will recognize that achievement is rewarded by the high school and that the school is more attuned to the way the real-world functions.

Educational psychologists tell school systems that *children* learn from the *concrete to the abstract*. First of all, high school teenagers are not *children*. Secondly, if teenagers were put on the board of education's payroll, then they could plainly see the relationship of achievement and academic excellence on a *concrete* basis rather then be perpetually puzzled by the nebulous abstraction of "psychological reward" as opposed to the easily grasped concept of "monetary reward" being set aside for college expenses.

Get psychologists and the detrimental influence of psychology out of education and the ponderous institution will automatically improve. Future teachers must stop hearing the mantra that "Intrinsic rewards are more desirable than extrinsic rewards (money)." When Jesus spoke to the masses, He used parables to express His intent. The masses could not grasp His abstract moral principles. So Jesus used *material* references such as sheep, shepherds', mustard seeds and good

Samaritans to represent His abstractions to His *mass* audience. Jesus did things right by truly going from the concrete to the abstract.

Students today are a part of *mass* America. They need reality education and not intrinsic, *democratic*, sociological and psychological preparation for an abstract ideal society that *they* have to build without any training or skill. It is about time that education gives both form and substance to the word *reward* instead of emphasizing an elusive phantom known as "intrinsic reward." Then all *students* will finally *visualize* the concept of reward when it is given a material image in the form of money for valid *academic* achievement being set aside for future college debts.

Grade level norms must be established and strictly enforced. Tenth graders should not be reading on a seventh-grade level and seniors ought to maintain a B average in all academic subject areas. Teachers should be allowed to enforce rigid standards that don't use grade inflation to dilute educational quality for the sake of quantity (passing everyone). But the educational power structure avoids grade level norms because precise grading standards would accurately reflect the inadequacies of the present sociologically oriented *democratic* comprehensive public schools. At present true grade level norms in various core curriculum content areas are cleverly disguised and camouflaged by enigmatic standardized test results using difficult-to-interpret terminology like "stanines" and "relative skill competency."

Critics promptly state that grade level norms would deprive school systems from having their own unique and individual curriculums, which incidentally hardly vary from high school to high school throughout the country. Educational pundits insist that grade level norms would have teachers teaching for standardized tests and not for the individual instructor's personal goals and objectives. So why can't teachers pursue both the standardized tests' goals and their own goals simultaneously while devising lessons that support both?

The miracle of television along with the radio and motion picture industries have more than erased "regional uniqueness" throughout the United States. When I was a teenager people in the Dixie states sounded very different than northerners did, but today the speakers on radio and *CNN* television news shows originating from Atlanta sound exactly like those *Fox* announcers in New York City. Kids in Palo Alto, California watch the same *CBS* cartoon shows and *MTV* broadcasts as kids in Emporium, Pennsylvania do. Teenagers in Kalamazoo get on the same color and model school buses as kids in Poughkeepsie. We don't need to preserve our local eccentricities as much as we need to reinforce our national commonalities, interests and beliefs.

It is true that local customs have given way to *mass* conformity but the educational establishment is generating more of this *mass* mentality mediocrity under the cloak of "*democracy* for individual *student* development" and the "comprehensive (code jargon for not being strictly academic) high school."

Educational gurus flirt with flimsy theories like "The child needs an educational environment where he or she can *create* and *experiment*." American education contains more fantasy than an anthology of *Mother Goose* nursery rhymes and it is really very much akin to a *Grimm* fairy tale.

Educators really mean *re-creation* and *re-experimentation* when they talk about *student* "creation" and *student* "experimentation." The *students* aren't really creating or experimenting anything at all but they are merely re-enacting what mankind already knows and they are merely repeating demonstrations that have been performed by scientists and authors millions of times in the past.

Classroom learning (as teachers know it) is really *students'* re-discovering and not discovering and *students* re-creating and not creating. Sir Isaac Newton and Albert Einstein were examples of *discoverers* and William Shakespeare and Mark Twain were examples of *creators*. Anything that *students* do in the classroom is really only imitation of what true creators and true discoverers have already accomplished. So in that respect *students* (no matter how talented) are not true creators or true discoverers at all. They can only be re-creators or re-discoverers or else they would be *masters* instead of *students*.

Experience is often not the best teacher' as many believe. A *student* could do something wrong a hundred times and have plenty of experience without performing a particular task successfully. True creativity (like authoring this book) and true experimentation are a lot of hard work and should *not* be easy chores that can be achieved by simply following a procedure that has been duplicated millions of times before. Big projects, writing books and great accomplishments require years of labor. *Failure* is an inescapable characteristic of true creativity and true discovery. Schools expose *students* to certain learning devices and after several superficial tries (designed to build their self-esteem) they succeed in completing a certain easy task. Educators prematurely label what the *students* have done as *discovery* and as *creativity*.

Most authors have to go through dozens of painful publisher rejections before their works are available to the public. Scientists must develop tests that fail hundreds of times before that one test achieves an objective or accurately diagnoses a disease. It was Thomas Edison who had eloquently said, "Discovery (a genius) is 1 percent inspiration and 99 percent perspiration." True creativity and true discovery involve years of dedicated research, hard work and plenty of rejection and failure. When learning is made (or disguised) to come easy kids get the wrong impression of what adult life and real success are really about.

By isolating *students* from failure in public schools, educators are insulating and protecting them from what they need to know most: how to adjust to failure and rejection and how to reconstruct the spirit after failing so that *confidence* is built and not *self-esteem* being continually reinforced. *Democracy* in education and modern school psychology are obsessed with the objective of eradicating failure from a *child's* experience to make watered-down learning come easier to him or her. By eliminating the *student's* "right to fail" individual accountability is being sacrificed for the promulgation of *student* irresponsibility in school, at home and in the society.

But to accommodate administrators, college professors and school psychologists, *academic* tasks are reduced to simple sociological experiences. And after a *student* has completed a task that has been performed millions of times before educators proudly declare that the *child* (even if he is eighteen with a beard, a tattoo and long bushy sideburns) has "created" or "discovered."

American education makes a big mistake when it gives little Johnny Jones in the first grade of Happyville PS #1 the same credit for discovering that 4 + 3 =7 as we do Christopher Columbus for discovering America or Marie Curie for discovering radium. If we mean learning or *re-discovering* when we say *discovering*, then I insist it's time for educators to call a spade a spade.

Leonardo DaVinci and Michelangelo were bitter rivals and that *competition* motivated each to attempt out-creating the other. True *creativity* is basically a selfish enterprise and has little or no sociological implication. I often wonder if Picasso painted because he wanted *to share* his fame or his inspiration with other less-motivated painters or if Thomas Edison was inspired to invent while being motivated to *share* his ideas with other less motivated or less gifted idle dreamers.

The truth is that most great contributors to civilization preferred to think and to work alone. This is why only advanced *academic students* should be involved with *creating* and *experimenting* because they are the only *students* in the high school remotely capable of creating and

284

discovering anything. American education slyly conceals its own failures by disguising them in fancy terms like discovering, creating, sharing, cooperative learning and self-esteem, all of which have little or no application in the dog-eat-dog real world that's out there after graduation.

The American educational idea' of *sharing* (as generated by airhead college professors and impractical school psychologists) is actually more Marxist (share all wealth) than it is Jeffersonian (individual pursuit of life, liberty, free enterprise, happiness).

Kids are babied and doted on by parents that want to be their child's friend. Schools don't demand too much of the already spoiled *students*. Teachers must dilute their *academic* courses to accommodate *students* that have sound-byte minds that give up too easily on hard items that require time, hard work and energy to solve or complete. Schools discourage competition and encourage sociological cooperation and group activity to keep slow-learners and unmotivated kids on the old "academic escalator."

High schools only ask of *students* to participate according to their ability and don't demand excellence by raising the bar. "*Students* must be understood and given assistance and support to build self-esteem," the Educational Aristocracy preaches to teachers. "The curriculum must be adjusted to meet each *student's* individual needs." Now let's pause for a minute, take a deep breath and analyze what evils are being perpetuated all across America.

"From each (*student*) according to his ability; to each (*student*) according to his needs." Does that sound familiar? This country's educational system has gone topsy-turvy! The slogan for dialectic materialism (communism) has become the hallmark of American *democracy* in education. This is George Orwell's *1984* revisited.

That nebulous eighty percent gray area that psychologists and *Constitutional* lawyers have created has erased most of the distinctions between right and wrong, between good and evil and between smart and dumb. Love is hate, peace is war, truth is falsehood and *democracy* is socialism. Nothing has clear distinct definition anymore. Everything is everything! So that is why it is so easy for liberal educational philosophers and psychologists to easily corrupt the entire American public-school educational system.

A turtle hardly seems to move at all. But after wandering for fifty years in a certain direction, that tortoise will definitely be far from its original starting point. And that is exactly what has happened to American education in the last half-century. It has moved slowly step by step until school curriculums are more socialistic than *democratic* and more sociologically cooperative than academically competitive. The public has not felt this fifty-year pendulum shift because it has been happening too gradually, too slowly yet very deliberately.

Other non-friendly nations and terrorist organizations believe that our country's resolve is turning soft because our schools are not demanding *student* excellence and *student* academic accountability. The powers-that-be in American education are too idealistic, too impractical, and too conciliatory and as a result the *students* of today are too wimpy to academically compete and the parents of tomorrow will be too wimpy to economically excel. Soon this infection will reach lofty places like *Harvard* and *Yale* where grades and subjects will have to be watered down to accommodate the wimpy nature of the high school *student* pool that will be filtering out of watered-down high school programs.

The frail theories of American educational philosophy are as naïve as a grateful Caesar giving Brutus a shiny new cutlery set as an *Ides of March* appreciation gift. Besides grade-level norms for academic college-bound *students*, high schools desperately need a workable two-track system that sorts out and separates vocationally oriented students from those going on to higher academic education. Each county should have at least two vocational schools where high school *students* could learn viable trades.

A two-tiered or two-tracked system has been attacked by the educational power structure for being un-American, *undemocratic,* un-comprehensive and unethical. But this is what is actually necessary to promote the true American way of life that is fundamentally based on competition, free enterprise and individual achievement.

After eighth grade *students* should be given a battery of tests and on the information gleaned be channeled into two curriculums: the local academic high school and the county vocational trades' high school. Grade level norms could be enforced in the academic high school and more readily evaluated. Local high schools would then be more academically efficient. The brighter kids could work independently in experimental labs'. The *students* that have been sorted into the county vocational curriculum could learn skills and trades applicable to their later adult lives and then graduate to become productive members of society.

Teachers in the academic high school would not be baffled by such enigmas as "motivating" *students* to learn in a "*democratic* comprehensive high school" and adjusting grades to accommodate "*student* self-esteem." Discipline problems would then all but disappear.

The dual tracked system would not deprive any *student* of his or her freedom of choice. The new two-tracked curriculum would be flexible enough for a *student* in the trades sector to switch back to the *academic* college preparatory sector if he or she can pass a basic language and math skills academic entrance examination and then successfully migrate into the other more demanding curriculum.

Vocational *students* should not be stigmatized or discriminated against. A *student* in the academic college prep' curriculum could also make the transition to the trades program if he or she so desires up to the start of the senior year. We know that a good plumber or a well' *trained* electrician could make a lot more in the American free enterprise economy than a good teacher or a good nurse could. Let's start valuing trades education in conjunction with *corporate training* to make American education more cost-efficient.

As the curriculum now stands easy general high school electives only pay casual lip service to true vocational specialist preparation. Instead of putting the onus for learning for all *students* squarely in the laps of *academic* high school teachers, American high schools and county vocational schools should teach teenagers about the wisdom associated with true freedom of choice.

Teenagers must learn the value of true individual responsibility, of personal decision-making and of individual accountability for his or her grade performance and his or her individual behavior. The ultimate decision of whether to be in either curriculum or to stay or to transfer from one to the other would be his or hers to make based on the *student's* overall performance and behavior.

As it is now, parents put pressure on school guidance counselors to place their sons or daughters in *academic* college prep' courses and when all the kids can't make the grade the teachers feel pressure from administrators and then practice course dilution and grade inflation. When too many *students* fail a course, it is the teacher's fault. College is not for everybody! We must elevate vocational training education to be on the same plane as the academic high school. The stigma connected with vocational education as not being equal to academic preparation must be erased.

Upon graduation eligibility the vocational diploma and the academic high school diploma should be given equal status. The achievements of each *student* along with the *student's* class rank should be indicated on *both* diplomas so that prospective college admissions officers will know the exact credentials of the class valedictorian and be able to distinguish him or her from the class vagabond in the academic program and prospective employers will be able to differentiate the class expert tradesman from the class clown in the equal-status vocational curriculum. Presently a future employer can't decipher anything by reading or examining a devalued high school diploma.

College education is no longer synonymous with earning capacity so why should the myth be propagated that a college education is advantageous and more prestigious than a degree from an advanced post high school trades' academy?

Americans live in an economic society where garbage collectors (excuse me, sanitary engineers) earn more money than beginning teachers receive who have to put up with more garbage (from administrators and rowdy *students*) than trash collectors do. Absolute *democratic* freedom without individual accountability or the assumption of individual responsibility translates into anarchy and that's where the present educational scenario is leading this great nation. Educators need to formulate a more practical and cost-efficient model of *democratic* education and abandon the sham that is now gradually bringing our great American civilization to its knees. In its present form *democracy* in education is actually *socialism* in public schools. Free enterprise and fierce competition are what has made America the greatest civilization world history has ever known and those wonderful aspects must in the future become the hallmarks of our American public schools.

"The Trouble with American Democracy"

Don't get me wrong! I thoroughly love American democracy and the abundant freedoms that it allows me to enjoy. I can be creative, individualistic, entrepreneurial, and I can unequivocally believe in my interpretation and practice of American free enterprise. American democracy allows me to be expressive and critical of politicians' positions on various issues and simultaneously pretend being intellectual without any palpable fear of government reprisal. I can publish fiction and non-fiction books and expound on my diverse opinions with impunity. I truly appreciate and value what my guaranteed liberties personally mean to me. But outside of myself' and outside my interests and needs I am genuinely suspect of the functioning of democracy in a contemporary mass society. Let me explain and elaborate.

American politicians want me to believe that democracy is the greatest thing going since the creation of oxygen and food but I know from history that the concept of modern democracy did have its origin in ancient Greece and not in 1776 Philadelphia. The more celebrated Greek philosophers (in the midst of their great polemics) heaped ample criticism on *democracy* as an honorable system of government (let alone even contemplating the notion of verbally attacking democracy as a viable form of mass education as we now practice in the USA). In the Athens of Socrates and Pericles, the Golden Age citadel of pure democracy, the esteemed philosopher Plato described democracy as "in every way weak and unable to do either great good or great evil for civilization."

According to most venerable Plato, "The will of the people (the masses) is the worst of all lawful governments and the best of all lawless ones!" In other words, democracy represents a median fluctuating in a twilight zone somewhere between great and poor. Plato believed that a *Republic* was indeed the best form of government as stated in his work *The Republic*. A democracy would be doomed to eventually gravitate towards mediocrity, and after examining what *democracy* has been doing to our bureaucrats in Washington DC and to our civilization and culture, what it has done in our public schools, in the family unit and to society in general, Plato's remarkable assessment was not far off the mark.

The central problem with costly American democracy (both in government and in the local public schools) is that *our* society's problems and weaknesses are allowed to thrive and proliferate unabated at the conscientious taxpayers' expense. Anyone that has avidly studied history realizes that *Republics* like the *Roman Empire* could last for millennia but democracies are usually short-lived.

Plato's strong timeless argument seems credible even today when weighing into consideration issues like social welfare, unemployment, crime, drug abuse, individual irresponsibility as *a human choice* (freedom to choose) and the weaknesses of politicians in Congress and bureaucrats sitting on local boards of education dispensing important and essential educational directives in every community in this great *Republic*. In many respects, democracy is the antithesis of the stability permitted by a prosperous capitalistic *Republic*. Here's the analysis in a nutshell! It is our *free* enterprise economic system that gives America stability and not so much our *democratic* government and education systems.

Plato wasn't the only brilliant ancient-times mind that had doubts about the viability of *democracy* as an effective and efficient form of government. Other brilliant Athenians such as Aeschylus, Sophocles, Aristophanes, Aristotle and Demosthenes distrusted the ugly problems that a democratic government (without a *Republic's* strong laws) might generate. *Freedom for everybody* usually means waste, expense and attendant social disorganization, especially when the more industrious citizens must always do *more* work to help, to provide for and to assist the ever-existent slackers. That's an inherent curse of democracy. Good industrious people must care for, feed, produce for and clothe *those* (other than the aged, the afflicted and the children) that lack self-motivation and those that eschew the self-salvaging spirit of free enterprise.

It has been the *American Republic's* traditional idea of respect for law and order that has constructively contributed to national stability throughout our country's two-century plus history and not the democratic principle of pursuing absolute freedom (anarchy) for the masses, many of whom depend on government assistance for daily sustenance. And when our U.S. public schools pursue and champion student *democratic* freedoms guaranteed in the *Bill of Rights*, another earthquake has shaken the foundation of our great American *Republic* when education mimics the role and function of our inefficient American government.

Freedom without respect for authority (parents, teachers, policemen, judges, the law) eventually means chaos, turmoil and cultural disintegration, and as long as militant left-wing reformers (revisionists) and naïve educational psychologists give more *democratic* freedom to criminals and *students* to defiantly misbehave

290

and then simultaneously transfer (steal) authority away from teachers and policemen, public school education and American society will continue to decay, crumble and rot from the inside' out. And as long as our American democracy promotes absolute freedom for all of its citizens (and alien non-citizens living in the U.S. too) the United States is undeniably heading down the road to socialism and ultimately on a course with anarchy and chaos should a national catastrophe such as a nuclear war or a massive depression occur. It is the idea of having a free enterprise system and an American *Republic* (respect for law and order and valuing the existence of others) that keeps the USA strong and independent and not the notion of us being a contemporary democracy (continuously championing the expansion of individual rights).

The basic difficulty with American democracy is that it tolerates and attempts to mitigate all aspects of negative human nature. Criminals, murderers, thieves, drug addicts and dealers, sex offenders, prostitutes and other types of immoral and/or irresponsible people are given the same equal rights as contributors, honorable individuals, volunteers, law-abiding folks and societal benefactors. Totally dysfunctional people (citizens) are thoroughly protected under the mantle of *Constitutional* rights and allowed to flourish and practice their negative influences on civilization while these same pernicious social predators are generally shielded and protected from punishment (and citizenship revocation) by laws and avaricious lawyers under the guise of the *First Ten Amendments*.

In our American democracy the *First Ten Amendments* are given the power to undermine the teachings of the *Ten Commandments*, thus destabilizing the foundations of a moral' (and Christian) *Republic*. Unless necessary countermeasures are soon adopted and employed, this fundamental hypocrisy of a surplus of democracy weakening our venerable *Republic* will eventually initiate the decline and fall of the highly envied American way of life.

And I'm sad to report that there are no demanding qualifications for becoming a United States' citizen if someone is coincidentally born in this blessed country. Being born in America should not be the only criterion for citizenship, but in the past and also currently in the present it is.

First of all a good citizen must be literate and know how to read and write with a degree of fluency and skill. Secondly, a good citizen must know essential knowledge about our nation's history, about its admirable free enterprise capitalistic system of economics and also comprehend pertinent ideas relative to American culture and traditions. These cited principles contribute to the cohesiveness (and longevity) of our American civilization but presently they are not requirements for a native-born individual, who automatically obtains citizenship. A person born in the United States should not be eligible for citizenship until he or she graduates high school and demonstrates a mastery of reading, writing, U.S. history and fundamental cultural knowledge. Then after exhibiting those essential educational skills an eighteen-year-old should then qualify for taking an obligatory test to certify his or her right to receive citizenship and voting privileges. Voting and citizenship should be *earned privileges* and should not be *assumed rights* conferred upon potentially irresponsible people at birth. As it now stands immigrants studying to be United States' citizens often know more about U.S. history than many "unworthy citizens" that had acquired *that* particular designation simply by fortunately being born within the borders of the United States of America.

Another very evident weakness of American democracy is the fact that on the average only 40% to 50% of the eligible population votes in national, state and local elections. This deficiency is both disgraceful and problematic. Those that do not actively participate in democracy should be excluded from citizenship and from voting. American democracy is based on several suspect premises: that man is good and that he can be trusted and that he or she cares abut himself or herself and about his or her country and world.

Conversely a Communist society believes that man is evil and therefore must be controlled. The ideal civilization (and/or most satisfactory government) would be a *Republic* where people have earned privileges and can maintain them through the exercise of honorable and constructive goals along with personal responsible societal behavior. In other words what we now understand as *rights* would be *privileges* that could be earned but also that could be lost or taken away because of illicit and/or immoral conduct. Illegal drug usage, abuse of self and others, criminal behavior warranting incarceration and general contempt toward other human beings (represented in hurting or harming one's fellow man) would automatically result in the termination of citizenship.

Just like actions generate good and bad consequences, so too should inaction. What is the sense of being a legitimate U.S. citizen if illegal aliens and non-citizens have the exact same rights as you do? The best solution to the ongoing democracy dilemma would be to create and maintain a society based on acquired or lost privileges rather than one heralding equal permanent rights for everyone, whether they be responsible or irresponsible individuals, criminals or ethical citizens. Our Founding Fathers were moral men whose model public conduct and independent spirit are deserving of our imitation. That philosophy should be characteristic of our laws and practices.

I firmly believe that all American citizens should be required and expected to fulfill much-needed roles promoting community and societal stability through volunteerism. Every adult man and woman should be required to belong to a service club like the Lions, the Kiwanis, the Rotary and the Exchange. As worthy alternatives a good citizen could be involved in their church, in public charities, in the local volunteer fire department or rescue squad, be a hospital volunteer, become a Big Brother or Big Sister or serve as a *Little League* coach. In the newly conceived privilege-oriented democracy/*Republic*, no healthy able-bodied person that also desires maintaining his or her citizen status gets a free pass. Every citizen (or citizen wannabe') would be required to give something back to society by loyally adhering to a form of volunteerism. Every citizen ought to be proactive in taking a vital interest in the continuation of the nation's culture (of course the *ACLU* would bitterly oppose such needed reform). The present "rights-oriented democracy for all" does not make any mandatory demands on its population, particularly on its indolent and unmotivated citizens. As a result, apathy has become the watchword for all-too-many societal freeloaders.

Another glaring disadvantage of American democracy is that elected politicians are increasingly beholding to their constituencies. In many instances pressure groups, special interest influences and ethnic minority factions constitute real obstacles to objective and effective governmental decision-making. Elected officials will instinctively openly placate and pander to these "special interest groups" to garner votes and support, and soon criminals, child molesters, reparations' advocates, those that broadcast sexual innuendo garbage over the airwaves, illegal Mexican aliens obtaining amnesty and unemployed welfare recipients will be able to achieve their political goals by manipulating local, state and national elected officials (who all want to get re-elected) on policies and issues that incidentally favor *them*.

And then radical *ACLU* lawyers and liberal activist judges are eager to distort the idea of "freedom of speech" to encompass lewdness, utterances of obscenities and vulgarities in public, nudity, hate speech, college professors voicing anarchy, insurrection, rebellion, class-warfare revolution and the dissolution of Christian holidays along with the elimination of symbols associated with

293

Christmas, Thanksgiving, Halloween, St. Patrick's Day, St. Valentine's Day and *Easter.* In its original context "Freedom of Speech" simply meant challenging arbitrary and capricious government edicts without fear of retribution. Its definition and implementation had little to do with the explicit obscenities indicative of rap music lyrics and of nude dancing and pornographic literature emporiums in American communities. When a country loses the stability evident in its past traditions, it begins losing its moral identity both in the present and in the future.

* * * * * * * * * * * *

Nowhere is the negative influence of too much democracy translating into mediocrity as much evident in today's America than that which is apparent in our lackluster public schools. In this new arrangement called "cooperative education" the teacher (authority figure) is reduced from being the significant knowledge person guiding the class through a lesson and now his or her new function is to wander from classroom group to group being a general resource person known as a "facilitator." The new educational democracy emphasis is on the *group* (instead of the professional authority individual) determining its own goals, roles and methods.

Now here's where quality time-on-task education ultimately suffers with this new "child centered curriculum." The classroom groups waste valuable time bickering, debating, selecting, compromising, and talking while *student individual will* (along with teacher authority) is surrendered to conform to *student* majority opinion. When teachers are compelled to divide classes into groups to engage in "cooperative learning" they are adhering to an educational trend that postulates "getting along with others" (in a newly established and recognized pecking order) transcends the need for "individual academic achievement and accountability." Just like in the American political structure, in public school education *socialism* is disguised and marketed as *democracy* and group dominance prevails. Many lethargic members (lazy *students*) of those classroom groups heavily rely on the group managers to do both *their* work and homework for them.

And so public high schools produce many "classroom welfare *students*" that can't read and can't write because someone in the "cooperative group" had done those things for them (just like in the political welfare system) since those other conscientious *students* wanted to get good grades for *themselves* on *their* report cards.

294

Schools are now producing many doltish graduates that are unskilled, untrained, and unprepared and unless they're going to college, the seniors are bound for and being herded into minimum wage employment. But despite those horrendous salient facts school administrators are edified to know that the graduates have learned how to get along with one another in cooperative *democratic* groups. The "group technique" in American education has dismally failed because the suspect method has been (and is) producing a society of empty-headed gossipers and not a nation of independent thinkers.

When *students* are divided into groups for "cooperative learning" the stronger-willed ones and the more intelligent ones will naturally dominate the group's power structure. The more dynamic *student* leaders tend to be ambitious and are concerned about doing well because they selfishly want to earn good grades for *their* group contributions. The more industrious *student* leaders not only determine the direction the group will take but also wind-up doing the bulk of the work for the "lazy classroom welfare *students*" in the group that lack sufficient motivation to achieve on their own.

But when the non-workers and the non-contributors become the dominant decision makers later in life in the American political structure, then mediocrity will prevail (just like Plato had asserted) and excellence is automatically stifled. Does this trend in American democratic education sound familiar? American education is redundantly mimicking the failed democratic (socialistic) welfare system that ensures the continuation of individual irresponsibility, a deficiency that is being increasingly rewarded by the U.S. federal and state governments for "citizens" habitually practicing a lack of motivation and/or bad habits! And please remember that the Marxist/Lenin Russian Communists used to call their failed agricultural system "Cooperatives."

When an educational scenario exists where the better-motivated *students'* produce work for the more lethargic ones and when the less motivated *students* profit from the labor of the more motivated gifted-*students*, then the endgame is *educational socialism* and not *educational democracy.* The same principle holds true in adult America where the influence of non-productive members of society on vulnerable and power-hungry American politicians has become the accepted standard. In our American democracy irresponsibility is rewarded and mediocrity is now the clarion call. This is basically why the health of America is in jeopardy.

Democratic education (as interpreted by educational psychology) has led to a very dangerous notion that "*students* should be equal."

295

Student academic performance and behavioral differences are minimized in today's public schools regardless of individual ability. Excellence is sacrificed and mediocrity results when both ends of the educational spectrum (A and F *students*) are forced by the system to gravitate toward a *sociological* median.

And in the functioning of American government, the productive members, employers and corporations (through their hard-earned tax dollars) must support those people (citizens) that are unmotivated and dependent on government assistance despite the fact that the social parasites had equal opportunity to learn in public schools and now have equal opportunity to advance in the American free enterprise system. The economic playing field is now available for ambitious minorities but first blacks and Hispanics must overcome the "irresponsibility and apathy syndromes" that prevail in the culturally isolated city ghettos. Just remember: there are some good teachers in inner city public schools and also some bad teachers in suburban public schools as well.

While the needs of the group are magnified in democratic education the input of the *students* that contribute the most is devalued in terms of individual reward in American education (the same truth exists in American politics). The smarter ambitious *students* in school and the smarter ambitious citizens in society then become subordinated to the needs of the group and must tow the weight of the weaker non-motivated *students* and unmotivated adult *citizens*. By craftily interplaying psychological and philosophical terminology like "cooperative learning," "*democratic* education" "social welfare," "equal justice" and "sharing," the truth becomes blurred and nebulous in the eighty-percent "middle area gray zone" and now it is especially more difficult for the average productive middle-class citizen to distinguish and fathom.

And so *socialism* (group work and re-distribution of wealth from the motivated to the un-motivated) is advanced and stealthily masquerades around disguised as *democracy* (individual pursuit of happiness) in both education and in American politics. Thus, our great *Republic* is constantly and egregiously being endangered by democratic (socialistic) initiatives.

I have been and right now am disturbed that if the prevalent practice in public school education and in American politics is indeed *socialism*, then *that* exercise ought not be labeled and marketed under the title *democratic* education or under the guise of American democracy. Our beloved country has drastically wandered from our original American *Constitutional precepts* (individual pursuit and

296

individual rights) as prescribed by our Founding Fathers' wishes but *those* sacred tenets are now contradicted in our society's daily welfare-oriented activities that have more recently been redefined and instituted in our public schools. This socialistic deviation from true democratic (free enterprise) principles has weakened our national moral fiber and has spontaneously and simultaneously weakened our American *Republic*.

Being politically correct and being influenced by sound-byte messages in popular American society have taken precedence over the need for individual sacrifice and individual accomplishment (resulting from hard work) directed toward attaining *a personal goal*. Smart *students* are labeled "nerds" and "geeks" and "freaks" by their dumber peers and the academically gifted teens are also labeled "selfish" by the educational powers-that-be because some smarter *students* refuse to *share* their knowledge with their' peer intimidators. And in the society at large those incentive-oriented individuals that practice free enterprise must also support those "vegetable citizens" that are perfectly content living at a lower standard while either doing little for themselves or for their fellow man or even caring to benefit or improve either condition.

Both our American society and our public schools are losing their sense of purpose, are shrewdly hiding their weaknesses and are destroying the sacred foundations of our American culture that were originally predicated on *self-sufficiency*. By attempting to accommodate the needs of those *students* that cannot measure-up to the rigorous standards of *individual pursuit of happiness*, free individual enterprise, the American dream and the pioneering instinct as ordained by Thomas Jefferson, public schools (and our deficient American democracy) have adopted the course to use socialistic methods to attain democratic goals, thus making our *Republic* vulnerable to weakness and now being in danger of eventually dissolving from the inside. Today's teenagers (and many of *our* un-inspiring dependent adults) misconstrue the pursuit of pleasure as the definition for the pursuit of happiness heralded in Thomas Jefferson's *Declaration of Independence*. As a result our American culture (in general) is becoming more hedonistic than intellectual and simultaneously more volatile and less stable.

* * * * * * * * * * * *

So, in conclusion our cherished American democracy is destined to wallow in mediocrity by tolerating individual misconduct, increasing crime, non-motivated people and by over-protectively looking out for *their* unmeritorious interests by sympathetically calling slackers "unfortunate citizens." I agree with Plato. The best form of government would be a no-nonsense *Republic* that treats rights as privileges that (first of all) must be earned through achievement and accomplishment and subsequently maintained by commitment and performance. There must be obligatory dedicated volunteer service to the society with the requisite understanding that those earned *privileges* enjoyed (along with citizenship) would be revoked should an *individual* fall into practicing bad habits and then persist (through bad conduct) in demonstrating continual irresponsibility.

A new governmental paradigm is much-needed and it should be one that manifests *citizen* privileges as opposed to espousing guaranteed "unalienable rights for everyone." A fundamental problem with democracy is that not everyone pulls their own weight and those that don't *are rewarded* with welfare and Medicaid (Guess who pays for this?)

In addition to the burgeoning welfare quagmire, evil malicious people cannot be trusted and ought to have their "privileges" revoked. The Communists were partially right: some lawbreaking people can't be credited with "equal rights" and must be controlled on the basis of past negative performance. Some people cannot be trusted with absolute freedom (and must be controlled), especially when their self-centered actions endanger the rights and/or safety of themselves and others.

American Representative Democracy is an inefficient form of government that makes hard-working upper middle-class citizens contribute almost fifty percent of their annual incomes in taxes to subsidize others (in terms of housing and public-school education) that live just a tier below them in terms of material comforts and medical and social benefits.

"Environmental Greenies Are Dangerous People"

My wife drives a Nissan Altima that gets 32 miles a gallon and I motor around in a Maxima that faithfully achieves 28. My spouse and I habitually recycle our paper, glass and metal county trash and keep it all separate from our town-collected "other garbage." We conscientiously maintain our property in a neat manner and keep our shrubs and bushes trimmed and our lawn well-manicured. Like the plurality of Americans, we respect the environment and try our best to protect it.

A fairly funny joke goes something like this: "Yesterday it was so cold outside that I actually saw a liberal with his hand in his own pocket!"

I happen to believe that hardcore "Environmental Greenies" are very dangerous people. The fanatics invent crazy modern mythological terminology like "carbon footprint," "alternative energy" and "global warming" and the overzealous charlatans expect to make the rest of civilization (including our easily impressionable and indoctrinated school children) feel guilty if *we* aren't voluntarily and gullibly deceived by their creative frivolous terminology.

But yes, it's my sincere contention that the on-a-mission Greenie extremists (along with their suspect unproven theories) constitute a major threat to American civilization because their radical militant movement is counter-productive to our already fragile U.S. economy and their perverted liberty-threatening agenda is a direct detriment to U.S. national security.

For the purpose of clarity, let me explain my seemingly bizarre position on this contemporary issue. In truth, the more radical militant Greenies want to restrict your (and my) automotive mobility and limit your (and my) "fossil fuel freedom" in order to make you and me become more dependent on electric-powered vehicles and state-sponsored mass transportation.

Generally speaking, radical Greenies are "extreme liberals" who don't like American dependence on either foreign or domestic oil in order to operate our automobiles. The crazed lunatics insist that we use "alternative energy" to replace the scourge of petroleum products and carbon emissions presently polluting the atmosphere.

Let's get real here! When is the last time you've seen an automobile passing you on the highway with a solar panel and a windmill on its roof responsible for propelling it? Not even the most devout environmental Greenie has one of these "alternative energy" babies!

"Alternative Energy" does not exist on any practical functional level! It's successful implementation effectively replacing standard auto' engines and fossil fuels is still decades away! The unique terminology "Alternative Energy" is really an anachronism, a misguided misnomer designed to goad the rest of us into feeling ashamed of driving around in gas-guzzling SUVs, Altimas and Maximas.

The so-called totally electric cars that are out there are abundantly overpriced modes of transportation. One popular version sells for 44 thousand dollars, that is, after the government gives you a rebate of 10,000 bucks.

Guess who pays for the ten-thousand-dollar rebate? You and I do! This Greenie-originated "rebate canard" represents a deliberate-but-strategic egregious redistribution of wealth designed to force and compel you and me to purchase plug-in cars that have to be re-energized every few hours and that have trouble accelerating over fifty miles an hour.

And this totally false notion of conserving the environment by having millions of electric-powered cars on American highways is both a farce and a hypocrisy. Electric cars do not constitute "renewable energy" like wind and solar power happen to represent "renewable energy" sources. Electric cars will have to be plugged-in in order to recharge their batteries every few hours, and guess where most of the electric energy they'll be using originates? From good old electric companies using good old efficient fossil fuels: oil and coal. How's that rather perverted strategy for protecting and saving Mother Nature? Pretty counter-productive those novel electric automobiles will be, wouldn't you say?

Here's another misuse of typical "Greenie" jargon, a disingenuous scoundrel idea called "Cap and Trade." Allow me to emphasize that wind and solar power are not examples of "Alternative Energy" as the shrewd Greenies ardently argue. Wind and solar are what can best be described as "Supplemental Energy" that will not replace coal-generated electricity anytime in the immediate future.

Now here's the problem with the recently proposed Cap and Trade legislation. The wind and solar industries cannot economically or efficiently compete with coal as a source of competitive electric energy. And so, the existing power companies must pay fines for polluting the atmosphere, the penalty money going to subsidize newly created (but financially unprofitable) wind and solar companies.

300

Again, beneath the Greenie ruse we have the deceptive hidden agenda of redistributing wealth from the practical "have corporations" to the impractical "have-not wind and solar companies."

Yes, according to the demands of Cap and Trade, good legitimate capitalistic money will be earmarked to slyly go from profitable electric companies to uncompetitive wind and solar corporations so folks, don't be surprised when your electric bill goes up an additional twelve hundred dollars a year to finance this extravagant government-oriented money grab that's custom-designed to assist the Greenies in accomplishing their warped goals!

Let's try a little theoretical one-month experiment! We'll use wind and solar "alternative energy" to replace oil, gasoline and coal for four full weeks. After those 30 days pass, how many U.S. cars would still be on the highways? How many U.S. houses would still have electricity, heat or air conditioning? So much for the pathetic lie known as "alternative energy!" Wind, solar and electric cars represent only 2-3% of total U.S. energy production, so logically and realistically, how could 3% "alternative energy" ever pretend to replace 97% oil, gas and coal?

And permit me to assert that the real villains in this progressive travesty of economic justice are the Greenies who are desperately attempting to paint the electric companies as the evil capitalistic culprits that are contributing to increasing the size of our "carbon footprints." I don't know about your singular attitude, but I'm perfectly satisfied with the size of my carbon footprint and I don't wish to see it diminished in any way.

When the boisterous Greenies eventually convince Russia, China and India to stop polluting the environment and the atmosphere (which just happens to travel around the globe to the USA), then that's the appropriate time for America to join the idealistic quixotic crusade to save the planet.

Indeed, our own national security is currently being jeopardized in the form of self-destructive unilateral economic disarmament. By listening to and legislating the Greenies' deleterious environmental program, industrial jobs are gradually going overseas to the new manufacturing countries of Russia, India and China, giving those three foreign nations (that obviously don't care too much about the environment) an international competitive advantage over the self-victimized United States, where it is estimated that two oil and coal industry jobs are lost for every "alternative energy" job that is created through wily socialistic wealth (and energy) redistribution.

Yes indeed, the radical Greenies are very possessed quixotic liberals that want to save the planet while naively and inadvertently destroying American civilization through ignorantly crippling the formerly virile U.S. economy. The one-track-mind Greenies truly desire middle class citizens to engage in an irresponsible class warfare game with the rich as John Doe's targeted combatants. Yes, tax the wealthy more so that we can more readily redistribute and share the common wealth!

By raising taxes on the rich to help support saving the environment, here's what's really occurring. The middle-class is in the act of spiting itself! The so-called rich control all goods and services produced in America so therefore, the cost of items the middle-class buys will conversely go up.

By redistributing the wealth through higher taxes on the rich (with some of the money going to the Greenie causes), we all can expect to pay more for soap, soup and meat at the supermarket and more for clothes, tools and paint at Wal*Mart. A tax on the wealthy is really a hefty burden on you and me, the American consumer!

Just objectively examine the economic statistics to further understand my point! In 2010, the U.S. trade deficit has averaged 41 billion dollars a month while Red China's trade surplus in October was in excess of 27 billion dollars. The ongoing and very dangerous Greenies' philosophy will make the United States export less and import even more by sending more industrial jobs overseas to countries that don't have the same reverence for a pristine environment as America does.

Is there any wonder that on-the-rise Red China holds 800 billion dollars in U.S. bond debt? Is there any Greenie out there that doesn't see this astonishing and growing ugly debt scenario as either a potential or direct threat to U.S. national security?

And around three billion people live in China, India and Russia. How could 310 million Americans (practicing intense conservation) ever offset three billion other not-so-concerned earth inhabitants randomly polluting the planet while the U.S. continues to give still other New World nations around the world economic advantages when it comes to *our* ecology-minded manufacturing and industry? Ten to one are bad odds at any race track or casino.

Just examine what the maniacal Greenies and their political influence have done to California's San Joaquin Valley, which was once the most productive agricultural region in the USA. Canal water is being dammed and diverted south of San Francisco in order to protect endangered fish species such as the delta smelt and the silvery minnow.

As a result of over 150 billion gallons of water being re-channeled annually, thousands of acres of cantaloupe, grapes, tomatoes, lettuce and onion crops have been sacrificed (along with over 40,000 agricultural jobs) while simultaneously generating much higher chain store fruit and produce prices.

Finally, the crazed Greenies insist that the Earth is in jeopardy because of an impending phenomenon known as "Global Warming." This is another hypothetical trick designed to scare the rest of us into believing the gross distortions of the asylum-oriented environmental gospel.

Ever since the Cambrian geologic age that had occurred on Planet Earth over 700 million years ago, scientists estimate that there have been over 300 Ice Ages. In fact, the last Great Ice Age ended only around ten thousand years ago when the Great Lakes had been scoured-out by the northern retreat of the tremendously thick layer of glacial ice.

Americans don't have to fear the Greenies' doomsday version of Global Warming nearly as much as they have to be wary of the prospect of Global Cooling.

Just imagine this rather frightening catastrophic rendition of events! A mile-high sheet of glacial ice again descends from the Arctic Circle onto the United States and soon every skyscraper in Seattle, Chicago and New York City is violently crushed and devastated during a 21st century three hundred and first cataclysmic ice invasion.

Don't listen to these dangerous Greenie environmentalists that want to control our everyday lives at our own expense, thus endangering our own individual independence and national prosperity! Global Cooling is a much more formidable potential disaster than Global Warming (coastal flooding) will ever be!

"Darwin, Einstein and John Dewey"

On the average, democracies usually last for up to two hundred and fifty years. That historical pattern gives the United States of America around three more decades until we're put on artificial life support, *our* systemic malady principally caused by moral decay, by legal and political corruption and by widespread economic inefficiency. Yes, since WW I we've created a grotesque-looking Ponzi pyramid,

In another thirty years government spending will drastically exceed GNP (Gross National Production), seventy percent of the burgeoning American population will not be paying federal income taxes, and also, more money will be going out of Social Security and out of Medicare than entering into those specific government program safety nets. At present, our U.S. total federal, state and local government expenditure is 39% of GNP, when 20% is the most desirable percentage ratio in order to fully assure national economic stability.

What obscure factors besides government waste and federal and state over-regulation will ultimately accelerate the demise of the USA? It is this writer's contention that the decline of America will be attributable to an extension of the philosophies and teachings of three currently venerated individuals: Charles Darwin, Albert Einstein and John Dewey.

Back in the early 1900s, Charles Darwin's Theory of Evolution was not exclusively confined to the scientific realm. Instead, Evolution's basic premise of continuous change (along with an expanding spiral progressively developing) bled over into such social disciplines as political science, psychology, the law and most dramatically, American education. Nothing in today's reality (not even God) is "absolute." Everything constantly changes and mutates into something else! Is not "change" the watchword of our time in American history?

Karl Marx and Vladimir Lenin were indeed highly influenced with the notion of Darwin's Evolution. Those two political intellectuals reasoned that in ancient times mankind had Aristocracies (warlords, city-state rulers and local despots). Eventually the existence of Aristocracy melded into Monarchy with one king controlling all activity within a certain region or country. And then in 1776, rebellion against King George III's tyranny resulted in the Revolutionary War, and with great inspiration, a fantastic rebirth combining Greek Athenian Democracy and the concept of the Roman Republic's law and order gradually integrated into what is now the United States of America.

Marx and Lenin (being affected by Darwinian Theory), believed that Democracy would surely evolve into Socialism and Lenin's successor, Joseph Stalin, theorized that Bolshevik Socialism should predictably evolve into another predestined disaster, Soviet Russian Communism. Just think of the millions of innocent victims that had (and have) died under the aegis of inflexible iron-fisted Communist doctrine!

Isn't it a marvelous miracle that the USA (along with its free enterprise and free market capitalist system) has over the course of the last century proven Marx, Lenin and Stalin to be total political frauds? And yet, with the obvious fact that Soviet Socialism and militant Communism have both miserably failed as evidenced with the crumbling of the Berlin Wall, ironically, the USA today is rapidly moving in the direction of Socialism to attempt solving its proliferating domestic woes?

But don't despair! There is still time for economic salvation once Americans come to their senses. If everyone in the U.S. took responsibility for their own lives and pulled their own weight in this land of abundant opportunity and free public school education, then government could wisely shrink-down to twenty percent of GNP from its current 39% level and our REPUBLIC (respect for law and order) could be effectively preserved and future financial disaster could be strategically averted. But first things first: For *our* time-honored traditions (Christmas, Thanksgiving, Easter, 4th of July, etc.) and our all-important historical heritage to adequately survive, political *evolution*, societal flux and class warfare must be removed from American culture.

Yes, Americans are truly living in the closest thing to a Utopia that can be manifested by man on this good Earth. When Judas Iscariot challenged Jesus, "Why do you spend *our* money on expensive oils when the money could be spent on the poor?" Jesus simply and succinctly answered, "Judas, there will be poor always!"

But unlike almost any other culture on this planet, the United States affords all its citizens the opportunity to take risks, to succeed (or to fail), and to engage in freedom of speech, freedom of the press, freedom of religion and finally, "individual opportunity" along with freedom of education to advance and to become upwardly mobile, all of these wonderful "liberties" based on individual initiative, individual determination, individual motivation and individual perseverance.

306

Let's examine history. The only real success at democracy (following a revolution) had occurred after July 4th, 1776 in Philadelphia's Independence Hall, and then over a decade of extremely difficult growing pains, regional rebellions and full-blown arguments over the tenets of the Articles of Confederation had ensued, but, finally, the U.S. Constitution had been drafted and signed in 1787, with the "democratic" Bill of Rights being completely ratified in 1795, nearly twenty years after the famous Declaration of Independence had been authored and proclaimed. All of *that'* exhaustive and dangerous establishment of American democracy (the Republic) required nearly two decades of great sacrifice to complete.

Now look at what had happened in France after the French Revolution: Anarchy, a Reign of Terror and the tyranny of Napoleon came to be. What about the Bolshevik Revolution of 1917? How about Socialism eventually evolving into Communism? Remember the film Dr. Zhivago? The good humanitarian doctor returns to Moscow after the "People's Revolution" and finds his house occupied by a rabble of belligerent dissidents that threaten to evict Zhivago from his own property if he doesn't abide by *their* mob-rule control.

And also, what about the infamous Nazi Revolution in pre-WWII Germany and the accompanying Fascist Revolt that had happened in Italy? How did Hitler and Mussolini ever improve their countries without thoroughly devastating Germany, Europe and Italy in the end? And how about the recent Iranian Revolution conducted against the Shah? How did *that* historical phenomenon work out for the still-dominated and exploited natives of Iran?

And how could *we* be naïve and gullible enough to assume that good things are now going to happen in Egypt, Libya, Algeria and Syria *after* their bloody "Revolutions!" More theocratic Mullahs sponsored by the radical Islamic/Muslim Brotherhoods perhaps! How about a little Middle-East separation of "Mosque and State" like we have a fundamental division of "church and state" right here in America!

And what about Albert Einstein's colossal impact on American culture? With the Theory of Relativity came the unique notion that everything in society is "relative": nothing anywhere in America (save death and taxes) is *absolute,* permanent and fixed. And so now we have such things as the Bill of Rights to the Constitution coming into conflict with widely-recognized traditional American family values. The First Ten Amendments (under the guise of freedom of speech and freedom of expression) are now insidiously undermining the Ten Commandments handed-down to Moses on Mt. Sinai.

Take this rather disturbing gay rights marriage issue for example in regard to what Einstein's relativity has mutated into. Remember: today everything is evolving and must be 'Relative" and not "Absolute" (God's Ten Stone Tablet Laws). Two iconic Commandments are: "Honor Thy Father and Thy Mother" and "Thou Shall not covet thy neighbor's wife!"

Just think about *those* two Commandments for a second. The principal purpose of heterosexual (man-woman) marriage is to biologically conceive children and then to nurture them through mature parenting skills. The very vocal gay and lesbian political activists want gays to get married, to adopt children and then to have loving families.

Now someone please explain *this* paradoxical situation to me. How could an adopted child with gay "parents" know who the mother is if two males are his or her parents? If two lesbians are his or her parents, which one is the father according to the very explicit Commandment: "Honor Thy Father and Thy Mother?" And if two gay married men are living next door, according to the Ninth Commandment, which one is "thy neighbor's wife" to be coveted?

Under recent gay rights' laws, the idea of certain "sins" against God has been totally eradicated and "sin" is now basically obsolete and "relative." And needless to say, a woman's right to choose or to have an "Abortion" too violates the Stone Tablets' ABSOLTE Commandments because a conceived child is sinfully *killed,* "Thou Shall Not Kill," and has no opportunity whatsoever to ever honor either a mother or a father. And indeed, if the very vocal in-your-face abortion rights activists had been themselves *aborted* before birth by a "Right to Choose" mother, we would not be having any legal wrangles with the whole lot of them at present. Was Sodom and Gomorrah a Biblical myth or could it soon again be happening right here in America? I'll let *you* be the judge of that!

Finally, John Dewey is the "father of modern-day American public-school education." Dewey was a sociologist, a psychologist in addition to being an educator, and his "Revolutionary" classroom theories had been drastically influenced by Charles Darwin's Theory of Evolution and by Albert Einstein's Theory of Relativity. John Dewey was undeniably a confirmed Socialist, and most of our contemporary public-school teaching methods and practices are based on the socialistic idea of "sharing" in a "community (commune) classroom" atmosphere.

Dewey espoused the idea that "children learn by doing," and I often wonder if *this* particular theory of his pertains to the literal teaching of sex education inside the classroom, for without a doubt, the rampant implementation of sex education seems to be quite pervasive among brazen and *in*discriminate young teenagers in numerous environments outside the classroom.

Socialism in our public schools is stealthily taught under the guise of ever-evolving "democratic education." American free enterprise in the form of student classroom *competition* is de-emphasized by modern educational psychology. *Individual* academic achievement is often discouraged in deference to group (class) accomplishment. Soon there will be no honored valedictorians or salutatorians at high school or college graduations because being "outstanding" or being "excellent" automatically makes the other lower-ability *students* in attendance look publicly bad and makes *them* feel inferior in comparison.

In order for *it* to be successful, mediocrity must be both promoted and maintained in John Dewey's anemic academic performance system, so when public school teachers put kids into classroom "groups," the students that want to succeed wind-up doing the bulk of the "group's work" so that *they* could get decent grades while the less-motivated (and socially deprived) freeloaders get by with almost the same recognition given by the teacher, and if you further examine our current American economic welfare system, the productive members of society are encumbered with carrying the weight of the un-motivated adult masses on *their* backs.

And so, classrooms all over the American landscape are slowly-but-surely evolving into miniature European-style socialistic "nanny states," both tolerating and promoting academic mediocrity to guarantee the continuation of John Dewey's counter-productive Socialist Education System.

Dewey's egregious educational quagmire and his associated quixotic child psychology enforcement has, over the decades, negatively led to child-centered families and to child-centered classrooms. Parents have been demoted in the home and teachers have essentially been demoted in the classroom and are now labeled in academic jargon as "educational facilitators." Free enterprise (student class and subject competition) has been conveniently junked to accommodate John Dewey's lunacy in regard to socialistic "class democratic" education. But forget the euphemisms! Students that aspire to academic excellence are wickedly stifled from doing so by Dewey-centered classroom mandates, those ambitious kids being falsely labeled as being "arrogant," "self-centered," "selfish" and "uncaring" about the "group."

Sure as oxygen, we do have plenty of students hibernating and vegetating in "group-dominated classrooms," idealistically wanting to change the world for the better, but those sedentary, callow, well-intentioned sorry souls lack the skill and the talent to successfully attain their dreams of a better America. It is only when *our* students learn to pursue their own self-actualization and to introspectively explore their own individuality through dedication and through ambition that *those* presently victimized young people will learn to mature (not evolve) into responsible adults, contributing to society and distinguishing themselves through community service, charity, compassion and a noteworthy career.

But first off, American education must reject John Dewey's detrimental "socialistic group-sharing" system and in keeping with competitive free enterprise capitalistic democracy, everyone attending public school must drop this "group-sharing nonsense" and modify their behavior to confidently believe in themselves. Is there any wonder why many astute parents elect to ignore lackluster public school education and send their children to private and to parochial schools?

While growing-up in New Jersey and in Pennsylvania, my father had taught me' several cherished principles that to this very day still govern my behavioral life. Be self-reliant and try helping others who are *temporarily* having bad luck, and then there was Dad's favorite bit of advice, "The world doesn't owe you a living so learn to distinguish yourself! Show some passion about achieving your personal dreams and goals!"

Americans must have both "the dream" and "the drive," but unfortunately, many of us lack *that* second vital and more necessary quality: that is, a deliberate plan to achieve "the dream" through strong labor and relentless desire. Yes, twenty-three-thousand or so dollars might now be the standard "Poverty Level" for a family of four, but if a motivated person living in the U.S. makes 50 thousand dollars and pays income tax on salary, property tax for a house, state income tax, state sales tax, gas tax, federal withholding tax, etc., then money-wise, he or she is as good as being on welfare too while simultaneously having the burden of working for a living to support a family!

And for those critics out there that will insist that I am guilty of discrimination, they are ABSOLUTEly right! I do possess discriminating tastes and values! Throughout history, right has always discriminated against wrong, good has always discriminated against evil and morality has always discriminated against immorality, otherwise, in stark contrast, there would be no distinct difference

310

between the two polarized entities, namely, good and evil, the two diametrically-opposed forces blending eventually into the same existence and also into the same definition, just as radical left-wing rights' activists want to legitimize and finalize!

So in the final analysis, thanks to Charles Darwin and Albert Einstein's theories as catastrophically interpreted by the disillusioned Socialist John Dewey, our present dysfunctional American public school educational system, our litigious-oriented legal system and our corrupt political system (along with our ever-evolving and ever-relative morality) are entirely convoluted and presently without clarity or focus, and consequently, the United States of America is soon on the verge of entering a self-destruct mode!

"Wall Street Protesters"

I maintain that the Occupy Wall Street protesters conducting lengthy rallies across the USA (and across the world) just don't understand and appreciate the United States of America, the greatest force for good that this Earth has ever known.

I suppose to begin with, I have a little trouble with the profoundly un-American operative word "Occupy." True "Democratic" protesters don't stubbornly "Occupy" anything that isn't their own personal property in the first place. They compliantly apply for a permit to publicly address their various grievances, demonstrate their major points of view between the reasonable hours of nine a. m. to five p. m., and then after conducting their peaceful demonstration, the bona fide protesters go home. Isn't extended loitering still against the law?

Whenever I ponder the terminology "Occupy," I think of Adolph Hitler and his crazed Nazis "Occupying" France, Holland, Belgium, Austria and Poland. My traditional mind contemplates someone actually taking and using something that is unlawfully his or hers. Genuine demonstrators don't "Occupy" anything. They peacefully make their public statement and then use the "democratic" method of the Election Day ballot box to actively change society to conform with their perspective's immediate goals and objectives.

When I further think of the suspect word "Occupy," my mind instantly contemplates a stark scene from the movie *Dr. Zhivago*. Zhivago returns home to Moscow after serving his country at the Russian WWI front. Meanwhile, the 1917 Bolshevik Revolution has occurred and Zhivago finds his formerly beautiful home "Occupied" by fifty irate dissidents. The Bolshevik "protesters/occupiers" tell Zhivago that he would be allowed to stay in his former home if he abides by *their* inflexible rules and if he gratefully pays for *their* food and for *their* basic daily necessities.

If the New York Wall Street protesters had their druthers, they would first take over Zuccotti Park, ultimately handicap Wall Street, next destroy "greedy" American Capitalism and then swiftly replace its "corruption" with a voracious and exploitative even more corrupt European-style nanny state.

But please don't expect productive and retired American adults and through-the-mill senior citizens to voluntarily provide for the abundant needs of mostly vocal young people, adamantly demanding privileges and "economic justice" (Socialism) that the all-too-vocal demonstrators have not legitimately and rightfully earned on their own.

313

Perhaps I can't satisfactorily identify with the mostly eighteen-year-old to twenty-four-year-old Wall Street protesters because I have diligently worked my' rear-end off for over forty-two years at all sorts of jobs, and have over that long span managed to borrow money and then faithfully repay it after taking several entrepreneurial risks owning and operating various business enterprises.

Not to sound too religious and too old-fashioned, the Wall Street protesters don't fully comprehend the Protestant Work Ethic. They quit too easily and lack the confidence and the fortitude to succeed. They don't like challenges or obstacles. They seem to despise competition and free enterprise. They interpret their "selfish" needs as being more important than and positively above the needs of self-reliant "selfish" Americans laboring and providing for their families, day in and day out. They appear to be saying, "The world owes me a living!"

When I was eight years old, I worked for my grandparents, who had a small concession stand inside their farm market. Work was consistently emphasized to me by my parents and grandparents when I was expected to ambitiously dip ice cream, fetch sodas, sell candy bars and electrocute hot dogs for prospective customers. Yes, I confess that in my formative years I had been exploited by my parents and by my maternal grandparents. I always had to work before I ever was allowed to play. Work and self-sacrifice for the good of the family always trumped and preceded the concept of "self-indulgence" and play.

When I was thirteen in the mid-1950s, my family lived in Levittown, Pa. My father was a stainless-steel fabricator whose company laid him off during one of several terrible economic recessions that had occurred during that explosive decade.

I had to find a way to earn my suddenly lost weekly "allowance." My dad lent me 25 dollars to purchase a daily newspaper route, which I soon paid off and then expanded from 75 customers to 125 within a year. I managed to make 10 dollars a week at my first adventure into free market capitalism. Ten dollars a week was a considerable sum for a thirteen-year-old kid back in the 1950s, equivalent to around 100 dollars a week in today's inflated money nomenclature.

But I could not keep all of my ten dollars a week. Half of my earnings had to be given to the family, twenty-five percent was used for my acquisition of shoes and school clothing and the remaining twenty-five percent I could use for my own "selfish" teenage pleasures. That's how I originally learned about the mechanics of "American Capitalism."

In high school, I worked in the back room of a delicatessen three nights a week and on weekends, spending plenty of time making

314

sandwiches and peeling potatoes. After graduating from a New Jersey high school in 1960, my dad got me a year's employment as a welder where he worked in Norristown, Pa. I decided I didn't like breathing in nasty gas fumes all day long, so the next year I attended a teachers' college in Southern New Jersey.

And my parents, through their own individual sacrifices, had saved enough money over the years to pay for my advanced education. I too have learned from their example and had saved sufficient cash to pay for my three sons educations, two at *Rutgers* and one at *Rowan University*. I just can't fathom how many of today's nanny-state "entitlement-oriented" college students are several hundred thousand dollars in debt and feel "entitled" to something when they had the option of attending inexpensive community colleges and rather minimally extravagant state colleges.

And yes, capitalism certainly does involve taking risks. I had borrowed money to start-up businesses on the Ocean City, Maryland, Rehoboth Beach, Delaware and Atlantic City, New Jersey boardwalks, worked fourteen-hour days for sixteen summers from Memorial Day to Labor Day and managed to frugally save sufficient money to pay for my home and educate my three sons. But if it weren't for me having the initiative, freedom and the opportunity to voluntarily engage in free-enterprise risk-oriented American Capitalism, I could have never successfully achieved *those* particular family and parental obligations.

And yes, I had worked for 34 years as a public-school teacher, so I definitely understand both the private sector business world and the public sector government world as well. My wife also worked for 31 years as a teacher in another school district to help me pay monthly household debts, so I really have trouble understanding a 21-year-old complaining about how rough it is for him or her to find employment or to pay for his or her college education.

And I didn't get the position of English teacher I had desired right away. For the first three years of my career I was a 6th grade all-subjects teacher and the next two years I patiently was the permanent substitute at the local high school before I finally earned my English teacher status. If "instant gratification" were my watchwords in the mid-1960s, then I might have become a disgruntled 60s hippie protester comparable to the current frustrated Wall Street protesters that happen to prevail today.

What disturbs me most about the misguided Wall Street protesters (and their movement in general) is that it is basically an economic socialistic "re-distribute the wealth" scheme where the advocates claim to represent the 99% of Americans who vehemently resent the 1% millionaires and billionaires. Well, I too am not in the top 1% income bracket, and these garrulous Wall Street protesters do not speak for me in any way, shape or form.

And for those insistent Wall Street objectors who have no employment and have accumulated massive advanced education tuition debts, the participants never explored the option of enlisting in the U.S. military, which would pay towards a college education after the young adult volunteers contribute several years of their lives loyally serving and preserving the security of the United States of America.

But regrettably, the mercurial Wall Street protesters don't appreciate the hand that feeds them, obviously the provider being American Capitalism. Free enterprise is the indispensable engine that affords economic stability to American democracy. If you only want "Democracy," then move to Iraq or Afghanistan. If you desire true "Democratic freedom" founded on solid "free market" economic principles, then live in and learn to contribute to the prosperity of the United States of America. Think about it for a moment. What would the world be like today if the United States of America (or American Capitalism) never happened?

When the Wall Street protesters profess that they desire to dismantle American Capitalism, those dissidents are actually vowing to destroy their own dreams of personal success and the goal of ever achieving personal economic prosperity. Talk about biting the hand that feeds them. Capitalism has created more wealth than any other economic system in the history of the world, including Marxism, Socialism and Communism. How's that 1959 social experiment going down there in Cuba, Fidel?

And capitalism has made America the envy of the world. But what other nation has freed so many millions of people in other countries and liberated them from cruel tyranny, from crazed dictators and from widespread oppression? What other political/economic system provides more for its citizens than American capitalism does? One thing is for sure. Being poor in America is like being upper middle class in foreign places such as Uganda, Indonesia, Libya and Syria.

But here's exactly what the Wall Street protesters fail to understand about the merits of American Capitalism. Wall Street (and the large banking and insurance companies) by itself did not cause the present economic recession. And if the protesters really want to take their animosity about the recent financial meltdown crisis out on the right people, they should be vigorously marching in front of the White

House and in front of the Capitol Building in Washington DC to forcefully express their twisted anti-money anti-capitalism sentiments.

I think that the Wall Street protesters inadvertently practice a warped inverted value system that idealistically espouses various abstract amalgamated causes. They worry about disadvantaged people living in Africa, about curing the international AIDS epidemic, about the salvation of the endangered world environment, about egregious corporate Wall Street greed while the very provocative demonstrators simultaneously are conspiring against the perils and evils of American Capitalism.

On the other hand, people like myself believe in self-reliance and the pursuit of individual success in a challenging and fluid free market-free enterprise economic structure model. In my own value system, I first want to "greedily" advance and help myself, then assist my family, then support my relatives followed by my community population, then performing charity for constructive national and international organizations, and after all of that is eventually responded to, finally I want to consider aiding the poor people of Africa and the shrinking rain forests of South America.

I humbly value the fact that I live in a stable, organized community, and quite frankly, *we* are proud and independent folks that don't need or wish for any community organizers and political activists around to *disorganize* my town so that *they* can reconstruct and re-organize the community according to *their* ultra-liberal activist economic and assumed legal justice standards.

But in reality, the Wall Street protesters just don't comprehend Wall Street and the myriad attendant benefits of American Capitalism, which argumentatively represent the only true hopes (the private sector) of getting this grand nation out of the current encumbering recession. Although the *public sector* performs an invaluable service to society, teachers, police officers and firemen basically consume wealth; they effectively don't produce wealth like the *private sector* Wall Street corporations do.

And policemen, teachers and firemen (along with most contributing adults) have pension plans and/or 401 K's that generate and accumulate wealth by investing in high grade stocks, bonds and mutual funds, all invaluable pillars of American "greed" and capitalism that the Wall Street protesters totally and explicitly abhor. And may I add that most American corporations are wisely structured "democratically" in that the stockholders vote on company policy and consequently decide executive salaries and compensations.

How many of the boisterous Wall Street protesters realize that the major banks that had been saved by the federal government have all repaid their TARP loans while in the process, the U. S. Government has made hundreds of millions on interest money paid on those same government loans when stock options, bonds and preferred stock had been finally redeemed?

How many Wall Street protesters realize that the bank bailouts were done to principally save Europe's fragile nanny-state economies from collapsing? AIG, Bank of America, Wells Fargo, Goldman and Citi Bank all have Gordian-knot types of entanglements inside the colossal global economy!

And how many Wall Street protesters realize that the U.S. Government coerced Wells Fargo into swallowing down Wachovia, which was in danger of defaulting on its mortgage loans, and the Feds also were engaged in forcing Bank of America to choke on dangerous Countrywide Inc. mortgages and also obtaining Merrill Lynch on the verge of tanking, *that* coincidentally grossly mismanaged in-jeopardy company also going belly-up? That's the main reason why Wells Fargo and Bank of America needed concurrent TARP assistance!

Republican George W. Bush was asleep at the wheel when he didn't observe that Freddie Mac and Fannie Mae were egregiously giving frivolous home mortgages with little or no collateral being offered by the buyers. Truly, everyone who is *not* credit-worthy does *not* deserve living in a home (forgive the double negative). That's why we have public housing apartments.

Now enter Chris Dodd and Barney Frank, both Democratic politicians overseeing wasteful government regulated institutions Freddie Mac and Fannie Mae. Low interest adjustable rates were quickly and generously offered to credit-unworthy mortgage recipients, and when the adjustable rates rose from three and a half percent interest to seven and a half percent, soon the mortgages and mounting debts became much greater than the houses' true value. Millions of unnecessary national foreclosures (since credit-worthiness precautions had not been originally defined and observed) soon became inevitable realities.

But perhaps the biggest travesty of all was when the large banks were told by the government that they also would have to offer low interest adjustable rates to credit-unworthy home buyers (just like Freddie Mac and Fannie Mae were doing) or else the Fed would cut down on issuing paper and electronic money to the B. of A., to Citi and to Wells Fargo.

318

The big banks reluctantly went along with the flimsy mortgage-lending Ponzi scheme, so to protect themselves, they quickly bundled the bad loans into complex derivatives, sold the derivatives to smaller investment companies, and when the housing bubble burst, the government determined that the banks were still responsible for the bundled derivatives when the smaller firms that assumed the bundled debts went insolvent. And so, *this* salient fact is why the Wall Street protesters ought to be demonstrating outside the Freddie Mac and Fannie Mae corporate offices, outside the Capitol and outside the White House, and not blaming the complicated mess specifically on Wall Street.

And then there was Stan O'Neal, the CEO of Merrill Lynch who had received a departure bonus of 161.5 million dollars soon before Merrill Lynch tanked and had to be acquired (by government coercion) by Bank of America. And let's not forget the 12 executives at Freddie Mac and Fannie Mae (all government friends) who in 2009 had received 42 million in taxpayer money in the form of remuneration.

On the topic of excessive compensation from Freddie Mac and Fannie Mae, and also in regard to Stan O' Neal and Merrill Lynch, I'm in absolute agreement with the Wall Street protesters. And yes, I admit that "greed" is the root of all evil, but I insist that "money" is honestly the genesis of all good!

I wholeheartedly believe that if a corporation tanks, then the CEO deserves little or no bonus compensation. However, if a corporation is profitable, then the executives should be rewarded at any reasonable level "democratically" determined and approved by the voting stockholders.

And in the final analysis, I suppose that what most greatly disturbs and disappoints me about these mediocre Wall Street rallies is the lack of American flags being proudly displayed. This obvious fact suggests that much of the Wall Street protest debacle consists of misguided cause-oriented youth, an array of anarchists, elements of nihilists, a mix of Socialists, Communists Environmentalists and U.S. Muslims, all being aggressively infiltrated and motivated by wily *public sector* union organizers, who are deviously mobilizing the angry demonstrators for the purpose of advancing *their* own unions' goals and objectives.

But what really hugely alarms me most about the Wall Street protests is that they have been inspired by the so-called Arab Spring phenomenon, a recent Mideast revolutionary upheaval which has no demonstrable "democratic track record," "democratic tradition" or "democratic history." What's next? Sharia Law replacing Constitutional Law? Social disorganization replacing community organization so that each defective American town and village will eventually require the services of far-left "community organizers."

When I watch the vociferous Wall Street protesters on TV, I see a conglomerate of folks that don't believe in their own individual potentials, a group that wants to see the government play Robin Hood and take from me (and people like me) to re-distribute wealth for the sake of "economic justice," young people who would rather believe in elusive remote causes than in themselves and in American opportunity, a lot of grasshoppers desiring to extort money from Aesop's fabled industrious ants, and finally, last but not least, I see Hitler's minions "Occupying" Europe and my wary mind still envisions that belligerent rabble of Bolsheviks commandeering and "Occupying" Dr. Zhivago's formerly beautiful Moscow home.

"Precedent Linkin's Get-Tease-Berg A Dress"

Wen eye wuz and English teacher *weigh* back *wend,* I *ewes two* tell my *stewdents,* "Abraham *Linkin* did *knot* invent the *Linkin* Verb, and he *did'ant* invent *Linkin* Logs *ether!"*

Pleas enjoy *Czeching* the spelling/homophones and *sea* the *misstakes inn* italics *beelow:*

For score *an* seven years *ego, hour farthers* brought *fourth,* upon this *incontinent,* a *knew neigh shun,* conceived in Liberty, and *deadicated two* the *preposition* that *awl* men *our* created *sequel.*

Now *wee* are engaged in a *grate Cybil Wore,* testing *weather* that nation, *oar* any nation *sew* conceived, *an* so dedicated, *Ken* long *enddoor. Oui r* met *hear* on a *grate* battlefield *of dat* war. We have come *too* dedicate a portion of it, as a *vinyl wrestling* place *fore* those who here gave *there* lives that that nation *mite* live. It is *alltogether* fitting and proper that we should *dew diss.*

Butt in a *lager cents,* we cannot dedicate, we *cant concentrate,* we cannot *hollow* this ground. *Da* brave men, living *end* dead, who struggled here, have consecrated it far above our *pore* power *two ad ore detrack.* The *whirled will lit-till* note, nor long remember, *watt* we say and *due* here, but *wood* never *foreget* what *day* did here.

It is *four* us, the living, rather *2 bee* dedicated here to *da* un-Finnished work *witch day* have, thus far, so nobly carried on. It is rather for us *2 B hear* dedicated to the great *tusk re-maneing B4* us that from *thesis* honored dead we take increased *devote-shin too* that *clause fore* which *day* gave the last *fall* measure of devotion, that we *hear hi-ly* resolve that these dead *shell knot* have *dyed* in *vein;* that this nation *shill* have a *gnu berth* of *free-dumb; an* that *diss goverment off* the people, *buy* the people, *fore* the *peoples, shoal knot parish* from diss urf.

"Manmade Climate Change: Mostly a Hoax!"

Climate change is *not* a hoax, but it is 90% caused by natural changes in the Earth's geologic development and not too much affected by the activities of "evil mankind". The advocates of the theory of man causing climate change tend to "only live in the moment of now" and not see the Big Pattern Picture. Yes, man's recorded history is a mere three thousand years old, but Earth's natural history goes back billions of years.

Ever since the Cambrian Era of Earth's history (500 million years ago), there have been five major Ice Ages, some lasting millions of years. In *that* same 500-million-year period, there have been several hundred mini-Ice Ages, the last one (well-documented) occurring in the early 1700s. Obviously Ice Ages (Climate Change) followed by Global Warming (Climate Change) followed by another Ice Age (Climate Change) repeating itself over 200 times is quite remarkable and indisputable. And how incredible! Climate Change happened over 200 hundred times *without* mankind's industry, cars, fossil fuels and CO2 pollution being key factors.

The Renaissance Period (1200-1400 A.D.) was a time of global warming that followed hundreds of years of much colder temperatures that had previously existed during the Dark Ages in human history. The Renaissance was actually caused by Global Warming. Because Italy became warmer, Venice emerged as an important trade capital sending its ships out farther to sea to do business. Ideas were soon shared between cultures because it is always easier to borrow than to invent. It was then easier for Marco Polo to journey to China and take back to Italy fantastic new ideas like paper money, gunpowder and spaghetti. Because both Italian Dukes and Popes suddenly became extremely wealthy as a result of the new-found trading scenario, those prominent men could now afford to commission geniuses like Michelangelo, Donatello, Raphael and the great Leonardo da Vinci to create fantastic works of art, all of that progress naturally occurring because of the wonderful benefits of Global Warming.

And because the Earth was still even warmer in Europe in the early 1600s, a unique variety of maple trees could then grow in Northern Italy, thus allowing Antonio Stradivari to manufacture the famous Stradivarius violins. If it weren't for Climate Change that differentiated the Dark Ages from the Renaissance Period from the Post-Renaissance, those special maple trees and the Stradivarius violin would have never happened. Of course, that 1600s Global Warming was followed by the "Little Ice Age" in the early 1700s.

Just think about it! Global Warming took Europe out of the Dark Ages and caused the Renaissance; the Renaissance led to the Age of Exploration and Discovery (Columbus, Magellan, etc.); which led to the Age of Enlightenment (Voltaire, John Locke); which led to the Revolutionary War and Democracy Era (Washington, Jefferson, Lincoln); which lead to the Industrial Revolution (Ford, Rockefeller, Edison); which then led to the current Age of Science and Technology (Bill Gates, Jeff Bezos, etc.).

If Global Warming (Climate Change) did not get Europe out of the cold and miserable Dark Ages, we all right now would probably still be wearing rags for clothes, living in straw and primitive stick huts and riding around in donkey carts if we were rich enough to own one.

Climate Change adherents claim that CO_2 being emitted into the atmosphere is extremely dangerous and is causing Global Warming to occur. Any public school 3rd grader learns that trees and plants breathe-in carbon dioxide and give-off oxygen; whereas, humans and animals breathe-out carbon dioxide and breathe-in O_2, a true symbiotic relationship existing between plants and animals. So with the excess CO_2 man is emitting into the atmosphere, maybe now the Amazon Rain Forests can be saved because the environmentalists all fear that those jungles are being shrunken and becoming lost.

And oh yes, we keep hearing about the North Pole glaciers dramatically shrinking because of atmospheric CO_2, but we never seem to hear from the ecology crowd that the South Pole ice is readily and coincidentally expanding around Antarctica.

A principal factor in causing Climate Change is probably an astronomical phenomenon known as Precession of the Earth's Axis. The last major Ice Age ended about 12,000 years ago, but every 26,000 years, the Earth gradually shifts from 25 degrees on its right to 25 degrees on his left, thus changing an amazing 50 degrees on its axis back and forth every 26,000 years. If the recurring pattern is again correct, the Earth is now midway between Ice Ages.

https://www.youtube.com/watch?v=CUZOXczMfMo

Finally, President Trump is absolutely right to get the U.S. out of the Paris Climate Accord. The Accord is another American taxpayer rip-off/canard where the Obama Administration was to initially put-up 1 billion dollars to get the Paris Agreement started, and the accumulated funds over time would then go to Third World Countries, which would be another form of worldwide Redistribution of U.S.

Wealth (Socialism) at the American taxpayers' expense. And of course, other countries would hardly pay anything at all, just like the U.S. is supporting the UN (paying 24% of its budget) while many other countries remain deadbeat contributors, and just like NATO where the U.S. pays 2.1% of our GDP and Germany (a prosperous country) only pays 1.1% GDP as one example.

And let's not forget that according to the bogus Paris Climate Agreement, the major polluters of the world, China and India, will get to increase their CO_2 emissions for the next decade and a half while the U.S. is expected to decrease emissions, thus giving a significant economic advantage to the world's biggest polluters over already handicapped U.S. industry.

So yes, the Earth is $9/10^{th}$ responsible for its own Climate Changes, and mankind causing Climate Change is at best a 10% hypocritical ruse being perpetuated by countries that either don't pay their fair share or don't follow the rules that the world community expects only the U.S. to follow.

Ever since the Post-WWII Marshall Plan of 1948, the U.S. has been subsidizing France and Germany in the UN, in NATO and in massive annual trade deficits. It's time for countries like France and Germany to pull their own weight and pay their own freight!

Jay Dubya (John Wiessner)

Google: Jay Dubya books

"Muslims & Islam Proliferating in the U.S."

Our Founding Fathers had installed the "Establishment Clause" in the U.S. Constitution because they did not want a repeat of the persecutions that had occurred in England after Henry VIII made the Anglican Church (Episcopalian) the official state religion. Thus, in the 1600s groups like Pilgrims and Puritans immigrated to the American colonies and settled in New England while Catholics did the same thing in Maryland (Mary's Land). The Freedom of Religion clause described in the First Amendment originally pertained to "Freedom of Judeo-Christian" religious faiths, since our Founding Fathers never imagined that Muslims would someday legally immigrate (invade) into America by the millions. Our 1776 Founding Fathers did not want to see a single Judeo-Christian faith become the official religion of the United States as had occurred with Henry VIII and the establishment of the Anglican Church being England's official religion in the 1600s.

The average American family has an average of 1.5 children per household; whereas immigrating Muslim families to the United States generally have 5 or more children. Sweden, which graciously accepts Middle East Muslim immigrants, is in big immediate trouble, since the population of Sweden is only around 10 million and the Muslim population will soon be burgeoning and taking over the country a generation or two from now.

1) POTUS Barack Obama had stated that Muslims have always been part of the history of the United States, but to my knowledge, no Muslim had signed either the Declaration of Independence or the United States Constitution. In fact, the first Mosque in the U.S. wasn't built until 1919 in Maine, nearly 150 years after the bloody American Revolutionary War and the signing of the Declaration of Independence.

2) In the year 2,000, there were 1,209 mosques in the United States. In 2015, the number had grown to 3,186 mosques.

Here are the states having the most mosques at present:

California	525
NY	507
Texas	302
Illinois	200
Florida	186
Michigan	139
NJ	104

3) Nearly 4 million Muslims (low estimate) are now living in the United States and of these, over 100,000 had immigrated in 2015 (Trojan Horse Theory). By 2030 that number will easily more than double to over 10 million if reasonable limits aren't imposed. Most Muslims in U.S. belong to the Democratic Party, and 68% of Muslims believe that the government should provide more services (free stuff, welfare).

4) The Islamic faith teaches that "No Muslim should ever speak unkindly or ungently about another Muslim". This is why Muslims do not communicate or cooperate with the INFIDEL police in the U.S. and in Europe. Because of their clannish beliefs and habits, Muslims do not easily assimilate into Western Civilization and tend to live isolated in urban "no-go" ghetto zones. And Columbus discovering America in 1492 was not nearly as significant an event back then as was the Spanish defeating the Moors (Muslims) in Spain, sending the invaders back to Northern Africa, thus saving Christianity and Western Civilization from becoming culturally and politically dominated by Muslims.

5) Unlike Christianity, the Muslim faith is only one/third of a religion. True, it has a Koran similar to the Judeo-Christian Bible. But a third of Islam (through its mosques) is a system of "Education Indoctrination Centers" where the stern and severe religious teaching is much more militant than the instruction taught in a regular Catholic catechism class. And one/third of an Islamic mosque's function is a "Legal Teaching Center" where Sharia Law is taught as being superior to U.S. Constitutional Law. And let's not forget, Islam has little tolerance for women's rights or for gays and lesbians.

6) Sunni Muslims (Saudi Arabia, Iraq) are generally wealthier and better off that Shi'ite Muslims (mostly living in Iran). The Saudis are Arabs and speak Arabic; whereas, the Iranians are Persians and speak Farsi. But both Sunni and Shi'ite Muslims have their own radical elements. For example, most of the terrorists involved in 911 were Saudis. On the other hand, the Shi'ites believe strongly in the 12th Imam, an Apocalyptic figure who had descended into a well around eight hundred years ago and who will emerge at the end of the world to defeat all enemies of Islam. This is why Iran is so dangerous, especially after the recent Iran Nuclear Deal signed by the Obama Administration. The Supreme Leader of Iran and his zealous minions will use the freed-up 150 billion dollars it had received from the U.S. and cause tremendous revolutionary and terroristic havoc all over the world. The Iranians don't have to develop a nuclear bomb; they now (thanks to the Obama Administration) have the money to buy them from North Korea.

7) Lastly, there are over 1.6 Billion Muslims living on this fragile planet. If only 1% of that population is radicalized, the number of potential terrorists (16 million) is incredibly astronomical, and this realization is not counting the additional millions who easily sympathize with the radicalized and extremely dangerous Muslim zealots. Muslim urban populations tend to be docile until they reach 10% or more of the citizenry, and then cultural conflict surfaces as civilizations clash in big cities when Muslims invoke the "Freedom of Religion" mantra, citing the U.S. Constitution. Muslims will continue to attempt being wily by using the United States Constitution to advance their civilization (Sharia Law) and to thwart the traditional American way of Judeo-Christian life.

8) President Donald Trump believes that the larger city mosques need to be closely monitored because those places are where Sharia Law is most likely indoctrinated and where Muslim men are being radicalized. When Muslim women wear hijabs and burkas, that garb represents "symbols of submission to male chauvinistic dominance" in Muslim culture. And if you ever see Muslims praying in a mosque or marching in an Islamic procession, notice that the women are in the posterior of the mosque or at the back of the procession. The Muslim faith regards women as being second class human beings that are the property of male privilege and dominance.

9) In conclusion, Islam functions best in a dictatorial/autocratic state where a strongman like Saddam Hussein in Iraq or Hosni Mubarak in Egypt rules with an iron fist, or where religious intolerance reigns supreme (over individual human rights) in a theocratic, Sharia Law state like with the Ayatollahs in Iran or with the Saudi King in Saudi Arabia. In short, Islam is antithetical to any Bill of Rights-oriented American Democracy or American Republic.

10) The Roman Empire lasted a little over 500 years from 27BC to 476AD, and three principal factors were responsible for its eventual deterioration and collapse.

1) Open Borders: (Visigoths, Vandals and Huns penetrating into the borders and first fighting among themselves and then fighting against the Romans).

2) Anarchy: (barbaric tribes rebelling against and eventually defeating Rome).

3) Corruption: (Roman politicians giving away the Empire's treasury in exchange for favors and votes).

The United States Republic is in jeopardy for the same reasons that caused the Roman Republic to disintegrate and fall. We have had an Open Southern Border and an influx of illegal Mexicans, Central and South Americans and Middle East Muslim refugees', most of whom do not assimilate into American culture. The U.S. has elements of internal Anarchy with such radical groups as Occupy Wall Street, Black Lives Matter, Code Pink, MS-13 and the KKK causing massive havoc and social disorganization. And naturally, Left Wing Democrats want the Free Stuff Welfare practice to continue in order to gain favor from immigrant Hispanics and Muslims who will vote in future elections, just like the greedy Roman politicians had done over fifteen hundred years ago.

"Why Mitt Romney Pays Only 15% Tax"

Of course, Mitt Romney only pays 13% and not 35% of his income for federal taxes. The 13% represents a number close to the current 15% capital gains tax as prescribed and enforced by the IRS. Romney is self-employed and does not work for an employer like most people do that have to pay 35% of their wages as income tax. Mitt Romney plays hardball (without the help of Chris Matthews) in The IRS Capital Gains Major League while most Americans play softball in the Earned Income Minor League.

And forget this left-wing FAIR SHARE nonsense! Anyone reading these words can do exactly what Mitt Romney does to only have to pay 13% and not 35% income tax; that is, if they have the economic guts to take major risks as Romney skillfully does.

Here's several hypothetical examples of how to play Capital Gains Major League hardball. First of all, according to recent tax returns, Romney contributed 13% to 20% of his yearly income to charities, so that statistic alone tells us plenty about the generous character of Mitt Romney and also about one of his large income tax deductions.

But what is this mysterious 15% capital gains tax that Romney is implementing? Well, YOU can do the same thing too. Buy a thousand shares of a stock for 10 bucks. Hold it for a year and then sell it for 20 dollars. You made a 10-thousand-dollar Capital Gain on your risk venture and therefore only have to pay 15% tax and not 35% income tax. You took a risk by saving your "earned income money" that had been taxed at 35% and now you are entitled to a 10,000 dollar "Capital Gain" that legally requires a $1,500.00-dollar tax and not a $3,500.00 "Earned Income" tax.

If you're frugal and manage to eventually save $100,000.00 from your "Earned Income" and then invested it in a business, and after a year sold that business for $500,000.00, then you would legally pay only a 15% tax because you had taken a risk, were successful, and Uncle Sam believes that you'll probably further stimulate the economy by re-investing most of your "Capital Gain" into another larger business enterprise and also hiring new employees.

Mitt Romney is not hiding anything in his tax returns. He's an accomplished risk-taker who succeeds over and over, time after time. That's why Romney pays only 15% capital gains income tax and not a 35% "Earned Income" tax like the average American employee does. Mitt Romney pays less because he has an employer's mentality and not an employee mindset, and he's not afraid to take big risks doing

Capital Gains investing that's incidentally given full legal approval by the IRS.

Anyone who thinks it unfair that Mitt Romney is not paying his fair share (35% of "earned income"), well, that person has an EMPLOYEE MENTALITY and obviously does not understand the true principles of American capitalism as evaluated and enforced by IRS accounting standards, That critical person seems to have more of a problem with the IRS Capital Gains tax laws than he or she does with Mitt Romney.

"The End of a Teaching Career"

Up until 1995 I had worked for administrators that were all older than I was. After 1995 my employment was under the dominion of less experienced superiors' that were somewhat intimidated by the veteran teachers on the middle school staff. I got the impression that the new generation of school executives wanted a faculty that was loyal to them and the school administrators were a trifle defensive when dealing with instructors that were in the school system thirty years before the new power elite had made their appearances.

I knew that the end of my teaching career was near when teaching methods gradually changed to sociological activity-oriented classrooms as opposed to the academic structured teacher-guided teacher-centered approach. Hostile parent conferences increased in frequency from around four a year to eight. I had taught over four thousand *students* in thirty-four years and I began thinking that I should go out while I was still on top of my game and remarkably still had most of my marbles.

I was not getting along too well with my supervisor and the vice-principal, who both were my junior by around two decades. The supervisor would always be putting *Mickey Mouse* memos' in my mailbox and I would correct all of the grammar and spelling errors (and there were many) and then return them. The vice-principal was catering to hostile parents and acting like their surrogate representative against teachers rather than deflecting the overprotective meddlers into oblivion where *they* rightfully belonged. I instinctively knew that the new school leadership wanted the old faculty to go and have teachers that *they* had hired and who' were beholding to *them*.

And most of my old buddies had retired from the *profession* including Bob Gordon, Tim Carley, Ron LeFey, Phil Tweston, Jim Kyle, Larry DeLancy and Rob Renbeck. Dean Miles had moved to another district in Pennsylvania, Tim Amoro had become a principal in another New Jersey' town, Ron Carputis was now a curriculum coordinator in my district, Joe Sacci was now a school supervisor and John Rizzo had gone into the oil business. Charlie Southard, John Magliari, Mrs. Finnian, Jack DeCicco and Bill Catello had all died.

Mack Fascito had wanted me to retire with him in June of '99 but I was hesitant. As the school year progressed, I soon became more and more interested in the prospect of living to see retirement.

"Mack, I want to stay around for one more year and retire in 2000," I said. "It's a nice round figure!"

"What difference does it make?" Mack maintained. "All the old guys are gone. The administration and your supervisor are gonna' make life miserable for you and besides, the board of education is offering a buyout for our sick days. How many have you accumulated?"

"Over two hundred and fifty!" I proudly answered.

"That means you're eligible for the maximum buyout!" Mack persuasively indicated. "I think the time has come!"

"I think you're right!" I agreed. "The principal told me that the accumulated sick day' buyout would be only a one-year-deal. Take it or leave it! The window closes on September 1st!"

I still kept my summer employment as a field manager at Atlantic Blueberry Company, the world's largest cultivated blueberry farm. I figured that since my wife was still teaching that I would try substituting two or three days a week starting in September of '99 to keep my mind and spirit active.

Substitute teaching was not exactly a royal cup of tea. And local school districts were only paying substitutes seventy dollars a day. 'Gee, if I work for a hundred and eighty days as a sub',' I thought, 'I can make a whopping twelve-thousand-six-hundred-dollars! The average cleaning lady makes more than seventy-dollars-a-day cash without deductions!' I mused. 'If it weren't for my pension and my sick day' buyout I would be eligible for food stamps!'

Substitute teachers really have their hands full when taking on an assignment. *Students'* eyes light up when they suddenly realize that the regular teacher is absent. The *children* have their own glossary of words to describe that festive realization: "Party!" "Kill!" and "Fun Time!" are some of the vernacular terms that *students* use while their eyes widen as if they are a pride of lions spotting a fat, wounded water buffalo the minute they see a substitute.

Substitutes encounter interesting experiences such as chalk in eraser grooves, tacks or chewing gum wads on the teacher's desk chair and *students* changing their seats to see if the sub' is smart enough to read a seating chart to relocate the *children* where they belong. *Students* will volunteer misinformation about where the regular teacher had left off in the textbook and will try to leave the room at every possible opportunity to make a phone call, visit the lavatory or take a stroll to the nurse's office. A hard day of substituting could wind-up being about as rewarding as a day touring the New York' sewer system.

"I would have to substitute one whole week to stay in a decent New York hotel for one night with meals included!" I told my wife.

334

"Grin and bear it!" she answered. "A day of substituting at least pays the television cable bill!"

"Yes, but that's not including any premium channels or a digital box!" I elaborated.

One of my first substituting assignments was at a neighboring district's elementary school. The principal told me that I was to be in charge of only one male *student* that had In-School Suspension.

"How old is the boy?" I inquired.

"Five years old! A kindergarten kid!" the administrator answered.

"What did this *child* do to warrant In-School Suspension?" I inquisitively asked.

"He became angry and kicked a male teacher in the testicles during cafeteria period," the principal replied. "I know you have plenty of experience and can easily handle the *child*!"

The kid cried and protested for an hour and a half in the detention office so I took him to the cafeteria and bought him plenty of snacks. After that "reward" I bent the rules, became his friend and we played *Bingo*, checkers and card games' until the 3: 15 dismissal bell finally rang.

Any time a substitute comes into contact with a hundred and thirty *students* in an eight-period day, that instructor is bound to have conflict with at least one. I was subbing at the local high school in March of 2000. After taking attendance, I was ten minutes into the lesson when a *student* stood up and started walking out the room. "Where are you going?" I asked him.

"Oh, I'm not a *student* in this class!" he answered. "This is my lunch period so I thought I'd just sit in and see how *you* were doing!"

"Enjoy your lunch!" I responded with a smile. I registered in my mind what the anonymous sixteen-year-old junior droll *child* looked like. Every time that same *student* was in a class where I was subbing, I would ask him, "Shouldn't you be in lunch now? The first time I had you in a Spanish II' class you were *out to lunch*!" The boy would always blush at my allusion and then slouch down in his desk in sheer admiration every time I mentioned those wonderful words as a reminder to him that I had not yet passed senility.

Another time at the high school I had entered a remedial mathematics classroom and all the *students* were milling around. "Please sit down so that I can take attendance and get the math' lesson started!" I implored the twenty-six seemingly uncooperative and disenchanted *students*.

Everyone abided by my' request with the exception of one haughty senior girl. "Mrs. Warner lets us walk around and talk to each other all the time!" she arrogantly insisted. "Why do I have to listen to you?"

"Because Mrs. Warner isn't here today and I am!" I answered. "Now just sit down so that things can start in an orderly organized manner!"

"You're mean! Do ya' know that?" the girl accused while still not sitting down.

"Look!" I exclaimed. "I think you're being very uncooperative under the circumstances! I don't think that asking you to sit down is too much of a demand!" I added. "Why do you suppose these desks are in the classroom? Waiting for termites to devour them?"

"I've had about enough of your rude shit!" the girl yelled. "You're an asshole!" the distraught girl screamed as she bolted out of the classroom honoring *flight* in the notorious "fight or flight" mindset.

No *student* in the class would tell me who the nasty girl was so I quickly took roll and figured it out for myself. I buzzed the office and reported the girl as being *AWOL.*

"Oh, she's sitting in the office waiting to see the principal or vice-principal right now!" the main office secretary replied over the intercom. "I believe she's complaining about *you*! Send down a Discipline Referral Card on the *student* after *you* have time to write one up!"

I assigned the day's math' lesson and then I wrote up the aforementioned discipline card. A girl' friend of the defiant young miss (now seated in the office) raised her hand and requested to go to the lavatory.

"Okay, I'll write you out a pass as soon as I finish with this discipline card," I promised.

"I have to go right now because I'm having my period and I gotta' get a rag' from the nurse!" the girl snottily replied.

"Look, I promise you you'll be out of here in just another minute!" I answered as I jotted down the final information describing the first classroom' incident with the other girl. "Please try to have a little patience and extend to me some basic respect and courtesy!"

"Fuck you!" the girl squealed as she insolently walked out of the classroom without a hall pass. "Asshole!" she yelled out into the otherwise empty corridor.

I had remembered the second girl's name because I had taught her when she used to be a respectful eighth grader three years before. I wrote down the second incident on the back of the Discipline Card and reported the second girl as also being *AWOL* from the math' class.

336

The office secretary called the classroom over the intercom. "Mr. Wiessner, the new school policy is that two *students* can't be listed on the same Discipline Referral Card," the voice specified. "You'll have to present two separate cards to the office for each of the incidents with the two different girls!"

I spent the balance of the period re-doing the first card and then writing up the second regrettable repulsive event. The class had become silent and cooperative once the remaining *students* realized that the substitute was not afraid to assert some authority and send *students* down to the vice-principal's office.

After the class was dismissed at the ringing of the bell I had a teacher lunch period so I had time to then drop off the two discipline cards in the main office. As I was entering the main office I observed two policemen dragging a girl I had never seen before out of the vice-principal's office.

When I got to the teacher's lounge to eat my brown-bagged lunch and to enjoy a *Coke* I asked the other faculty members at the table if anyone knew what had happened with the girl being taken into custody by the police.

"Oh," a social studies teacher said, "she had called Mr. Jackson an *asshole* because she didn't like the way he had graded her essay question on a test!"

"So regular teachers receive that kind of back-talk just like substitutes do!" I laughed.

"Yes, Jackson wrote her up," the female social studies teacher continued, "and the vice-principal told the *student* to go to In-School Suspension because she had accumulated a whole series of violations, but the girl refused to budge from the chair in *his* office!"

"And then the vice-principal called the police?" I asked.

"Yes, I was in the main office at the time," another teacher seated at the lunch table politely interrupted. "The assistant-principal told the girl that if she didn't get up and go to In-School Suspension that she would be trespassing in his office! The girl was stubborn and refused to get up so the cops hustled her out of the building while she was screaming like a maniac!"

"You don't know how lucky you are being retired!" the first teacher added. "I wish I were *you* right now!" she honestly congratulated my thirty-four-year career.

I glanced around the crowded high school faculty room and noticed only one familiar face that I had known from the past. I felt like *Rip Van Winkle* must have when he had returned to his native village after sleeping for twenty years in the *Catskill Mountains*. All of *his* old chums and cronies were gone from the village.

I walked to the men's room and noticed that one thing hadn't changed in the last thirty years. The same *Coke* machine that Bob Gordon, Tim Carley and I had moved to trap John Magliari in the teachers' lounge's men's room was still situated in the exact same spot.

On my way to instruct the next class I noticed a destructive-minded *student* walking down the crowded C-Wing corridor breaking four balloons in a row with his long fingernails. The decorations along with crepe paper were festooning the hallways because the high school football team was to play a major opponent later that week in an important league game.

'Let another teacher notice and report the balloon breakings!' I thought. 'I've already written out two too many discipline cards today! Give me a break!' I pleaded as my eyes rolled up to briefly view the C-corridor's ceiling panels.

Twenty feet ahead down the corridor Mr. Joe Wilkins intercepted the *student* breaking the balloons and started escorting the young violator to the main office for a ride on the familiar discipline carousel.

Eighth period study hall was an absolute nightmare that afternoon. I was alone and in charge of fifty restive but lethargic *students* that just wanted to fool around and talk. I separated them into sets of two at various cafeteria tables despite their protesting. Two girls and a boy refused to break up and move to another table. Finally they did and the young ladies then tried grossing me out.

"Hey man, did you ever have sex on a washing machine when it was runnin'?" the first girl asked me.

"That's too personal of a question," I answered. "Now please move to another table or I'll have to write you up."

"Once I had sex with my boyfriend in the back of a church while a service was going on!" the second young lady disrespectfully informed me.

"Look young lady, there are at least three ambitious *students* in this mass study hall that want to do some work!" I reprimanded. "Now please show more consideration for them. Not everyone wants to hear about your lackluster personal life. There's more to living than a mere biological existence!"

One of the girls and the boy then got up and moved to another table. On my next rotation of the cafeteria mass study hall I stopped at the table to where the two *students* had switched. "Say Mr. Wiessner,

338

did you know that Peggy and I like to have sex together with Greg here!" Jenn guiltlessly and shamelessly stated. "We like threesomes!"

"Maybe by the time all three of you mature into normal adults," I calmly said, "you'll finally realize that you all also have hearts', minds and souls besides just simply having physical bodies!"

My comment appeared to have an impact because all three *students* actually opened books and began reading. I glanced out the cafeteria's back windows and saw the board of education president, the principal and the superintendent sitting at a picnic table eating barbecued meat. 'I wonder if any of them have any clue as to what has been going on for nearly forty-five minutes in this cafeteria mass study hall only fifty feet away?' I wondered.

I was happy that no further incidents happened in that eighth period cafeteria mass study hall. I thought about how cafeteria study hall *students* back in 1975 had mocked Jack DeCicco by calling him "Meatball!" and I quickly realized that things had not really changed that much in the past quarter-century. The only thing was that I was the new elderly Jack DeCicco on patrol. When I checked out at the office the principal asked me, "Did you have a good day Mr. Wiessner?"

"The best!" I falsely replied. "It was without a doubt the absolute best!"

"Glad to hear everything went smoothly for you!" he cutely answered.

As I left the building and proceeded to my car in the A-Wing parking lot a red-haired *student* exited the high school and yelled, "Fuck this shit hole!" at the top of his lungs.

'I can relate to that!' I thought as I entered my automobile. 'This has been my worst day of subbing so far. Now where's the nearest bar? I think I need a double *Southern Comfort* on the rocks right away! I'll dedicate my first double shot to the memory of Jack DeCicco!'

In June of 2000 I received a phone call from the new middle school principal (my old middle school principal was now the new high school chief executive and the old high school vice-principal was now the new middle school head honcho).

"Say *John*," he enthusiastically began, "how would you like your old English teaching job back from September to *Thanksgiving*? Mrs. Grasi will be out on maternity' leave and I figured I would give you the nod."

"Okay," I replied. "I think I could handle that assignment. It sure beats regular subbing in certain subject' areas I'm not that familiar with!"

When I had left my position as the major eighth grade English teacher in June of '99 I had a hundred and ten *students* scattered over six class periods. Now my attendance roster read a hundred and thirty-five *students* condensed into the same six classes. Special needs *students* requiring individualized attention had been *mainstreamed* into the regular academic English classes.

Five of the classes had twenty-seven *students* each. The *children* generally were quite immature and many of them were outright obnoxious. 'This is going to be a very challenging assignment!' I thought on the first day of school. 'It's a good thing this stint will be over in less than ninety days! I hope my heart holds out!'

I didn't win too much favor with the new school administrators when this substitute replacement' English teacher criticized and slammed the basic unfairness of the *GEPA* writing test to eighth graders' parents on Open House Night.

And then the new middle school vice-principal was my' old supervisor whose frequent handwritten memos' used to receive my critical grammar and spelling corrections. Trouble was about to explode because the new Educational Aristocracy at the middle school embraced everything that *this manuscript* has been attacking from page one.

The vice-principal was acting like a surrogate representative of aggressive overprotective concerned parents that thought I was being too stringent and severe with their *children*. Just about every day a memo' would be in my mailbox that Mr. or Mrs. so-and-so was complaining about something "insensitive and sarcastic" I had said to their son or daughter in class or about me being too harsh in grading his or her *child's* compositions.

In mid-November the vice-principal came up to the second floor to briefly discuss a parental concern with me' between seventh and eighth' periods. I had just had a challenging session with the seventh period general English *students*, a class of twenty-seven *students* comparable in many ways to the old 8-6ers.

A seventh period *student* seated in the back of the first row next to the teacher's desk hadn't done homework or class work for the entire marking period. I was standing in front of the room at the lectern when the child stretched out his arms and loudly yawned as I was addressing the abominable seventh period' class. The fatigued *student* had inadvertently knocked the set of metal bookends off the teacher's desk onto the floor.

"Would you please pick up the metal bookends from the floor and place them back on the teacher's desk?" I politely asked.

"No!" the *student* adamantly replied and then put his head down on the desk feigning sleeping.

"Look, if *I* had accidentally knocked the bookends on the floor and then asked *you* to pick them up," I said, "I could then understand your refusal. But *you* have knocked them on the floor. Why don't *you* simply pick them up?"

"Stop buggin' me man!" the *student* nastily replied. "Get off my damned case!"

When the vice-principal accosted me out in the hallway I told the school administrator that I would be writing out a discipline card on the defiant *student* that had refused to put the metal bookends back on the teacher' desk.

"Okay Mr. Wiessner, but I'm really here to tell you that Mrs. Larson had called and thinks you shouldn't have embarrassed her son by reprimanding him so harshly in front of his peers!" the paranoid school' administrator related.

"Well, I handled the situation just the way I always have in the past," I said. "I've never backed down to any *student* and I don't think I've going to start at this stage of the game!"

"Try being a little more sensitive!" the vice-principal suggested. "The times are changing!"

"Look!" I replied. "The classes *are changing* from seventh to eighth period and right now I've got to get back to my primary responsibilities."

When I re-entered the upstairs classroom, I immediately noticed that the roll and grade book had been stolen from the lectern in the front of the room. While the vice-principal had been distracting me about a parental grievance some *student* in the seventh period class had pilfered the teacher' records and I had a good hunch that it was the same *student* that refused to pick up the metal bookends off of the floor. I immediately buzzed the office and requested that the vice-principal come back up to the classroom.

I explained what had happened and the vice-principal said that the major suspects would be interviewed the next day.

"Interviewed?" I asked. "Valuable teacher records, school property has been taken and *you* want to *interview* the suspects tomorrow? Get the police over here right now and have them *interrogate* the *students* and let's crack this mystery wide open today!"

'I'll *interview* the *students* first thing tomorrow morning," the politically correct vice-principal related. "I can't keep them after school and have them' miss their buses unless they've been given a full day's notice! It's school policy in the *Student* Handbook!"

On Thursday morning I was on early morning bus duty when the on-a-mission vice-principal approached me. *"Mr. Wiessner*, it is the administration's position that if the grade book can't be found that you'll have to prepare a new book with the grades in it for when Mrs. Grasi returns after *Thanksgiving!"*

"Well, I'm just a substitute teacher' fill-in and I'm not going to do it!" I answered. "The first marking period' grades had already been submitted to the guidance office two days before the grade and roll' book had been stolen from the lectern!"

"I think you're being quite difficult!" the vice-principal admonished. "Didn't *you* take the time to make a copy of all the grades in the grade book?" the school executive indicted.

"Look," I angrily replied, "in my thirty-four years of teaching I have never had a grade book stolen! And I only remember it happening once to Mrs. Finnian back in the early 1970s at the high school when I was teaching there!" I emphasized. "A *student* has committed a punishable *crime* by stealing school records and *you* want to reward that *student* by having *me* rewrite the grade book!"

The vice-principal realized that I couldn't be coerced into re-doing the roll and grade' book, which was an impossible task because all of the first marking period individual test, homework and writing grades for the hundred and thirty-five *students* were missing. Later that day I telephoned Mrs. Grasi about the theft and she agreed to make up a fresh roll and grade book starting with the second marking period.

On Friday morning I was in the office during my *PPSA* picking up my paycheck. I had just signed out to leave the building to drive to the bank and deposit my hard-earned wages into my checking account.

"Mr. Wiessner," the vice-principal said, "I'd like to see you in my office!"

"Well, I'm on my way to the bank right now so why not make it later!" I answered while thinking that I never wanted to see or hear the vice-principal again ever in this life or in the next one.

Two periods later happened to be my teacher lunch break. The vice-principal entered the teacher's room and said, "Mr. Wiessner, I want to see you in my office right now!"

"Does it involve the roll and grade book?" I asked.

"Yes!" the vice-principal testily replied.

"Has it been returned?" I queried.

"No!" was the terse response.

"Do you want to see me about a parent calling?" I questioned.

"Yes, now come to my office immediately!" the school official inflexibly demanded.

"Well then," I said, "the school has a definite procedure that the parent must follow. Have the parent call the Guidance Office and schedule a conference! Let the parent be inconvenienced by having to come in and complain about something instead of using the telephone and having *you* do his or her dirty work!" I suggested. "A parent has never to my knowledge called the school to arrange a conference to praise me! No, that has never happened in thirty-four years! This parent wants to have a hostile conference! And in two days I'm outa' here!"

The vice-principal felt that I was being *insubordinate* and also a bad example in front of other younger teachers having lunch in the faculty room. One could easily hear a pin drop at the end of our heated disagreement. The school executive left the faculty room virtually in tears.

Five minutes later I marched upstairs to set up the *VCR* for a film I would be showing the following period. The principal entered the classroom and slammed the door behind him in anger.

"*Mr. Wiessner*, this is one of the hardest things I've ever had to do," he anxiously but firmly stated, "but I'm going to have to ask you to leave the building because you have been *insubordinate* to the vice-principal."

"But I only have two more days until *Thanksgiving* break!" I replied. "Why don't you just let me finish my assignment *we* had agreed upon?"

"Sorry, but I can't tolerate teachers being *insubordinate* to administrators!" the principal declared. "You must leave the building immediately!"

"Well, I just want you to know that I told the vice-principal off because I don't think that school administrators should be the surrogates of overprotective parents!" I succinctly stated.

I knew that I had not signed a contract but had only made a verbal agreement with the principal to teach until the *Thanksgiving* holidays. I left the school building where I had taught for twenty-seven of my thirty-four years in a stupor. I had been exiled for being *insubordinate* to administrative discretion while the vice-principal was acting as an undesired parent' surrogate. 'Evicted from the school system I had worked with all my heart to *professionally* represent for thirty-four years!' I pondered.

I was happy that I had not surrendered my convictions and my principles right up to the end. When I explained to my wife what had happened, she said that she was not-at-all surprised at the outcome and sounded pleasantly optimistic about the future. "The administration wanted you out because they believed you were influencing the younger teachers by setting a bad example!" my wife intelligently concluded. "You were a definite threat to their authority! You've always been sort of a rebel!"

"Joanne," I said, "I'm just sick and tired of hearing bells ring all day long. The school bells ring seventeen times a day. Times that by a hundred and eighty days a year and that comes to over three thousand times a year," I indicated. "Multiple three thousand times a year by thirty-four years and I've listened to bells blast over a hundred and five thousand times in my career. No wonder why *you* say I'm deaf!"

"And that's not counting the fifty thousand times you also heard bells ring between classes as a *student* before you ever became a teacher!" my wife impressively elaborated. "And don't forget the over seven hundred fire alarms you've listened to!" my wife reminded. "Look at the positive side," my spouse suggested. "You've taught over four thousand *students* in your educational career!"

The principal and the vice-principal taught the six eighth grade classes the last two days before *Thanksgiving* break. My mother's cleaning woman's daughter was in one of the Accelerated English classes and related that the administrators had told the *students* that Mr. Wiessner had taken sick and could not teach them the last two days before the four-day-holiday' vacation.

'They lied to the kids!' I considered. 'Education is not really about academics, or teaching, or learning or knowing right from wrong. It is just a big American power game where administrative might makes administrative right!' I sadly concluded.

"Maybe *you* can begin that writing career you've always dreamed of doing!" my wife recommended and consoled.

"You're right Joanne, my pension is safe and secure and now that I'm no longer a teacher," I added, "I can actually be an ordinary citizen with genuine freedom of expression and other remarkable *Constitutional* rights! I might even produce several PG-13 type books with graphic content!"

I knew that I had written sixteen manuscripts from 1974-1999 while I had been an instructor and this book *So Ya' Wanna' Be A Teacher* has become the sixteenth work.

"You're absolutely right!" I reiterated and agreed with my wife. "Teaching is over in my life and it's time for a new career! There *is* life after teaching!" I laughed. "Thanks to the principal and the vice-principal now I finally have a good ending for book number sixteen! No more teacher serfdom!"

"At last you've come to your senses!" Joanne answered with a smile. "Writing should be much more relaxing than teaching was. It's time for someone else to step up and fill your big shoes!"

"Being Gay Versus Being a Practicing Gay"

I am not frightened or scared of gays, and I do not suffer from homophobia. I believe it's more like "homo-dislike-ia" of homosexual behavior. Proponents of gay rights have their nasty habit of labeling anyone opposing gay behavior as being homophobic, and they expect me (or anyone like me) to feel guilty about my "discriminating." In my mind, there's a big difference between someone being gay and someone practicing gay behavior, which I personally find abhorrent and immoral.

Let me explain my position. Let's say that I own a restaurant. If two men come into my place of business, I don't know if they are gay or straight, so how could I possibly discriminate against them by not providing service? The same observation would hold true for two females sitting down at a table. If the two men or two ladies act like normal restaurant customers, even if the men show effeminate mannerisms or if the women seem to have masculine appearances, I cannot prove that they are "gay" and must cordially give them the benefit of the doubt.

Gay is okay! But there's a caveat here in my moral reasoning! Gay is okay if the gay person is celibate and engages in abstinence. In other words, I have no problem accepting gay folks if they are professed "gay virgins."

But if the two seated men (or women) begin holding hands incessantly and then lip-kissing for prolonged periods of time in "my restaurant," offending either my other patrons or myself, then I would definitely insist on evicting them. My conscience (moral compass) would determine that their practicing of "gay public behavior" is both inappropriate and unacceptable. Conversely, if the two men or two women were acting in more traditional restaurant etiquette, blending in with the crowd, then they would be more-than-welcome to dine in my establishment.

Now let's say that a photographer having strict Christian moral values is approached by a same-sex couple planning their wedding pictures. The photographer automatically knows that the same-sex couple desires being "practicing gays" so he refuses them his services and hands them a business card of another photographer who would gladly accommodate their wedding day needs. But the same-sex couple does not honor the photographer's moral values and the adamant pair unreasonably threatens to sue him and destroy his business for wickedly violating their civil marital rights. I believe that such blatant discourtesy and inflexible disregard for another person's moral value system is both reprehensible and totally selfish, especially if the photographer had tried to peacefully resolve the issue by politely referring the vindictive same-sex couple to another more liberal-minded photographer. But in most cases, the two very militant same-sex gays will attempt to destroy the photographer's livelihood simply for the purpose of stubbornly advancing their "immoral" agenda.

Let's say that a gay couple enters a bakery. The owner suspects that the pair happens to be gay but will gladly sell the twosome doughnuts, bagels, bread, cookies, Danish, cream puffs, eclairs, buns, rolls, muffins or even a birthday cake. But the intolerant gay couple wants the baker to cater their wedding and provide a reception cake, which is obvious code language for the duo being "practicing gays". The baker refuses, so a day later a vigilante mob of gay rights activists pickets the bakery in an effort to economically punish the Christian-oriented owner and consequently shut the business down.

As for my own personal behavior, I feel no need to publicly announce over and over my sexuality yelling-out the statement, "I am straight! I am straight!" Conversely, I can't lucidly fathom why it is so necessary for mostly "practicing gays" to repeatedly tell the world all about their unorthodox sexual orientation by shouting "I am gay! I am gay!" Who really cares?

Ask yourself several elementary questions to fully comprehend the absurdity of "same-sex marriage." "Was my grandfather a woman?" "Was my grandmother a man?" "Was my father a female?" "Was my mother a man?"

The gay and lesbian advocates are endeavoring to rewrite the dictionary, making opposites have the same definitions. These' obdurate social revisionists desire to create a 21st Century Tower of Babel where basic gender descriptions are virtually identical and where all differentiation pertinent to traditional male/female gender references are erased.

Years ago a high school friend of mine came "out of the closet" and announced to his former classmates that he was a "homosexual" at the high school reunion. This old friend told me that he now is retired as a social worker and presently often performs nude "gay entertainment shows" up in western Canada.

My old friend came back to my town to visit his only living aunt, who immediately got in touch with me and related the news. I contacted the fellow and invited him to a restaurant nicely situated near a local river. My wife decided to tag along for a delicious meal.

During the dinner, I innocently asked my friend, "Tell me, how long have you' been officially declared gay?" Surprisingly, my benign inquiry sent my homosexual past acquaintance into a terrible verbal tirade. "Why do you call me gay?" he obnoxiously screamed out loud. "I'm not gay! I'm queer!" he boisterously ranted.

My wife and I were extremely embarrassed at his loud outburst occurring inside the crowded dining room. My old chum's unwarranted holler was indicative of "indecent gay public behavior," and if I were the establishment's manager or its owner, I would have either reprimanded my old pal or thrown him off the premises.

Even if a gay is a "practicing gay," it's okay with me as long as either he or she doesn't shout it in my face. I don't like wild and raucous gay parades, and I would never attend a raucous straight one, either. I contend that one's sexuality is private knowledge that is unfit for public consumption. If someone engages in homosexual conduct, I prefer that it be performed in a bedroom or in a hotel room, but please be sensitive to my "discriminating sensitivities" when out in public. Gays should exercise discretion and prudence when navigating around in public or in mixed company.

I suppose the principal reasons for my basic "homo-dislike-ia" are as follows:

Homosexuality goes against nature, or against the "natural order." Humans and animals reproduce through natural sexual intercourse. I have a problem with the "gay practice" promulgating that another man's rectum is an entrance and not the obvious exit that's been effectively designed by nature. Furthermore, let's assume that all animals were suddenly transformed into homosexuals. Cherish your dogs and your cats. Within twenty-five years, most animal species would cease to exist. And if all humans were homosexuals, then human existence would quite possibly disappear into oblivion after a century.

Oh yes, I know all about sperm and egg fertilization outside the womb and then having embryo implants inserted into the uterus. But don't we straight folks get it? Since practicing gays can't reproduce "naturally," adoption is the next logical and predictable step on their radical agenda.

Yes, I certainly know that married gays love each other very much, but how they practice their gay love (sodomy, etc.), well quite frankly, most religious-value-oriented people find the enactment of homosexual physical love to be egregiously offensive, repulsive and distasteful. And I just have to wonder how many same-sex marriage "adopted children" will grow-up being straight "traditional marriage" adults?

Yes, I suppose that Christian morality does "discriminate" against "the practice of gay behavior." Throughout recorded history, morality has always "discriminated" against immorality; good has "discriminated" against evil and moral right has "discriminated" against moral wrongdoing. The main objective of the uber-liberal left and of the gay rights activists is to cloud the prominent line between morality and immorality (under the surreptitious guise of Constitutional Rights), cleverly blurring the difference so much that soon it will be impossible to distinguish the contrast between "religious morality" and "legal immorality."

Forget all of the redundant, hackneyed legal arguments! Someone please explain to me exactly what is moral about homosexual-sexual activity? Or is gay the New Morality? In many cases, legalizing gay marriage is a government permission slip to immorally practice sodomy.

Much of this new 21st Century interpretation of the legal rights of gays (along with woman's rights' abortionists) can actually be attributed to the theories of two famous scientists, Charles Darwin (everything in animal life must evolve and change) and Albert Einstein (relativity). In effect, the Ten Amendments in the U.S. Bill of Rights are presently in direct conflict with the Old Testament's Ten Commandments.

Who can deny Albert Einstein's colossal impact on American culture? With the revolutionary Theory of Relativity came the unique notion that everything in society is "relative": yes indeed, nothing anywhere in America (save death and taxes) is absolute, is permanent or is fixed. And so now we have such things as the Bill of Rights to the Constitution coming into clashing conflict with widely-recognized traditional American family values.

The First Ten Amendments (under the guise of freedom of speech and freedom of expression) are now insidiously undermining the original Ten Commandments handed-down to Moses on Mt. Sinai, simply because now all truths (gay rights included) must be *relative* and not *absolute.*

Indeed, Darwin and Einstein have inadvertently affected the change in American values from absolute moral truths to relative values. This stunning societal switch happened when scientific thinking bled over into the social sciences in the early 1900s.

Take this rather disturbing gay rights marriage issue for example in regard to what Einstein's relativity has mutated into. Remember:

everything today is rapidly evolving and must be "Relative" and not "Absolute" (for example, God's Ten Stone Tablet Laws). Two iconic Commandments are: "Honor Thy Father and Thy Mother" and "Thou Shall not covet thy neighbor's wife!"

Just think about those two simple-but-sage Commandments for a second. The principal purpose of heterosexual (man-woman) marriage is to biologically conceive children and then to nurture them through mature parenting skills. The very vocal gay and lesbian political activists want gays to get married, to then adopt children and next to have loving families.

Now someone please explain this rather paradoxical situation to me. How could an adopted child with gay "parents" know who the mother is if two males are his or her parents? If two lesbians are his or her parents, which one is the father according to the very explicit Commandment: "Honor Thy Father and Thy Mother?" And if two gay married men are living next door, according to the Ninth Commandment, which one is "thy neighbor's wife" to be possibly sinfully coveted? Evidently, the sixth and the ninth Commandments are being blatantly violated by "practicing gays actively engaged in gay marriage."

Under the Charles Darwin "evolutionary pattern" and under Albert Einstein's politically correct "relativity law," which have both morphed into gay rights' laws, the idea of certain "sins" against God has been almost eradicated, and "sin" is now basically obsolete and simply a "relative" insignificant matter. In order for Biblical teaching to survive in this modern era, Ten Commandments' morality must gradually evolve into immorality, or else it is destined to perish when contradicted by perpetual "gay and freedom of choice immorality."

And needless to say, coincidentally, a woman's right to choose having an "Abortion" also very obviously violates the Stone Tablets' ABSOLUTE Commandments because a conceived child is sinfully killed, "Thou Shall Not Kill," and the fetus has no opportunity whatsoever to ever honor either a mother or a father, or for that matter, ever coveting a neighbor's wife.

And indeed, if the very vocal in-your-face abortion rights' activists/hypocrites had themselves been aborted before their sacred births by "Right to Choose" mothers, the conservative Christian community would not be having any legal wrangles with any of them at present.

Was Sodom and Gomorrah a Biblical myth or could it all soon again be happening right here in America? I'll let *you* be the judge of that! But still, acceptance of gays, lesbians and tolerating a woman's

351

"right to choose" are currently being taught in our all-too-liberal socialistic public schools, thus affecting and influencing young impressionable minds, thanks partially to the impact of Darwin's Theory of Evolution and Albert Einstein's Theory of Relativity, both scientific principles ironically skewing American Constitutional Law and thus, changing former absolute tenets of morality as exhibited and taught for over two millenniums in the Bible's Ten Commandments.

No, I am not an integral part of the invented left-wing propaganda nomenclature "homophobic." Instead, I am merely "dis-like-ia" of boisterous, bellicose, arrogant, obnoxious, egocentric, intolerant radicals who proudly practice sodomy and other gay and lesbian homosexual behavior. I mean, quite succinctly, does it totally defy standard definition and traditional explanation? What part of the precise dictionary word "immoral" do practicing gays not understand?

"A Self Analysis"

From my perspective, everyone has two basic psychological needs: a need to socialize with others of his/her species and secondly, a need to be alone by oneself. I, like most introverted writers and authors, much greater prefer the latter to the former. Confidentially, I totally enjoy being removed from social clutter for my self-motivated brain to quietly explore the development of new story plots and themes. When I'm preoccupied writing, my fleeting thoughts at that intense moment are just as indispensable as oxygen and food. To preface my personal observations, I maintain that an author's examination of conscience is both a meritorious and a healthy sort of worthwhile enterprise.

As a young boy attending the afternoon black and white cowboy movie matinees at the Rivoli Theater on Bellevue Avenue in downtown Hammonton, New Jersey, I quickly comprehended the valuable concept that is readily apparent in the nomenclature, "It is better to make dust than to eat it." In other words, I always admired either the Sheriff or the Marshal leading the on-a-mission posse and simultaneously felt sorry for the poor deputies having to eat the dust of the head guys up front chasing the dastardly outlaws across the cactus-laden wilderness. And oh yes, Rule #1 of being a nationally recognized author is that no one will take either you or your writing seriously until *you* first take you and your writing seriously.

When I was a New Jersey teacher of literature for thirty-four years, one of my favorite tales that I used to orally read with my classroom students was the mythological story of "Perseus." One fine day the young Greek hero was curiously standing on a mountain cliff when the goddess Athena appeared and soon approached upon a floating cloud and imperatively asked, "Before I send you on a dangerous challenge to slay the formidable monster known as Medusa the Gorgon, I'd like for you Perseus to courageously answer this one simple question. 'Which would you rather have; a soul of clay or a soul of fire'?"

Perseus did not hesitate to answer the odd interrogative by intrepidly articulating, "A soul of fire, because most vain cowardly men commonly possess souls of clay. Dear goddess, pardon my audacity but I won't ever want to be greedy and weak like most other craven humans behave on this rather corrupt planet!"

And so, I wholeheartedly maintain that to be the proud-but-humble owner of "a soul of fire" happens to constitute the very essence of my literary philosophy. A mortal in quest of literary excellence must search for and find a viable writing voice to adequately complement his or her writing style, and then the aspiring author should avoid being timid and next boldly address any relevant issue that should enter his or her psyche.

While vacationing with our wives ten years ago on the West Coast, a professor friend and I stepped into a Palm Springs, California bar to savor a few cold drafts of beer. Being gregarious, we struck-up a conversation with two other elderly retired tourists, and the topic of discussion soon changed from "the pleasant weather" to the subject of "property." The two wealthy gray-haired gentlemen each bragged that they had owned houses in Florida and California, and each respective fellow extensively cherished his coveted lengthy stock portfolio. "What kind of properties do you own?" the first zealous capitalist bluntly asked me.

I pondered the conceited guy's direct inquiry and soon carefully replied, "Most of the property I own is 'Intellectual Property'." "I am the author of 52 copyrighted books, and every idea, every character, every plot scenario, every conflict, every aspect in the stories' constructions is owned exclusively by me. I honestly mean Guys," I paused and deliberately emphasized, "I do own my New Jersey home, I have some blue chip stocks and bonds, and my wife and I have an acre of land in the Poconos along with several building lots in Florida, but believe me, the most priceless properties I value still are the intellectual properties I own that nicely exist in my fifty-two published books."

Naturally, my strange unexpected declaration made my new bar acquaintances pause and stare blankly at me with their dual mouths agape as my New Jersey pedagogue/companion giggled profusely and then anxiously proceeded to swallow-down another gulp of his delicious cold beer.

Eminent New England nineteenth century writer Ralph Waldo Emerson had imaginatively invented the now-obsolete "Theory of Transcendentalism", the romantic notion that Emotion should "transcend" Reason in order for a regular person to ultimately experience true satisfaction and complete fulfillment in life. On the contrary, I staunchly subscribe to the principle of what I describe as "Reverse Transcendentalism", or the requisite speculation that Reason should valiantly triumph and dominate over Emotion in a story presentation.

Yes indeed, it is true that one could have emotion demonstrated in the content of one's story, but the evolution of the plot along with the accompanying vital subplots ought to be both logical and plausible in construction for the captivated reader to easily grasp the tale's scope

354

and sequence. The prescription for a terrific story is quite elementary from my lifelong writing point of view. The appropriate literary formula to faithfully apply is this: Quality + Quantity + Author Discipline + Perseverance = Eventual Success. In the final analysis, *that* particular recipe has loyally worked for me.

Being a public-school English teacher for thirty-four years, I had been fully aware of distinguished educational psychologist Abraham Maslow's Theory of Hierarchal Needs, represented in a standard pyramid illustration. At the bottom of the isosceles matrix is any living creature's need for food, shelter and clothing (fur or other external protection). Then above those fundamental essentials is a definite need for basic socialization, recognition, love, acceptance "emotional security" and group or family approval.

And now inside the triangle formation we get into the more complicated and intricate "lower thinking skills," which along with important problem-solving ability, dramatically and intellectually separates mankind from the lower animals. Here's where I selectively believe the strict differentiation between writers and authors comes into stark focus.

I strongly insist that *authors* write fiction novels and fictional short stories, and on the other hand, *writers* systematically research and organize non-fiction books, term papers and newspaper and magazine narratives. Non-fiction writing (in its architectural format) involves the explicit use of general description. The whole process is akin to newspaper front page articles that are characterized by the creation of "a hook" introduction to gain the reader's instant attention. Next the non-fiction *journalist* accurately exploits the presentation of "Who? What? When? Where? How? and "Why?" in his' or her' newspaper article. And then to add a personal non-fiction touch, a few direct quotes are slickly thrown into the *writer's* process of front page narrative construction in order to add a distinct degree of "human interest" to the initial exposition being adroitly fabricated and communicated.

On the periodical's Editorial Page, certain higher-level thinking skills are evident with the deft utilization of Opinion, Interpretation and Analysis, three distinct thought synthesizes that are significantly emblematic of us mortal humans and which are not widely present anywhere in the lower animal world. College term reports and theses papers are very similar to a *writer* preparing a serious newspaper or magazine task. One must austerely employ lower-level thinking skills encompassing the methods of Research, Description, Interpretation, Analysis and possibly Opinion/Conclusion.

But conversely, *fiction authors* take their thinking dynamics to a higher level than non-fiction writers do. They perilously enter the lofty realms of Imagination, Creativity, Originality and Invention, thus attempting to fearlessly imitate the Glorious Creator. Renowned Abraham Maslow calls this highest level of thought ascension "Self-Actualization," and *this* coveted perch is the thinking plateau that authors audaciously pursue and that non-fiction writers dare not enter or tread.

Three areas of human classification represent the population of American academic organization ranging from lowly kindergarten up to the prominent university niche. It has been statistically established that around 75% of the people associated with American education are students, 22% are dedicated teachers, aides, librarians, instructors, administrators and professors, and the remaining 3% or so are the gifted creators and inventors of knowledge.

By consistently producing quality fiction as being an elevated dimension of accepted literature, authors are conscientiously competing for respectable inclusion into the revered 3% "creators and inventors" who are superbly contributing to the advancement of modern civilization.

Even though I consider Non-Fiction scribes as "Writers," and despite the fact that my literary efforts venture mostly into "Fiction," I insist that I am not yet an *author* in the same sense as Mark Twain, O. Henry, Jack London, Edgar Allan Poe or Nathaniel Hawthorne, but if people are reading and relishing my works a century from now, I will have then satisfactorily risen my accumulated literature up to international fame and therefore, my fictional works will have earned me the coveted designation of finally becoming an "Author."

A certain nebulous facet of fiction writing is the obscure enigmas of Creativity, Imagination, Invention and Originality. Exactly what are the defining characteristics of these often-elusive authorial phantoms? In reality, it's fairly easy to explain but rather difficult to fully fathom.

First of all, I realize that I first require a suitable outline to effectively arrange and present a well-structured story in a rational manner. What I'm about to disclose is my former secret method that predictably always had worked for me, and I hope I'm not precariously jinxing myself by hereby revealing its former surreptitious mechanics. The up-to-now reliable practice ordinarily determined how something inside my head mystically connects like an electrical extension cord into the Universe's master wall socket AC power plug.

Allow me to first sincerely divulge that I am not a particularly religious human being. Now in my home's computer room there are three lamps (two identical table ones and the third light located upon a tall thin stand), which I mentally reference as 'the Father, the Son and the Holy Spirit'. Like a submissive suppliant, I reverently invoke each lamp individually to assist me in my writing endeavor, obediently reciting in a silent prayer, "Lamp of wisdom, lamp of light; please help me' to create a new story idea." Amazingly, this unique, mysterious and esoteric technique has always enabled me to become spontaneously erudite and capable of "Inventing" numerous outlines and subsequently, of scheming-up quite "Original" characters, settings, conflicts and noteworthy story patterns.

Essentially, I acknowledge that there are two types of Creativity: "Reactionary Creativity" and "Imaginative and Original Creativity". Reactionary Creativity is rather easy to perform. A good example is shown in the biography of L. Frank Baum, who was sitting as a restless patient inside a doctor's nondescript office. According to the legend, Baum was thinking about what should be the name of a fantasy land that would be the functional title to a new children's book he had been contemplating. Out of sheer boredom, L. Frank glanced over at the doctor's metallic filing cabinet of patients' information and then perceptively noticed two ordinary-looking drawers. The first compartment was labeled "A-N", and the bottom one remarkably read "O-Z." 'Oz!' Baum mentally exclaimed. "That's it! My new book has both a title and a very neat setting!'

Here are several instances of Reactionary Creativity from my own life's mundane adventures. While I had been authoring the novel *The Great Teen Fruit War*, I was driving my auto' on Fairview Avenue in downtown Hammonton when the railroad crossing gates began descending along with the objects' corresponding flashing red lights. Immediately I "Imagined" the Blueberry Gang kids tying two Peach Gang teens to the already descended gates as the extended passenger train speedily whizzed-by. When the gates eventually ascended (in the novel), the two Peach Gang kids were elevated to straight vertical positions, giving the victims the appearance of being primitively crucified to the all-astonished motorists encountering and passing-by the bizarre prank scene.

Another occasion of Reactionary Creativity was when my wife and I were vacationing in beautiful Taormina, Sicily. We were staying at the quaint Hotel Villa Schuller, which had a terrific penthouse lounge that allowed a fantastic view of distant Mt. Etna. I 'Imagined', 'Now I really have discovered the ending to my latest detective story.

Terrorists are captured by the local Mafia. The U.S. government had hired the Mafia to perform the critical service and pays the awesome Messina and Palermo crime syndicate a handsome stipend to conveniently dispose of the diabolic villains. The Sicilian Mafia rents a huge helicopter, and then the notorious mobsters toss the alarmed handcuffed terrorists into the steaming lava crater of the gorgeous island's constantly active volcano.'

A third situation where Reactionary Creativity is identifiable was when I had ventured on an excursion through Bristol, Pennsylvania on my nostalgic way to Levittown, where my family had resided from 1953-'59. Immediately a worthy story title popped into my head "Doing Bristol," and then thanks to my knowledge of United States geography, I recollected that in addition to Bristol, Pennsylvania, there is a Bristol, Virginia, a Bristol, Connecticut, a Bristol, Tennessee, a Bristol, England and a Bristol Rhode Island. I 'Imagined' that the main character of the story would go to sleep in one Bristol (Pennsylvania) and then each night would surprisingly wake-up each morning in another Bristol until the protagonist gradually would wind-up back in a familiar motel in his original destination, Bristol, Pennsylvania.

Another form of Reactionary Creativity that I habitually employ is when I satirize or parody the serious works of acclaimed writers like William Shakespeare, Edgar Allan Poe, O. Henry, Mark Twain, Jack London and Nathaniel Hawthorne. This type of "Reactionary Creativity" comes easy to me because all I have to do is rewrite what already has been expertly organized as quality literature.

However, since "Original Creativity" is much harder to achieve than "Reactionary Creativity" happens to be, that's precisely where and when the three magical, admirable, aforementioned computer room lamps come into play. Quite candidly, I often seek (and obtain) inspiration originating from outside myself. As I've already indicated, the lamps (along with my special personal incantations of solicitation) were always a trilogy of fabulous charms for me to be able to accomplish my central authorial ambition. But I cannot guarantee (toward the end of my writing career) that my little treasured secret would magnificently work for everyone or anyone else.

Throughout my life, I've always been a rather persistent, stubborn, and obstinate individual, and coincidentally, the general thrust of my exerted energy was specifically to prove the venerable Albert Einstein wrong. Einstein is reputed to have confidently stated, "A stupid person keeps redundantly committing the same silly mistakes over and over again without ever obtaining any favorable results."

Well then, after I had written my first book *Enchanta,* the overall sales effect was absolutely negligible. After my thirtieth book, Einstein's genius was still essentially infallible with me having dismal sales' results from my frustrating labor. But after my forty-eighth book *Hawthorne: Hazed, Hooked, Hammered and Hijacked,* the popularity of my previous literary products suddenly began to proliferate. For the past fifteen years, I just felt totally compelled to prove Einstein's provocative declaration to be (in my extraordinary case) erroneous.

Since childhood, finding my environment rather lackluster and horribly mediocre, at every opportunity I've attempted to "think outside the box". But conversely, morally speaking, I've always tried my best to "believe inside the box". Sometimes I've discovered my subjective conscience to be at continuous war with my objective-oriented mind. At times, even to this very day, this ongoing mental struggle is a troubling disappointment to me, and the battle causes my intelligence to be plagued with both mental and emotional turbulence. In truth, many authors are hapless tortured souls of their own doing.

I conjecture that three elements have over the years formed my spirit's core philosophy. Sometimes the three items are compatible; sometimes the triple ingredients are combative adversaries. To be sure, I've always honored the ancient teachings of the Ten Commandments, especially adhering to the principal tenets "Thou shall not kill; Thou shall not steal; Honor thy father and mother; and Thou shall not covet thy neighbor's goods."

But then my thinking has also been influenced by Ancient Greek thought, an afflictive effect that encourages me to literally doubt almost anything and everything. The sterling expressions of Socrates, Plato, Aristotle and Aristophanes have suggested to me that I should chronically be cynical and mutually skeptical of most things, including religious history and the Bible's *Old Testament.*

And in retrospect, the third feature prevalent in my ambivalent personality, Jeffersonian thought, is thoroughly embodied in the Declaration of Independence and also in the Bill of Rights. This American "freedom of thought" perspective often puts my mind at odds with prevalent religious teachings and with their "absolute truths".

But in the final analysis, my moral compass (hammered into my vulnerable cerebrum for eleven years by various Catholic school nuns and priests) is usually victorious over Reason, the Commandments trumping both Greek Thought and the alluded-to Ten Amendments to the United States Constitution.

359

In conclusion, I generally try to behave in a humble/modest life style even though I'm relatively proud of my abundant stories and novels. But to authentically communicate with the outside world, I needed a nom de plume in a similar fashion that Samuel Langhorne Clemens needed to be Mark Twain, William Sydney Porter needed to be O. Henry and Mary Anne Evans needed to be George Eliot. Lacking full confidence writing as John Wiessner, I respectfully summoned the very necessary assistance of the magical "Trinity 3-Way Illumination Lamps" stationed in my upstairs computer room, and then in a sudden inspiration, my brain incredibly came-up with the all-too-obvious pseudonym "Jay Dubya," which is a genuine corruption of my very common "J.W." initials.

"Social Security: Government Rip-off"

The average American Works 40 Plus Years: He or She Should Die A Millionaire! Here's Why and How!

1) Under Federal Law, each EMPLOYEE must pay 6.2% of his or her annual wages into Social Security (up to $118,500.00 in salary). The worker's EMPLOYER must pay a matching 6.2%, totally 12.4% of a person's wages going into the Social Security Fund. (This 12.4% does not count additional Medicare Contributions). On the other hand, SELF-EMPLOYED individuals must pay the full 12.4% (up to $118,500.00).

2) On August 24th, 1935, President Franklin D. Roosevelt signed into law the Social Security Act. In the 1930s, 1940s and 1950s, mostly men were employed in the national work force. Women mostly stayed at home serving as mothers and housewives. In 1935, the average life-expectancy of men was 58 years; for women 62 years.

3) Thanks to advances in medical technology, today both men and women live to be 70 years of age or older. The point here is that Social Security had been government-created so that few Americans would be able to collect at age 62-63 because most eligible men would have already been dead at age 58 in 1935.

4) If an American retiring today in 2016 had worked for 40 years, his contributions over that four-decade span would have exceeded $40,000.00. Add to this $40,000.00, the employer's $40,000.00 matching contributions, the joint sum would raise the total to $80,000.00. The government trick here is that NO ONE has an INDIVIDUAL SOCIAL SECURITY ACCOUNT with the indicated total amount that had accrued over 40 years. The Social Security FUND is a "general pot" consisting of all contributions of all workers.

5) Over the span of 40 working years, $80,000.00 in total contributions, if prudently invested in government bonds, telephone and electric utility blue chip stocks paying at nominal 3.5% dividend, should grow from 80 thousand dollars to around a million dollars with the yearly incremental dual employee/employer contributions.

6) The annual interest paid on 1 million dollars (at 3.5%) would be $35,000.00 a year. But instead, Social Security pays about half the sum (17-18 thousand or less) to the average American at age 63.

Theoretically, the average American gets systematically cheated out of around $18,000.00 dollars a year.

7) Even with the annual payments of $18,000.00 or less for Social Security, there still should remain the one-million-dollar PRINCIPAL AMOUNT (3.5% growth a year over 40 years) in the individual worker/contributor's accumulated account. But since the S.S. FUND is a GENERAL FUND and is NOT based on INDIVIDUAL ACCUMULATION AND DISTRIBUTION, instead of $1,000,000.00, the spouse of a deceased former worker (you or me) receives a paltry "Death Benefit" of $255.00.

8) Now if you aren't already angry, this next item should make you totally furious! There are two existing divisions in Social Security Benefit Distribution. The first has already been described, YOUR S.S. The second division of Social Security is identified as "DISABILITY PAYMENTS". When Barack Obama took office seven and a half years ago, 4 million people were on Social Security Disability. Today, there are over 12 million people on S.S. Disability, an increase of 8 million recipients who are DRAINING the system. And to top it all off, these additional 8 million people are NOT counted on the National Unemployment List, thus keeping the artificial number at around 5%.

Many Congressmen want to save the present Social Security System by first raising the retirement collection age from 62-63 to 70 and then by raising the top employer/employer contribution from 12.4% of $118,500.00 to a much higher amount. (Please bear in mind that the employees or self-employed workers making over 118 thousand would never get back their contributions in terms of benefits received, thus making the designed BENEFIT a TAX).

Donald Trump will rescue Social Security from its present monetary dilemma, which ought not exist in the first place if bungling (or conniving) Washington bureaucrats had managed the program properly from its outset!

362

"The Liberals Three Card Playing Deck"

The very vocal American left-wing political entity consists mostly of the ultra-liberal Main Street Media, Far-left Democrats, the archaic and self-patronizing NAACP, Black Lives Matter agitators, Radical Feminists, anarchistic Occupy Wall Street fanatics along with various militant Socialist and Communist affiliates. These various "Grievance Industry" factions are not playing the U.S. Game of Life with a full deck, their overly aggressive poker hands featuring three major playing cards: the Race Card, the Victim Card and the Slavery Card. And any fair-minded conservative traditionalist who challenges the validity of the repetitious 3 Liberal Playing Cards is automatically labeled a Racist, a Bigot, a Fascist or a Neo-Nazi.

Misguided Liberals erroneously think and believe that the United States is a "Democracy". But our colonial Founding Fathers created "a Republic," featuring a very just and reasonable Bill of Rights. Individual DEMOCRATIC rights are specifically outlined in the U.S. Constitution's First Ten Amendments, and these honorable covenants grant individual citizens an array of privileges ranging from Freedom of Speech to Freedom to Worship; from Freedom of the Press to Freedom to Bear Arms. The wisdom principle of "A Republic" (including the American Republic) is that this enduring form of government is primarily based on "the Rule of Law," and our American form of government also heavily relies on the preservation and continuation of the nation's culture and traditions for its survival. A "Democracy" tends to foment defiance of established Law, enacts opposition to "Old Morality", believes in the dismantling of time-honored traditions and finally, the Far-Left desires a quixotic "Revision of America's Culture and History".

Our very wise Founding Fathers aptly understood that historically, "Republics" last much longer than do "Democracies". For example, the Athenian Democracy lasted for only 186 years while the Roman Republic lasted for over five centuries, finally falling because of the same debilitating conditions that our current American Republic is detrimentally experiencing: Open Borders, Anarchy and Government Corruption. The Roman Empire had long been besieged with invading Visigoths, Vandals and Huns (Open Borders), barbaric tribes who later fought among themselves and then battled against the Roman Legions (Anarchy), while avaricious Roman Government Officials and Politicians bought votes from citizens by accepting bribes and simultaneously raiding the Empire's Treasury (Corruption). Yes,

History tends to repeat itself! The U.S. Republic is presently being negatively besieged and affected by Illegal Aliens (Open Borders), clashing Left-Wing and Right-Wing coalitions (Anarchy) and most obviously, modern-day avaricious Politicians (Corruption). These three present-day catalysts are the same malignant factors that had led to the gradual fall of the once-mighty Roman Republic.

Concepts such as "Democracy" and "Equality" are excellent ideas when those two principles relate to Constitutional Rights and to the implementation of U.S. Justice and Law, but "Democracy" and "Equality" are terrible practices when the two abstractions pertain to the American Economy (everyone gets Equal Pay) and to American Education (all students have Equal Academic Ability). Did you ever hear of a Civil War song titled "The Battle Hymn of the Democracy"? Of course not! It's "The Battle Hymn of the Republic!" And in the memorized Pledge of Allegiance, do we say "and to the 'Democracy' for which it stands"? Obviously no! We recite, "and to the 'Republic' for which it stands, One Nation under God with Liberty and Justice for all!" Astute observers must fully understand that the main goals of the Radical Far-Left are to relegate Christianity, to weaken the Republic while interpreting our Founding Documents as Democracy, and finally in the process, dangerously attempting to relegate and diminish most aspects of Western Civilization in America.

Vociferous Far-Left liberals don't really pragmatically practice the U.S. Constitution and the Declaration of Independence, which the latter document advocates the promotion of INDIVIDUAL "Life, Liberty and the Pursuit of Happiness". Far-Left Liberals COLLECTIVELY believe in GROUP CAUSES rather than espousing the conviction of each person being directly responsible for his or her actions, which is what the U.S. Constitution and our Founding Fathers were all about: Citizen Responsibility balancing the deployment and enjoyment of abundant Citizen Rights! In essence, each INDIVIDUAL is a free-thinking Sovereign Human Being, a small model of our Sovereign Nation.

As has been already indicated, the Liberals myopic 3 Card Playing Deck redundantly advances the Race Card, the Victim Card and the Slavery Card. Liberals have a short-sighted perception of human history when they think that only blacks had been slaves. Let's journey back into the ugly past a thousand-years or so. Most anyone reading this essay more-than-likely had ancestors in the year 1,000 A.D. who were slaves, serfs, servants, chattels, vassals, peasants, indentured workers or poor sharecroppers. A millennium ago people (the masses) were stratified into virtual caste systems without any chance for any upward social mobility or "individual accomplishment". Humans were classified either in the wealthy 2% noble class or into the 98% exploited fiefdom servitude class.

Then on June 15, 1215 a political miracle began taking shape in Runnymede, England. King John (brother and successor to King Richard the Lion-heart) was compelled by the threat of bankruptcy to sign the Magna Carta (Great Charter), which granted certain rights and privileges to Norman Barons, which over the next several centuries evolved and led to lower-class Saxons eventually obtaining their own individual right to own property and to not be dependent on wealthy Norman Nobles for security and protection in exchange for their grueling labor. Over the course of several-centuries, the English economic/political progress (began by the Magna Carta) slowly led to the Age of Exploration (Columbus, Magellan, etc.) and then the Age of Enlightenment (Voltaire, John Locke), the influential predecessors to the Age of the American and French Revolutions.

Beginning in 1776, our Founding Fathers finally freed the suppressed inhabitants of the original 13 colonies from the vile tyranny of King George III of England. The Revolutionary War along with the Declaration of Independence and the U.S. Constitution wonderfully granted colonial men the civil rights that elevated the general population from second-class subject-of-king status to citizens being able to have free enterprise, to participate in upward economic mobility, and to basically enjoy the benefits of both reward and profit through INDIVIDUAL initiative, thus allowing free members of the NEW REPUBLIC to engage in the unique experiment of American Capitalism.

What the Far-Left must fathom is that the White Man had to emancipate himself from British Monarchial Despotism in 1776 before the White Man could ever LIBERATE the black slaves from their plantation masters 70 or so years later. And yes, it was a Republican President named Abraham Lincoln who had authorized the Emancipation Proclamation, and yes, it was Southern Democrats who (after the Civil War) created the KKK to deliberately intimidate the recently freed slaves.

The Liberal Race/Victim/Slave Card peddlers don't have a monopoly when it comes to being discriminated against. For example, I never knew my Polish grandparents, descendants of Slavs (Slaves, Serfs and Peasants). My father's father had been a logger in upstate Michigan. A raging forest fire destroyed his camp, and not having any property insurance, my paternal grandfather was devastated after going bankrupt, and died shortly thereafter. No welfare safety net or food stamps existed in the early 1900s. My (also legal Ellis Island)

Polish grandmother, who I had never known had later died from the horrendous influenza epidemic that flourished in East Coast cities from 1917-1919.

After my paternal grandfather's death, my father's family had moved from Michigan to Baltimore to be near Polish relatives. English and German people had settled in America decades before the Poles immigrated, so consequently, Poles had trouble getting work from the already established British and German employers. A nearby Baltimore business named the John F. Wiessner Brewery (later defunct in the 1920s because of Prohibition) affected the opportunity for my family surname to be changed from the Polish Wiesniewski to the German Wiessner so that my discriminated against father and his five sisters could more easily get factory jobs in Baltimore City.

My maternal Sicilian grandfather (who also legally came to America via Ellis Island) daily operated a fruit and vegetable pushcart on Ninth Street in Philadelphia. My maternal grandmother's family was so poor that she had to wear her father's old tattered and weatherworn shoes to school and was egregiously mocked and scorned by the other more fortunate children whose families were of better means. After my grandparents married, Grandpop Antonio diligently saved and finally had enough money to buy five acres of ground on Route 30 in Hammonton, New Jersey, where he and Grandmom Annie built a small roadside farm market. An established British farm family owned the adjacent property and proceeded to build a much larger farm market only 50 feet away from the one constructed by my grandparents, obviously in a strong effort to run "the Sicilians" out of business and out of town. After 3 years of intense competition, my maternal grandparents prevailed and were able to proudly buy the larger farm market from the disgruntled English farm family.

And then there was my wife's Sicilian father and uncle who in the early 1940s were shunned and ostracized from playing baseball and football by other area Italian kids because the two brothers happened to have a darker complexion. Like my maternal grandparents, my wife's father and uncle prevailed in a hostile social environment and eventually became very successful businessmen, not because of any COLLECTIVE POLITICAL CAUSE but because of their own INDIVIDUAL DETERMINATION to overcome discrimination. They refused to be "victims"!

In the early-to-mid 20th Century, America was a true "Melting Pot". The immigration system worked because the new ethnic arrivals were predominantly from Europe, were of the Christian/Catholic/Jewish

366

faiths, possessed and fervently practiced the Protestant Work Ethic, and were mostly Polish, Irish and Italian Caucasians who (overcoming difficulty) gradually blended-in with the already entrenched English and German early settlers.

But then in 1965, Democrat President Lyndon Johnson implemented the Immigration and Nationality Act, which in 1968 soon morphed into the Hart-Celler Act, a law that changed the Immigration Quota System from being 90% White European newcomers and 10% People of Color to a reversal of 10% European and mostly new people from Africa, from the Middle East, from Central and South America and from Asia. That 1968 experimental "Melting Pot" is not working too well in the year 2018, and its unintended consequences are burgeoning our very beleaguered Welfare System, our schools, our hospital Emergency Rooms, and our prisons because many of these new clannish arrivals are not assimilating swiftly and smoothly into our American culture, principally because they have DIVERSE religions, languages, cultures and more relaxed "work ethics" carried-over from former dependency lifestyles in their previous countries. The current "Diversity Movement" is actually CULTURAL DISUNITY and WESTERN CIVILIZATION DILUTION in disguise.

The Democrats appear to relish putting new U.S. arrivals on Welfare and Food Stamps, thus insuring the Liberal Party of future votes in future elections. But honestly, Republicans also like having the new arrivals (especially from Central and South America) for cheap labor, and the GOP too shares the blame in this illegal immigration matter because these aforementioned migrant populations are a good source of higher company profits.

The Liberal Dems often criticize American Capitalism as being "Trickle-Down Economics", but someone please explain to me exactly how anti-economic-gravity "Trickle-Up Economics" is supposed to work? If the Democrats are so concerned about "Income Inequality", don't they realize that "Income Equality" in code language means "Socialism?" But Socialism (which had failed miserably in the now-extinct USSR) is the gospel of countless college professor demagogues, many of whom could never survive in the highly competitive "free PRIVATE-SECTOR markets of Wall Street and Main Street". I can still hear my father lecturing, "Son, if you listen to and advocate the indoctrinating words of your Liberal college professors, you'll never make more money than they do lecturing from their PUBLIC-SECTOR Ivory Towers!"

The major legitimate reasons for foreigners to secretly cross U.S. borders is defined in the need for them to escape Religious Persecution and Political Persecution in their native land. Natural disasters would also be legitimate reasons to enter the U.S. without a VISA or PASSPORT. Economic Opportunity and Receiving Welfare are not bona-fide justifications for encroaching into the United States illegally, for most of the world's six billion "DREAMERS" would prefer living in the United States than in their current country. But as already stated, Democrats gladly welcome "Open Borders" because their existence almost guarantees more future Dem "DREAMER and CHAIN MIGRATION" voters at the ballot box.

The Far-Left elitists sanctimoniously claim to have the High Moral Ground, when actually their conceited High Morality is a bane of Immorality where the First Ten Amendments to the U.S. Constitution are being systematically utilized to dismantle the Ten Commandments handed-down to Moses on Mt. Sinai. Consider these circumstances:
Old Morality: Thou Shall Not Kill New Left-Wing Morality: Have 2 million U.S. abortions annually.

Old Morality: Honor Thy Father & Mother New Left-Wing Morality: Get rid of sexist terms Father & Mother.

Old Morality: Thou Shall Not Covet Thy Neighbor's Wife. New Morals: Your neighbor's wife could be a male.

Old Morality: Thou Shall Not Commit Adultery. New Morality: Let's have total sexual & homosexual liberation.

Old Morality: Thou Shall Not Steal. New Morality: Make Government Politicians steal for you by more taxation.

Finally, President Trump has been greatly criticized for saying that "Both Sides were equally to blame at Charlottesville". True, the Alt-Right consisted of White Supremacists, White Nationalists, KKK Members, Neo-Nazis Ultra-Conservatives "and some good people". But conversely, the acrimonious Alt-Left doing battle at Charlottesville was composed of Antifa Anarchists, Black Lives Matter Insurgents, Occupation Wall Street Maniacs, Neo-Socialists, Neo-Communists and "some good people". Charlottesville was a classic 2017 version of WWII's Adolf Hitler versus Joseph Stalin, with both warring "Fascist" sides acting extremely belligerently in an Anti-American fashion.

It's been eight generations since the terrible Civil War and the abolishment of Slavery. And as far as U.S. Blacks are concerned, I think that the aggregate minority incessantly calling themselves "Black Americans" and "Afro-Americans" fundamentally alienates their CAUSE from the remainder of our great society. When Blacks simply begin to call themselves "Americans", I firmly believe that a better harmony could be attained between Caucasians and Blacks.

Now imagine that your life is graphically represented as an isosceles triangle. At the apex is you; then immediately below is your spouse; then below you or him/her are your children; then below your offspring are your relatives, your community, your church and your charities; then below that level are the people around the world, and lastly at the bottom of the triangle, are climate change and the people with AIDS around the globe. The Liberals want YOU and ME to invert or reverse that "Traditional Triangle" and have us concerned mostly about CAUSES such as climate change, the people around the world with AIDS, and at the bottom of the newly-established inverted triangle, the least important elements are you and your spouse. Liberals want you (and me) to sacrifice your (my) entire existence for everything else besides yourself (myself), for if you or I don't, you and I are labeled "greedy capitalists". Contrary to Liberal Belief, the United States was founded on the idea of "Self-Reliance".

In conclusion, the Great American Experiment so adequately described in the Declaration of Independence and in the United States Constitution is primarily about the right of the INDIVIDUAL exploring his or her own potential in a highly competitive, risk-oriented Free Enterprise economy. On the other hand, Democrats and Socialists believe in SOCIAL CAUSES being the necessary agenda mechanisms to elevate various minority groups into more prosperous life stations through incessant dependency on government handouts, food stamps, redistribution of wealth and "free stuff welfare". Most Democrat voters don't fully realize that the free market/free enterprise PRIVATE SECTOR creates wealth and prosperity in America and that the GOVERNMENT PUBLIC SECTOR consumes wealth through excessive taxation and through inefficient redistribution of wealth. In the final analysis, it's the longtime struggle of the INDIVIDUAL PURSUIT OF HAPPINESS principle versus the COLLECTIVE Robin Hood REDISTRIBUTION OF WEALTH philosophy that are relentlessly engaged in chaotic, contemporary political warfare. In a nutshell, Democrats and Socialists desire to artificially and COLLECTIVELY manufacture a Bureaucratic UTOPIA. The LEFTIES don't truly comprehend that "UTOPIA" can only be achieved on an INDIVIDUAL basis through personal sacrifice and through determined perseverance, ultimately leading the pursuer to success.

In my lifetime, I had been an English teacher for 34 years, had been a field manager on the world's largest cultivated blueberry farm for 18 summers, had owned boardwalk businesses (after borrowing money from relatives and banks and taking financial risks) on the Ocean City, Maryland Boardwalk for 16 summers and on the Rehoboth Beach, Delaware Boardwalk for 8 summers and on the Atlantic City Boardwalk for 3 summers, and I have written and published 54 hardcover/paperback/ebooks. If I was Black or if I had been a foreign-born "Person of Color" living in America, I believe that I would have likewise accomplished my goal of authoring 54 books. The specific manuscripts might not have been exactly the same content as the present ones, but with steadfast desire and INDIVIDUAL resolve, the 54 books would still have been written, even if Hillary Clinton would falsely claim that the government had written those particular 54 books for me.

And in summary, I profess that over the years I've been blessed by proudly exercising my own 3 Card Playing Deck, "INDIVIDUAL Life, Liberty and Pursuit of Happiness!"

"Trump Is Best for America's Future"

Written Prior to the November 2016 National Election.

Frankly, I'm getting tired of reading and listening to the same old redundant "attack Trump tripe" that's being reported as objective news on Cable TV and in various big city papers and national magazine articles. Pretentious "full of themselves" writers like Peggy Noonan and Bill Kristol are being unmasked by DJT as being weak public parasites who want to maintain the past and present status quo. But we are rapidly entering into a "New Age of Enlightenment." Trump supporters now understand the basic corruption problem that prominently exists and continues to proliferate throughout this crippled country: Establishment political RINOS and their surrogates, newspaper writers and the rest of the lousy Main Street/Wall Street media (Fox News and Wall Street Journal included) along with the always hungry tax and spend Democrats are all playing on the same team. Why are these political partners all basically so excessively opposed to Donald Trump?

As an author, I have learned to have little respect for print journalists. They have LITTLE IMAGINATION or PROBLEM-SOLVING ABILITY. "Journalists" like Noonan and Kristol only DESCRIBE the false RINO/DEMOCRAT political gospel to which the pundits want you, me and Trump to adhere. These apprehensive "journalists" fear Trump and are working overtime to make sure that the future will continue to be corrupt "Business as usual." And the talking head TV pundits are avid Trump critics too! ("What is art without a critic?") Critics don't contribute anything important to anything; for instance, they can't write Broadway plays or great novels; they can only criticize the creative works of others while they themselves wallow in brain-dead mediocrity!

What do journalists contribute to the "Real World?" If Noonan or Kristol and their myriad colleagues had any guts, the verbose cynics would run for office like Donald J. Trump is doing and attempt to reshape the grotesque reality that their flawed liberal political persuasion represents! The left-wing pundits espouse the European model of governing: "Problems must be MANAGED. Trump is a threat to the left-wing media and the feckless "Establishment" because DJT believes that problems need to be addressed and SOLVED! You might fear Donald's methods, but in the end, the problem (Illegal, Immigration, Muslim Jihadists, ISIS, high taxation, trade deficits,

National Debt, etc.) will be SOLVED and not simply awkwardly MANAGED by incompetent boobs.

Most Donald Trump supporters think the same way I do about the biased Press, about cowardly RINOS and about greedy Democrats! Trump is the only Republican out there to maintain that George W. Bush was a flawed President who had been asleep at the wheel during the horrendous housing crisis that nearly killed the USA economy, who did NOT prevent 9/11 (despite intel' warnings from the CIA), who allowed the National Debt to grow from 5 trillion to ten trillion dollars during his 8 years in office, and who allowed extensive illegal immigration across the Rio Grande (and from VISA overstays) to flourish after Reagan's "final amnesty."

Similar chaos coming from Washington DC is still going on as I organize this protest missive, and all the while the predatory Press almost solely wants us to focus our entire attention on Trump's caustic demeanor, on Trump University, on Melania's GQ photo' op' years before Trump ever married her, on Trump's comments about Rosie O'Donnell and also on Trump's affair with Marla Maples (whom he later married) while he was still wed to his first wife. CNN, MS-NBC, Fox News, and yes, the venerable Wall Street Journal are in unison stooping to communicate National Enquirer tabloid journalism for the hidden purpose of deliberately taking-down Donald Trump's Republican candidacy. There's an ugly conspiracy going on to stop Trump, and for once, a good portion of the American electorate is finally figuring-out this obvious concerted RINO/DEM/Press coalition.

True, loyal-to-their profession journalists should write their subjective political opinions on the newspapers "Editorial Page" and not present their "anti-Trump views" as if they are genuine objective facts appearing on the periodical's front page "above the fold!"

All that the MSM, the Establishment RINOS and the Democrats want to collectively do is as follows:

a) Maintain the status quo and systematically increase the National Debt. These dangerous enemies of the REPUBLIC selfishly value Globalization first and America second!

b) Keep their power structure together and at every opportunity smear Donald Trump, who effectively threatens their now-vulnerable and partially exposed power architecture.

c) Intentionally cause a political circus tabloid war between Trump and Ted Cruz over picayune nonsense matters so that

Kasich, Romney or Hillary will eventually become President to keep their corrupt power structure intact.

To me, Donald Trump is the only viable solution to quantitative tax reform, to the salvation of capitalism, to the preservation of Christianity in America and to the protection and advancement of our American and Western Civilization. Cruz, Hillary, Bernie, Rubio, Ryan, Romney (along with Mitt's gutless "superior Mormon morality"), along with folks like Noonan and Kristol need to be neutralized and have their corrosive mass media influence diminished. Only Trump can achieve this requisite and adroitly dismantle the malignant factors (RINOS, DEMS, MSM, Lobbyists, PACS, Special Interest Groups) that are harmfully hurting our beloved country.

Who is the only one running on either ticket that will reduce the National Debt (that is destroying this Nation)? Who can best reduce the trade deficit? Who can best stop Illegal Immigration? Who can best defeat Muslim jihadists across America and around the world? Who will best lower taxes for the U.S. work force and for corporations? ·Who is best equipped to create PRIVATE SECTOR jobs? Who will reduce wasteful PUBLIC SECTOR jobs by shrinking money-sucking departments of the federal government? Obviously, the only acceptable answer is our New Era Republican Donald J. Trump!

Please remember, the DC federal government PUBLIC SECTOR cannot create wealth; it can only consume wealth created by the PRIVATE SECTOR'S taxpayers. And when the Fed prints excessive paper money, this means that the dollars in *your* wallet are worth less and less!

Most everyone currently involved in DC power fears Donald Trump and is desperately trying to bring him down. Trump happens to be the most true-blue patriot running for President out there. Think about it. Trump has the ideal life! He loves this country and wants to see it prosper again and not turn into a Second-Class Banana Republic like Obama, Clinton and the gutless GOP Establishment (either intentionally or not) are causing. Yes, Donald J. Trump will thrive no matter who is President! Why does the man sacrifice the perfect life he's been enjoying and as a result encounter all of the terrible grief from all directions being rendered upon him? There's only one viable answer: Trump truly wants to "Make America great again, greater than it has ever been before!" If you oppose THAT basic premise, you are not giving Trump a fair shake. If Trump is elected President, the public should react to his performance. Until then, critics should stop negatively hypothesizing about a Trump future that hasn't yet materialized!

To my mind, Trump is a contemporary Stephen Girard: he's someone who is willing to risk his fortune and his reputation (and even his life) to salvage America from imploding from within! Noonan, Kristol, Paul Ryan (a loser), Hillary Clinton (a lawbreaker), Bernie Sanders (a dumb-ass Socialist), and Ted Cruz never accomplished anything significant in the REAL PRIVATE SECTOR WORLD, and Kasich (a weak political Caspar Milquetoast) will only exacerbate this country's REAL WORLD and REAL DOMESTIC problems. Globalization is the real culprit that's the USA's principal nemesis, and folks, we all have to pay dearly for helping the rest of the world and the UN mandates, giving those foreign items priority over America's vital national interests. Remember, the more taxes we pay, the less freedom we have to "pursue happiness" and to help our families.

Without a doubt, the so-called "qualified experienced politicians" have gotten us into the 21 trillion-dollar mess (when Obama leaves office) we're currently drowning in, and now the Establishment (Noonan, Kristol, TV pundits, RINOS, Media, Democrats) is saying that Trump is unqualified because he lacks political experience. So-called sophisticated elitists like Noonan & Kristol have totally lost my respect, faith and trust, and I no longer care about what clumsy and stilted journalistic propaganda they are spewing in order to prevent Trump from winning the Republican nomination. These pundits know (and fear) deep-down inside that Mr. Trump is very capable of handily defeating Hillary Clinton in the upcoming election!

But then several months ago I realized something rather important. The Establishment GOP RINOs don't really care if either loser Mitt Romney or loser Paul Ryan is the 2016 Republican nominee; just as long as the nominee isn't Donald J. Trump.

Even if Mitt Romney and/or Paul Ryan were to lose again in November to a Democrat, it really doesn't matter to the up to now all-too-comfortable DC GOP crowd. The wily connivers still will have the corrupt system power structure intact, still will have their corrupt lobbyists and special interests to "grease each other's wheels", and with Hillary as the new President, the RINOS can still play the Washington political power game with the MSM and the Democrats while conversely, pretending to be "patriotic and Constitutional Republican conservatives".

In the past 30 years since Ronald Reagan, American voters have not been given a clear-cut honest Presidential choice. It's been a RINO

374

(Bob Dole, George W. Bush, George H. W. Bush, John McCain, Mitt Romney) versus a similar-minded tax and spend Democrat. Do you remember the egregious KKK charges levied against Reagan by the Democrats of his era? Remember how Reagan was painted by the press as being grossly stupid and quite incompetent? It's the same type of garrulous B.S. all over again with Trump, but this time, it's being maliciously administered through 24/7 cable TV "news" outlets and by the ultra-liberal social media websites to the tenth power!

Already in Louisiana Ted Cruz is trying to steal delegates (with the RINO Establishment's blessing). Trump won the Louisiana Primary, but the delegate distribution was exactly even between DJT and Cruz (18 each). Now Cruz is trying to WIN Louisiana by stealing Marco Rubio's 5 delegates and pilfering 5 more of Trump's delegates that DJT has already won.

And as far as Trump not acting "Presidential" is concerned, only the duly elected President can act "Presidential". When (or if) Trump becomes President, he will act Presidential in his policy decision making. Until then, it's a brutal matter of participating in "King of the Republican Hill", and Trump has methodically knocked 14 RINO candidates from the political summit. After he masterfully takes-down Cruz and Kasich, he'll then adroitly deal with the all-too-treacherous Hillary. If she doesn't get personal with Trump, he'll be "Presidential" and will stick to debating the crucial issues. If Hillary obnoxiously dares to attack his personal life or character, Trump will counter-punch twice as hard, no matter whether she's a woman or not!

Now this is why the MSM, the RINOS and the allied Dems almost hysterically fear Trump in a totally paranoid way. Donald will absolutely defend himself to the hilt. He'll deftly double and triple-down if he has to do precisely *that* style of attack in order to win, which is the only thing Trump understands in any intense competition. Trump doesn't obediently apologize (on demand), and he won't go on any international "Apology Tour" like wimpy Barack Obama had done throughout the Middle East. Trump can't be controlled by big donor PAC money, and this is why Noonan and the rest of the MSM perceive him as being especially DANGEROUS (to their avaricious interests!) All other candidates on both sides constantly seek PAC money. Up to now, Trump is self-funding his campaign and owes no one anything!

And lastly, not to sound too repetitious, I highly admire Donald Trump because he doesn't cave, but instead the man boldly and confidently increases the pressure upon his targeted opponent when aggressively challenged. Take the matter of Trump University for example. The main "student complainant" gave Trump University all "Excellent" grades on HER final evaluation of the educational business course (Trump has conveniently produced the documentation for public scrutiny). Trump never settled her plaintiff lawsuit, and the disgruntled woman and her greedy attorney finally dropped the prosecuting case because they realized that in the end, their bogus political charges (disguised as valid legal charges) would be totally futile and unproductive. Why aren't Peggy Noonan, Bill Kristol and the other "objective journalists" writing about *this* very recent Trump victory development?

In closing, Trump is the only viable candidate who will staunchly fight for America's vital interests upon the World Stage. And I only hope that the FBI doesn't start to prosecute Hillary until February of 2017. This belated action will prevent Obama from giving H. Clinton an undeserved Presidential Pardon. Then after taking his Oath of Office in late January, Trump will soon clean-house and drain the swamp, and hopefully with a newly appointed Attorney General, Hillary will be aggressively prosecuted for the e-mail scandal, for her violation of federal rules and regulations and also for her lack of response to the Benghazi consulate catastrophe, thus allowing our Libyan ambassador and three other brave Americans to die unnecessarily. If the FBI presents charges BEFORE next January 20th, then Obama will probably pardon Mrs. Clinton the same way that Gerald Ford had pardoned Richard M. Nixon!

Lastly, I am overly tired of this detrimental "business as usual" political fiasco from the toxic Media and from the DC elitist class! There's only one person running for President who will boldly save the "Republic" from the egregious and detrimental ongoing "Democratic/RINO/MSM Corruption" (PACS, lobbyists, special interest groups), and that on-a-mission zealous candidate is Donald J. Trump! Peggy Noonan, Bill Kristol along with their self-serving band of confederates realize that if Trump wins next November, it's game over for the malignant influences that THEY uphold and perpetuate by means of endorsing those in both parties who are repugnantly (or incompetently) propagating the vile destruction of this great country!

And please, I don't want to read any more holier-than-thou pundit trash being generated from opinionated elitists like Peggy Noonan and Bill Kristol. Let the election process play-out fair and square (if that's at all possible), and then objectively judge Donald Trump (if he wins) on the merits of his accomplishments or on his failures, but in all fairness, give the man a fair and unbiased shake in the meantime. In my humble opinion, Peggy Noonan and her TV and media friends are just one level above the pathetic women spouting their daily lackluster jargon and anti-Trump diatribes on "The View"! To fully fathom the real Donald J. Trump, pay close attention to what the man does and not to what he opines or Tweets on Twitter.

Epilogue: 21 trillion-dollar National Debt means: $63,000.00 per person, or a family of four owing around $250,000.00. Do you have this kind of spare change in your pocket?

"How Socialism Is Destroying American Culture!"

Socialist Bernie Sanders had almost won the Democrat Party Nomination in 2016, and would have been the Dem' candidate if Hillary Clinton had not rigged the Super Delegates to endorse her victory at the Party Convention held in Philadelphia. At present 35% of people living in the USA are on some form of government assistance (welfare) (113 million), and 15% (17 million) are on food stamps. How did this debilitating set of circumstances ever happen? It did not develop overnight, but instead evolved over the course of the past one-hundred-years.

Ken Langone, a zealous capitalist and co-founder of Home Depot, offered to have proactive college students who advocate Socialism in America to board his private jet and fly down to Venezuela where Socialism presently abounds, inviting on TV the gullible idealists to eat out of garbage bins and dumpsters and compete against wild street dogs for scraps of food. A side trip to Cuba could serve as verification of the perils and failures of existing Socialism as a form of parasitic government. Quixotic and naïve Democrat/Liberal university students (free health care and college education for all to surely bankrupt America) are quite realistically the same kind of indoctrinated, foolishly deceived and misguided ilk that are tearing-down Confederate statues on Southern campuses, the hypocrites not realizing that the represented Civil War soldiers were also Democrats, but only depicted from another era. "Liberal/Progressive" college professors seldom (if ever) lecture to their captive, receptive audience one iota that a Republican President Abraham Lincoln had freed the plantation slaves with the Emancipation Proclamation and that conspiring Southern Democrats had formed the Ku Klux Klan to actively terrorize the recently freed former subservient slaves.

How did this Socialism infestation of America ever get started? The obstinate Progressives and the determined Socialists of the early 1900s aggressively went to war against the practice of religion being taught along with Biblical readings being recited in American public schools. Might I remind you, the words "Separation of Church and State" are nowhere mentioned in the U.S. Constitution. *That* particular skewed and altered interpretation is solely based on the "Establishment Clause" which reads: "Congress shall not establish a State Religion".

This "State Religion" documentation of our Founding Fathers goes back to Henry the VIII in England. When the Pope would not grant the British king an annulment to marry a second wife, Henry VIII established as the "State Religion of England" the Anglican Church, which is the Episcopal Church in the U.S. Other British denominations *persecuted* by the Anglicans like the Pilgrims, the Puritans and the Calvinists fled England in the early 1600s and settled in New England. Quakers fled England and settled in Pennsylvania, and Catholics fled England and settled in Maryland (Mary's Land).

Our Founding Fathers did not want a dominant "State Religion" to prevail in America like the Anglican Church had dominated as a State Religion Church in England, so they authored "The Establishment Clause" in the Constitution to avoid religious persecution of other religions by one ascendant, dominant faith.

In the late 1800s, the Liberal Progressives and the Far-Left Socialists then deftly hijacked the existing Constitutional "Establishment Clause" by claiming and interpreting the particular distorted nomenclature as "the Separation of Church and State". By successfully taking the Ten Commandments, the Psalms and the Golden Rule out of public schools and next substituting *those important moral principles* with John Dewey Educational Psychology and Sociology, the subsequent baneful results being defiant teens in the schools and belligerent teen rebellion in the home, together mutually causing heightened friction between modern-day hostile "students/children" and their very perplexed teachers and stressed-out parents.

Now let's go back to the year 1920 when Socialism in America had its real genesis. Democrat President Woodrow Wilson, the father of Economic Progressivism (redistribution of wealth) and a friend of Socialist/Atheist John Dewey, needed a mechanism to pay for the U.S. participation in WWI: Wilson imaginatively introduced Federal Personal Income Tax, and he promised that the new tax would go away after the war debt had been satisfied; quite to the contrary, the tax never did go away, and its negative implementation over the years has led to the colossal growth of the avaricious Federal Government. Today 50% of the average person's income goes to federal, state and local property taxes. Because of the great tax burden, two people (mother and father, husband and wife) in the family have to work simply to make ends meet. This very necessary survival activity disrupts family unity with grandparents, aunts, uncles and various strangers babysitting kids so that the two workers in each family can contribute to paying for the ever-expanding American welfare state (now at 35%). Progressive Woodrow Wilson & Socialist/Atheist John Dewey have cunningly initiated a malignant government/education system that has caused dysfunctional teen rebellion at home and comparable teen hostility at school when you evaluate the failures and full impact of the "Student-centered classroom" along with the equally disastrous "Child-centered home".

John Dewey wanted to dismantle capitalism and replace it with socialism. Ask any school Superintendent, "What do you think of student academic competition for grades in the classroom?" They will more than likely answer, "It is better that students learn to cooperate than to compete for grades; it is better that they must *share* (Socialism) knowledge in the classroom."

It must be comprehended that *competition* is the lifeblood of American capitalism; a school system's dislike of INDIVIDUAL ACADEMIC student competition is fundamentally undermining the American economic system (capitalism), which *is* by definition, based on competition.

"Competition" in education is often regarded by Administrators and Supervisors as a "dirty word". It's only used by schools when the football team and band *compete* against other schools; but competition in American education is not used in terms of *individual* students competing for grades or pursuing high honors against other students. Many high schools are getting rid of Valedictorians and Salutatorians because recognizing high honors makes the lesser motivated students feel badly and emotionally hurt at graduation ceremonies simply because ACADEMIC achievement is rewarded to "selfish" and "greedy" Valedictorians and Salutatorians. Schools and most classrooms are now mostly about GROUP THINK SOCIALIZATION (Socialism) and not about INDIVIDUAL ACADEMIC ACHIEVEMENT (Competition, Capitalism).

Student EQUALITY in the Classroom is also a harmful problem in regard to *Democratic Education* (Socialism in disguise). Equality is a great word when it comes to the U.S. Constitution and to EQUAL justice under law. Conversely, equality is a terrible word when it comes to economics (Socialism) and to Education (Educational Socialism: all students are equal).

"Group work" has taken the place of INDIVIDUAL student academic performance in the classroom. Teachers often divide a class of 25 students into 5 groups of 5; two kids who want good grades are strategically placed in each group and wind-up being the group captains doing the bulk of the task/assignment while the other three in each group do little or nothing. All 5 kids get the same GROUP work grade: This sort of common practice is Educational Socialism demonstrated at its best.

When I had taught 8th Grade English up to June of 1999, there were 2 *homogeneously* grouped Accelerated English classes and 5 General English class sections in my school. Now in 2018, all the 8th grade students are *heterogeneously* grouped with all ability levels represented in 7 different classes. When "group work" is done in the classroom, the former *homogeneously* grouped Accelerated English-type kids will do the bulk of the work in the *heterogeneous* class group work (academic welfare, Educational Socialism).

Once in the late 1970s I was assigned a Student Teacher in 8th Grade English. The student teacher taught a great "teacher-centered-classroom" lesson with very good discipline and terrific classroom discussion that I sat in on and witnessed as well as being accompanied by the student teacher's college coordinator. The student teacher received a C grade from the college professor for the very orderly lesson observation.

I told the Student Teacher, "Next time divide the class into 5 groups of 5 and go from group to group (station-to-station) as a 'facilitator' to monitor student progress." The Student Teacher did what I had suggested and got an A on the second classroom observation lesson. This specific development was evidence that the college student teacher coordinator wanted to see John Dewey Socialistic "Group Think and Share" being employed as opposed to student INDIVIDUAL ACADEMIC PERFORMANCE based on "competition for grades" in a "Teacher-centered" classroom environment.

Many high school graduates attending community college must take remedial courses. Why? Because there is a lack of skill development in high school from Socialistic education that is not working especially well. Dewey "group think" education has "the Idea Curriculum" being taught in Elementary School. Instead of basic skills being exclusively instructed, students are supposed to learn Algebra in 2nd grade and the Theory of Relativity in 3rd grade, with spelling, grammar, punctuation and times table memorization being deemphasized in favor of the impractical "Idea Curriculum".

When I had been teaching, toward the end of my career, if a student earned a 50, 40, 30 or less on a test, I was instructed by my Supervisor and Administrators to record the grade of 60 in my roll book. Then I had to figure-out how an unmotivated *student* with an already-inflated 60 average could pass with a 70 (low D). Therefore, I creatively implemented things like "Classroom Participation Grade," "Group Work Grade" that was fraudulently obtained with more motivated kids doing the bulk of the labor, "Class Attendance Grade" and "Group Project Grade to be Done at Home (mostly by the self-motivated students)."

In 1998 the English and Reading teachers at my middle school were asked to vote on a new Literature textbook series. We chose a series having traditional authors' and short stories like those written by Jack London, Washington Irving, O. Henry, Nathaniel Hawthorne, H.G. Wells, James Thurber, Mark Twain, Edgar Allan Poe, etc. Over the summer, the Supervisor (and with the approval of the Administration) overruled the faculty vote and instead ordered a Multicultural Literature Text with entries by virtually unknown foreign authors. The newly selected stories had shallow, unsophisticated plots along with weak vocabulary and were but another indication of the encroachment of John Dewey Socialism "dumbing-down" literature studies.

Required Smutty School Readings Part of Dumbing-down of America

Have you ever watched Jay Leno seriously interview young adults in TV skits? "How many Senators are there?" (Answer: 50). "Who was President at the start of World War II?" (Answer: Ronald Reagan). These types of questions and answers are indeed bold evidences of the ongoing dumbing-down of students in American Public Schools. This educational craziness all started in the early 1920s with the Father of Modern American Education, a Socialist/Atheist named John Dewey. This Marxist's deleterious theories and methods are still prevalently practiced today in public schools in the year 2018.

John Dewey (1st Honorary President of the NEA) believed that American students should be "socialized" instead of being "academically and morally strong". This influential social philosopher believed that a Utopian Socialistic State could evolve if over time the younger generation would be dumber than their parents. Hence, "capitalism" could be systematically dismantled, and "group think Socialism" would slowly and eventually replace it, with the majority of the passive Utopian population (over ten decades) becoming dependent on government economic support (welfare). Dewey never comprehended that Utopia can only be accomplished through "INDIVIDUAL initiative and personal pursuit of happiness" and not by means of Socialistic Mass Dumbing-down Educational Design.

As we are gradually discovering in 2018, a bureaucratic "Deep State" exists (and has existed) in various departments of the U.S. Government, where high-ranking officials in the FBI and DOJ, who incidentally are not elected by citizens but are entrenched in high positions for decades, have recently attempted to undermine the Trump Administration.

Another less-apparent Deep State exists in American Education, and most of the players (Superintendents, Administrators, School Board Members, Teachers) are not quite remotely aware of how "the Educational Disease" they are inadvertently promoting is like a dead fish rotting our society from the head-down.

This current profanity-laced, low-value, inferior plot, lack of sophistication assigned summer reading book titled *A Short History of the Girl Next Door* is the first piece of pus that's now locally being squeezed out of a colossal century-old contaminated pimple that began with the twisted and detrimental theories of Socialist/Atheist John Dewey. And the NEA, the NJEA, school supervisors and curriculum coordinators throughout New Jersey are all willing (or unwitting) accomplices in advancing this extensive, slow-rolling, academic decline.

The staunch defendants of the *Girl Next Door* will argue that this type of reading represents "academic freedom". What this "academic freedom" over time methodically morphs into at its extreme is "student anarchy" exhibited all throughout the school. One such example from the *Girl Next Door* rubbish rag is on Page 24 where Matt (the main character) describes his impression of his father: "I have HIM to thank for my general awkwardness in any and all social situations." Hey Matt buddy; you are an INDIVIDUAL and your father might have given you genetic features but he certainly didn't cause your social awkwardness!

Just ask your local school administrators how many fights and suspensions occurred last year? Yes, and it all commenced with the John Dewey Socialism theme, which in the '60s and '70s evolved into "the student-centered classroom". Teachers are relegated and diminished to the role of being "facilitators" instead of being the *subject authority* in the classroom. While getting away from "teacher-centered" education, discipline problems are proliferating wildly because some students now are emboldened to openly and overtly defy teacher authority because of "the student-centered classroom" plague.

384

John Dewey's "student-centered classroom" also negatively breeds student anarchy and numerous school fights principally because power in the classroom is taken from teachers and given to students under the false guise of "developing student responsibility". This unhealthy transfer of authority causes school and society disorganization to proliferate.

In the 1940s Dr. Benjamin Spock advocated the "child-centered family" as opposed to the "parent-centered family." His famous book *Baby and Child Care* also contributed to social disorganization both at home and at school. Fortunately, Dr. Spock towards the end of his life had the decency and the courage to recant this toxic Socialistic believe because he ultimately recognized that the John Dewey "psychology approach" had caused widespread teenage rebellion in the home along with student dysfunction throughout the school. School Psychology (based on Dewey's Socialistic theories) has proven to be no adequate substitute for the simple Judeo-Christian Commandment, "Honor Thy Father and Thy Mother".

Book Review: Analysis of Local High School Summer Reading book
A Short History of the Girl Next Door

This required summer reading at the nearby high school is what truly motivated me to author this essay/article, and I was inspired to do so because my granddaughter and my nephew (a junior and a sophomore respectively) were assigned the mandatory summer reading task. The same book was assigned to students in grades 9-12, and the freshmen, sophomore and junior students ages 15-17 are obviously, under the law, actual minors being exposed to having their morals corrupted by literary obscenities.

Forget the 398 profanities/vulgarities (124 F-words, 90-SH words & 83 A-Hole words & variations) explicitly stated in the required high school summer reading *A Short History of the Girl Next Door*. The book has little literary merit or redeeming value and here are some reasons why.

1) The main character Matt. W. is not a PROTAGONIST, a good person who wants the best for his peers and for the world. Matt is an ingrate, an ungrateful egotistical teenager who resents everything that his parents have provided for him. Matt is a "stealth ANTAGONIST" and not a decent role model for any teen reader to imitate. M. W. shows few (if any) admirable character/personality traits and curses incessantly when upset or frustrated.

2) Matt. W. never mentions any constructive or realistic goals or future in his life and how to work hard to achieve them. The entire first 160 pages is about Matt (a freshman) liking Tabatha L. (a freshman); Matt despising Liam B. (a senior) for dating his neighbor Tabby (Tabatha) whom he desires; and Matt liking to play basketball at which senior Liam excels. Matt also likes playing with his toddler brother Murray.

3) Matt W. is lazy outside of his limited interests as indicated in #2. He does few (if any) chores around the house and has never worked a summer job for any neighbor or relative (mowing lawns, etc.). He mostly sulks and curses about not having Tabatha, about Liam dating Tabatha and about Liam being better at playing basketball.

4) *A Short History of the Girl Next Door i*s evidently a book *about* Socialization and anti-Socialization (Socialism) and not about Matt W. pursuing Academic or Moral growth or excellence. A high school book should be about ADDING to what students know instead of TEACHING-DOWN to the negative aspects and language of some of the readers' peers. Literature should be UPLIFTING: not contaminating or toxic.

5) After Tabatha is killed along with her father in an automobile accident, Matt W. becomes even more antagonistic and hostile towards Murray, towards his parents and towards his teachers, and this is where his anti-social cursing habit increases. Matt becomes an instant atheist, questioning the existence of God and regarding the minister's words at Tabatha's viewing as meaningless and shallow. Showing amoral and atheistic tendencies are not good role models for high school students. The book's message conveyed to young readers: Religions, Church, religious teachings and the Ten Commandments are irrelevant and false. Matt W. never recants *these* egregious and dangerous suppositions.

6) Not all families have kids who intolerably curse and swear relentlessly, so it is no wonder that many parents will find this book absolutely offensive. With the usage of a plentitude of F words, SH words and A-hole words, this book is without a doubt smut with a capital S. At the end, Matt seeks to have an awkward peace with Liam, but this small change in behavior is too little too late for the unmeritorious work to succeed. Since freshmen, sophomores and juniors are between the ages of 15-17, they are not considered adults under the law, and so, *A Short History of the Girl Next Door* just might be Corrupting the Morals of Minors and be a case of Mass Child

Abuse, either situation being a felony crime being thrust upon most of the impressionable student body.

All one has to do to obtain a list of classic novels is to search on Google and find at least 100 ACADEMIC titles such as *Don Quixote, The Grapes of Wrath, Fahrenheit 541, The Old Man and the Sea, House of 7 Gables, The Odyssey, 1984,* etc. These sorts of titles are ACADEMICALLY appropriate and not *Socialistically* oriented to "dumb-down" like *A Brief History of the Girl Next Door.*

Now after reading this essay/article, everyone should fully know and understand precisely how the synthesis of Woodrow Wilson's Progressive Political Movement combined with John Dewey's Educational Socialism have been dually ruining America and Public-School Education along with American culture for the past hundred years.

About the Author

Jay Dubya is author' John Wiessner's pen name. John is a retired New Jersey public school teacher, having diligently taught the subject for thirty-four years. John lives in Hammonton, New Jersey with wife Joanne, and the couple has three grown sons.

John has written and published fifty-six books. Besides *Thirteen Sick Tasteless Classics*, *Thirteen Sick Tasteless Classics, Part II*, *Thirteen Sick Tasteless Classics, Part III* and *Thirteen Sick Tasteless Classics, Part IV*, Jay Dubya has written *Pieces of Eight, Pieces of Eight, Part II, Pieces of Eight, Part III* and *Pieces of Eight, Part IV*. All four *Pieces of Eight'* works contain short stories and novellas that feature science fiction and paranormal plots and themes. *One Baker's Dozen* is a collection of twenty-six short stories. *Two Baker's Dozen* also contains sci-fi themes. *So Ya' Wanna' Be A Teacher* is a non-fiction autobiography of the author's teaching career, and *RAM: Random Articles and Manuscripts* represents another (mostly) non-fiction writing endeavor.

Other Jay Dubya adult-oriented fiction are the works *Black Leather and Blue Denim, A '50s Novel*, and its exciting sequel, *The Great Teen Fruit War, A 1960' Novel*. *Frat' Brats, A '60s Novel* completes the "coming-of-age" trilogy. Jay Dubya also has produced two irreverent Biblical satires, *The Wholly Book of Genesis* and *The Wholly Book of Exodus*. A third satire *Ron Coyote, Man of La Mangia* is also a parody on Miguel Cervantes' classic novel, *Don Quixote* published in 1605. *Mauled Maimed Mangled Mutilated Mythology* satirizes twenty-one classic myths and *Fractured Frazzled Folk Fables and Fairy Farces* and *FFFF&FF, Part II* satirize famous stories from children's literature.

The author has also penned a young adult fantasy trilogy, *Pot of Gold, Enchanta* and *Space Bugs, Earth Invasion. The Eighteen' Story Gingerbread House* features original children's tales.

Jay Dubya really likes '50s music, and he also listens to songs by the Beatles, *ELO*, the Carpenters, the Beach Boys, Fleetwood Mac, the Eagles, the Rolling Stones, John Mellencamp and John Fogerty.

When not listening to popular music, Jay Dubya prefers watching *76ers'* basketball and *Phillies* and *Yankees'* television baseball games.

Author Biography

Born in Hammonton, NJ in 1942, John Wiessner had attended St. Joseph School up to and including Grade 5. After his family moved from Hammonton to Levittown, Pa in 1954, John attended St. Mark School in Bristol, Pa. for Grade 6, St. Michael the Archangel School in Levittown for Grades 7 and 8 and then Immaculate Conception School, Levittown, Pa. for Grade 9. Bishop Egan High School, Levittown Pa was John's educational base for Grades 10 and 11, and later in 1960, the aspiring author graduated from Edgewood Regional High, Tansboro, NJ. John then next attended Glassboro State College, where he was an announcer for the school's baseball games and also read the nightly news and sports over WGLS, GSC's radio station.

John Wiessner had been primarily an English teacher in the Hammonton Public School System for 34 years, specializing in the instruction of middle school language arts. Mr. Wiessner was quite active in the Hammonton Education Association, serving in the capacities of Vice-President, building representative and finally, teachers' head negotiator for 7 years. During his lengthy teaching career, John had been nominated into "Who's Who Among American Teachers" three times. He also was quite active giving professional workshops at schools around South Jersey on the subjects of creative writing and the use of movie videos to motivate students to organize their classroom theme compositions.

John Wiessner was very active in community service, being a past President of the Hammonton Lions Club, where he also functioned for many years as the club's Tail-Twister, Vice-President and Liontamer. John had been named Hammonton Lion of the Year in 1979 and in 2009 received the prestigious Melvin Jones Fellow Award, the highest honor a Lion can receive.

John also was a successful businessman, starting with being a Philadelphia Bulletin newspaper delivery boy for two years in the late 1950s in Levittown, Pennsylvania. After his family moved back to New Jersey in 1959, John worked at his grandparents and his parents' farm markets, Square Deal Farm (now Ron's Gardens in Hammonton) and Pete's Farm Market in Elm, respectively. He later managed his wife's parents' farm market, White Horse Farms in Elm for three summers.

Also in a business capacity, for 16 summers starting in 1967 John Wiessner had co-owned Dealers Choice Amusement Arcade on the Ocean City, Maryland boardwalk and also co-owned the New Horizon

Tee-Shirt Store for eight summers (1973-'81) on the Rehoboth Beach, Delaware boardwalk. In addition, "Jay Dubya" was a co-owner of Wheel and Deal Amusement Arcade, Missouri Avenue and Boardwalk, Atlantic City. And then, for 18 summers beginning in 1986, John had been the Field Manager in charge of crew-leaders for Atlantic Blueberry Company (the world's largest cultivated blueberry farm), both the Weymouth and Mays Landing Divisions.

After retiring from teaching in 1999, writing under the pen name Jay Dubya (his initials), John Wiessner became the author of 56 books in the genre Action/Adventure Novels, Sci-Fi/Paranormal Story Collections, Adult Satire, Young Adult Fantasy Novels and Non-Fiction Books. His books exist in hardcover, in paperback and in popular Kindle and Nook e-book formats.